Crossed Lines

A Novel of Love, Lost

By J.T. Marsh

CROSSED LINES: A NOVEL OF LOVE, LOST

First Edition. May 2019.
Copyright © J.T. Marsh 2019
ISBN 978-1-989559-09-3

Written by J.T. Marsh
Published by Queensborough Books

I'll never forget you

1. Past (2002-2007)

When I was fifteen I left the smoky, wide-open skies of Dallas, Texas, for the rain and the thick, grey clouds of Vancouver, British Columbia, Canada. It was less than a year after the twin towers in New York had fallen, and I'd spent that year living with my father before deciding, finally, to return home to live with my mother in a little apartment block somewhere on the city's east side. That year, I kept mostly to myself, managing a tenth grade quick and painless, turning sixteen along the way. Then, sometime through the eleventh grade I fell *in love* with my thirty-something Spanish teacher, Karen Thoreson, through the twelfth grade starting an affair with her. It was an involuntary act for both of us, to fall *in love*, and it scared me more than I've ever been scared of anything else. But even after all that's happened, after all the suffering it's caused and all the lives it's destroyed, I still don't know if I can say I'd have given up what we had. It's not that I don't think we made no mistakes. There were a lot of things that happened that I would've done differently if I could go back and do it all over again. It's just that what we had, for the time we had it, was so beautiful that I would never give back that feeling of having been with her.

In the last week of the classes in the eleventh grade, I'd slid onto her desk one afternoon when there was no one else in her classroom, took a deep breath, and then, in the middle of listening to her describe her summer plans, I'd asked her point-blank: "why don't we go out sometime?" She'd stopped, laughed, and said: "maybe next year." But her laugh almost hid a nervousness that led me to replay that little conversation over and over in my mind through the summer, looking for any hidden meaning, finding none, instead seizing on the obvious, the plain, until I'd convinced myself to try again. Soon the twelfth grade arrived, that first day after Labour Day seeing the halls bustle with life. Arriving at her first-period Spanish, I was the first student there, and walked in on her standing at the side of the class, with one hand reaching for a tin on the top shelf of a cupboard. Easily I took the tin and handed it to her, instinctively flexing my biceps underneath the small, white shirt I wore stretched tight across my chest. "Thanks," she said, quickly looking me up and down. "Anything for you," I said, with a wink and a nod, before turning and making for my seat near the back of the class. With her fresh face, white teeth, and brown hair tied back neatly into a bun, she looked not yet resigned like the other teachers to a lifetime of stale coffee, red tape, and disappointment. That first day back, I'd caught a glimpse of her looking my way from the head of the class, a little glint in her eye making clear her feelings in ways that words couldn't. We'd exchanged sneaky little glances from across the room before; some part of me was worried that, over the summer, she might've forgotten about me—no, not forgotten, just lost interest in the little game we'd taken to playing, where I'd push the boundaries of the normal student-teacher relationship and she'd give some weak rebuke, feigning disinterest even as the light behind her eyes made clear her true feelings. That night, after having gone home to a cold, dark, empty home, I sat back on the living room's couch and thought of her. Later, months later, with Karen in my arms, I'd kiss her, and when I'd kiss her it felt like we weren't so different after all.

But our little game had been playing itself out for more than two years by the time we'd first *make love*. At the start of the tenth grade, I'd re-enrolled in Eastmount Secondary, the school I'd attended for the eighth grade before spending the ninth in Texas. (There was no middle school in Vancouver; it was elementary for grades K through seven and secondary for eight through twelve). Having started taking Spanish in Texas, I'd kept on with the subject on returning to Canada rather than go back to French, Canada's other official language besides English. Most of the students in her classes were there because they'd become tired of studying French, required from grades four through eight, and on being offered a choice had defaulted to Spanish. I sat somewhere near the back of the class, watching as Miss Thoreson worked her way through her first year on the job, one day letting my eyes linger lovingly on her shapely, curvaceous body as she was turned to face the whiteboard, standing on the tips of her toes as she reached with one hand to scrawl verb conjugations in the last available space at the last possible moment before the bell rang to end the period, chairs screeching against the floor and a stampede to the door as she shouted homework. The last one to leave that day, I stopped at the door and looked back, looking at her wiping the day's work off the whiteboard. Later, in the twelfth grade, after we'd begun seeing each other, there were these little moments when I'd find myself alone with her, resting my hands on her wide hips, our foreheads touching as we leaned into one another, standing, bodies swaying slightly, hers seeming to fold snugly into mine. But I was so much bigger than her, the width of her shoulders fitting between my biceps, as though we were complementary pieces. I thought we were made for each other.

As the twelfth grade got underway, the summer's warmth faded, replaced by the cold, hard rain marking winter's impending arrival in the Pacific Northwest. But it was never too cold or too wet for me to wander outside in a t-shirt and jeans, meandering along the path hugging the building, stepping right through puddles as I came up to Karen's room. Watching her through her classroom's window, I'd approach and gently knock. When she turned to look, I raised my palm and blew her a mock kiss, the gesture seeming to strike her as though it were a real kiss. She took a half-step back, then smiled, offering a little wave in return. These were the little moments that stood out, emboldening me to press further. I was only obeying instinct, without restraint, even as I fully believed I knew exactly what I was doing and that I was in full control of myself. Soon, I'd spend hours plotting half-seriously the next time she and I would cross paths, whether in the halls between classes or in the parking lot in the morning or in the library at the end of the day, going over every little detail, rehearsing every line, on coming across her completely forgetting myself and just wind up *looking* at her. In love with her, I'd developed a need to be near her, like every moment I wasn't had rapidly become hard to stand. These were the little games we played, the little games we'd keep on playing even after we'd come to be together halfway through the year, when I'd be close to eighteen but not yet over that line, in her little apartment those months later *making love*, I thought, like any other couple. But it was all an act. We were both scared of each other, and of ourselves.

As the month of September drew to a close, there came a day when I'd had the chance, but squandered it all the same. I stood, leaning against a locker among a group of my classmates in the hall, when Karen appeared from behind a corner. Our eyes locked for a moment, causing a flustered look to appear on her face, seeming to almost stop her for a half-moment. But as she walked past, I sensed in her a flourishing heat, like she couldn't hide the need she had for the attention I gave, as she allowed a momentary smile that only I seemed to see. Turning away from my classmates, I faced her at exactly the moment she stepped past and I said under my breath, "you're so fucking hot," as though it was the most natural thing in the world to say. What I really wanted to say to her was *I love you*, but couldn't bring myself yet to form the words. As she passed, she looked back briefly but said nothing, seeming to take it all in stride, then walked away. *It was a game*, I thought, *it was nothing more than a game*. If only I'd known, then, that I was like an open book, that everyone around me could see exactly how I felt and what I was thinking, then I might not have wound up making the leap from harmless flirtation to propositioning Karen, from there to *making love*. But I couldn't just *be* with her, even as it was plainly evident from the way she *looked* at me and from the way she seemed to go out of her way to let me *look* at her; it took a months-long build up, in that time she seeming more sure of herself, patient, but not without her own doubts. When we'd finally *make love* months later, she'd take me in her apartment, pull me down on top of her in bed, and, when it was over a half-minute later she'd hold me, as if she was afraid to let the moment go.

Through the first couple of months of the school year, the rain lingered, rainwater pooling in places, never seeming quite to dry. But inside the classrooms and halls at Eastmount there wasn't any relief, my assignments handed in, sometimes late, often late, usually late, almost always late, handed back drowning beneath a storm of red ink. In every course except Karen's Spanish, I soon fell behind the rest of the class, to stay behind until the last months of the school year. In history, one afternoon, having stayed late to make up for missed coursework by writing an in-class essay when Karen walked in. My eyes traced a little path along the curvature of her hips, lingering lovingly on her ample bottom while she walked past, leaning over slightly at the history teacher's desk and dropped the folder lightly on it. They exchanged some small talk, she half-looking at me with a glance once, twice, and I couldn't help but think she was taking her time just to give me the chance to eye her up, as though to savour the attention. It was confusing, deeply confusing, and once she'd left I hurriedly finished the essay and left, hoping to catch her in the parking lot, though I had no idea what I'd say to her if I did. By the time I made it to my car, though, hers was gone, and I swore at myself under my breath for letting another chance at her slip through my fingers, even though it should've been clear to me by then that she'd keep on giving me as many chances as I needed. Although I'd never been more scared of anything in my life, I knew, somehow, to push through the fear, take the little openings she gave me here and there, and make them as wide as possible in the hope of having my chance at her. Months later, after we'd *made love* for the first time, I might've thought we could've become like a couple, like *boyfriend* and *girlfriend*, albeit in secret. But it wouldn't be that easy or simple, and through the rest of the twelfth grade I grew to become more confused about it, even as I was absolutely certain I had it all figured out.

Back in the first week of classes that year, I walked, one afternoon, along the hall outside Karen's classroom, chancing a look inside. She wasn't there. It was hardly halfway through that Wednesday, and from the year before I'd grown used to seeing her sitting at her desk as she worked through lunch. Turning, I walked right into her, papers fluttering to the floor. Dropping, each of us gathered up the papers, starting on either side of the little mess and working towards the centre quickly. She reached for the last sheet, and just as the tips of her fingers touched the floor, I let my hand brush against the back of hers, touching her only slightly, the kind of touch where it was almost as though we weren't touching at all. Later that afternoon, between fourth and fifth period, I thought to try at touching her again, but there was a moment's doubt lingering in the back of my mind. The hallway was full of students between classes, but as I headed around a turn and down the main stairwell I spotted, from a distance, Karen exiting the main office, locking eyes with her for a half-second before she turned and headed in the opposite direction, disappearing out of sight. On some level, even at the age of seventeen I must've sensed the indecisiveness in her, the hemming and hawing between the part of her that wanted the attention and the part of her that wanted to be left alone. Later, I went home, driving back to the little apartment complex I lived in with my mother, Lisa, arriving to find her in the living room, spending her day off smoking a cigarette and watching television, bottle of cider sitting half-empty on the coffee table in front of her. She didn't seem to notice that I'd been gone overnight, and took no note of me as I walked in through the door. Then, as I turned and started up the stairs, she called out, "dinner's in the fridge!" Later, I came downstairs to find her gone, in the fridge finding some leftover Chinese.

At home that summer, I'd become like an afterthought, as though I was just *there*. Lisa worked as a waitress at a diner nearby, her shifts keeping her out until late at night, leaving me to fend for myself. One late-August's evening, the sky was aflame and it was just past eight. As it was hot and humid, I had the windows open and a little black fan pointed right at me while I sat in a t-shirt and shorts, watching the Expos tee-off on the Phillies. At some point I fell asleep, only to be woken by Lisa thumping through the front door. The sky was dark and the drapes swayed gently. There was the sound of snickering, of a man's voice I didn't recognize, of people making their way inside, then the halting, disjointed gallop of heavy steps up the stairs. But at the last moment, the footsteps took a hard turn and thumped into the next room, the creaking and groaning of bedsprings suddenly under a heavy weight, contracting and expanding rhythmically, faster, faster, faster still, groaning, then sudden silence. But I'd grown used to it by then; it was just a noise, like the wailing of a police car's sirens and the pattering of an autumn's rain against the streets.

We lived in a little subsidized housing complex just a few blocks from Eastmount. We'd lived there as long as I could remember; it had two bedrooms, and in mine a bunk bed that hadn't yet been replaced. The summer between the tenth and eleventh grades, I'd kept working at a local thrift shop, midway through July spending a few hundred saved-up for a used car, an Oldsmobile Eighty-Eight, a big, hulking battleship of a car. The morning after Lisa had come home, I woke a little early and headed downstairs, on my way casting a glance back through the door to Lisa's bedroom, spotting her still in bed with someone. At least, I thought, the Oldsmobile was *mine*, a private space where I could imagine Karen sitting in the passenger seat, consumed as I was by the act of obsessively thinking about her, exactly as anyone else might've been. But I never stopped to think about what might've been going through her mind, acting on instinct alone. In the months that were to follow, it was instinct that would wind up changing our lives forever.

In her little apartment, months later, we were in bed, naked, her body draped across mine, her head resting on my muscular chest. It was dark, with only the pale orange glow of the streetlamps bleeding in through the blinds, a slant of light striking her just right, bending along the curvature of her body. With one hand, I reached for her backside, kneading with a grip that was awkward and uncertain, probably too hard. At seventeen, nearly eighteen, I was half her age, but fully believed it didn't matter. (I still believe it didn't matter). After having *made love* that night, it seemed almost anticlimactic to not know what was supposed to happen next, but then I think, now, that she, then, didn't know either, that she'd put everything she had just into crossing that last line and hadn't anything left to figure out her next move. She stirred, pushing herself off me and rolling out of bed, and I thought to reach after her, to take her by the hand and pull her back, but a self-conscious feeling kept me from doing anything but lying in place, propped up on my elbows, and looking after her. Then, I listened as she made across the room, the floor groaning as her feet struck the little seams between the beams, the door creaking as it swung open, then silence as she stood in the doorway and tossed a half-nervous glance. Neither of us knew what to expect, what should've happened next, what either of us should've done next. I don't remember exactly what happened after she'd left the room but before I followed her out, only that, even after we'd *made love*, I was still scared of her, that bolt of fear still twisting up from a pit at the bottom of my stomach until I couldn't stand it and had to get away from her. But all it took was our touch, her hands on my chest while I rested my hands on her hips, to reassure me, in her bathroom, she and I in each other's arms, the fear still there, but subdued, muted, as if it had withdrawn and let me have the moment.

Then, it was back on one of those late-October mornings, unseasonably cold, just before the start of classes for the day, and what best I can remember about it was the perfectly cloudless sky which made the near-freezing temperature feel all the more surreal. Looking across the faculty lot, I spotted Karen stepping out of her green CR-V. She hadn't yet spotted me when she began towards the building's south entrance, my eyes tracking her all the way there. Then, as she reached the door, she turned and looked back, scanning the lot for something, anything, her eyes finding mine. *I love you.* I mouthed the words. I couldn't tell if she made out the words for all the distance between us. She seemed to nod slightly before heading inside, leaving me to lean back against my car for a little while longer until I couldn't stand myself any longer and followed her in. But when we next ran into each other, later in the day between periods, she seemed distracted, as if she was looking through me and down the hall. That night, I dreamed of her.

1. Present (2015-????)

Ten years later, when I was twenty-eight, I found myself standing, one night, in an aisle at a grocery store, comparing one brand of fabric softener to another while somewhere in the back of my mind I wondered just where it'd all gone wrong. It was late at night, and still I had the muck and the grime of a day's work on my hands, while my feet were tired and sore, the hardness of the store's floor felt through the soles of my steel-toed boots. I spent a little while pretending to read the labels before giving up and dropping one box into the basket I carried in one arm, then made for the cashier. On my way out of the store, I turned a corner and ran into her. On her phone, with one hand fidgeting in her purse, dirty blond hair framing her face, but with a bit of the colour faded from her skin. Then, her eyes swept up, linking with mine, and suddenly it became obvious that we'd been staring at each other. "Keith," she began. "Karen," I reacted. Soon, not that night but some days later, we were in my apartment, in bed, *making love*, her ragged breaths, the lewd slap of skin against skin, and the rhythmic creaking of the bed's springs the only sounds as we had each other again as we'd done before.

After our first night together, she insisted it was to end there. "I'm a married woman now," she said, sitting on the edge of the bed, before putting her earrings back on and straightening her hair. Yet, as she looked back, tossing a glance my way, the little glint in her eyes hinted at the weekend trysts, the early morning couplings, the secret, after-work rendezvous to come. Six months slid by, our covert meetings reawakening a fondness for her, stirring those old feelings, until, sometime halfway through that year's summer, our intimacy seemed to make each and every day worth looking forward to. She became an addiction, with every moment spent either with her or thinking of her. It was like I was a teenager again, given a second chance with the woman I'd fallen in love with hardly ten years earlier. It was in this frame of mind that I rose one morning, steam rising from the mug of coffee in my hand, and looked out from my apartment perched precariously on the edge of the road, across the street from a whorehouse disguised half-cleverly as one of those little, hole-in-the-wall hotels, my thoughts reaching through the pre-dawn darkness towards her.

Even as we carried out our covert affair, it was difficult to think of her just as Karen, part of me still wanting to think of her as Miss Thoreson, Spanish teacher. (She'd kept the last name when she'd married, but I never asked if she'd liked to be called Miss or Mrs.). I told her what I'd been up to in the ten years since we'd seen each other, what I'd done, the degree I'd earned in Sociology. "I'm glad you got yourself sorted out. I always knew you had it in you," she'd said, "you just needed to rise above it." It made me proud to hear her say that, even if she hadn't yet known what I'd been through in my years we'd been apart. Arriving at her seaside condominium one morning, I soon stood in front of her, the room dark but for the orange haze of the streetlights bleeding in through the closed, slanted blinds, silent but for the thrum of traffic rumbling along the street outside. Hands on her hips, I gently slid my palms along the curvature of her figure as she leaned forward, pressing into me, her small, firm breasts pushing against my broad, hardened chest, lips joining with mine, my back against the door to her bedroom, until we fell back onto her marital bed, that lewd slap of skin against skin again filling the room.

In public, at work, she'd always projected the image of an educated woman, prim, proper, her hair tight neatly into a bun, tight, taut, her blouse, white, freshly ironed, every creased edge sharp, her jet-black skirt accentuating her shapely figure, extending below the knee, her high-heels clicking on the smooth, hard linoleum floors, her face configured into a permanent look of disapproval as she looked over a classroom full of students, eyeing each with a guarded suspicion. Yet, as she called me into her arms, taking me to her bed whenever a spare night presented itself here and there, she would let down her hair, tear off her clothes, in an instant leaping upon me, pressing herself down upon me, taking me inside her as we worked towards our mutual climax, the image of her as prim and proper coming apart in an instant, bursting at the seams, her hair soon a matted mess as she lay upon me, still but for the gentle rise and fall of her chest. And on pushing herself up off the bed, she'd flash an impish grin before turning and making for the bathroom, her figure stark against the darkness, her skin blemished, imperfect, my eyes drawn to the little teal butterfly tattoo etched on the side of her shin. Whenever I found myself with a spare moment at work, I'd find a quiet little corner of the warehouse to park my dock-stocker, pull my phone from my pocket, and read over the texts we'd exchanged, satisfying my craving for her even as it made me want more.

But like a fantasy, we never had much time together, our lives divided by the gulf between a twenty-something man and a married-with-children middle-aged woman. Whenever we found the time, though, we'd abandon the pretense of respectability and surrender to each other, giving in to the pleasure our *lovemaking* provided. It was easy enough for me to forget, during those times, that she was married with a young son, a mental trick which allowed me the fantasy of being with her as more than a lover. Of course, she'd likely noticed the hints that gave away my lifestyle; the twin-sized in my one-bedroom apartment, the little Ford Ranger I drove, the bottle of antidepressants sitting in my bathroom's medicine cabinet, the fridge stocked only with enough food to last a week and the kitchen sink half-filled with the last night's dishes. Mercifully, she'd never asked, allowing an implicit understanding that our personal lives were off-limits, that ours was an affair, nothing more, despite us having been together before. This time it was different, she seemed to say, this time it was just *sex*. And then it wasn't.

One night, a steady rain pattered against the windshield as I rolled up the street in my truck, slowing at just the right spot, parking close enough, I thought, for a quick walk the rest of the way, but far enough not to draw suspicion from her neighbours. Her husband was not due back from a trip out of town until the next day, but still I gave a quick look up and down the street before stepping out of my truck and starting towards their home, walking through the rain without an umbrella or a coat, getting wet all the while. Arriving at her front door, I raised my fist to knock; at exactly the moment I was about to strike, the door opened, Karen standing there, pulling me inside before she closed and locked the door. One, two, three seconds she waited, then turned back to me, in an instant us taking each other in our shared embrace, my hands resting on her hips while her arms reached around the back of my neck. We kissed, her taste flooding my mouth. Reaching behind her, I held onto her bottom as I picked her up, her legs locking around me, her feet crossing against the small of my back, and carried her down the hall and into her bedroom, heaving her onto the bed, waiting a half-second before taking off my clothes and setting myself on her, her hands clutching at my back as I entered her, at once immersing myself in the warmth, the pleasure of her, her body, her touch, the feeling of closeness no one else had ever given me.

Afterwards, we lay there for a little while, she lightly rubbing the back of my neck while I rested my head on her chest, listening to the beat of her heart. In the months since we'd begun our affair, I'd been wanting to tell her the way I felt, but'd never found the courage. Every time I'd tried, the words became lodged in my throat. That night, it was no different, the two of us lying in bed, basking in our *lovemaking's* warm afterglow for a while, eventually, falling asleep to the sounds of the city fading in through the open window. Late next morning, I woke to find myself alone in bed, from the bathroom the crackling hiss of a stream of water striking the bottom of the shower. Sliding the door gently open, I stood in the doorway for a minute or two, watching the shower's curtain rustle, before stepping forward, drawing the curtain open slightly, and stepping inside, her hands finding my sides as we shared an embrace. I tried to speak, "Karen, I..." but couldn't find the right words. "Shhh," she said, placing a finger against my lips, then turned and ground her bottom against me, my erection pressing against the softness of her skin. Kissing the back of her neck, I gave in, driven by instinct to push at her until she reached back, took my length, and guided me inside her, until our bodies were flush with one another. Stilled, I held myself against her, rocking slowly on my heels, savouring the moment, until I couldn't hold myself back any longer.

In the shower, we stood, she grasping the shower's hose, leaning forward, looking back as I let my hands run the length of her back, the soft hiss of the hot water streaming around us as we pushed against one another, my movements against her building, faster, faster, faster. Her breaths drew shorter, sharper, until her back arched and her whole body stilled, her eyes squeezed shut, and she shuddered, quivering, writhing in place. And as I held myself against her, jaw clenched, fists balled, my climax peaked, my mind blank as I strained into her, until it was finished. Spent, I leaned over her, into her, the both of us panting, the moment having been won. Still, as she turned to face me, reaching round to rest her hands on the back of my neck, we looked into each other's eyes, pulled each other in close, and held ourselves against one another, our lips joined, our tongues mingled, the hotness of her breath blending with mine, her taste sharp, her warmth spreading between us in a wave of heat that could scarcely be felt against the stream of water flowing around our bodies, steam rising all around. It was a little moment of satiation, of a hunger sated, a craving quieted, a purpose fulfilled. Then, pulling back until our foreheads rested against one another's, I spoke, with a whisper. "I still love you," I said. She stilled, cradling my bulk in her arms, seeming to take my larger frame in her grasp, as if we were swaying in time to an imagined song.

Against the hiss of the shower's piping hot stream, it seemed as though she might've not heard me, might've instead sought to bundle herself up within a protective warmth. But as my hands found their way along the small of her back and came to rest on the sides of her hips, she turned slightly, raising herself until she rested back against me, her shapely, curvaceous figure steadying against my bulky, muscular frame. A breath drawn in, then, she spoke. "I know." An exasperated sigh let out, barely audible against the soft hiss of the shower's piping hot water striking the tiled floor. Placing my lips softly on the back of her neck, I planted tender kisses up towards the side of her face, settling gingerly behind an ear, nibbling, her back arching as she pressed back, until there was only our skin to separate us, a warmth all around.

Then, a slam, the sound of the front door swinging open. Her eyes widened, and in the seconds it took for either of us to process what'd happened, a series of footsteps sounded out, drawing louder, louder, nearer, nearer. Neither she nor I moved from each other, even as the full weight of the situation dawned on us, each of us remaining frozen in place until the washroom's door swung slowly open, its hinges creaking, doorknob squeaking, a man's voice speaking from beyond the hall. Karen pulled forward, reaching for a towel and draping it around her body before handing one to me, her motions halting, disjointed, frenetic, as though some small part of her thought it possible to escape undetected, that part seizing control, while I stood, watching, silent.

A child's voice. "Mum?" Daring a peek from behind the shower's half-closed curtain, I found her young son standing in the doorway, husband behind, his jaw hanging open slightly, eyes wide, shock on his face crumpling into a jagged, ragged anger. Soon, shouting, crying, the slamming of the front door behind as I sprinted, naked but for a pair of underwear and a t-shirt, towards my truck parked on the side of the street, clutching my clothes under one arm. Soon speeding along the highway and across a bridge into town, I could not hear my own thoughts against my heart slamming against my chest, while my hands gripped the wheel, tight. By the time I made it home, the sun had set, and I arrived to a cold, dark, empty apartment, and I arrived without knowing when, or if, Karen and I would see each other again.

2. Past

A little over three years had passed since the September 11th attacks. Still living in Texas at the time of the attacks, that day saw me at school with the rest of my classmates, watching news footage replay scenes of carnage over and over again, images seared into our memories of fiery explosions, of metal beams tossed into the air like splinters of wood, of men and women leaping to their deaths, of hundreds of thousands of tons of concrete pulverized into dust. Soon after they had us recite the Pledge of Allegiance in class every day at the start of the second period, with our hands over our chests as we read aloud in perfect unison, the ritual marking clearly the end of one era and the beginning of another. *I pledge allegiance, to the flag, of the United States of America, and to the Republic for which it stands, one nation under God, indivisible, with liberty and justice for all.* A few weeks later, I met a senior girl named Melissa outside the front entrance to Hebron High School. Even though it's been many years since she and I have last spoken to each other, I'll always, always, remember what we'd had. Through that one year I'd lived in Texas, we met every day out front where the school buses unloaded, until, sometime halfway through the month of March, Melissa and I finally had sex.

We lived in Carrollton, a middle-class city just north of Dallas where my father had settled with his second wife (they split up before I moved in with him; it's a long story). It was the exact picture of the all-American suburb, with the same four or five houses built a hundred times over to make a neighbourhood, the same neighbourhoods built a hundred times over to make a city, and the same cities built a hundred times over to make a way of life. Every house stood exactly the same distance from the street, and was painted one of the same three or four colours, each seeming like a shade hardly darker or lighter enough from the next to be distinguished by the naked eye. Every lawn was cut down to precisely the same height, watered so as to not sport even the slightest, smallest patch of brown that might've drawn the eyes of neighbours whose names one never learned. Every garage held the same car, truck, or SUV, each one of the same three dull, dark colours, every morning all of them jammed onto the same highway heading in the same direction, and again back the other way at night. It was a place of crushing conformity, yet one which was confident in its own superiority; *this is the life*, it reassured itself, *this is the life the world wants.* As she and I had the house I lived in to ourselves, we explored each other's bodies, clumsily, but like we were the first people to do it. She wasn't thin, she wasn't pretty, and she wasn't popular, but for the time we were together, she was mine.

We'd met one morning when she'd spotted me getting off one school bus wearing my Canucks jersey the day after they'd thrashed her Red Wings, and we struck up an instant friendship. Though she was a senior and I was a freshman, hockey gave us a shared interest, so many nights that year spent at my house watching one game or another; as my father spent his weeks working in Houston, returning to spend the weekends with me, I had the place to myself, making it easy to invite her into an entirely private space. It was during one of these weeks that Melissa and I had each other's virginities, *fucking* on the living room's couch, stilted, awkward, fumbling through the act, without a clue what we were doing, sure we were doing *something.* Though I'd only just turned fifteen, I thought I'd fallen *in love.* But at the end of the year, she moved away to go to college in Ann Arbour, Michigan, leaving me again without a friend, loneliness prompting me to ask Lisa if I could've returned home. Months later, shortly before the start of the new school year, I moved back to Canada and in with my mother. I've never told anyone why I'd chosen to move back after only a year in the States; Lisa never asked, taking me back as she'd grown used to over the years, the act of moving between her and my father so well-rehearsed by then it hardly registered as anything at all.

In the twelfth grade, in Canada, as September gave way to October, there came a moment when I'd come across Karen standing in the office at Eastmount, my eyes lingering lovingly on her skin tanned just so, her eyes brown, her lips thin, her dirty blond hair framing a face shaped by gently curving cheeks. She seemed to notice me looking her over but chose not to look back, her eyes fixed on something else. It was as though she had allowed me the moment, and for the short time it was mine I was grateful. Every time we crossed paths a bolt of fear shot through me and I was nearly overcome by the urge to look away. But I'd always push past it, always, on instinct alone.

Months later, it was the new year after classes had resumed following the two-week Christmas break, and the time came when she and I were together, taking place in the back seat of my car, with her knee-length hiked up around her hips and my jeans pulled down to my thighs as she moved against me, her hands grasping at my shoulders and her lips over mine as I came too quickly. Later, not too much time later, she sat atop me as we took in the moment, the car's windows fogged up. As the sound of the rain's chatter filled the air, Karen pushed herself off me, then turned to sit back, a look of uncertainty on her face suggesting she'd done something she'd soon regret. Acting, I leaned over and let my hand caress her cheek, bringing her lips to mine as we shared the lightest of kisses, her strain fading, giving way to that sly, impish grin I'd come to think of as hers. It wasn't our first time together, of course, and it wasn't our second either, but in my car, in a forested area halfway up the mountains it seemed *different*. She'd picked the spot, on Vancouver's north shore, and it was the first and only time we'd have each other in a public place, she, later, telling me the risk of being caught wasn't worth the thrill of *making love* in that clearing not far from where she'd once had an old boyfriend when she was in high school. She didn't say it exactly like that, of course, but I put it together from what she had said; at the time, though, I only looked forward to the next time we were together, and it didn't matter to me at seventeen or eighteen where our next time together happened; it was only important to me that it happened, someway, somehow.

Some weeks into the twelfth grade, and already we were at an impasse. "We have to stop," Karen had said (and not the first time she'd said it, having alternated between meekly resisting my advances and quietly urging me on for a while), as we stood outside Eastmount on the little sidewalk that separated the faculty and student parking lots, "or this is going to get me in trouble." But the tone in her voice suggested she didn't mean it, that she wanted me to keep going. Having taken up working out sometime the previous summer, I spent an hour in the morning three or four times a week in the weight room. So early, I had the room to myself, feeling the slow, rhythmic contractions of my body's muscles as I worked my way in a horseshoe-shaped path along the weight room's equipment, my body like a machine. Every now and then, I'd come across Karen in the halls as I headed from the locker room to my first class, first once, then a second time, soon she going out of her way every day to approach, passing just to give herself the chance to exchange glances with me. My heart lifted a little each time, and I knew from the furtive look she gave me that she felt the same way. She wanted me to stop, but she couldn't bring herself to stop. At the same time, I looked at her and knew, just *knew* that she wanted me to press forward and cross the line she couldn't cross. After I'd begun working out in the morning, she and I crossed paths in the hall one morning between the gym and the locker-rooms, the two of them separated by a single narrow hall. Though this routine had begun only recently, I hadn't been in altogether poor shape before, and this brief encounter marked the first time she'd seen me in shorts and a t-shirt, a small t-shirt which seemed to cling to my biceps and my barrel of a chest. She stopped, and I stopped, her eyes sweeping quickly from my chest to my feet, then back up again. "Keith," she said, her voice wavering slightly. It then occurred to me that I'd been sweating, a thin film of moisture covering my face, neck, a dampness pulling my shirt taut against the firmness of my chest. Instinctively, I flexed my biceps slightly, and she seemed to take a half-step back. "Miss Thoreson," I said, suddenly aware of myself. "Karen." "What?" "It's Karen." I'd known her first name for a while, but it was the first time she'd asked me to call her by it. "Oh." It was all I could think to say. She looked away, then turned slightly and continued walking towards a door at the end of the hall, while I stood and stared after her, watching as her shapely, curvaceous figure receded into the distance and disappeared behind the door. Though I didn't have her class that day, the rest of it saw the school's floors seem a little smoother, the air a little richer, and the weight landing on my feet with each step a little lighter. I hadn't even touched her yet, not in the way that lovers touch each other, and already I believed I was hopeless *in love*. I'd come to learn she believed she was *in love*, too. But that wasn't all we had in common. We were both terrified of each other, even as either of us worked to put on the most confident front possible, she afraid for her job, while I was afraid just for the twisted, sick feeling in my stomach whenever we were near, whenever I thought about her, whenever I was about to approach her and feed her some line that sounded smooth and suave in my head but probably came out awkward and insincere.

"About yesterday," I'd began, working to keep my voice steady and the knot in my stomach from rising, "I didn't—" "It's fine," she'd said, turning from the whiteboard to face me, leaning back on its edge, "you're not the first guy to have a crush on his teacher." It was the next day, in her classroom, before classes had started for the day. Approaching her, I'd advanced until there was hardly a half-metre between us, her stance relaxed, loose. "C'mon," I'd said, "just one?" At the time I was scared, frightened in a way I'd never been. I wanted to run away and hide from myself. My heart pounded against my chest and a bolt of fear had lodged itself in my gut. "Keith," she'd said, seeming to steady herself against my advances, "don't do this to me." But her voice seemed full of uncertainty as mine. Though it would be some time before we'd *make love* already I'd drawn a little bit of courage from the way we looked at each other whenever our paths crossed. In her apartment, months later, not the first, not the second, not even the third time we'd *made love* but *sometime*, we were in bed and I was looking for a reason, any reason at all, to leave her, to be anywhere other than where I was, that intense fear of *her* making it suddenly impossible to be there. But then she turned and kissed me on the cheek, before reaching across my chest and resting one hand on the other side of my face, then gently bringing my lips to hers, our kiss pushing the fear from my stomach for a moment, only a moment, just long enough.

It was just weeks into the twelfth grade, and already it felt, in ways, like I was fading. At home I was largely left to myself, Lisa having devoted herself to the new man in her life. His name was Randall. They'd been seeing each other since first meeting while I was living with my father in Texas, and since I'd moved back home she'd spent most of her time at work or with him. As far as her boyfriends went, Randall seemed like he was the most benign one yet, as he ran his own business, a little local delivery service which looked to be on the level. Then she came home one day with a bruise on her arm. When I asked about it, she'd said, "oh, that's nothing," quickly and nervously, followed by, "he treats me right," rubbing the bruise as she spoke. But all I thought to do was watch as she came and went, until the day came when she showed up one afternoon with him standing next to her, holding her hand. It was one mid-October day, the skies cloudy and the pavement outside still wet from a heavy rain. Wearing thick-rimmed glasses and with his balding hair more grey than brown he looked much older than her. He offered me a handshake, but I didn't take it. From that point on, whenever we crossed paths, I couldn't help but look him right on the eye for just a half-second and put on the sharpest scowl I could manage. Look, I hadn't the slightest clue what I was doing. I just couldn't stand him. He was a prick, a foul-mouthed, drunken prick. It just so happened that he'd wind up giving me exactly the right reason for seeing him as the enemy, but it made no difference, as I would've made sure to find a way.

Late one night, past midnight on a Thursday, I came home from the thrift shop to find our little townhouse cold, dark, and empty. But I'd hardly made it in through the front door when a taxi slid to a halt in the street outside, Randall and Lisa staggering out of the backseat. There was some pause as he leaned over the taxi's roof and seemed to have a word with the driver, before turning and heading towards home. Quickly grabbing a few things from the kitchen, I headed upstairs and ducked into my room just as the front door swung open, the sound of its scraping across the linoleum floor scratching through the night. But that night, there was no sound of footsteps thumping up the stairs, no sound of bedsprings squeaking and no sound of grunting or groaning. No, sometime after midnight I made my way downstairs to see what was happening, finding Lisa on the couch, asleep or passed out, Randall nowhere to be seen. It was an odd sight, one I haven't quite gotten used to, to see her sitting there silently, still in her clothes from a night out, her hair a mess. Tiptoeing across the living room's floor, I reached for the clock-radio and set its alarm for eight o'clock in the morning. Then into the kitchen, where I found booze in a cupboard and poured it out into the sink. Withdrawing back upstairs, I couldn't help but wonder if there was more than I could see going on, the night darkening until I woke, still in my clothes, still-undone homework on the desk, the fog slowly lifting. It was confusing; I couldn't know when he'd be there. Every time I came home, whether after school or after work late at night, I had no way of knowing what I was coming home to.

By the time I made my way downstairs Lisa was up and about, getting ready for the day. She had her coffee, no crème and three sugar, while I sipped on a can of Coke. We exchanged a few words, small talk, deftly avoiding the topic of the night before. "Working late tonight?" I asked. "Yes," she replied, "well, er, sort of. Randall's picking me up after I get off." "Again?" "Yes." Sitting at the table, we said very little, until she looked at her watch and announced that she "had to go," then reached for her coffee and downed the last of it in one quick gulp before grabbing her coat and heading out the door. It was the last we'd see of each other for a few days, in the meantime the place yielding to a silence. There were dirty dishes piled up in the sink. A pile of undone laundry so big the basket had disappeared beneath sat outside the washroom. A stack of unopened mail lay on a cabinet in the living room, waiting to be thrown out still-unopened. But it was the little things that bothered me. The pictures hung on the wall only slightly askew. The thick film of dust covering the tops of the TV stand and the exposed surfaces on the bookshelf. The hole in the wall where a foot had cratered in the plaster and the drywall months earlier, mostly hidden behind a couple of strategically-placed boxes, still visible when I walked past on the way into the kitchen and looked to the side at just the right angle. It made me aware of myself, as if it was something I'd done wrong, or if it was something I could just stand up and fix all on my own.

That morning (or maybe it was a morning a few days later) I'd hardly made it out through the front door myself before I began to have thoughts about the rest of the year, imagining myself somewhere, anywhere but there. There hadn't been a time when I hadn't been an outsider, memory holding scorn, contempt. I remember always dreading schoolwork done in pairs or groups, knowing each and every project or presentation would see me awkwardly paired with some other outcast, or just plain left on my own. I suppose it was in this mindset that I found myself taking up working out in Eastmount's weight room every morning for an hour before classes, sometime halfway through the tenth grade. It offered a peace of mind that came from being in a safe space, safe not from harm, but from the relentless self-doubt and the insecurity that would run rampant through my mind if only I'd ever give it a chance. Through early adolescence I'd never been small, and the three-to-five-times-a-week workouts soon turned me thick and sculpted, making me feel exactly more assured of myself as I walked the halls of Eastmount and drew the sly looks and the furtive glances here and there. But I was still an outcast, spending lunches alone, sometimes reading, sometimes pretending to read. That morning, as I put myself through the paces on the weight room's machines, I pushed myself hard, every muscle's rhythmic contraction smooth, repetitive, like a well-oiled piece of machinery running itself through a routine, until my biceps burned, ached, only to push myself harder still, until I couldn't manage even one more rep, then pushing through another, then another, then another.

At home, Randall became more and more common a sight. Look, I never really bothered to ask how they'd met. It made no difference to me. He and Lisa were in and out of sight, there, but not there, with weeks of their absence punctuated by the seemingly random bursts of shouting and crying, crashing and smashing that marked each of his stays over. In the span of a few months I came to steel myself against the possibility they'd be there at the end of the day, my stomach knotting up each and every night as I took the corner onto that little side-street where we lived, calming at the sight of an empty space where his beat-up white van always parked, finally settling as I found our little home empty and quiet. But then there were the days or the late nights he was there. Quickly, my safe space shrank to the size of my bedroom, until one night even that little box of air became unsafe. But so long as I had the little moments I could retreat into fantasies of being with Karen, I still saw myself having an escape.

Months later, in her apartment we'd *make love*, finally, after having put ourselves through so much melodrama just for the sake of our *feelings*. In the weeks following that first awkward time we'd *made love* in her apartment she asked me to keep my distance at Eastmount for reasons I thought I understood but didn't, couldn't have. Even as we'd become, well, *something*, in public we reverted to our old way, hiding our feelings behind the roles of teacher and student. There came a day, after we'd first been together, when I stood in front of my locker, fumbling with the combination I'd suddenly forgotten, until turning away and finding myself walking right into her as she'd approached me from behind. She looked right at me. Nodding slightly, I looked right back, holding the stare for a half-second before she turned and walked away, her heels clicking as she kept a deliberate pace until disappearing around a corner and out of sight. Later that night I lay atop her, she gently stroked the back of my neck, causing me to feel a stirring sensation that quickly spread throughout me, and again I was energized for her. She said, "you just don't stop, do you?" And I said, "only for you." "To be eighteen again..." "Seventeen." "Whatever." She laughed warmly and pushed me off her, rolling away to rise from bed and make for the washroom. Following, I joined her, and in her apartment's little washroom we kissed again, the moment reassuring either of us there'd be more nights just like that one, if only we could learn to be better than we were. We *made love* again that night, she pulling me back down on top of her, kissing me, reaching to guide me inside her, as I began to move against her in awkward, stilted motions she breaking the kiss to bring my head into the side of her neck, she, then, whispering something indistinctly into my ear, as I came she rubbing her hand in long, slow circles on the back of my head. In the afterwards, as I began to fall asleep, I heard her say, "I wish I didn't love you." When I woke up the next morning, she was already up in the kitchen, and I quickly and quietly took my leave without knowing when we'd have each other next, but sure it was to be sometime soon after.

Early in the school year, though, as I walked through the hall on the way to first-period English, binder under my arm, Karen and I crossed paths, as we did so often, well before we'd first had each other. At just the right moment I looked her in the eye, and she raised her eyebrows tellingly, the little twinkle in her eye making her feelings perfectly clear. Some months later, maybe three or four, we'd *make love* in her little apartment, and I'd have my peace, like any other man might've after having found love. But, in the meantime, I'd soon find things at home in a state of change as Lisa told me, one night over a rare supper at home together, that she and Randall were moving in with each other. Well, he was moving in with us. How she planned on fitting him and all his junk into our little townhouse wasn't something I asked. It wasn't really the point. No, the slight edge to her tone of voice suggested she'd agreed to let him move in some time ago and had just avoided telling me until now. They'd been together for two years by then, and I don't think I'll ever understand why it took so long for the two of them to take it to the next step; all that mattered to me, then, was that it meant a sudden invasion of one of the few safe places I had left.

2. Present

That night, Karen and I exchanged texts, hers short, choppy, as if she'd found the time, here and there, to sneak a moment, chancing detection, risking it for the sake of sparing a thought. Still, she didn't explain what'd happened after I left, and I didn't ask, nor when we'd see each other next, if ever. As the night passed, her messages grew longer and less frequent, until finally, just past midnight, they ceased altogether, leaving me to spend the night lying in bed, gazing through the window as if to project myself into the sky beyond, to immerse myself in the orange haze cast onto the street by so many streetlights. Still, with the constant thrum of traffic slowly dimming to a dull roar, the night slid past, with only the shadows dancing on the ceiling to mark the progress of time inching forward, groaning and straining as it edged toward morning, bending and warping as it folded itself into nothing, until suddenly it seemed as though I turned over and found myself staring into the day, looking into the future but unable to see any further than a foot in front of me.

Then, it happened. A call from Karen, the first I'd heard of her voice in the six months since her husband had walked in on us. "Richard and I are getting a divorce," she said, "we tried to keep our marriage together but the trust just isn't there." It came as quite the shock to so suddenly have her back in my life, and at first I half-wondered if I'd gone crazy and just imagined her call out of the need for *someone*. "Keith," she said, "don't stop this now." Her voice was firm and gravelly, guarded and tired, but with a weakness just behind it that seemed so unlike her. We met that night, that very night, in the parking lot outside of a Starbucks, sharing an embrace that was warm but firm. Later that night, I was atop her, my whole body moving in long, slow strokes as we *made love*, but unlike any other time, as if we were younger again, she thirty-five and I seventeen, both of us trying to re-enact the very feeling we'd had after falling in love ten years earlier. But it was a fraud. We'd lied to ourselves, we'd tricked ourselves into believing we could've felt that way about each other again. As I looked into her eyes, I knew right then that we couldn't stop, that we were to act out our *love* because of a vague compulsion to do *something*, because it was better than doing *nothing*, because we were made to do so by something that came from a place deep inside us, something in need of a satisfaction neither of us could've ever provided to each other.

A breakthrough. Morning came, the day after her husband had walked in on us, with it a message from Karen left on my voicemail. Her voice was nearly hoarse. "I can't see you anymore," she said, "goodbye." In an instant, cast out, left adrift. With nothing left to be gained by continuing our affair, she had to end it, focusing her efforts, instead, on salvaging her marriage, her family. She had not said this exactly, but that morning as I sat in my truck and listened to her message over and over, a certainty seeped into the moment, calm, measured, uncomfortable but not altogether out of place. Having only so recently come to terms with my own thoughts, my own feelings, at that moment I did not know what to think, to feel. Instead, as I turned into the future, it seemed as though circumstance had reached out and brought me back to square one. In bed, months later, or maybe it was months earlier (I can't remember), with Karen, she lay underneath me with her legs hooked onto my backside, the warm, pleasant afterglow of our lovemaking still lingering in the late night's darkness like the setting sun's last light. "Mmm..." she moaned as I kissed the nape of her neck, my lips finding her ear, taking her lobe between my teeth and gingerly, lightly biting down. After the separation that'd followed her husband walking in on us, that first night back together was like finding an oasis in the desert, enough to make me forget, for at least that one night, all the pain I'd caused her, all the upheaval I'd been responsible for, all the hardships that surely lay ahead in both our lives. That was some time in the future. In the days that'd immediately followed our sudden separation, though, I had only my half-lucid daydreams to satisfy my need to be with her. In my truck I spent the early afternoons and the late, late nights driving along a highway, back and forth between work, putting myself through the motions, even as I couldn't keep myself from thinking ahead to the time Karen and I were to be together again, some part of me in the grips of an almost religious fervor, a certainty it was to be. But other concerns soon intervened.

Without Karen to distract me, I soon found myself wandering listlessly through the days. Hardly a few weeks had passed and I still thought there might've been some small chance she and I would be together again. We'd gone our separate ways before, ten years earlier, only to wind up together again, so, I thought, why not then? It was exactly this mindset that led me to look back through the texts we'd exchanged and the pictures I'd taken of her with the expectation of seeing her again, like a poor person looking through listings of luxury homes and imagining himself buying each and every one. Before work one afternoon I sat in my truck with the windows rolled down and the seat tilted back all the way while listening to Nirvana on the stereo. It was an unseasonably warm afternoon, with the skies clear and the wind rolling in from the west rustling the trees gently. At the age of twenty-eight I worked in a warehouse, a cavernous building that sprawled over an area the size of three or four city blocks, belonging to a company called CylinderWorld. It was one of the largest warehouses of its kind in the province of British Columbia; no matter what they say, in the logistics business it *is* the size of your warehouse that counts. We received containers directly from the port and forwarded their contents to other companies in Canada. Our main game was auto parts, coming from factories abroad, from places like Thailand, Taiwan, and Tanzania. That night, my shift at the warehouse sped past in a blur, my body moving in a series of rhythmic motions repeated a thousand times each shifts. It was mindless work, picking orders from a voice-activated computerised system, the kind of work that my body had learned to perform without any input from my mind; every motion smoothly executed from memory, every word spoken into my headset with the same flat, level tone of voice, every case of product picked up and slid into exactly the right place, my body moving in a cadence that allowed my mind the freedom to wander. It was as though my body was a piece of machinery, put to work mechanically and methodically by my employer, with my person watching from a distance. A call to my cell from a number I didn't recognize, on my lunch break, around the time most people were sitting down for supper with their families. "Keith, it's me." Lisa. "I'm leaving Randall." The first time I'd heard her voice in eight years. "I...need your help." Soon, I'd agreed to meet her, hanging up without a clue what to expect. It was new ground, even as I couldn't escape the feeling that there was something eerily unfamiliar about it all.

Then I was suddenly in bed with Karen, having her in the little twin-sized bed I kept in my apartment's bedroom. We were in the midst of *making love*, but it was hard, determined, as though we were trying to wring that old, familiar pleasure from each other's bodies like blood from a stone. All the little details magnified themselves a thousand times. The thick stench of sweat soon filled the air. The rustling of the bedspread underneath. The soft, mellow orange of the streetlight fading in through the blinds, striking her body, lending her stomach, her breasts a sickly glow even as her face, her neck, her hair remained shrouded in the darkness of the night, faintly visible through the dim. The last doubt left my mind as Karen and I began to move against one another, our motions gathering intensity, she seeming like a woman possessed. Forward, back, she pushed, her soft, supple flesh grinding against me. She was the love of my life. "Karen, I..." Rocking back and forth, she rolled her hips, her body moving against mine in long, slow strokes. With each stroke, her small, wideset breasts rocked, and her loosened hair jostled. "Karen, I..." Bringing herself down, she arched her back, grasping my shoulders with both hands, kissing the side of my face lightly, then harder, working her way towards my left ear, licking, nibbling, her voice soft, warm, thick with lust. "Fuck me," she said, "fuck me," before burying herself in the side of my neck. This was lovemaking, instinctive, like two animals rutting against one another. "Fuck me..." It was all she could say. Even as the last fear had left my body, an anxiety grew, an intense worry that I was somewhere I shouldn't have been. Though it'd been some months since we'd last had each other, it felt, then, like it'd been only days, hours even, the warmth of her skin against mine suddenly making it feel like we'd never been apart.

Karen rode me with a frenetic energy to her movements. Almost as soon as our lovemaking had started, I began to thrust up into her, all thought having left my mind as I'd surrendered myself to her so completely, my movements ragged, disjointed, my body uncoordinated, its rhythm halting, disjointed. As I built rapidly towards my climax, she pushed herself up until she was riding me, then reached with one hand between her legs to the place where our bodies had joined, where she'd taken me inside her and made us one. It was as though we had become one person, the act of making love having removed the flimsy distinction between us, our body working as a single thing towards its goal, our mutual release. I saw her place her hand between us and touch herself, but no more, for with her other hand she took me by the chin and made me look her in the eye, a silent understanding passing between us. Losing control, I came inside her, my mind blanked by a raw, electric pleasure, seconds later she bringing herself to orgasm, her strokes slowing, stopping, her whole body quivering, then falling still, our lovemaking having been won. It seemed as though it'd lasted forever, though it can't have been more than a couple of minutes. Then, as the fog cleared, she and I still thrust against one another weakly, our bodies working the last bit of sex out of themselves, until we lay there, silent but for the pounding of our hearts and the gasping of our breaths. The anxious feeling was still there, though, and I suddenly became aware of myself, feeling very much like a teenager living in an adult's body, fearing only the coming day and the inevitable separation from her. Lovesickness. It was lovesickness, the same feeling I'd had ten years earlier, but this time as an adult pursuing a relationship with a married woman whose marriage was in the midst of a spectacular implosion.

One day during the months Karen and I were apart after being walked in on by her husband, I received in the mail an envelope containing election material from the union I'd belonged to for years. At work, I was a member of the International Brotherhood of Roadsters, one of the largest unions in the world. In the midst of an election cycle, our local had begun sending us glossy magazines filled with election pitches from every candidate, praising their own platforms and denouncing the others'. For a while, I'd taken every pamphlet, envelope, and postcard they'd sent and discarded them on the coffee table in my little apartment, letting them pile up next to old novels I'd read and an empty pickle jar repurposed to hold loose change. It wasn't that I thought my vote didn't matter; I hadn't thought about it at all. (I'd like to say it was because my affair with Karen had commanded my attention, but that would be a lie). And then, I held in my hand the ballot I was meant to turn in, the election being conducted by mail. At work, I'd fill in the gaps between thinking spells devoted to Karen with spells devoted to our union and its long, slow march into irrelevance. It made me angry. Sometimes my anger got the best of me. Sometimes I'd let someone have it, when I'd gone off on one of my supervisors, Maya, for instance. I can't explain it. When something upsets me, I go into a state where I lose the feeling in my fingers and toes, where the blood rushes to my face, and then where I get a headache that lasts into the night. But nothing would happen, nothing much. Our union, the Roadsters, protected me, but, when the dust had settled and I'd returned to work, I was still confronted, in those six months when Karen and I were apart, with that very union standing idly by while the company had its way, on the floor a story making the rounds of our rep golfing, every now and then, with the company's owners on weekends, that image stuck in my mind of him smiling as he teed off with company officials, the thought causing that feeling to take hold again, causing the blood to rush to my face, again, amplified by the knowledge that I was powerless to do anything about it. Only I wasn't. they just wanted me to think I was. That's all they want. Everyone wants you to be angry at someone; it's just the way things are. It could be the only way to overcome them is to not get angry at all. But that's not what I did, at work or with Karen. With our agreement due in less than a year, our rep (a role filled by a new person every time we saw him, or so it seemed) had begun to work on the next one, leaving the rest of us to wait and see what he could come up with, knowing as we should've that it was to be just a copy of what we'd had. But I shouldn't have complained. It's not the way of things. It might've been the way I wanted things to be, but that didn't matter, and doesn't matter now.

It was only by chance that I'd found myself having wound up working a union job when there were so few of them left, at least in warehousing, itself a line of work I'd just happened into after graduating from university. It made up for a lot of missed time. The truth was that I didn't know what to think about our union, and I still don't. This time around, the magazines were the same, the ads and the promises and the words printed on the glossy, professional-looking pages might as well have been directly copied from the last election. Instead of setting it down on the coffee table, I wedged it between the pages of a book I'd been reading, and carried to work, intending to spend breaks looking over the ballot. But instead, at work, I wound up setting the book aside, pulling out my phone, and scrolling through the texts Karen and I had exchanged for months, reading over each and every one, as if to remind myself those months hadn't been a figment of my imagination. It was during just such a day that I witnessed the arrival of one of our union reps, a man by the name of Gerald Wang; he was there, I'd learn, for a meeting with the head of the company, and found himself set upon by a group of concerned workers, five or six or seven of them in the lunch room on arrival. Sitting at the end of a table in the break room, he looked to be talking with a group of workers, each of them listening intently as he walked them through our union's latest legal battle with the company while I only half-listened, devoting the other half of my attention to figuring out just when exactly I'd hit a foul ball. I didn't know, then, what that battle was, and it was only over the months that followed that I learned, our union's work unfolding in the background as I found my focus drawn irresistibly to Karen's sudden withdrawal from my life. This, all this, made me feel lonelier than ever, and it was in my lonely state that I looked, one evening after work, at my phone and saw a missed call from Lisa, in my voicemail a brief message from her asking me to call. I admit, now, that I thought about deleting the message and blocking her number on my phone, and that I came very close to doing just that. But, having been drained by spending so much time apart from her, I just couldn't muster the energy needed to keep up the act, choosing, instead, not to call her back, but to wait for her to try again. The next day, she called, and this time I picked up. There'd been so much she'd missed in my life during the years we hadn't been speaking to each other, and slowly, bit by bit, it all came out.

After having found myself cut out from Karen's life, I looked back on the past years with apprehension, but not regret. I'd stumbled from one milestone to the next, enrolling in a local university as an English major before emerging, somehow, five years later with a degree in Sociology. Some people put their degrees in frames and hang them on the wall, but I left mine in a little paper folder stuffed in a desk at home, underneath a pile of birthday and Christmas cards that'd accumulated over the years. No one at work knew I had it; it wasn't that I wanted to hide it from any of them, rather, it'd just never come up in conversation. Once, I'd sent a letter directly to the head of our local complaining about some of the company's practices, but received a reply instead from Gerald Wang which offered no new information and used the sort of stale, antiseptic language of a bureaucrat that seemed calculated to say as little as possible. That was, of course, in the months before I'd run into Karen in that grocery store's aisle so late at night, after which I'd completely lost interest in anything but being with her. It was like a disease, commanding my attention, leaving me suddenly aloof from the affairs of my brothers and sisters in the Roadsters. If they noticed, they didn't let it show. They wouldn't have. Being that I was one of the company's more junior workers, it sometimes seemed I was an afterthought anyways, every day left to put my head down and turn into the wind, working my body through the motions, rhythmically, mechanically, while I imagined that Karen was to be there at the end of the day to see me.

It went back further than that, actually. Years seemed to fold into days, until there came the day when I woke up and couldn't remember how I'd let the world pass me by. It's hard to explain; at some point, time just seemed to pass faster, faster, faster still, until whole years had left me trying, failing to figure how I'd come to be twenty-eight and with nothing to show for it. And then I met Karen in that store's aisle late at night. (Karen was a member of a union herself, the teachers' union, though we spoke only once or twice about it and only in passing). Then, after she and I had been caught in the act by her husband, I was back to my old ways, struggling just to get through the day. It became common for me to leave work early because I couldn't keep myself from breaking down, vision blurring behind the beginnings of tears, wiping them away before pulling myself back together. In the meantime, I watched as the union lurched into action, feeling adrift, rudderless, leading me to do something I'd never seen myself doing. That day, after having watched our union rep talk, talk, talk himself out of a corner and then walk into a closed-door meeting with the head of the company, I took out my frustration on someone else. As a supervisor, a short, brown-haired woman named Maya, took me to task for some small mistake I'd made, I lost control for a half-moment and told her to stop treating me like a "complete idiot." Taken aback, she complained, and the next day I found myself in a meeting with a shop steward and the company's head of labour relations, stammering out an apology. Soon, I found myself on the receiving end of a lecture, not from Maya but another supervisor, where I was told my attitude needed a major adjustment, that if I had such a problem then I should quit and find somewhere else to make people miserable, while I just stood and listened, saying nothing at all. Later that day, a few minutes later, actually, I left early, complaining I wasn't feeling well, able to make it barely into my truck before breaking down, the incident nudging me over the edge. As it was a Friday, I knew to look forward to another meeting on Monday, and through the weekend I could only calm my nausea by imagining myself somewhere else entirely. *Don't worry about it*, I thought, *it's not going to be your problem much longer.* But it wasn't to end there. I wish I'd paid more attention to these goings-on back when I could've made a difference. Six months later, when Karen re-entered my life a second time, I let these matters fall by the wayside, and it's only after recollection and reflection in the years since that I've come to appreciate what's happened.

It was around this time that Lisa called me out of the blue and asked for my help. The day I was to be handed discipline by the company, I wound up calling in sick to drive halfway across the city, meeting her in the parking lot outside one of those little, hole-in-the-wall coffee shops where we didn't talk a lot but still managed to say so much. It might've looked like I skipped work just to avoid discipline, but I didn't care, having thought about the day I'd finally see Lisa again. But when the dust settled, the company took no action against me, letting me off with a polite, carefully-phrased talking-to. Looking back on it, I was lucky just to keep my job, though at the time all I could think about was my sudden ejection from Karen's life, and the fantasies of the next time we'd meet. Sometimes I thought we might've run into each other again, and it was under the influence of this little daydream that I drove to that very same grocery store at the very same time of day and on the very same day of the week as we'd once, by pure coincidence, reunited after ten years apart, and stood in that very same aisle for a while as I half-expected and half-dreamt she'd appear from around the corner and we'd share an embrace. Later, months later, when she called me again, it was almost anticlimactic, but when I first felt the warmth of her touch after months apart I took it as vindication in my steadfast commitment to love.

3. Past

It all happened so fast. If it seems like Karen and I just fell into each other, well, that's just the way I've remembered it, as though it's the way some part of me has chosen to remember it. I don't think there was any one moment when I fell *in love* with her, in the way a teenager can; it was as though I just woke up one day in the eleventh grade and realized I was *in love* with her. In the halls at Eastmount, it was like we could go days without crossing paths. Then, we'd be in her class, surrounded by thirty-two of my classmates, she walking past, then leaning over slightly to point out a mistake I'd made on an assignment, some verb I hadn't conjugated properly, at the right moment seeming to look me over, while I looked at her, not at any part, just *at her*, a silent exchange taking place, as she walked away my eyes locked on her, tracing a path along the curve of her wide hips, when she reached the head of the class turning and tossing a glance back my way, the whole affair playing out in full view of the rest of the class, yet, still, secret all the same. It was these little moments I kept in the back of my mind in the months that led up to she and I *making love* for the first time, our affair culminating so rapidly, but with long periods of nothing stretching between those seemingly random bursts of activity, weeks passing without either of us looking at each other, then she taking a pass at me, walking past me in the hall and, at just the right moment leaning forward just so slightly, seeming to give me a look down her blouse, drawing my eyes down, then back up, her little half-grin making it clear these chance encounters weren't accidental. Then, months later, we were alone, my hands on her chest, through that very blouse cupping her small, wideset breasts, awkwardly exploring, fumbling, until she took my hands in hers and moved them away so she could lean in for a kiss, the taste of her mouth flooding mine, her regrets seeming to fade as she threw herself at me, I've since realized, out of a need to convince herself that what she was doing was only *illegal* and not *wrong*. It was a nuance lost on me at seventeen but which came to weigh on my mind heavily in the years after we'd parted ways. I wish I'd done more to reassure her, but I was only seventeen, then eighteen, and I was at that age when there wasn't anything, more or less, I could've done.

Towards the end of November of the twelfth grade, Karen and I started to become fodder for the rumour mill around Eastmount. Classmates had seen us trade little glances, had seen me spend more time than absolutely necessary in her classroom, and that'd been enough to start people talking. If anyone had asked, I'd planned to admit a crush on her, but no one ever asked, not even my old best friend, Adrian, not yet, anyways. It must've seemed unbelievable; after having fought with her early in the eleventh grade, my classmates might've been skeptical that I could've fallen *in love* with her so soon after. But so far, they were only rumours, and Karen seemed oblivious to them. Between periods, we'd cross paths; Eastmount was a large school, but there was only one hall that ran the length of the building, in a horseshoe shape, on both floors. And Karen's classroom was located right in the middle on the second floor, making it all but impossible for me to avoid her, not that I would've. We'd not yet moved past flirting, the exchanging of glances, the propositions and the half-touches that went along with drawing closer and closer to having at each other. "We should stop this now," she'd said, once, after it'd gone too far to be stopped so cleanly and easily, "before I get in trouble." We were in her classroom, after school had ended and the halls outside were mostly deserted. It was deeply confusing, to see her go from harmlessly flirting with me to actively spurning my attention in the span of just a few weeks. I don't remember what was said next. In a flash I'd left her classroom, heart slamming against my chest in time with every foot brought down on the ground. It was only a few weeks, six or seven before we'd be together, and already I was beginning to lose my mind. Nothing had happened, but suddenly it'd gotten out of hand, and she knew it. One look at her from across her Spanish twelve classroom and I knew it felt to her like she'd just suddenly woken up and found herself in the midst of an escalating crisis, about to have an affair with her student and about to risk everything she had for nothing at all. But it was too late to stop it. It'd gone too far for it not to go through to its end. And with my home being rapidly taken over by a strange man, I didn't want it to stop, the idea of having Karen a distraction from the war at home.

The next time I walked into Karen's classroom, I realized an apprehension had set in, an expectation that she would have more to say. We were so close, but still so far from each other. But as I took my seat at the back of the class, on my left a guy from El Salvador who needed no study, on my right an Asian girl with hair extensions and half a kilo of makeup, Karen said nothing, looking down on me and offering a flat look and raised eyebrows, her jaw tightening slightly before she opened her mouth, as if ready to speak, the bell then ringing, starting the period. The moment taken away, she turned, took a marker, and made at the period's lesson, scrawling verb conjugations on the whiteboard, slashing angrily. When one brave student raised her hand to ask a question, Karen shot her down with nothing more than a scowl. There were no more questions. She seemed to hide behind the strict, prim-and-proper professionalism of her role as teacher, using it as a mask to conceal herself. Avoiding her classroom in the mornings, I spent the hour before classes each day in the weight room, working the feeling from my body as though I was a machine, lifting weights in a series of repetitive motions until I could stand it no longer. After she made me promise to stay away from her, at least for a while, and I'd reluctantly agreed, but for going to her Spanish class keeping myself away from her. Where once I might've gone out of my way to walk the hall outside her classroom, now I plotted elaborate, roundabout paths through the school to keep myself from her room; I had math a couple of rooms on one side of hers, and biology a couple of rooms on the other, walking between them by heading outside and around to the other side of the building before doubling back. It was silly, I've since realized, to think that I could've simply switched off my feelings for her, but at the time it seemed like something I had to do. Even as we avoided each other, in the back of my mind I was already looking forward to the next time we'd touch. It was like an elaborate dance that neither of us knew, and it made me terrified of myself. But whenever we crossed paths, I couldn't keep myself from drawing my eyes along her shapely figure, down her wide, curvaceous hips, concealed as they were behind her tight, black skirts that extended well past the knee. It seemed a challenge. I liked to imagine that she was wearing such outfits just to challenge me, as if to draw me closer even as she'd told me, point-blank, to stay away. It was all a game. It was all a game. Even today, I can't quite convince myself of it, much as I'd like to try. Later that day, I don't know what might've happened, who she might've spoken to, what she might've said, but she'd changed, her attitude had changed, and she'd gone, in the span of just a few hours, no, a few days, a week or two at most, from trying me away from her to approaching me, when no one was looking, and telling me she wanted to see more of me. I can see now that she was just as confused as I was, and in her confused state, she was vulnerable, the instinctive part of me seizing on her vulnerability, seeking to exploit it, to work my way into her arms, her bed, wherever I was supposed to want to be. I wish I could say it was clean and simple, that we were just *together*, but I can't. At the time, though, I bought into the illusion that she knew what she wanted and that she couldn't bring herself to take it because of things like the law and her career standing, forcing me to act. It was back and forth, up and down, side to side, neither of us having a clue what we were doing even as we both knew that we had it all figured out. But it was all an act, as though she was suddenly trying to convince herself not to do what she knew she couldn't stop herself from doing.

Later that year, in the new year, not long after we'd first *made love*. It was only her third year at Eastmount, and she'd managed to find a job teaching Spanish and Social Studies at Carlisle Secondary in North Vancouver, a well-to-do suburb pushed up against the mountains, on the other side of the Burrard Inlet's waters. She'd attended Carlisle when she was a teenager, and she wanted to go back, in the way that she was about to. When I asked her why she wanted to teach there, she shrugged and said, "I grew up on the North shore. I want to go back there." This had actually been in the works for a while, she went on to say, and her time at Eastmount was never meant to be permanent but the in-between time, something temporary until she could do what she *really* wanted to do. I couldn't understand it. At the age of seventeen, almost eighteen, I wanted to be anywhere in the world but where I was. She must've known what I was thinking, as she edged a little closer in her chair to mine and reached for my hair, giving it a tussle, then stood and walked away, making into the bedroom before turning and tossing an impish grin my way. In a flash, I became aware of myself, feeling out of place, and suddenly I wanted just to leave the room and be somewhere else. We *made love*, and it was over quickly, like it'd been every other time we'd *made love* in the secrecy of her apartment. Sometime later that night, when I was sure she'd fallen sound asleep, I rose from her bed, quickly and quietly dressed, then left, ducking out down her building's fire escape, clumsily finding my way through the dark streets to my Oldsmobile, heading nowhere but in a rush to get there, fast. I hadn't the slightest clue what I was doing, and, now, after all these years have passed, I can see that she hadn't the slightest clue what she was doing, either. It's all an elaborate sham. Just weeks earlier, she'd tried to let me down; that wasn't what she was trying to do. We met, once, around the beginning of December, not far from the waterfront, but in a forested area. She'd called me there, she'd followed me there, I don't remember what happened exactly, what set of circumstances conspired to place us together in that little clearing along the shore of Vancouver's Burrard Inlet, only that we were there, together, but still I couldn't think, couldn't think, couldn't think, a blinding white fear blotting out all thought, even as we weren't touching, hadn't yet touched, alone as we were in the middle of a city of millions of people, protected only by a little forest of evergreen trees on three sides and an expanse of water on the fourth. It was just a couple of weeks after she'd faked me out by half-heartedly insisting we stop, and it seemed almost time for us to cross that last line.

It was weeks before we'd first *made love*, but weeks after she'd belatedly started to put up half-hearted resistance to my attention. There, in that forested clearing we played our imaginary game, listening to the waves chopping against one another. "Keith," she asked, standing aside the Oldsmobile with her hands in her pockets, "I know this can't happen," she paused, and looked away, then back at me, "but why can't I stop it?" She seemed to be asking herself as much as me. "We can be alone here," I said, "no one can see us." Silence, for a moment. "Keith," she said, then looked as though she couldn't figure out what to say, instead letting her voice trail off. Reaching into my pocket, I drew out a little box and handed it to her, another gift. It was a small heart-shaped box of chocolates, bought at a Shopper's Drug Mart for eight dollars. "I shouldn't even have come here," she said, "but I have." I sat on the hood of the Oldsmobile, and she sat next to me, perched delicately on the lip with her legs hanging over the lights. "This is impossible," she said. "What?" I asked. "You make me feel like I'm going crazy." "Is that a bad thing?" "I haven't got a clue." She looked right into my eyes, in an instant turning the moment against me. Vividly, memories flooded my thoughts, memories of the setting sun and the bright grey clouds and the snow-capped peaks towering over the city, holding up the sky. Karen, I just can't help but imagine you were in love with me every bit as much as I was in love with you. The look in your eyes, that little twinkle that flashed whenever you blinked, it's one of those images of you I'll keep forever in my mind's eye.

We sat on the hood of my car, taking in the cold, salty air, watching as the wind whipped at the waters of the inlet, little whitecaps cresting atop the waves. A speck of rain fell on my cheek, then another, then another, soon the chattering and the hiss of a hundred thousand raindrops striking ground filled the air. We took refuge in the Oldsmobile. Her hair was a mess, ragged, wet locks clinging to the sides of her face. In a cupholder sat an empty paper cup from McDonald's that'd been there for weeks. A cracked CD and crumpled-up papers lay on the floor, with more trash unseen beneath the seats. Dangling from the rear-view mirror was an old air freshener no longer freshening the air. And in the passenger seat next to me there was a voluptuous, full-figured, thirty-five year-old woman, soaking wet blouse clinging to her chest. With the suddenly heavy rain chattering against the roof of my car, we were together, alone, and she had a look on her face that seemed to invite me to make the next move. I'd planned it exactly like this, right down to the very last detail, but in the heat of the moment I was nearly paralyzed with fear. Though I was almost two hundred pounds of muscle, and over six feet tall, so much bigger than her, at that moment I felt so small compared to her. I was filled with terror and confusion. But I felt as though I had to press on. Reaching over to her, I let my hand caress the side of her face, lightly pulling her to me, kissing her on the lips with only the faintest of touches, as though we were a hair's width from each other, an electric charge building between us, as though to force us apart. "Look at where we are," she said, "look at this." She seemed to be talking to herself, as though to talk herself out of what she was about to do. "Keith," she said, turning to me, resting her open palm on the back of my hand, "I wish you were a couple of years older." "Just imagine I am," I said, "I won't tell anyone." "If only it was that simple," she said. "Why isn't it?" I asked. She forced a laugh, a nervous laugh, one which, I've since realized, came from her seeing me as so naïve as to think it was so simple as just keeping a secret. "What the hell am I doing?" she asked. In the distance, a foghorn sounded out, or at least so my memory says, while a hundred thousand thoughts scattered themselves across the back of my mind, each seeming so much like the others, filtering through like grains of sand seeping through a tightly-clenched fist.

Kissing her again, this time on the side of her cheek, I let the kiss linger for a moment too long, sampling the taste of her skin, the smell of her hair, then planting a little row of kisses down towards her neck, turning to whisper into her ear. "You are so beautiful," I said. She said nothing, seeming to draw in breaths sharp, fast. "You're so beautiful," I said again, murmuring this time. There was a lump of fear in the pit of my stomach, rising, while my heart slammed against my chest. At any moment I could've thrown up. We were so close together, that it seemed our bodies were straining at one another's, the tension in hers evaporating even as mine intensified. But the fear made me stronger, as though I could've powered through it and had Karen right there in the front seat of my car. In the glove box were a couple of condoms, from a box I'd bought and left there for this very reason, but I think if we'd had sex then I would've been too caught up in the moment to stop and put one on, and she too beside herself to insist. At the age of thirty-five, Karen was a woman, a real woman, not a girl. At the age of seventeen, almost eighteen, I was becoming a man. Her hand found the side of my face, brushing my cheek, making for my hair, the tips of her fingers tracing lightly behind my ear. Her other hand felt itself along my thigh, stroking firmly against my jeans, slowly working towards my groin, with each motion drawing nearer. Leaning in, I felt her breath on my skin. We kissed. But it was a lover's kiss, our tongues dancing, our breaths mingling, her taste flooding my mouth.

She began to try and push me back, but lightly, applying the slightest of pressure to my chest. "Stop," she said, mumbling through our kiss. With one hand, I reached up and gently cupped one of her breasts through her blouse, prompting her to break our kiss for a moment, gasping, before I kissed her again. My nimble fingers found their way inside her blouse and underneath the strap of her bra, and I began to stroke her bare skin, my hand clasping gently, her soft, smooth breast seeming to fit perfectly into my palm. She'd tensed up and pulled back slightly even as her hand had reached my groin and she stroked my erection through my jeans. "Stop," she said, as much to herself as to me, "don't stop." Scared, never more scared in my life, I wanted to run away, that bolt of fear curling around my insides, turning my blood to ice. But then, just as we were about to kiss, she abruptly pulled away. "Keith," she said, "stop." I stopped.

I came home one afternoon to find Lisa and Randall, she sitting on the living room while he stood in the kitchen in front of the stove, the smell of cigarettes mixing with the sting of booze. It all happened so suddenly. As I was about to turn and head upstairs, Randall called me back down. "Fuckin' get in here," he said, "get in here and sit your ass down 'cause you've had this coming a long time. Your fuckin' ass is grass and I'm a fucking John Deere." "What?" I asked. "You fuckin' heard me," he replied. From Lisa, silence. Caught off guard, I walked into the living room, Randall following close behind. He had in his hand a bag of chips, and when I sat on the couch he threw the bag, hard, almost right at me, landing it on the end table, nearly knocking over the lamp. "You fuckin' think you can just come and go whenever you want, well in this fuckin' house you better show some respect or else." "Or else what?" I asked, forcibly injecting an edge into my voice. "When I was your age I was already working full time," he said, "and you—" "I am working," I said, "what do you think I do all the week?" "Oh yeah?" "Yeah!" "Well fuckin' move out then," he said, "get your own place to live and quit ridin' it here like you can just show up whenever you please. You eat my food and you sleep under my roof and you don't show me any fuckin' respect. Well I've had it!" All this time, Lisa sat silent, perfectly still, while Randall and I had it out.

"The fuck is wrong with you?" I asked, "what did I do to you?" He pointed at the kitchen. "You fuckin' know what you did," he said. It occurred to me he was talking about the rum I'd poured out. "That's right," he said, "you know." "What are you gonna do about it?" I asked. "You wanna have a go with me?" he asked, stepping at me, his hands open. "What?" I asked. "Take it, take a shot," he said, "I'll give you one free one." "Are you fucking nuts?" "If you've got the guts to do it." "Oh, fuck this." Fed up, I stormed out, slamming the front door shut before getting back in my car and peeling off down the street, blowing through a stop sign and running a red light, drawing honks, my driving soon attracting the attention of a cop car, the wailing of sirens and the flashing of red-and-blue lights soon behind me. Of course I had to go home, but I couldn't just go home, I thought, half-expecting Randall would be there with a baseball bat, ready to take a swing as soon as I walked in the front door. I don't know. But the drive just made me feel tired, my grip on the wheel loosening and my eyes losing focus on the road before I gave up. I don't know what I was expecting when I walked back in, only that the worst had yet to come.

It was after sundown by the time I finally went home, tip-toeing through the front door, closing it slowly, quietly behind. The whole place was dark and silent. Into the kitchen, it was only when I opened the fridge that I noticed Lisa, still sitting on the living room's couch, the narrow pane of light from the fridge casting a sickly, pale glow right on her. I couldn't think of what to say, so I said nothing. Turning, I made it halfway to the stairs when Lisa called out. "Please," she said. Stopping, I looked back. She stood in the dining room, half-obscured by the shadows, looking right at me. Then, I walked up the stairs and into my bedroom, shutting the door firmly, twisting the lock until I heard it click into place. In the morning, Randall was there, but Lisa wasn't, and he hardly paid any attention to me, sitting on the couch as he looked up from his drink and tossed a glare my way, muttering under his breath, "fuckhead." The next time we'd cross paths, it wouldn't end so easily. With months to go until I finished high school, I had at least that long until I could move out. It never seriously occurred to me to just move out then and there, to drop everything and walk out the door, never to come back; I don't know why. After having found myself in a state of war every minute of every day, whether against the alcoholic who'd shacked up with Lisa or against myself, it was like I'd become paralyzed, stuck, frozen in time, frustrated. It was in this frame of mind that the month of December drew slowly, slowly past, Karen and I playing our little game, until given a break.

Christmas had arrived, and with it two weeks without classes, a relief after the previous months had taken their toll. Karen left town, off to visit family on the island. A plastic Christmas tree had been erected in the corner of our living room a couple of weeks earlier, pulled from its box deep in the back of a storage closet and stood precariously in its mount before being decked out with a smattering of ornaments and lights. Actually, it looked perfect, right off the cover of a special holiday issue of one of those home and life magazines. But for the chipped, faded paint on the walls behind and the worn, frayed carpet underneath, there might've been photographers beating down our door to commit the image of our tree to memory. But I didn't like it. It seemed so forced, so fake, so lacking in all the little details that might've made it a real family's tree, that might've made it look and feel like the focus of a real household's Christmas. And on Christmas day that year, my mother and I occupied the living room, unwrapping gifts with the thrift store's tags still attached, she on the couch, half-smoked cigarette dangling from her lips, the sting of cheap vodka lingering in the air. Then, Randall arrived for dinner, bringing a fifth of vodka again, the day soon spiralling out of control, with shouting, swearing, and the sound, only the sound of the back of a hand striking a woman's face, hard. The rest of the day is not worth recalling. The rest of the break I spent thinking of Karen, whether I was working a shift at the thrift shop or at home, replaying that last afternoon we'd spent together in my mind over and over, searching for the exact moment I'd let that chance slip through my fingers, at the same time looking ahead to the next.

3. Present

"Don't be that guy." This was the warning from a co-worker, a twenty-something man named Jordan, a man with bulging biceps and tattoos snaking up the back of his neck. He'd claimed to have had sex with something like twenty or thirty women in the past year (I can't remember the exact number, but then if it was true then he probably couldn't either), and this claim had been made shortly after having described his apparent love affair with all sorts of drugs. But he never drank alcohol, he was very firm about that. "Booze just fucks you up," he'd said. All this came as six or seven of us were standing on the warehouse dock, dock-stockers and streaks parked in a haphazard semi-circle while we waited out the last minutes of our shift. The truth was that for all his friendliness and all his good-natured badgering, I didn't like Jordan because his life seemed to revolve around drugs and sex, to the extent that he came across not as a real person but as an over-aggressive caricature, a parody. Yet we listened as Jordan described some fanciful sexual encounter, the way he'd been on the balcony of a downtown hotel with a prostitute, his ejaculation firing at the very time the fireworks show in the bay reached its own climax. Or at least that was how he'd described it, not in those words, though. It wasn't all that unlike a time Karen and I had *made love* in the cab of my truck, she riding me while I held onto her bottom, at exactly the moment of my orgasm a bolt of lightning ripping through the sky, flashing a bright white light over us both. "Don't be that guy," he said, cocksure, certain of itself. "Don't be that guy." A horn blared, a forklift drove past, and the chattering of a thousand and one hammers striking a hard surface, each leaving a small, shallow indentation in the warehouse's bare, barren floor. At any time, I could've turned and walked away, excusing myself to tend to the day's work, the hundreds of cases' worth in orders left to pick. But I didn't.

Randall was there as Lisa and I went back and forth carrying boxes of her things out to my truck. He said nothing, pouring drinks in the kitchen and taking them into the living room where he had some sitcom on the TV, the canned sound of a laugh track playing over the clinking of ice against glass. It didn't take long. Lisa had little to move. But when we'd finished loading for the day, I went back inside, telling her I had to use the washroom, on my way up the stairs peeking around the corner to look into the living room, finding his chair empty. He wasn't in the kitchen, either. Theirs was a small house, too small to be a home, lacking as it did in all the little touches that made one, plastic flowers where there should've been family photos, a hole punched in the wall where there should've been a dresser or a drawer or a little table. Soon, Lisa and I were on the road, making our way for her new place, when I felt the telltale thrum of my phone vibrating in my back pocket, my gut telling me it was Karen, as I gunned the engine to catch the tail end of a yellow light the vibrations stopping, drowning beneath the rumbling and tumbling of the road underneath. But my gut had lied. As I drove with one hand on the wheel and the other resting on my knee, there came to mind the second-to-last time I'd had Karen, the last time we'd *made love* before that night we were walked in on, neither in her bed nor mine but in my apartment's little kitchen, her back to the wall and her legs hooked around my hips as I held her up, my hands gripping her ample bottom while I thrust inside her slowly, again, and again, and again. "Keith!" Lisa said, my attention returning in time to stop, quickly, at a red light, narrowly avoiding rear-ending another car. "You alright?" Lisa asked. Nodding, I tightened my grip on the wheel, and looked ahead. That night, and I don't know why I remember this now, when I was up well past any reasonable time, I saw, from my apartment three or four police cars pulled up, their lights flashing, at least as many officers standing around a homeless-looking man, seeming to interrogate him. There might've been a woman holding a young child in her arms behind a little chain-link fence, talking to another officer. The only thing I can remember hearing them say to him clearly was when a female officer's voice asked, "what's your status in Canada?" Having had interactions with the police when I was a child, I watched, for a moment through the my apartment's blinds, only looking away when it was clear that nothing was going to happen, that there'd be no fighting or shouting or handcuffs snapping onto wrists. Later that night, as I turned the light off and went to bed, I wondered what the police must've thought, whether they'd felt exasperated at having to solve another domestic dispute. They'd always had that look that seemed to say *the animals just can't keep it together* whenever they'd been called out to my home when I was a young child; it's one of those little details I might not actually remember but might, instead, imagine, as if I'd been taught to see myself that way.

After we'd dropped off the last of her things for the day, Lisa and I had lunch at a diner halfway up the King George Highway in Surrey. "Thank you," she said, "for your help." "I haven't done much," I said, "moved a few boxes and a couple pieces of furniture." Nursing a cup of black coffee, I let the tips of my fingers rest on the mug's side until they burned sharply, then moved them slightly up towards the rim, making long, slow circles while I thought of something to say. It wasn't the first time we'd seen each other since she'd called, but it was the first time we'd had a spare moment to just sit, an awkward silence there, broken only by the chatter of a TV's squawking in the background and the murmur of the diner's other customers. "You were right about him," she said, after we'd sat nervously for some time, "and I wish I'd listened to you. It's not that easy, but it's a start, isn't it?" Nodding, I sighed and looked into my cup, taking a sip. She looked tired, worn down, the bags under her eyes a shade darker, her hair greying here and there, and the wrinkles etching her face like an old spider's web. She looked so unlike the person I'd had a falling out with and I couldn't help but entertain the notion, for a half-second, that she might've been someone else altogether. "Don't you think we've got some work to do?" I asked, thinking out loud. "What do you mean?" she asked. "It's gonna take a long time to get everything back to the way it was." "I'm tired, Keith." "I can see that." "No, that's not what I mean." "What do you mean?" "This is uncomfortable for me too, you know." "Well, I suppose that means you're on the right track." "Huh?" "If it's making you uncomfortable then you're pushing your boundaries, right? Stepping outside your comfort zone, you know? I guess it seems kinda strange coming from a guy like me, but I'm really glad that you're finally doing what's right for you. I just wish it hadn't taken you so long to realize it." "Actually, that's not true..." The truth was that I fully remembered my actions from all those years before, that I shared the blame for all that'd gone wrong between her and Randall; but, then, as she'd later tell me, I was only seventeen, then eighteen, and I couldn't have known what I was doing. It was deeply confusing. I wanted to take my share of the blame, but I couldn't disagree with her. There's some truth to the idea that I was just doing what I did; I think it applied to her, too. We were all just acting out on learned behaviour. It was the way we did things, the way we always had.

Looking back on the six months Karen and I had spent together after that chance encounter in a grocery store's aisle late at night, I began to consider her thoughts and feelings in ways that made me step outside myself. For some reason, I envisioned her standing in front of a kitchen's sink, wearing rubber gloves and holding a sponge as she scrubbed slowly, deliberately at pots and pans, staring out the window and into the sky. In those six months we'd *made love* perhaps two dozen times, slow and passionate, fast and hard, as if we were exploring each other's bodies like a pair of hungry teenagers awkwardly fumbling our way through the act. In the shower was her favourite place to *make love*, the piping hot water filling the air with a steam so thick it seemed hard to breathe. It was a release for her, I've since realized, not an indulgence but a compulsion through which she could have some temporary escape from the tedium of her steady advance through middle age. She had everything, a life worthy of the Dick Van Dyke Show, and yet she had nothing. This, I've come to appreciate in the time since we've last seen each other, Karen, and I want you to know I couldn't ever have found the little piece of happiness that I had without you.

But it was hard to forget what'd happened between Lisa and me. At the diner, the waitress walked by, topping up our coffee from a mug she seemed never to put down. "What's not true?" I asked. "You liked him at first too..." she said. "No, I never liked him," I said. "He bought you a bike before he'd even met you." "It got stolen like three weeks later." "Still, he bought it..." "I don't see what this has to do with anything." Then, I asked, "what does he do these days anyways?" She said, "he still has his delivery business. It's just fallen on hard times. The economy hit everybody pretty hard, you know." I don't remember exactly what I was thinking at the time, but for some reason I can remember clearly dipping the tip of my finger into the freshly-poured coffee until it was submerged to first knuckle and holding it in for one, two, three seconds until it burned painfully. Lisa said something reassuring, or at least she tried, then reached into her purse for her phone. "I'm trying to do the right thing," she said. "Why?" I asked. "Keith, I've got nothing left," she said, "I'm at the end of my rope. It's why I'm here." Suddenly I noticed the clothes she wore were faded in places, loose threads here and there, and when she reached for the sugar at the centre of the table her sleeve revealed, for an instant, a bruise on her arm near her shoulder. More than anything, I wanted to know the truth, but couldn't bring myself yet to handle it, something in the back of my mind that I couldn't see keeping me from just reaching out to her. Looking back on it I can see, now, that it wasn't Lisa who couldn't let go. It was me. It'd always been me. Even, that night when Karen and I had *made love* for the second-to-last time, after we'd come down from our post-orgasm high, the little glint in Karen's deep brown eyes made her look like she *knew* she'd done something she'd regret. We said very little then, and I hadn't found the courage to just tell her I *loved* her, and after briefly showering I left and drove home, with only the promise of another secret tryst to keep me going through the grind of the week's work, mindless, rhythmic work, work like the kind that sustains, but only.

There was more that afternoon, but little of it meant anything, the point having been made that Lisa, after years, was back. But at least it was *something*. We left with little more than a promise, but it was a promise worth having, I think. But on the way home that afternoon, I suddenly realized that it'd been exactly ten years, give or take a few months, since Lisa and Randall had married in a little ceremony I hadn't been invited to. But, honestly, even if they'd invited me I still probably wouldn't have gone. The date had snuck up on me, and as I drove up the King George towards home it seemed as though the road was a little longer, a little harder than before, the truck's engine groaning and whining as I pushed on the gas to head up an incline, the little truck jumping and jolting with every bump, every groove in the road, making it over the hump, Surrey soon behind as I drove deeper into the city. Arriving home, I changed into a ratty old shirt, a pair of shorts, and my hi-vis vest, then, already tired from a long day, made it to work with seconds to spare. It was all a fraud though, and with real people's lives at stake, fraud left us with little room to maneuver. At work, weeks earlier, one of our shop stewards had excitedly announced a deal having been made with the company, a deal that would give us everything we wanted, that would address each and every grievance we had. (Though I wasn't a part of the meetings, I'd imagine they went like this). At work, the lights flickered overhead and the cold winter's wind swept through an open bay door and across the hard floor, the racks of product channeling the wind like canyons, creating a powerful storm that surged through the warehouse with each gust pushed inside. In the middle of unloading a full container's worth of product, I turned and sped away in my dock-stocker, the floor clicking under my machine's wheels as I made my way around the building. The next time he was there, Gerald Wang had said, "it's done," speaking to a few workers who'd sort-of cornered him and looked to him for answers. "We're going to vote on the revisions soon, maybe next week." Confused, and not at all relieved, I approached and asked him, "why do we need to revise the agreement?" He said, "what do you mean?" "The agreement's good enough as it is. Why can't we just get someone to enforce what we have?" "That's not the way things work." "Why not?" "There are always two sides to an issue," he said, "it's better to work it out on our own instead of going to an arbitrator. You never know, the arbitrator might side with the company. We could get a better deal if we're willing to compromise." Speaking to Gerald Wang, and I know this is going to sound odd, made me nervous and scared, and it gave me the same flustered, heated feeling I felt whenever I was angry, or when I was a teenager and approaching Karen, then my teacher, to take another shot at her with a slim chance of success. Some of the workers scoffed at him, but at the time none could seem to come up with anything else to say. It was only in the years to come, later, much later, that I came to realize the truth about what'd happened, even without much in the way of facts, compiling a series of half-truths and innuendos in my mind into something only vaguely resembling the facts of the matter.

After Karen and I had reunited a second time, there seemed an implicit understanding that it was not like the first. We imitated ourselves, in the shower, scalding hot water following the contours of our bodies, hands clutching, fumbling, grasping at each other as we put ourselves through the act of *making love* as if, put together, we could recapture the intensity of the *love* we'd shared so many years earlier. But it proved hard to adjust to the new way of things, as if I couldn't break out of the role of being her secret *lover*, the one she turned to when she wanted a passionate release from the boredom of domestic bliss. This, I've come to appreciate, was her compulsion. And yet I was in *love* with her all the same. In the time between her husband walking in on us and Karen calling me back into her life, I imagined what kind of man he was; I'd caught only glimpses as the family photos in their bedroom, their living room, and the balding, suit-and-tie wearing man I'd seen couldn't have matched with the sensual, vivacious Karen I'd fallen in love with. I spent a lot of time at work thinking these things through, using the distraction to avoid, mostly, the rumours that'd begun to make the rounds in the warehouse's narrow aisles, every now and then, though, the distraction failing and the rumours taking its place. But I could never figure out what the rumours were, exactly, everyone having a different version of them, everyone except me.

No matter what happened, it seemed everyone was only telling me what they thought I needed to hear. There were a lot of rumours that made the rounds at CylinderWorld. The people who seemed never to be talking were always the ones who talked the most; an older worker named Donovan had always made it a point to tell everyone he liked to avoid spreading rumours, but then nearly every day he had some story or another cooked up from some half-truth he'd heard. Gerald Wang was in the break room at the start of our shift, and he sat amid a group of five or six workers, all seeming, at a glance, to be listening intently. He had this way of speaking that was confident and convincing, like the lawyer who could passionately argue for a client's innocence even as he was certain of that client's guilt. He was there, a shop steward was to tell me that night, to settle complaints the workers were having. His recent regular appearances at CylinderWorld should've been a hint, but at the time I was thinking about Lisa, and later Karen, and I only noticed him there. It might seem strange to talk of *feeling* a particular way, but as I pushed myself through the evening's shift, I *felt* like a little piece of nothing whenever I dutifully went into work, and it was. If I dropped dead right then and there, it wouldn't have meant anything to the company. This isn't some stunning revelation, nor a stroke of genius; we all come to terms with this feeling at some point in our lives. At the age of twenty-eight, working in a warehouse and driving a little white pickup truck along a highway five days a week, it was around this time that I finally realized what I was. It didn't sit right. Whenever I thought to just accept myself as a piece of equipment to be used by the company, it set off a chain of thoughts that wound into the night and took me to a place hardly connected at all from where I'd started. I may never know, but that very night I took to the floor and made sure I'd think of *something* that could make me feel like a real person again. Then, some time later, Karen reappeared, her own life in the middle of its long, slow disintegration even as she worked to keep it all together.

At some point, months before I'd begun my secret affair with a married woman, Jordan began to ignore me, which suited me just fine as it meant no more questions from a virtual stranger probing the depths of my sex life. But it was an awkward silence, the kind that clearly meant to convey a message, but I couldn't tell what the message was. No. After having suddenly reconnected with Lisa, it seemed like I could've looked at Jordan, or Donovan, or any other person working in that warehouse and seen a little piece of the puzzle, as if each of my co-workers held part of the answer. There were so many of us. Some had names like Bhulwinder, or Paramjit, or Bhupinder, while others had names like Scott, James, Samantha. It's hard, looking back on it, to really put myself in their places and see what each of them was up to, but as I approached Maya and offered her, again, an apology for having lost my temper with her, it seemed like I could've if only I would've tried. (Maya was short, her eyes hardly coming up to my chest.) But, all the while, I let my thoughts be dominated by the things that'd happened with Lisa. One look back at me and I could tell Maya knew there was *something* going on in my head, and that she knew, in the vaguest way possible, that it was something she had gone through herself. "Forget about it," she said. In time, we would come to see eye-to-eye. But first, Karen.

Suddenly filled with a confidence, I began working faster, harder, picking orders in minutes that would've taken anyone else half an hour, my body seeming to channel the frenetic energy with which I'd pursued Karen in secret and in public so many times, as if I was in relentless pursuit of the very same *feeling* as I'd been. At the end of my shift, I found myself picking orders in the same aisle as Jordan; we stepped past each other without a word exchanged. But then I tossed a glance back, the look on his face telling me we'd cross paths, so to speak. The warehouse was so large, its cavernous insides like a bunch of aircraft hangars haphazardly bolted together, and sometimes days passed without ever seeing half of my co-workers. Looking at him out of the corner of my eye, I wondered if he might've ever been *in love* with anyone or if, with him, it really wasn't an act. It wasn't my place. It was somewhere between arrogant and presumptuous even to wonder, but I couldn't help it. The night passed, and soon I was on my way across the parking lot towards my truck, parked about as far as possible from the employee entrance. It was a little moment of silence after having spent the entire day locked up in my own thoughts, allowing a peacefulness to intervene. Some of my co-workers were walking to their cars, their vests glinting under the pale orange lights illuminating the lot with a dim, sickly glow. Still I felt confident in myself, as if there was some part of me that looked into the future and knew exactly what I needed to do to earn my way out of the rut I found myself stuck in.

Sitting in my truck, I pulled my nearly-dead phone out of my pocket to plug it into the truck's charger, and in that half-second between the screen lighting up and going dark Karen's name and number flashed across. She'd called. Seized, I waited for the phone to charge, waiting as the rain intensified until it struck with the sound of a thunderous barrage and as the parking lot around emptied until I sat alone in the darkness of the early evening's night, minutes passing until the phone at last powered up, that picture of her and I together on its home screen appearing. Careful not to unplug the phone, I unlocked it and selected 'Miss Thoreson' from my contacts, and for a moment hovered over her number, afraid. It rang. It rang, it rang, it rang, then clicked over to her voicemail. Hanging up without leaving a message,

I turned back and dialled again, this time the call making it halfway through the second ring before it cut out, the call declined. With the night having set itself on the scene, I left. Whatever might've happened to her since we last saw each other, I wanted to speak with her, to hear the sound of her voice, like I was starving and fantasizing about my next meal. It was as though an important step had been taken, which put me, as I saw it then, *closer* to *something*, even if I hadn't the slightest clue what. *You're on the right track*, intuition seemed to say, *just keep doing what you're doing.* But I wasn't, and I knew it. Whenever I clocked out at the end of the day, I left the warehouse wishing I'd done something different, that I'd worked just a little harder or a little faster, that I'd not given the time to those who were telling me different things, that I'd just put my head down and pushed through the day without stopping to think about what could've, should've, even would've been.

After Gerald Wang had made his visits, he took a vacation, leaving us waiting until he'd come back to hear whether he'd done any good in meeting with the head of the company. I wish I'd done more back then. It'd just been a rumour that'd spread when one worker had heard something and repeated it to a couple others until, like a bunch of kids playing telephone, it'd become something it wasn't. It didn't really matter, anyways, as it was all a distraction seemingly meant to pull me off the straight and narrow, to entangle me in a web of deceit. You know, Karen, I still don't think I'll ever understand what went wrong, but if it means anything to you at all (that is, if you ever read this), I want you to know that I always wanted you to be happy. Vaguely, as if behind a thin mist, the drive home saw me looking back and trying to decipher some hidden meaning from the shop steward's question, the amateur psychologist in me parsing out his words, going over each in isolation, considering so many possible meanings, then reading into his tone, the vaguely crooked look on his face, at once losing sight of him, the person living inside me at once reducing him to the level of an object, ascribing to him a motive, thinking forward, thinking back, thoughts blending, blurring, bleeding into the night. It was all so much to think about, and at once, as I pulled into the little side-street on which my apartment building sat, I chided myself for overthinking the matter. With holes in my socks and dirt under my nails, I climbed the stairs towards my third-floor apartment, finding it all exactly as I'd left it. There were messages on my cell phone's voice-mail (I'd forgotten it at home that night), but I let them be, falling onto the living room's couch, lying on my stomach for hours until a restless sleep took hold. Not the next day or the day after, but a few weeks later, Karen called, and we were together again.

4. Past

One night in the new year, not altogether long after Karen and I had touched each other in my car, Lisa and Randall went out drinking, returning sometime past midnight, stumbling through the front door, the giggling and the gleeful shrieking soon giving way to the shouting and the breaking of glass. As I made my way down the stairs, the wailing of police sirens drew sharply louder, drowning out the sounds of the night. Soon, Randall was cuffed, in the back of a police cruiser, while Lisa and I stood on the side of the road listening as a constable explained what was to happen. "He'll spend the night at the station," the constable, a young, blonde woman said. "In the morning, if he's cooperative, we'll go from there." Then, the constable handed Lisa a card for some local counseling service, before turning and making back for the row of cruisers parked along the side of the street, leaving the night quiet, slow.

Later, after an hour or two of staring at my bedroom's dark ceiling, I made for the stairs, intent on raiding the kitchen, stopping with the tips of my toes hanging off the edge of the top. Crying, the sound of soft, hushed crying hung in the air. Slowly, delicately, I inched down the stairs, tiptoeing around the spots which I knew creaked and groaned under my weight, until, from the last step at the bottom I had a clear view into the living room, Lisa sitting on the couch, clutching a tissue against her cheek as she stared off into space, as though she were caught in a daze. Soon, I sat next to her, one leg pulled up, listening, waiting for an opportunity to say something, for her to let me in. It might've seemed like an odd thing, to be in the middle of a warzone, but then I'd—we'd been through much worse, so we both knew how it went. Being as I was seventeen, though, I couldn't think of anything to say, instead letting silence settle, a silence broken only by her sobs, softer and slower until she fell quiet. Then, she looked at me, and spoke.

"Well I guess you're happy," she said. "Why would I be happy?" I asked. Forcing a snicker, she said, "don't you hate him?" "Yeah, but..." Silence, for a moment an awkward silence. Yet, I was conflicted, too, as every part of me believed he was wrong for her, for us, resenting his intrusion into the unit we'd made up for so long. He had no right to be there. He had no right to be a part of our lives. And yet, it was her choice to invite him in, to give him a place in our home. Though these are the ways I've come to express the way I felt, then, at the time all I understood was anger, resentment, shame. "He's not a bad person, you know," Lisa said. As it was the time to listen, I sat silent, waiting, allowing the truth to draw itself out of her and into the space between us, to bare itself for us both to see. "He wants me to be happy." She folded her arms and rubbed a thumb gently against the side of her elbow. "He's a good person. He just, sometimes..." Right then, the phone rang, snapping Lisa out of her self-imposed trance as she reached for the cordless and answered it halfway through the second ring. It was Randall, of course; I could tell immediately from the way she seemed to perk up on hearing his voice, the dull, aching look behind her eyes flashing into a bright whiteness. She didn't ask for privacy, so I stayed to listen in, taking in her half of the conversation, imagination filling in the rest. "Where are you now?" she asked. Of course he was in jail, having been thrown into the drunk tank for the night. "When will you be out?" In the morning. "They'll just let you go?" Yes, he was to be set free without any charges. "I'll be there." A moment's pause. "I love you too." Then, it was finished, the cordless sliding back into its charger, Lisa looking over at me. *This is happening*, the look on her face seemed to say, *with or without you*. Soon, I was alone, again, watching the night's darkness slowly bleed into the morning's light, a lingering doubt burning my insides like a corrosive acid melting its way through a weak, brittle surface, exposing underneath it all something rotten and black.

A couple of weeks earlier just before Karen and I had that fake-out kiss in my car, I'd met Adrian—more like, ran into Adrian—in the hall at Eastmount between periods. We kept in touch mostly by way of ICQ, an old instant messaging program that'd already fallen out of use by most people. (He was in the International Baccalaureate program, Eastmount being one of the few schools in the area hosting the program, while I just happened to live in Eastmount's catchment area; we had none of the same classes and none of the same classmates and none of the same friends). He hadn't seen me online in a while, and waved me over from across the busy hall, and soon we were sitting outside on the soccer field bleachers, talking about nothing in particular. Look, I don't remember exactly how it came out, but that's not important. He didn't even believe me at first; "and you're serious?" he asked once it was clear I wasn't just talking shit. "I'm in love with her," I said, "like, I really love her. I don't know what to do." He thought I was just infatuated with her, that it was a case of unrequited love that'd taken hold of me. But then they all thought that, each and every one of our classmates who'd seen me spend mornings, lunch hours, time after the school days had ended in her classroom, sitting on the edge of her desk, trading playful barbs and coy glances with her. "Just be careful," Adrian said, "or you'll wind up doing something you might regret." He'd always been the practical type, and for a moment I thought he might've seen right through me, might've spotted the little cocksure glance I gave Karen every time we crossed paths. But he let it be. We stayed out that afternoon, as late as his tightly-planned schedule allowed, until he was needed at a meeting for some club he chaired, leaving me to wander home. Without a shift at the thrift shop that night I was needed nowhere.

     All I could think about was being with her. Adrian was on the lookout for me; he sent an instant message the night after I'd told him, but I let it sit without reply. It might've made me look aloof and distant, but I couldn't quite figure out how to make myself look. "Don't do anything stupid," Adrian said once, "I don't know if you know it but pretty much everyone can tell what's going on with you and Miss Thoreson." He said it in the parking lot after classes one time, and at first I was sure he meant that the rumour mill had begun talking about us. It was true, but it wasn't true. Some were saying we'd slept together, while others that I was just *crushing* on her, hard. It mattered little to me who said what, and, looking back on it, even if some of my classmates were *telling* each other we'd slept together it didn't mean they *knew* we'd slept together many, many times. The difference was important to me then, even if, more than a decade later I can now see there was hardly a difference at all in the damage they could've done to her should the rumours have found the wrong ears. But we hadn't slept together yet, and that was the critical fact. "It doesn't matter," I said, "nothing's happened." "Maybe not," he said, "but just so you know, people are talking." The next time I saw him, he was holding his girlfriend's hand, walking between classes, and when I saw them together I felt a sudden pang of jealousy that all but compelled me to have another go at Karen, and that's exactly what I wound up doing next.

In the morning, I made it to Spanish class with seconds to spare, quickly and quietly taking my seat under Karen's watchful eye. She might've forced the meanest of glares my way, then made a cutting remark, something like, "...and for those of us who couldn't be bothered to make it to class in good time, we're starting with chapter two today." Behind the menacing tone I could detect the slightest hint of feeling, but a feeling I couldn't figure out. It was frustrating, and it left me searching for a way out. Look, I wonder, now, if she knew just how my sudden expulsion from her love life had made me feel; but I took it on the chin, managing the same blank, impassive look on my face whenever we crossed paths, whenever I sat in her classroom for the day's lesson, every now and then allowing the slightest hint of feeling to creep back in, softening my stare. But as the twelfth grade drew nearer to its end, I couldn't see more than a half-metre in front of me, thinking only of the next opportunity for adventure, wanting to be anywhere but where I was. Karen had once told me she'd spent years teaching English in Mexico after graduating from university, where she picked up fluent Spanish, and for a while I thought of doing something like that. Except, I thought to head to the other side of the world, picturing myself hopping on a plane to Bangkok and riding around on old, creaky buses carrying monks sitting next to chickens in wire cages, until I found a place that struck me just right, some little hole-in-the-wall town where I could live a simple life eating out of street stalls every night and drinking cheap beer and smoking cheaper cigarettes. It seemed like a picture worth seeing. But, in the meantime, I had to make it to the end of the world, one way or another. Even though Adrian had told me to be careful, and even though I knew he was right, I struggled to keep myself from just walking up to Karen, taking her by the hand, and telling her, in front of a class full of students, that I loved her.

The next time I went to Karen's class, I made it a point of walking through the door exactly as half the students had already entered, hoping she'd notice. Things were coming to a head. Having turned in so many assignments late or not at all, I was only scraping by. My counselor had worked out a deal where I'd receive credit, but no grade, for the math course I was failing badly, in exchange for completing a little book of coursework that I'd left in the trunk of my car for most of the year. But then, halfway through of April, I'd find the little book wedged underneath a half-empty carton of antifreeze, its edges frayed, but every page intact. Skimming through it, I'd realize it was just long enough to complete, and I took it home with me that night after a shift at the thrift shop, tucked into a binder, intending to work on it into the early hours of the morning. I'd eventually finish it, and hand it in just in time, jammed with loose-leaf paper and solutions written illegibly, but receiving credit anyways; it's only in the years since that I've realized I was allowed to pass because my counselor had likely made a personal appeal to the math teacher to let me through and on from high school. At home, as I parked on the street outside our little townhouse, I noticed ours was the only unit whose windows were brightened a dull orange by the lights inside, like a single Christmas light on a string flickering for a half-second after the plug had been pulled out from the socket. Still thinking of Karen, I withdrew into fantasies of *making love* with her mixed in with re-enactments of all the little moments we'd shared when passing each other in the halls, working to keep my mind's eye there as I walked through the front door and into a war zone. We'd kissed, we'd put our hands on each other, and from the corner of my eye whenever we passed in the hall I could see a little glimpse in hers that made it clear she was feeling exactly the same way for me that I felt for her. Of course she was. It seems, now, like an over-elaborate and roundabout way to think, when she'd already let me touch her then I should've known to just reach out and have her, but, at seventeen, I was exactly as unsure of myself as she was of herself, if for different reasons. She'd laughed, half-nervously, she'd looked and she'd glanced, she'd stared at me before catching herself. If only she wasn't my teacher, we'd have been together already. But that tension, that apprehension meant we couldn't have plainly what we might've. It's all an act. Of course we were to be together, but the act of crossing that last line seemed so difficult just to do, my teenaged awkwardness and her apprehension about us being together taking what should've been quick and drawing it out, even as it was leading only to one place.

Rapid action, Lisa, Randall, the slamming of doors and the thumping of feet up and down stairs. They were at it again; they were always at it again. But this time, I stood on the stairs, just high enough to be out of sight but just low enough to allow a peek at what was happening downstairs. It was hot, a late-spring heat wave opening every window. He yelled, she yelled. He stood, she stood. He took her into the kitchen and then there was the pouring of booze into a cup and the clinking of ice cubes against glass. It doesn't really matter what happened next. There wasn't any violence, and in fact it seemed like they were having a *good time* by yelling at each other like they were. I couldn't understand it then, and I don't understand it now, and I don't think I'll ever understand it. Living with the two of them, together, was like walking on eggshells, Randall having turned Lisa into someone I couldn't recognize, a total stranger who thought only of how much booze she could put in her body. But that was the night; I couldn't take it anymore. I had to get out, I wanted to get out, I needed to get out before *someone* did *something* that couldn't have been taken back. Falling asleep at my bedroom's desk that night, I woke the next morning with sheets from my math workbook stuck to my forehead. With my head full of intoxicating ideas of adventure, I secretly and silently picked a date the coming summer when I'd leave, July 31st. It was to be, I thought, my escape. I wouldn't wind up making that date, and when I wound up leaving I wouldn't make it very far, but that wasn't the point. Immediately, my mind filled itself with fantasies of rolling up mountains in rickety old buses, of scorching heat and parched, brown fields stretching to the horizon and beyond, of miming my way through conversations with shopkeepers and clerks at dusty bus stations in little towns here and there. Then, Karen.

In the dead of winter, it was cold enough outside that you could see your breath, and the skies had become concealed by an almost permanent layer of thick, grey clouds. I spent whole days in a daze, alternately lost in thought and staring out the window listlessly, imagining little shapes and patterns in the smoothly undulating sky, plotting the next time Karen and I were to see each other. We passed each other in the halls that day, once or twice or three times, each encounter lasting a few seconds, but seeing an exchange of looks that were in some secret code, like a silent language reserved for us. But I kept myself in check, suppressing, for a little while, the urge to just act out. Let's back up a bit. In the eleventh grade when I first fell in *love* with Karen, I was caught in the middle of an impossible situation, trapped under the weight of an ongoing crisis, with every night seeming to threaten a new battle waged at home. There were holes in the walls. The first had been my doing. I was angry, and no one was home; let's leave it at that. The second had been Randall's doing. The third, the fourth, the others were no one's in particular. (I think one of them might've been me moving furniture). It became a regular event for me to be sitting in my room, forcing my way through overdue homework, when muffled shouting would sound out from below, interrupted only by the crashing of broken dishes and the slamming of doors followed by the smack of the back of a hand against a cheek and then the rapid creaking, squeaking of a bed's springs. But I'd trained myself to ignore it, instead wondering what it would take for Lisa to finally break free of the spell Randall had cast over her, to see him, at last, for what he plainly was. Then, it happened. On my way up the stairs between the end of a day at Eastmount and the start of a shift at the thrift shop, I heard him mutter, under his breath, "fuckhead," at me. Stopping halfway up, I stood in place for a moment, thinking to turn back and confront him, before carrying on up, leaving him be. By the time I came home, well past midnight, he was asleep, our home dark and cold. As I turned into the kitchen and switched the light on, I noticed, out of the corner of my eye, Lisa was sitting in the living room on the end of the couch, crying silently. She was in pain. Turning for bed, I closed the door to my room, shed my clothes onto the floor, and climbed into bed, pulling the covers up to my neck before drifting off to sleep. That night, I dreamed of holding Karen in my arms, only to wake and find myself trudging through the mud between the parking lot and the school, looking for the sight of Karen to spark a new day alight. But she wasn't there. Her classroom was empty, dark, locked. She'd stayed home for the day, taking a personal day, I'd later learn, and in her place there was a stodgy old woman who wore thick-rimmed glasses and had curly grey hair. It was a relief to have the day's Spanish period free from the distraction of being in the same room as her, even as I craved to be as near to her as I could possibly have been. I was in love with her and she was in love with me. When she came back to Eastmount, I made another try at her, seamlessly linking our kiss and our touch with the next time we'd be together, and already she seemed to draw nearer to me even as she pulled away further than ever. It was almost time.

At home, there were bottles in the cupboard above the kitchen sink, whiskey, vodka. When I first found them, I poured them out into the sink, then screwed their caps back on and put them back in the cupboard. Later, he came home, and I listened as he trundled up the stairs and into the second-floor kitchen, then back down and out the door, returning a little later clutching a brown paper bag. Later, after Lisa had come home from a late night at work, she and Randall were getting into it again, and from beyond the kitchen's wall I heard him shout, "and if you fuckin' pour my fuckin' drinks out again you'll be fuckin' sorry!" "I don't know what you're talking about!" Lisa said. It would later emerge that Lisa told him she did it after he'd—correctly—decided I did it, and she'd done so just to get him off my case. But I let it happen anyways. Opening my bedroom's door a crack, I peered across the hall and into the kitchen, watching as they stood a half-metre apart, his back facing me, partly obscuring her front. There was more shouting, and then he took an empty glass and threw it against the wall, hard, shattering it into a hundred little pieces. "Please..." she cried. He took her by the shoulders and shook her, and when she tried to break free he raised the back of his hand and struck her across the face. It was then that I leapt forward, fists clenched, then spun him around and cracked him square in the jaw. The last of the night that I can recall was Lisa's crying as she pulled at me with all her strength, trying to get me off him. I recall this, now, but still I can't help but wonder how much of it has been thatched together by memory, bits of truth tied together by lies.

In Karen's classroom after school one day, the last day of classes before the two-week Christmas break. I'd waited until after the halls had become largely deserted so no one would walk in on us talking; so long as we kept our voices down, I thought, no one would know a thing. Leaning against the whiteboard, I tried my best to loom over her while she kept on wiping the last class's verb conjugations and half-pretended to be listening to me, half-pretending to be ignoring me. Turning to me, she quickly looked me up and down, then turned back and made for her desk, sitting down, pulling out a pen, and going at the papers and the handed-in assignments. Following, I sat on the edge of the desk, leaning in slightly, without a clue what I was doing, without a clue what to do next, just sort-of leaning there, the moment awkward, she seeming to let the attention sink in until she looked up and let the smile fade from her face. *Don't think*, instinct seemed to tell me, *just keep doing what you're doing.* She looked down at her work, slashing red ink across the pages, but at some point she'd stopped, leaving us at an impasse, neither of us able to take the next step, she out of fear for her career, me an ordinary fear of myself. In the face of my feelings, Adrian's words repeated themselves in my mind, *just be careful,* but almost silent compared to the instincts telling me to press on. Not all that long before the two-week break, I felt time was running out on my chance to be with Karen, even though, looking back on it, she would've kept giving me as many chances as I'd needed. She was waiting for me to make a move. There was some part of her that could only step aside and let me push, slowly, each push forward bringing us closer to being together. It was like a psychological hang-up, as if she'd determined to decide what to do next once I'd made the next push at her, whether to give in then or hold off for a little while longer. "Karen," I said, "about last time…" She said, "it's fine," without looking up. Enough time had passed that the halls outside had become largely deserted, and although we were in public I felt emboldened to try, not to touch her or kiss her but just to talk. But back on the very first day of classes in the year of my twelfth grade, I walked the halls fully expecting to find Karen around every corner, beyond every door. In the eleventh grade her Spanish class had been my home-room, but in the twelfth it was an English class held in a room halfway across the school. By force of habit, I went, that first day, to Karen's classroom, stopping myself a half-metre from the door. It was all so deeply confusing. But I was sure, confident of myself. In her room, Karen sat at her desk. Outside, in the parking lot after classes had ended for the day, she approached from a distance and struck up a conversation. "Don't you think you should put a shirt on?" she asked, sly grin across her lips. "Maybe," I said, mind drawing a blank as I looked at her, eyes quickly drawing from her head to toe and then back up again. But my body seemed to respond, my biceps flexing and my shirt tightening slightly, already skin tight against my hardened, barrel of a chest. "Well," she said, beginning to walk past but tossing an impish grin back, "if you don't...I wouldn't mind." A wink, then she kept walking. It's only in the years since that I've realized she was, then, as scared as I was, scared for the feelings she'd come to have for me. Though she tried to conceal her fear beneath the veneer of confidence. We're all afraid of *something*. Some people just hide it better than others. "God, I love you," I said when she was safely out of earshot. But at just the right moment, she turned and looked back, for a split-second seeming to have heard me. I chose to imagine she'd heard me. She flashed a grin, then kept walking, her brown hair swirling a half-second behind the turn of her neck, making her look caught in a camera's lens at exactly the moment of capture. That was then. "Keith, you're going to be the end of me," she'd said once, months later, but with a soft, playful tone that came from the lingering after-sex haze as we lay atop one another in her little apartment's bed. But as we kissed, she held her hands on my chest, as if to pin me in place, to freeze the moment forever. She had come to fall in love with me. She wanted me. It made me feel so good to have someone want me. She'd gone out of her way to have me, to make herself mine, myself hers. But first, months earlier, she'd forced herself away from me when it'd become too much to bear, as if it could've been so simple.

4. Present

"Don't be that guy." But Jordan had a point, I thought. After having found myself unceremoniously cast out of Karen's life I realized, suddenly, that I'd devoted myself so completely to my affair with her that I'd let nearly everything but my job fall by the wayside, and if I could've paid the rent without having worked I'm sure I would've let that fall by the wayside too. But, you see, it made little difference. All the phone calls I'd neglected to return through those months amounted to three or four from the union about the election, another from the psychiatrist I'd been seeing. It was like being pulled from a warm bed and thrown outside, naked, into the middle of a frigid winter's storm, being so suddenly cut off from Karen that I'd found myself confronted with the reality I'd been so avoiding. Alone, so very alone, I couldn't just call her, couldn't text her, couldn't show up at her home like I'd done, secretly, so many times before. I know it makes me seem like an idiot to have expected, whether I was aware of it or not, our affair to last, or to become something *more*, but after having been with her, off and on, in one way or another for more than ten years, I just couldn't keep myself from *believing* that we'd keep on being together, someway, somehow, forever.

"Don't be that guy." At home, in my apartment's bedroom closet I kept plastic totes stacked one on top of the other. In one of those totes there were some old textbooks from university, and sandwiched between a geography textbook and a biology lab manual was my old high school yearbook. I'd like to say I found it by accident, but in fact I went looking for it, spending half a Saturday afternoon going through tote after tote until happening across it, leafing through it until I found the page I was looking for. Mine. Each grad had one. We'd all written a little paragraph. Mine had been shorter than most. I couldn't have said what I'd really wanted, anyways, couldn't have offered any reflection on the best and the worst of my experiences back then. Not that it matters. No one really reads those things. Near the middle of the yearbook was the faculty's group photo, and in the third of three rows stood Karen, only her face visible to the camera, smiling, her teeth white and her hair a darker brown than I remembered. That photo had been taken before we'd first *made love*, before she'd crossed that red line and broken the law. But I looked on that picture as if it was one she'd taken just for me, maybe in one of those old instant photo booths in malls where teenaged couples would put their arms around each other and make funny faces for pictures they'd keep pinned to the insides of their locker doors. It's stupid. Even then, as I looked on that picture I knew it was stupid to think of it that way. But I just couldn't help myself. There had to have been something there, I decided, before closing the yearbook and placing it back in the tote where I'd found it, then the tote back in the closet. She'd told me so, back then, that she thought about me all the time. She must've been thinking of me when that picture was taken, just as I'd been thinking of her when they'd dressed me up in a black robe and mortarboard and taken my picture for the yearbook. Everyone had been so nice and understanding to me, but I couldn't see it at the time. No one can.

"Don't be that guy." Only a few of my classmates had signed my yearbook. "Keith! Take them one at a time. Hope you're able to achieve your dreams and help people. Make sure you have fun. Later man." "Thanks for your comment the other day. I've seen you as a very enthusiastic person in volunteering & history and I'm sure you'll succeed on the future. Have a great summer, and good luck in whatever you are planning." "Man, it's kinda tough putting so many years with you into words, but I'll try to write as much as I can! I still remember when we were in elementary and we'd use to go over to each others – I remember that time in spring break when I went over like everyday! I also remember the sleepovers, the hanging out, the movies and all the fun we had! Without a doubt, you were and you are still one of my best friends. From the time when you weren't doing so great, to now, I'm still around to help you out whenever I can. Just remember, everyone has their talents and I truely believe that if you think you can do something, you can. Although I have to say I'm kinda =(you live so far away now and that you'll be moving away one day, I hope we can keep in touch! If you ever need a helping hand, anywhere with anything, you can be sure that you have one of your best friends back home! Best of luck! – Adrian Chan" He wound up leaving, first to Toronto, then San Francisco, while I wound up living in a little box of an apartment not all that far from our high school. They were all so good-hearted and well-meaning, but I didn't see it at the time. Karen signed it, too. 'All the best – Miss Thoreson.' For years I'd thought it was code for *something*, but in my mind whatever it *was* code for changed over time. As close as she could come to acknowledging our *love*. A wink and a nod to the private affair we'd been carrying on. A half-hearted try at signalling the end of our affair. A plain, honest well-wishing. It became no clearer after we'd reunited a decade later, but I'd never asked. Never occurred to me. It'd have felt odd, sitting with my old Spanish teacher, with her going through my old high school yearbook as if she'd been a student, too. That rainy afternoon, in the middle of those weeks before Karen called me back into her life again, I suddenly felt a surge of regret, not for having lost her a second time in less than ten years but for the crushing realization that the only picture I had of her from our time together back then was the distant shot of her smiling face framed by the faces of other teachers, middle-aged teachers whose names I couldn't remember and she probably couldn't either. It might seem—it seems, now, after all that's happened to not have taken any pictures of her, back then, but that was the sort of illicit affair we'd had.

In Karen's new apartment, weeks later, boxes were piled high and countertops were covered in half-unpacked dishware and little packets of soap. Karen had taken to wearing her old 'Property of the University of British Columbia' sweatshirt whenever we were at home, alone, even sometimes with only her underwear else on, making it look, when she stood, like she was wearing nothing at all below the waist. But the flustered, tired look on her face seemed not at all hers, as though a stranger's face had imposed itself on her body. It was unsettling, in a subdued sort of way, and as she sat on her living room's couch I approached from the side, sitting next to her, gently taking her by the sides and pulling her into my lap. "Keith, I'm tired," she said, even as she pushed back, nuzzling into the nape of my neck. "Then just rest," I said, "let's just rest." "'Kay," she said. But the tension that'd worked its way into her muscles wouldn't unwind, and as I linked my hands around her stomach I felt her insides twist themselves into knots. We spent the night together, that night, but we didn't *make love*, instead sleeping spooned on the couch, all the while an intimacy had begun to quietly creep away.

Winter ground slowly past, the bright, grey skies darkening, unleashing a torrent of rain, pausing occasionally to gather strength before releasing yet another deluge. There came a day, though, sometime halfway through January when the skies deigned to let loose a flurry of snow, a thin layer of whiteness soon coating every rooftop, every open field, every road, crunching beneath my feet as I walked along that concrete path snaking around the back of the warehouse's parking lot, every breath exhaling a wick of hotness that blended, faded into the frigid, wintry air. Arriving, I stepped inside, a blast of warm air rushing over me, striking every patch of exposed skin, the marked contrast between cold and hot sending a shiver running the length of my spine. Shifting my stance slightly, I brushed the last flakes of snow from my hair, pulled tight my hi-vis vest's loose left strap, and headed in, navigating the building with all the deftness of a blind man following a familiar set of steps from memory alone. Work that night was hard and long, but the only real detail I can recall was the looking forward to a night with Karen. (No, I don't remember anything about it, because it was just another day at work. But let's imagine I can.) After work that night, I drove to Karen's, finding her in the middle of taking a bath, reading a Danielle Steel novel and sipping on a glass of red wine. When I walked through the door to her washroom, she put the book down and lifted herself out of the bath, standing naked for a moment before wrapping a towel around her body and stepping towards me. Still covered in the muck, the grime of the day's work, I felt so coarse, so unrefined, contrasting sharply with the shapeliness, the femininity of her hardly-concealed body. In her bed that night, we *made love* exactly like we once had, her legs hooked around my backside as I moved against her, my hands holding hers above her while we kissed, her back arching and her body tensing up as we had our release. But it was a fraud. In the dim of the night, the little imperfections that age had wrought on her body couldn't be seen, making her look exactly as she'd been ten years earlier when we'd first *made love*. For a moment, I forgot all that'd happened between us, convincing myself to indulge in the fraud.

But after we'd been walked in on by her husband, the fraud had been revealed to us and to everyone around us for what it was. Turning inward, I sought escape. But I couldn't. Sitting near the top of a pile of books in my apartment was a copy of 'Endless Love' by Scott Spencer, a book I'd first encountered in an intro-level university English course. Back then, I'd only thumbed it, passing the course with an unearned B-minus. Years later, I plucked it off the shelf and read through it in a day, and it became one of my favourite novels. In it, a young Jewish man, the son of committed Marxists, is cut off from his lover, and remarks that it's only a cliché, the idea that you begin to see your lover's face everywhere after being so suddenly and unceremoniously expelled from her life. Yet, it was true, for me at least, that in the time between Karen's husband walking in on us and Karen calling me back into her life, I went about my days looking on every thirty- or forty-something white woman whose hair was brownish, shoulder-length hair and a shapely figure with an anticipation, never mistaking any of them for Karen, but some subconscious part of the mind for a moment inciting me to imagine her there, on the other side of a grocery store's aisle, looking for her preferred brand of fabric softener, not finding it, thinking on whether to settle for a substitute or shop elsewhere. Even once I went to that very grocery store and stood in the same place in the same aisle at more-or-less the same time at night half-expecting her to be there. At twenty-eight I was eighteen again. There was a woman who appeared at the end of the aisle, but much too young and much too thin to allow me to indulge in fantasy that it might've been her. I realize how that sounds; as if the young woman, then, wandering down the aisle was there only to have me look on her and think about Karen. No matter how many people there were in the world, I knew, I *know* I'll never find anyone else like Karen, even though there are probably a thousand and one women like her. In those months after Karen and I had been walked in on, it was like a part of me had been instantly removed. It might seem—it might've seemed silly, melodramatic even, to have allowed myself to fall *in love* with a married woman, to a woman with a young son, to the woman I could've never had anything more than an affair with, but then I never fell out of love with her even in our years apart.

To Karen's neighbours it must've been obvious she'd been carrying on an affair. A truck, a white pickup truck with a bald tire and a thin layer of dirt and mud crawling up its sides parking so often on the street in front of her home, but only when her husband's sedan wasn't there, the same young man with blond hair and blue eyes and a worn hi-visibility vest and work boots with torn, tattered laces entering her home only to leave hours later, before her husband returned in his jet-black BMW and his blue-patterned tie. But she knew none of her neighbours all that well, at most a quick wave and an exchanged 'hello' in the morning on her way to work, or so she'd said. Hers was a world of white-picket fences and carefully-washed SUVs and weekly soccer games standing on the sideline with the other parents cheering their young children on. And for the six months I was in her life, there'd been a point where, our *lovemaking* seemed to recall the way we'd once, ten years earlier, found so much in common despite our differences.

At work, I'd stopped making excuses for myself, and began avoiding my co-workers, spending breaks sitting in my truck, sometimes reading, sometimes with my phone in my hand, ready to reply in an instant should Karen have sent me a text. Then she'd text me, just as I was reading her old texts, so that I needed only to scroll down a bit to reply. But I never replied, not right away, thinking about her the rest of the evening, deciding what to say and how to say it, the shift passing in an instant as I suddenly found myself flashed forward to standing in line at the punch-clock waiting with the others for the shift's last seconds to pass. At home, I'd wait until the early morning to reply, sure that she wouldn't right away, only to receive her text immediately. It was awkward, uncertain, like I was a teenager again. It became rare for us to *make love* in my apartment, rarer still for her to be there at all, but, again, we were there, *making love*, this time awkwardly fitting ourselves onto the little twin-sized bed, she on her back while I was on her, her skin soft, smooth, warm, her little gasps coming in time with my movements against her, the sliding of my length inside her in one smooth motion, then withdrawing in another, she seeming to fit around me perfectly every time I bottomed out. But then, "ow," she said, and I stopped, realizing she'd struck her head against the wall behind the bed. "Sorry," I said. "It's fine," she said.

Then I reached underneath her, grasped her by the bottom, and lifted her with me, inching back before setting her back down, kissing her, she kissing me, then in one hard movement pushing back inside her. Coming inside her, I'd pushed in to the hilt and held myself still, but in the aftermath I realized that I'd kept the moment away from her, that I'd hurt her in the little what that I had. She hadn't come. I hadn't made her come. But it was a small thing, a little moment, and in those months after she'd called me back into her life a third time it seemed like a, like a progression, looking back on it like a step towards *something*, I'm still not sure what.

Text messages were exchanged, hers still short, terse, mine punctuated by long periods of time between them. Still I rose in the morning, replaying that scene in my mind like an old war film, its frames flickering, its colours drained, some part of me wondering if it'd all been a dream, a premonition, an omen that'd presented itself That night, as I undressed, discarding clothes so dirtied, so torn, so dulled in their colours by a day's work, thoughts of Karen clouded my mind, filling each second, each hardened, lightened moment with an aching sensation, a longing that seemed to intensify, gaining strength with each beat of the heart. Casting my shorts, my shirt, my safety vest onto the bedroom's floor, I made my way into the washroom, turned, and leaned forward, gripping the sides of the sink with both hands, pushing a gaze through to the world on the other side of the mirror, no small part of me wondering on the person staring back. At my apartment, after a rare night out, unknown to either of us the last time we'd see each other for more than three weeks. Being that my twin-sized bed was too small for us, we *made love*, that night, on my living room's couch, she atop me, my hands holding her bottom, her hands gripping the couch to either side of my head, her small, wide-set breasts heaving with each of her strokes against me, our bodies fitting flush with one another's for a half-moment before she'd withdraw with a quick pull of her hips away from mine. But it wasn't a rhythmic, rehearsed set of motions, Karen seeming to use the act of our *lovemaking* to work a tension, a stress from her body, her movements quick, frenetic, her hands finding my shoulders, then sliding to my neck, one taking my chin, holding, kissing, her teeth on my lip, biting gently, her whole body seeming to still while she spasmed underneath me, her head tilting forward, my lip sliding almost-out, the tips of her teeth biting onto the edge of my lip at exactly the moment to trigger my release as I came inside her. It was the last time we'd see each other for more than three weeks, with so much left to happen in that time.

The truth was that I'd just *happened* into the job which meant joining the Roadsters, tossing a resume at a random job ad I'd seen on craigslist after a lengthy stint as a part-time *package handler* with a package delivery company. It'd been the kind of long, meandering journey that couldn't be planned. It'd been my choice to rack up thirty thousand dollars in student debt. It'd been my choice to cultivate few marketable skills, and instead spend my time fantasizing about *making love* to women (not just Karen; there were others) with whom I had no chance of fostering a real *relationship*. At the age of twenty-eight, almost twenty-nine, I had nothing to show for myself, and little hope for much of a future. Despite it all, I was certain of only one thing: my *love* for Karen, the one woman in the world it seemed fate had conspired to draw me towards even as she remained only just out of reach. But after Karen and I had begun seeing each other again, I was still kept at an arm's length, staying away whenever it was her turn to take care of Lucas, reappearing only when she'd texted or called me to come and be with her, only when she'd handed Lucas off to Richard for the week. It was on exactly such a night, halfway through my shift, when Karen called and said our weekend together was off; at first, she wouldn't go into the details. Then, just past midnight, a series of texts explaining, in not so many words, she'd leapt at the chance to have an extra week with her son, with Richard suddenly called to Edmonton on an unexpected business trip. I texted back, capping it off with, "I love you," but received no more texts from her that night. It was a cold winter's night, but still I left my bedroom's window wide open and slept on top of the covers, waking every couple of hours to check my phone, never finding any more replies. Don't think this wasn't happening. It was. It's just that I'd—we'd been through this all before, and it was frustrating, to me, how little it all had changed. I had become the other, just as I'd always been the other. Don't think, but make sure to think it all through.

Her divorce, she hadn't told me when they were getting divorced, only that they were. But even when she'd said that, the almost-quiver and the half-anger in her voice made me think, not then but in the weeks that'd come after, that even this might've not been true. (Looking back, I can see, now, that this was the moment when it'd begun to end; when you let suspicion contaminate trust, then there can't be anything else. Though our affair had been based on a lie, cheating, since we'd run into each other in that grocery store's aisle, so I can't really talk of trust. Then again, she was lying to herself by being in a marriage she never *really* wanted, a cheat on itself. I don't know. I still can't figure out what to make of it all.) I didn't know anything about divorce, except the things it does to the child. And it was exactly that realization, as I was stuck in traffic on the highway one afternoon, that made me feel suddenly guilty for myself. I don't know why that feeling of guilt hadn't set in until well after it should've. I knew what we were doing in the six months we'd kept our affair secret. I knew the risks, and so did she. But it's like I'd been so immersed in the passion of our affair that I'd come to half-believe we'd never have to deal with the consequences of our actions, even as I'd half-expected it all to fall apart at any moment. Then I'd been given everything I could've reasonably wanted; Karen, to myself, even though that's not what I had at all. Yet it all had left a bad taste in my mouth. After work that night, I went home and drank, the next morning waking up to a throbbing headache and another text from Karen inviting me over the following day. Actually, for a half-second I was sort-of dreading the evening with her, not the *lovemaking* but the act of waking up beside her the next day, the conversation, the stepping around each other in her bathroom, the little moments after the warmth had faded.

After we'd had a few weeks apart, the separation had built a sexual tension between us like a dam holding back water. Then, together. Late in the afternoon, Karen and I were in her little apartment's bedroom, capping off a day of hauling heavy boxes and furniture up from my truck by *making love*, in bed she on all fours while I took her from behind, she bucking slightly as she slid back in time with my thrusts, our bodies seeming to work against one another's. Leaning forward, I rested my hands on the bed next to hers, our *lovemaking* raw, animalistic. With my head next to hers, I took the back of her ear in my mouth and bit down, hard, prompting her to scream out in pain even as her whole body was wracked with an electric orgasm, her back arching and her whole body seeming to convulse, while the dull, metallic taste of a drop of blood was on the tip of my tongue. Then, I held still, buried deep, coming inside her. Then, she seemed, for the moment, satisfied, swaying her wide, ample hips slightly from side to side while I lay still buried inside her, a soft, low purr emanating from the back of her throat. In the warm, after-sex glow, I collapsed onto the bed next to her, nearly asleep when she lay against me and seemed to fold herself into my arms, turning her neck slightly, as if to look back, and said, "I don't know what that was..." "Me neither," I said, mumbling. "I'm going to lose my mind," she said. "Why?" I asked. She said, "you're going to make me lose my mind all over again." In the months that were to follow, that small moment took on a new significance, that time together maybe, I'd like to imagine, I gave her the only real, physical thing I'd ever had to give. But neither of us would learn about it until later, in the meantime too much left to sort itself out in both our lives for either of us to see that far ahead.

5. Past

A few days passed, the first couple of weeks in the new year blending into one another. Somehow, Karen returned to class the next day as though nothing had happened. It must've been all about appearances; she couldn't have been seen to have allowed herself a moment of weakness. Still, from that day forward, there was an implicit understanding reached between us: if I could commit to not antagonizing her then she would allow me an isolation, a measure of freedom in class from the unwavering glare to which she subjected the rest of the class. Over the next few weeks, it seemed as though Karen's piercing scowl softened whenever she looked at me, her frown relaxing for a half-moment into something vaguely resembling a smile, evidence there of feelings behind the prim and proper, before again hardening as she shifted her look of vague disdain back out over the classroom. All the while it seemed I could only look up at her and imagine myself holding her in my arms, the two of us swaying gently in time to a silent yet elegant waltz, just a short while later the two of us holding each other exactly as I'd imagined, right down to the last detail, the loose strands of her hair and the colour of the white-and-grey sweatshirt she had on, almost as though it'd been a vision I'd had.

None of it was real, but it was fully real at the same time. You have to understand that now, as an adult, I look back on this first time I'd fallen in love with another as something special, unique, different, in the same way that, I'm sure, everyone feels the first time they fall in love. It was a feeling of intense longing, of a vague but impossibly strong need to be near her, perhaps so strong only because I, in my youth, was so weak against it. Actually, earlier in the school year, maybe in late October just after Thanksgiving, Karen and I had spoken, briefly, in the parking lot, far enough from anyone so as to be out of earshot, but she looking just as nervous as if we were standing in the middle of a crowd of people. I'd propositioned her, directly, again, and she'd, again, rejected me, but this time chose to keep talking. "What if we, what if you and me went for coffee sometime?" I asked, "just to talk," I said. "I don't think so," she said. "Yeah, but..." There was more, and in the new year after I'd first told her outright that I was *in love* with her, I couldn't help but re-enact that little half-conversation in my mind, parsing out the words, in vain searching for some hidden meaning, coming up only with the obvious. But her sudden reluctance was enough to make me wonder if I'd imagined it all, every shared glance and every hint of affection.

Sometime that fall, I'd taken to walking past Karen's classroom on my way from English to Biology, going out of my way to walk at just the right angle to allow me to look through the open door at her desk and see her, there, looking right back up at me as though she'd come to expect it. It was a small thing, a little ritual I'd come to value, for it gave me the chance to have those extra few seconds of looking on her, of trading furtive glances and of sharing the secret knowledge that *something* was there, even if neither of us knew exactly what. And then, there came a day halfway through October when she wasn't there, in her place a thin woman wearing thick-rimmed glasses and a flannel shirt. Even though she wasn't there, I couldn't help but keep up my little routine of walking past her classroom at exactly the right time to look through the door, but found only that glasses-wearing fill-in, who looked back with a sideways expression on her face, until a few weeks later when I managed to break myself from the habit and began spending my spare time at Eastmount alone. She came back hardly a week later; a friend had fallen ill and she'd taken the week off to go out of town, she'd later tell me. Over the next few days, I fantasized about her constantly, spending time in class looking off into space as I imagined seeing her again, kissing her, touching her, as if it would make her return to Eastmount right then and there. And it worked better than I could've hoped. She returned. Weeks, months later, even after we'd begun to see each other at her apartment, *making love* whenever the chance presented itself, I *still* couldn't stop myself from fantasizing about her. It was, I thought, exactly like a disease. Little did I know that we, Karen and I, were so close to a breakthrough, that only days were to pass before we'd finally have each other. Love, when you're that young, is like a disease. But I can't say what it was like for her at thirty-five.

In the parking lot outside Eastmount, Karen was there, working herself out of the passenger seat of an old Cutlass Ciera driven by a grey-haired senior who I'd later learn was her grandmother. As I parked my car in the student lot, I couldn't take my eyes off her, watching as she made her way towards the school's side entrance, turning, as if on instinct, to look back my way. I managed to catch up with her as she headed along the narrow hall leading from the side of the building towards the office, and stopped her halfway there. We were in a narrow hall, with no one around to see us. I don't know what prompted me, but I stepped in front of her, seeming to loom over her, and asked, point-blank, for her phone number. She looked me up and down. Then, she jotted down her number on a scrap of paper and handed it to me, looking half-sure of herself. I took the paper and shoved it into my pocket, later taking it out so I could enter her number in my phone even as I'd already committed it to memory. Looking back, I don't think I'll ever know what motivated her to give me her phone number, to allow me that first, crucial inch into her personal life, and it was an inch I intended to make into a mile. I don't know what'd happened to change her mind so suddenly; in time, I'd learn, it wasn't anything at all, anything other than her having re-enacted that kiss over and over in her mind, until she'd given into her feelings and taken that one advance, that one of many, as I'd applied a pressure she'd let up. It's hard to explain unless you've been there, but if you're reading this, Karen, then you know exactly what I mean. It made no sense then, and it makes no sense now, but it was, looking back, the only possible way for things to happen.

Eventually, I made it home, sneaking in while Lisa and Randall were on the back patio smoking and drinking. Having forgotten my cell phone among a pile of papers on my bedroom's desk, I retrieved it and found Lisa had called several times. This I'd sort-of expected, but not a tearful apology asking me to come home. Then I'd called Karen. After a shower and a shave, I slowly made my way downstairs, in the main room crossing paths with Lisa, the flat look on her face suggesting she knew I'd come home. We said nothing as we crossed paths, but then, as I was halfway out the door, she said, "dinner will be on the stove when you get in later," then a pause, "if you get in later." I wish I could tell you I didn't know what to make of her sudden about face, on her change from screaming at me to leave to wishing me to stay, but it was the same as it'd always been. As I turned away, I felt something strange, something I couldn't quite understand, and it's only in the years since that I've realized the lingering sensation I felt that not all was well had come from inside me. It was only later, much later that I'd learn Lisa knew I was up to *something* with *someone*, she trying, in the way she was, to figure out *what* with *who*, events seeming to blend seamlessly into one another, as I left to be with Karen the thought occurring that maybe, just maybe it was all linked someway, somehow, that the whole bunch of us weren't all that different from each other after all. It's a strange feeling, but as I took to the streets of Vancouver, I felt safe, like I could've walked back in at any time, all the yelling and the screaming and the swearing gone, as I neared Karen's apartment those thoughts fading, fading, fading, my heart thumping against my chest and my stomach twisting into knots, as I parked in the street and made my way around to the back entrance the fear so overwhelming I nearly threw up. It was hard, then, for me to understand why she seemed on a daily basis to go from rejecting my advances to tacitly encouraging them, but then, I suppose that was our way.

She lived in a little apartment in South Vancouver, not far from the airport. She'd later tell me she liked to go for walks and watch planes taking off, imagining she was on them. As I reached the building's back door, she was there, standing with the door half open, her face brightening when we locked eyes, she taking me by the hand and saying, "you made it," with an edge to her voice that suggested, in my self-conscious state, she might've been about to do something she knew she'd regret. But it was a fleeting moment, she leading me inside, both of us wordlessly understanding what was to happen next, she sitting me on the edge of the bed, then starting out of her clothes, pulling her blouse off, her breasts concealed only by her bra. Never more terrified of anything in my life, I could feel my hands shaking slightly, until she leaned down, took them in hers, and rested my palms on her breasts, through the fabric her breasts seeming to fit perfectly in my grip, as though we were made for one another. Reaching behind her, I made to unhook her bra, fumbling at it slightly, until she smiled warmly and reached back, quickly and neatly undoing the hook, her bra falling, revealing her bare breasts. But I couldn't know what to do next, sitting, every muscle in my body locked in place, as if I was too scared to move. She leaned in, taking my hands and placing them on her thighs, then slid her palms along my arms, seeming to sample the feeling of my biceps, while I could only watch, the moment building to something, anything, when the fog had cleared she lying in bed next to me, her body fitting snugly, perfectly into mine, as though we were made for each other, as though we were meant to complement each other, that moment, that perfect moment, I've since realized, one we've both been chasing ever since, that one moment the source of all our missteps, all our successes, sustaining us like air and water.

      In her apartment, sitting on the edge of her bed we kissed. Never more than a game, it was as though we were watching ourselves from a distance, like disembodied spirits looking down on their bodies ambling into the night. We *made love*, she taking me on top of her, her legs hooked behind me as I began to awkwardly moving against her, until she reached with one hand down, took hold of me, and guided me inside her. I began to push, my motions stilted, the sensations suddenly too much. It was over quickly. Afterward, she lay atop me, and I wondered right away if she'd come, a little part of me worrying she hadn't, an insecurity growing. At Eastmount, we were like any other student and teacher, avoiding each other like we hadn't, yet inseparable, spending every moment of spare time together, under the flimsiest of pretences, making it obvious to the world that there was something going on between us even as we went to great lengths to hide our *love*. No one knew. Everyone knew. It was an impossible charade. Even today, Karen, I don't know how we ever got away with it. Maybe we just got lucky. It was the middle of October and then it was five months later. "Karen," I said, standing in front of her desk as she stood behind it, "I don't think I can ever love anyone like I love you." It was a stupid thing to say. Everyone believes they've found *true love* when they're a teenager. Then they look back on their adolescence, ten years later, and cringe at themselves for being so naïve, so simple-minded at having believed themselves. Karen, even after all that's happened between us since, I want you to know that I'm still in love with you, that you're the love of my life, and although I doubt we'll ever see each other again you'll always be my true love, my soul mate, my greatest hope and my gravest fear. It seems stupid, and it is, but at the same time it's never been any more than a game.

Some months earlier, towards the end of the eleventh grade, there came an afternoon when I sat on the edge of her desk while she pretended to busy herself with work, until she stopped, looked my way, and asked. "Keith," she said, "do you ever think about what's ahead of you?" "Sometimes," I said, sipping a bit on a can of Coke, "what do you mean, exactly?" "The future," she said. "When I was younger I wanted to be a fighter pilot in the Royal Canadian Air Force when I grew up," I said. "What's stopping you?" "Dunno," I said, shrugging, "my dad always said it was stupid. He said everybody wants to be something cool like that when they're a little kid." She was listening intently, having leaned towards me slightly, her gaze focused. "Maybe he was right," I said, then asked, "what did you want to be? Did you want to be a teacher?" She laughed. "Oh God no," she said, "that just sort of...happened." "How?" "After I graduated from university I had nothing to do so I went to Mexico and taught English for a few years. I saw an ad in the UBC school paper and called it. Actually I'd just broken up with my boyfriend and I wanted to get away for a while and teaching English in Mexico seemed like a good idea back then. Before I knew what I was doing I was on a bus passing through the states. I arrived in a city called Zacatecas." She let her voice quiet, as her eyes wandered wistfully. "Have you ever been to Mexico?" she asked. "No," I said. "Not even when you were living in Texas? Not even a day trip?" "Nope." "That's a shame," she said, "it's an amazing place. And I don't mean Cancun. Sometimes I wish I hadn't left. And believe me, I almost didn't. There was a time when I thought it might be a good idea—might have been possible to just stay in Mexico forever." "So why didn't you?" "Well, you can't just live out of your backpack forever," she said, then let out a sigh, "much as you'd like to." In the middle of the afternoon, it was as though she'd momentarily lost herself in memories of adventure, excitement, of living by the seat of her pants, of rising in the morning every day without knowing or caring what might happen by nightfall. It was mostly lost on me at the time, but even in my adolescence I'd come to appreciate at least one part of her life: the need to *live*. Even if you're doing something already done by many people, so long as it still seems new, so long as it *is* new to you, then you're still satisfying the urge to do *something* new.

Then, a change in tack. "Do you still want to become a fighter pilot?" she asked. "No," I said. "Why not?" "Karen," I began. "What?" she asked. "Doesn't everybody want to be something cool when they're little?" I asked, meaning it as a serious question, as though there was some instinctive part of me that *wanted* her to tell me my father had been wrong. Then, before she could answer, I asked, "what about you? What did *you* want to do with your life?" "Keith, let me explain something to you," she said, quickly looking past me at the door, then back, "there's something that happens to you when you become an adult. It's not about reaching a certain age. There are people out there who are in their forties, fifties who are still just overgrown children. It's not about that. I'm thirty-five and even I still don't know what it's about. But I can tell you what it's not, that's for sure. It's not..." An unsettling silence. "You're a good kid," she said, reaching over with one hand to muss up my hair a bit, "I think you'll be alright. You've still got time to get yourself together. Nobody knows what they want to do with their lives when they're seventeen anyways. And those who tell you they do are lying to themselves." It all seemed to come out of nowhere. So late in the afternoon, the deep, dark orange of the setting sun bled through the blinds, casting a glow on the floor that seemed to advance towards us, moving across our bodies. In the middle of a late-winter's thaw, the evening was almost on us, and with it the promise of the darkness of a night's sky.

"Karen," I said, "I know what I'm doing with my life." She laughed. "You sound so cute when you say that," she said, then letting out a sigh, "I remember when I used to think like that. Actually I don't. I just remember that I did. But real life is more complicated than that." In the distance, the wailing of an ambulance's siren faded in, piercing the thrum of the city, reaching a shrill, sharp pitch before fading back behind the growl and the grumble endlessly rising from the streets. It was phrased so that it had an edge to it, as if she was looking to cut through to me. I answered, but I don't remember what my answer *was*. As a young man, at the age of seventeen, almost eighteen, I couldn't understand the way she felt, couldn't put myself into her frame of mind and see the way she saw, but that didn't stop me from looking on her and wondering what might've been. Still I was scared. I didn't know what I was doing. It was intimidating to be in the same room as her. It was one of those little moments that'd taken place just as I was falling hopelessly *in love* with her, but while she still hadn't yet made up her mind about me, whether I was just another slacker or if there was something in there worth looking into.

"It's more than just work," she said, looking into the distance, then back, "it's trying to handle fifty different things all at once and forgetting how to just be yourself. It's like you have to look at black and convince yourself it's white. It's making yourself into something less than a person just so you can make some money and be a success so you can show up make it seem like you're a respectable person who's doing something worthwhile with your life." She'd looked out the window and into rainy, grey sky. On her desk was the little lovebird figurine I'd secretly given her; she'd taken to displaying it, a covert display that wasn't covert at all. As she'd spoken, her look drifted to the figurine, until it seemed like she was talking more to herself than me. We were so unlike each other. Hers was a world filled with people who had mortgages and RRSPs and credit ratings and meetings with this advisor and that counsellor. Mine was a world where the only thing that mattered was having some wheels and having some fun. That afternoon, as I walked across the parking lot on the way to my car, I caught a glimpse of Karen sitting in hers, faintly visible from behind the driver's side window. Reaching my car, I stopped and raised a hand in a half-wave, while she put an open palm flat against the inside of her car's window, and I imagine, now, that at that moment she must've felt we weren't so different after all. Less than a year later, after we'd first *made love*, it was like a formality marking the connection that'd been more than a year and a half in the making. Lying in bed with her, I felt like I was living entirely in the moment, the fear kept at bay. With one hand I pawed at her hair, letting strands flow around my fingers, while she seemed lost in thought, gazing past me with a sort-of distant look in her eyes. For a little while, it was like we were people other than who we were; I can't explain why, but I can say that I didn't know it then. At the time, all I could *know* was a vague feeling that not all was as it seemed, its true meaning only becoming clear in all the years that've passed. But I wonder, now, what she, then, thought of it, whether she, too, experienced that *feeling* of becoming someone other than who she was, or whether she, instead, had been someone other than herself all along.

Again we *made love*, under the pale orange glow of the streetlamps fading in through her bedroom window's blinds. In her apartment's little twin-sized bed she held onto my shoulders with her hands, lying back with her legs hooked against the backs of my thighs, clutching at my body, holding me so close that we seemed to move together in a halting, disjointed rhythm, burying myself inside her, withdrawing, kissing her, my mouth open, our tongues mingling, pushing myself inside her to the hilt, losing control, withdrawing, pushing in, she pulling my head down, whispering something indistinct into my ear, seeming to coax it out of me as I pushed inside her and held myself in. It was just as awkward and clumsy the second time, but that didn't matter. As the fog cleared, I found myself staring into her eyes, her hands gently holding me by the back of my neck while I let my grip on the bedsheets loosen. The smell of sweat and the sounds of panting breaths filled the air. Though I didn't know it at the time, couldn't have known it at the time, I've since realized this was the moment of happiness which we've each been chasing, risking so much for so little.

Later, we lay against one another, her head against my chest while I let a hand rest on her stomach. The blinds rattled against the windowsill, and at some point one of us (I don't remember who) had gotten up to slide the window open a half-centimetre, just enough to let in some air, then laid back in bed. A lit cigarette dangled from my lips, a thin tendril of smoke snaking towards the window's opening, fading into the night's sky. The smell of cigarette smoke mixed with a lingering after-sex and cheap cologne. For a little while, I wondered if she might've fallen asleep. When she stirred, pushing herself off me and rolling to sit up on the edge of the bed, I also sat up, took her hand, raised it to my lips, and lightly kissed its back. We talked, for a bit but said very little. Pulling her back down, I whispered "I love you" into her ear, and she let out a low sigh before she said "I know." We fell asleep that night, for at least that one night able to be together without having to worry about what might've happened next.

5. Present

"Don't be that guy." In the six months that Karen and I were apart after we'd been walked in on, life had lost its colour. Before work, it became a routine to pull myself out of bed an hour late, with just enough time to down a mug of jet-black coffee and make myself vaguely presentable. It took all the energy I had to push myself out the door and down the stairs to my truck parked in the street, sometimes the early-afternoons seeing me sit for a moment with both hands on the wheel while I said a little chant to myself, something like, "you can do this, Keith," or, "just get through the day." The truth was that I'd battled these demons before, and I was sure I'd come to battle them again, with or without Karen in my life. From my vantage point, parked on the side of the street, facing downhill, I had a view of a little cluster of forest, from behind the green a paper mill's squat, boxy structure rising just high enough to be seen, from its roof sprouting red-and-white smokestacks spewing a bright grey smoke that blended into the cloudy, mid-winter's sky. Sometimes, I'd look into the distance and imagine that when I turned the key it'd take me not to work but to be with Karen, the obsessive fantasy of being with her having taken hold of me so completely that it was like I'd reverted to the teenager I'd been, now living in an adult's body, surrounded by the trappings of adulthood, a job, a credit rating, a net payment of taxes every April having made me, for all intents and purposes, into a functional, productive grown-up. But then there was Karen. There was always Karen. Though she'd told me it was over, the last time we'd spoken, the adolescent living on in me couldn't, wouldn't accept it. Sometimes, even then, I thought Jordan's half-serious—not advice, but his warning was meant in good faith, not as a backhanded suggestion but a momentary concern; not concern, but not care either. I couldn't take it, then, because I couldn't see past it. Fully confident in myself even as I was as uncertain as ever about my place, I put myself out, each and every day.

"Don't be that guy." At work, it became a routine to shut down, to look ahead and simply push through the days. If anyone noticed, no one said a word. Thinking, I recalled a time Karen and I had each other in those six months, in the secrecy of my little apartment, *making love* with her back to the wall and her legs clasped tight around my sides while I held her bottom with both hands, struggling to move into her, as she came scratching her nails, hard, along my back. This was how I worked through the days, retreating into memory. In those months, we'd *made love* on nearly every surface in my apartment, her lying back on the kitchen table while I stood, me sitting back on the couch while moved atop me, in the kitchen she standing, bent over, hands clasping the countertop while I took her from behind, on every forward thrust burying myself in her to the hilt, then withdrawing nearly all the way, in smooth, strong strokes building to my own climax, my hands clasping her hips tight while she mewled and gasped with her own release. But, at work, this became a way to pass the time, to make the endless hours seem to pass in an instant, the act of having retreated into my own memories seeing me, soon, standing in line, waiting to punch out, another evening alone, at home, confronting me, Karen still not yet back in my life. Outside, in the parking lot behind the building, I sat with both hands clutching the wheel, the car motionless, noiseless. The sky had brightened, but still its darkness hung in the air, refusing to yield its territory to the steadily advancing dawn. A bland, tasteless musk drew itself into my body with each long, slow breath, spoiling my innards with a sinking sensation that wound its way through to a pit at the bottom of my gut, like a solid mass caving in on itself. Still I remained, gazing ahead into the dim, grey morning's sky, thoughts swirling about in a violent maelstrom, seeming at once to blend into one another, reducing themselves to an indistinct noise, a screeching fury, leaving me but a single, simple person, a man standing under a bright, white light. After sparing one last thought for Karen, I drove away, that night, I don't remember which night exactly, that night seeing me the last to leave. Though much had happened, much was still yet to happen, stuck as I was in that place between.

After work, it became a routine to drive along the highway for home imagining myself heading not home but to another secret rendezvous with Karen, as if I could've willed myself back into that happy state of mind. For most of the drive home, I thought, the route I took along the highway was exactly the same as the route that'd taken me to Karen's, and until I made that last exit off the highway before the Ironworkers' Memorial Bridge, the drive home replicating all the sights and sounds of the drive to her place, taking me under the same dull orange lights, over the same bumps and grooves in the highway's surface, all of it just enough to satisfy me, in some place in the back of my mind, that Karen and I weren't *really* apart. I know, I know. She was a married woman, and I was an adult well past the point when I could've been excused for indulging in quixotic fantasies about finding happiness with a woman who had so many reasons *not* to be with me. Even to this day, after all that's happened, there's a part of me that can't help but lapse into fantasy, now and then, of her. But after work I took that last exit and made my way home to a cold, dark, empty apartment, routine taking over, forcing me into bed each night and out of bed each morning, the person I'd become having learned at least to imitate the habits of a well-adjusted adult even as the person occupying the back of my mind kept clinging to the need to drop the pretenses and let it all out.

But when we'd stopped seeing each other in those six months, I'd taken the time and used it not to reflect on where I've been and what I've done, but instead to clinging to the possibility we'd be together again. Rising, I stripped from my ratty work clothes, soon standing in the washroom dressed only in socks, with only the rushing of water from the faucet to interrupt a silence. Then, after I'd turned the shower's faucet on, the room filled with steam, and when I'd stepped into the shower and leaned under the head, I lost control. My chest heaved and my innards contracted rhythmically, until nothing remained in my stomach and I lay bent over, face down, the tub's faded whiteness blurred behind tears. Bringing one palm up to my face, I closed my eyes and let the hotness of my breath beat against the hardness of my hand. Trying her number, I couldn't get through; I'd been blocked. I stood in the middle of my small, simple apartment's living room, a sense of dread grew, welling up from a pit at the bottom of my stomach, until the softness that'd only moments earlier covered every flat surface had faded, the walls, the white walls hardening until they seemed to tower all around, encasing me in a little box of air. I know it seems melodramatic to think and act like this, at twenty-eight years old no less, but, when no one was looking, when I was safely alone in my apartment I sometimes couldn't help myself but let it out, careful to make myself presentable, to shower, change clothes, and, if necessary, put on a pair of sunglasses to hide my reddened eyes before going back out again. Call it one of the benefits of living alone; there's at least one place where you don't have to hide anything. At work, we were all required to wear hi-vis vests; during the six months Karen and I were apart, I'd discarded my old, ratty vest and bought a new one, my old vest yellow, this new vest pink. I'd gone to a hardware store looking for parts to fix the pipes under my kitchen sink, and on seeing the pink vest for sale near the register I decided instantly I had to have it. Being that I worked with mostly young men, at least one of my co-workers asked if I was gay for wearing it, while many others, I'm sure, didn't ask. I liked that they thought I was, not because I liked the idea of them thinking or saying I'm gay but because I liked people trading rumours about me, I liked people ganging up on me. It's what I've been used to all my life, it's what I've known, even today it makes me comfortable, it puts me inside my comfort zone, it surrounds me with the familiar, the ordinary, it means I'm playing the role that I was born to play. But then, it made me seem like that kind of person, the kind of guy who shows up, one day, wearing a hot pink vest but doesn't want to answer any questions about it and who acts just as he acted the day before, who thought he could put his head down and push through the day. Even at work, Karen, I made myself into a target, even as I just wanted to be left alone.

And then, in the background, our union's work. In those months we were apart, I came very close to losing my sanity, our affair having turned me back into a teenager living in an adult's body. I became irritable, at work arguing with anyone over anything, whenever the opportunity presented itself taking a strip out of someone's side. At the time, I justified my actions (in my mind, at least) by judging the company in violation of the agreement, and the union in dereliction of its duties to the agreement, in my state of mind connecting the two to my actions. But then I'd take a step back, look at myself, and realize what I was doing. Months later, I'd found myself suddenly immersed, again, in Karen's life; it was like being instantaneously submerged in a vat of near-boiling water. I'd taken to bringing her little gifts, now and then, a stuffed owl I'd picked up from the dollar store, but with the tags carefully removed so she wouldn't know where it came from. But when we'd met, after I'd come home from work tired, sore, and just a little closer to the end of my fuse than when the day had started, she seemed to step into me, without saying a word taking the owl from my hand, kissing me on the lips, and for a moment it was as though we were, again, ten years earlier, caught up in the heat of our secret, forbidden love. But we weren't. Taking me by the hand, she sat me on her couch, then turned and made back across the living room, stopping halfway. It was then that I realized she'd moved into a two-bedroom place, down the hall, not far from the front door a second, smaller bedroom holding a child's bed, a bookshelf, the bedspread not yet unpacked, boxes piled in a corner. This all I took in when she was in the kitchen, poking around for a couple of wine glasses. Then she was standing behind me. I turned to face her. "It's Lucas's," she said. "I thought so," I said. "It's not done yet," she said. "He's with—" "Richard this week." "I'm sorry." "For what?" "I haven't got a clue." "I'm sure you don't." Little of it seemed to matter, right then, but despite the closeness we'd had, I couldn't quite figure out how to tell her that it was all familiar to me.

       Months earlier, after we'd re-united for the second and final time. By then, summer had arrived, the days long, the skies a vast expanse. As we walked along the waterfront of the city of North Vancouver, her dog, Tango, walked between us, trying his best to keep up while she told me about the changes that'd taken place in her life since we were caught by her husband and her son. But Tango was old, nearly sixteen, and he just couldn't match the healthy pace they'd used to walk, and soon we'd stopped at a bench, she on one knee to give him a scratch under the chin. "...he's left," she said. "We're getting a divorce. We tried to work it out, but we couldn't. The trust just..." A pause. "...it's just not there anymore." "I don't know what to say," I said. "No," she said, without missing a beat, "I'd imagine you don't." Another pause. "So why are we here?" I asked. Turning, she looked into my eyes and smiled weakly before saying, "I've missed you." More was said, but little of it meant anything except in its ability to draw us closer together and push us ahead as one. It was as though we were working together towards some mutual outcome, each line, each word exchanged marking a movement at our desired end. She slept over that night, then left in the morning, without saying whether we'd continue with our affair, whether we'd become something more. In bed, it'd become almost possible to forget who we were. Ten years earlier, the heat and the thrill of our secret affair had been enough, I think, to sustain her, while I, well, I'd been just a teenager madly *in love* with a beautiful woman of a teacher. But then, ten years later, we were just two people who the outside observer might've looked on and seen as having made a series of huge mistakes.

The trust, she'd said, *it's just not there anymore.* The way she'd said it convinced me she'd tried, in the way that she had, to redeem herself, for the sake of her young son trying to keep a loveless marriage together. Though I hadn't yet met her husband (not counting that night we were walked in on), I'd come to believe he'd somehow induced her through his own negligence to seek the passion and the romance provided by our affair. It was as though she'd been liberated, she'd later say, from a stale, lifeless marriage, by virtue of our affair having been given a new lease on life. Even her husband, Richard, had noticed the spring in her step, the light behind her eyes, the way she'd seemed to take to the days just a bit more readily. (She hadn't put it exactly this way when she'd been talking to me, but that's the gist of it). Maybe it all made him suspicious. No, he never suspected a thing. Maybe he was on his way home, early, with their son hoping to surprise her with a nice dinner he'd have cooked himself, spurred on by her having become so much more outgoing and pleasant and happier in the six months since she'd begun secretly having an affair. To find her with me must've felt like a knife in the gut. He'd done nothing wrong. Neither had she, I think. It's all kind of blurred together. It's become hard to separate what she'd told me had happened to her from what I'd known to happen to me, when I was younger, when my parents were going through exactly what Karen's son's parents were going through right then.

But she was confident in herself, sure as ever that she knew what was right even if she didn't always do it. At least, she'd been that way until then, the moment the door to her bathroom swung open and revealed her affair with me to her husband and her son seeming to have changed her forever. We kept meeting surreptitiously whenever a spare bit of time made itself available as though our affair was still something to be kept under wraps. Our *lovemaking* took place sparingly, perhaps once a month or more, her time consumed by the slow, methodical disintegration of her marriage, mine by the futility of the struggle to get ahead with so many forces arrayed against me. She asked, once, if I'd been with anyone else since we'd been caught by her husband in the shower. "No way," I said. It was later, as we stood on the edge of the Lonsdale Quay watching the summer's sun set behind the deep, dark urban forest set across the inlet in Stanley Park, that Karen still seemed indecisive, hemming and hawing over whether she was making the right choice. As my hand found hers, I made for a kiss, my lips finding the side of her cheek, her tense feelings palpable. "What on earth are we doing?" she asked. "We're..." I said, thinking, "...I don't know what you mean." She broke the embrace, then pushed me away slightly. "I shouldn't be here," she said, "this isn't how it's supposed to be." "How what's supposed to be?" "My life. Getting a divorce, cheating on my husband, messing up my son probably for life. It's not right. It's just not *right*." It was then, despite (or maybe because of) all that'd happened between us, that I realized we weren't so different after all. "Look what I've done," she said, "now my son is going to grow up with parents who hate each other. We couldn't stand each other in the first place but at least we had something. Now it's all gone and it's all my fault." I didn't know what to say, not right away, so I let her speak her piece, listening, only listening. If you ever stop and think of the way your life was before we met in that little classroom in that little high school in the city of Vancouver so many years ago, it might look like you've made little headway, but I don't think that's true. Karen, no matter what's happened, I still think you're a strong person. I think you'll always be a strong person.

But when Karen and I had walked along the quay and had looked across the inlet at the city's skyline, it was as though she'd become someone so unlike the woman I'd fallen *in love* with a decade earlier, but still a woman I was *in love* with anyways. She looked at me and said, "I'm sorry, Keith. But I'm just not sure about myself." After a long silence, I spoke. "Karen," I said, "I want to be with *you*. I've always wanted to be with *you*. I never want to be with anyone but *you*. I've thought about you every day since the day I met you when I was in the tenth grade. And I'll never stop thinking about you for the rest of my life. I love you more than I've ever loved anyone and that's never gonna change." Sighing, she let the unease fade from her face, a softened look replacing exasperation, until she leaned back in and gave me a kiss. "I know," she said, "I know." We agreed to keep seeing each other for so long as it seemed right, leaving at least some small hope that we might've been for the rest of our lives. That small hope was all I needed. Then, I put my arms around her and pulled her in, she reaching behind to rest her hands on the small of my back. For a minute or two we just stood in place, sharing each other's warmth, until she took a half-step back from me and began to turn away, leading me back to that little green CR-V she still drove after all those years. After she'd fastened her seatbelt I shut her CR-V's door, then looked at a plane flying overhead, tracing a white slash across the sky. It was a small moment in the grand scheme of things, but, whenever I stop and consider what came from it, sometimes I look back and think of it as the calm before the storm.

II

6. Past

"I know what you mean," Karen had said, once, sometime in the month of October during my senior year, after I'd shown up one day at her morning's Spanish class without having done an assignment due that day. I'd had a fight with Randall the night before, and I'd hardly slept. When she'd asked why the assignment wasn't done, I'd just said, "I've got some things going on," in turn prompting her to say those five cryptic words. For weeks, as we kept playing our little game towards its end, the self-conscious part of me went through those words, over and over, parsing them out, looking for some kind of hidden meaning. Then, in the new year, after we'd *made love* for the first time, those five words suddenly came to mind as I woke up in bed with her, she still asleep but beginning to stir. That morning, we acted like any other couple, stepping around each other in the bathroom, awkwardly reaching past each other in her little kitchen, sitting at her dining room's table, from opposite sides looking at one another, while I wondered just what was supposed to happen next. Eventually, I left, spending the day at home, alone, wondering whether to call her or let her be, the next day, a Sunday, on finding myself still alone in an empty home, giving in to the urge and calling her, letting it ring once, twice, six times, half-hoping she'd let it go to voice mail. A click. Silence. "Karen," I said. "Keith," she said. "What happens now?" I asked. She laughed, half-nervously, and said, "come over," and in an instant I was there, climbing the stairs to her little third-floor unit, raising my fist to knock on the door, at exactly the right moment the door swinging open, Karen standing to the side while I stepped past her, on hearing the door shut and lock turning back to face her, taking her hands in mine while we kissed. It felt like we'd been apart for years. "I've missed you" I said. "It's only been a day," she said, murmuring. "That's too much," I said. "Keith…" She let her voice trail off as she leaned back in until we were resting out foreheads against one another's, neither of us having a clue what we were doing but, at the time, neither of us caring. We *made love*, but it was over quickly. Afterwards, we began to talk, and as we talked it became clear just what she'd meant when she'd said to me, months earlier, that she understood what *I'd* meant when I'd told her, without telling her, that I'd had a home life that felt like it was getting worse every day.

"I know what you mean," Karen had said. Lisa and Randall, in the weeks before Karen and I had first *made love*, were at each other's throats over anything at all, like we'd become used to, their arguments having become background noise on those nights I'd spend alone in my bedroom. Sometimes, sometimes I'd come home and find Lisa sitting alone in the living room, sipping on her bottle of cider, Randall sitting alone at his desk, neither of them speaking to each other, either of them only getting up to get another drink. Sometimes Lisa wasn't home, usually Lisa wasn't home, but Randall always was. It was on just such an occasion that I came home to find Randall playing the living room's stereo so loud the music's lyrics could be heard clearly even in my bedroom, with the pillows over my head and the door shut. Lisa wasn't home. Of course Lisa wasn't home. It was a challenge. Actually, I'd walked in the door, not then but a few days earlier, and walked right past Randall without saying a word to him. He muttered, "fuckhead," under his breath, but this time I didn't just keep on walking, this time I looked back and said, "go have another drink," and *then* walked up the stairs and into my room, half-expecting him to shove me from behind or throw something at me or even just scream at me. But he didn't. In the months to come, I'd learn why, but until then, I'd think I'd finally made it by standing up to him, in some small way, having forgotten about all the times we'd gone at it in the meanwhile. I don't know. It all happened so fast. But it was all about to get so much worse.

"I know what you mean," she'd said. Back in the eleventh grade, there happened something that made it seem Karen—then still known to me only as Miss Thoreson—and I were enemies. This was probably why it became possible for us to carry out our forbidden love without the rumours becoming anything more; no one could've believed we would've fallen in love after what'd happened. It was an early morning, on the second or third day of November. I'd gone to Eastmount that morning under a black cloud, looking for a fight, finding one with my first-period Spanish teacher, then known only to me as Miss K. Thoreson. It doesn't really matter what she'd said to provoke my outburst; it's enough for me to say she was only doing her job. As she pulled me aside and led me to the side of her portable classroom, I took the pen in my hand and threw it, hard, at the far side of the room before turning to face her and shouting, as loud as I could, "what the fuck is your problem?" She stepped back, blinked, and pointed at the door, saying, "get out." "Fuck you!" I said, and stormed out. Running home, I sealed myself in my room, threw my bag on the floor, and lay in bed, shaking all over. In my room I was alone. It might seem odd that after what I'd done she and I would come to fall hopelessly in love with each other, but then very little of either our lives had ever been the way things were supposed to be. Karen, my Karen, she was the love of my life and the object of my desires so deep, so powerful that even with her I couldn't help but feel an intense craving for her, like I'd never felt for anyone before and I'm sure as I've been of anything that I'll never feel for anyone else again. As a young child, though, it was like I'd been pegged as the problem no-one wanted, shuttled from one grade to the next by teachers tired of having to deal with me; fitting, maybe, that I should've fallen in love with a teacher. It was all linked by that common thread needling through the lives of so many people, just happening to touch Karen and I at the time it did. And, that afternoon, the day after we'd *made love* for the first time, but before we'd *made love* for the second time, I stopped, turned, and said, "I'm sorry." "For what?" "You know." "No I—" "For yelling at you. Last year, I mean." "Keith, I forgave you for that when I read in your planner that you were in lo—that you liked me." "You shouldn't have." "Why not?" "I dunno." She stood on her toes and leaned up, kissing me on the cheek.

Reaching into the little backpack I'd brought, I drew out a little velvet box and handed it to her, she opening it and half-gasping when she saw the little diamond necklace I'd bought for her at a pawn shop. (It wasn't real, but that wasn't the point). I don't know why I didn't give it to her before we'd *made love* that afternoon, except to say that I might've thought it better to, I don't know, break the ice first. "D'you like it? I asked. "It's beautiful," she said, then turned and held her hair up while, with my hands trembling slightly, I put it on and fastened it at the back. Whatever she might've thought, then, she didn't let it show the next day at Eastmount, the Monday seeing her revert to the strict, prim-and-proper Miss Thoreson everyone knew so well as the school's Spanish teacher. Whenever we crossed paths in the halls, I'd glance at her, like I did, but she'd seem to look right through me, When it rained, the halls at Eastmount filled with the squeaking of wet sneakers against the hard linoleum floors, while around the doors there appeared muddy tracks reaching out from the mats placed inside, haphazard lines stretching down the halls, disappearing a metre or two in. It was on just such a day that I arrived early, like every other day, but chose not to head for the gym, instead squeaking my shoes against the floor deliberately as I made my way into the school, looking for Karen, checking this way and that, quickly sweeping my eyes up and down the hall, finding no trace of her. It was as though I'd expected her to be just around every corner, every turn, at the foot of every stairwell and at the top of every step. In the halls of Eastmount, I stood, one day, at the top of the main stairwell, leaning slightly against a wall, when up the stairs climbed Karen, her hand sliding along the rail as she approached, her hair tied back into a long ponytail and her eyes hidden behind a look I couldn't understand. It might've been like any other passing, but as she reached the top of the stairs she turned and tossed a glance back at me that seemed to ask me at her, like the glances she'd sent me so many times before. Staring at her as she walked away, my eyes drew themselves along her figure, curving around the shape of her hips, down the roundness of her backside, drinking in the sight of her one last time before she disappeared around a corner, almost pulling me after her like a fish hooked on a line. It happened later, not that day but soon after, and when Karen and I touched each other again, weeks later, it felt as though we were touching each other for the first time. The apprehension, the fear seemed to build, releasing itself as I put my hands on her naked body, cupping her small breasts in my palms, until she reached up, took my hands in hers, and gently pulled them down to rest on her hips, our bodies swaying lazily in time with an imagined waltz. It was all so deeply confusing, but, at the time, I couldn't do anything but let it be.

But after that first weekend, something changed in the way she'd acted, nothing noticeable at first, just the way she'd carried herself, the little spring in her step having become a bit heavier. She redoubled her efforts to be focused and no-nonsense. Some of my classmates in her Spanish twelve class noticed the way she seemed to become, again, stern and businesslike, as if she'd slowly let her classroom's decorum slide only to, without warning, crack down on the looser tone, every idle conversation in her class squelched, every minute accounted for, every free-study session turning back into a straight lecture on verb tenses or conjugations. But only I knew why. And I wasn't telling anyone. By then, it'd been weeks since our first weekend together, and already I'd begun to wonder if she'd put it behind her; if I'd have had the courage to call her, again, I might've been able to move on a little faster. In the hall, one day, I was leaning against a locker, not mine, and chatting with a short, Asian girl named Isabella Lam, when Karen walked past, clutching a file folder stuffed full of files against her chest, in the split-second we shared a glance a silent understanding passing between us, only later the realization occurring that it might've looked like I was flirting with that little Asian girl. The next time I saw Karen in the halls, not far from that spot, she was standing to the side, seeming to idly chat with another teacher, one of the buff gym coaches, she glancing over at me, that same silent understanding passing between us again. Suddenly, it was as if that weekend we'd spent together hadn't been spent together at all, just like the one after it, and the one after that. No, that wasn't what happened. We didn't exchange any text messages, and I couldn't work up the courage to call her again. (I'd later learn that she, too, couldn't work up the courage to call me). It was stupid and crazy, but then stupid and crazy was exactly what we had.

It'd later emerge that she'd been, off and on, seeing someone, a thirty-something guy with whom she'd been set up by a mutual friend; she'd slept with him for the first time after she'd slept with me for the first time, but learning this didn't make me jealous, just curious. Sometimes, I wondered what she must've been going through, what might've been thinking. She'd slept with him, she'd begun seeing him during those weeks we were apart to see if she could ease her feelings off me and onto someone else. It didn't work. It wasn't to be the first time she'd try it; his name was Richard (the very same Richard who'd walk in on us ten years later), and she'd wind up marrying him just over a year after she and I would see each other for the last time in almost ten years. But when I walked past her classroom at exactly the right time and exactly the right angle to catch a glimpse of her inside, I'd always find her looking out, as if for me, so that all I had to do was pass by and our eyes would lock, a moment passing between us that made it feel like there was no one else left in the world but us. At seventeen, almost eighteen, I was crazy, the sudden and, then, unexplained separation from the woman who would become the love of my life feeling like a clawing at the inside of my chest, as though there was a little part of me trying to escape. It was just the way I felt, and I couldn't, at seventeen, control the way I felt, just as I can't, now, so many years later. But it wasn't to last for much longer. It gave an impetus to the need to be with her again, a need that would see me through the months to come, every minute of every day seeing me struggle to make it look like we weren't together at all.

Then, one Friday afternoon, as I stood next to my car, holding the door open, I turned back and, acting on a gut feeling, cast a glance across the lot, finding Karen sitting in her CR-V with the window rolled half-down. Looking right back, she nodded, and then I nodded, and soon we were off, she leaving first, me following. I lost her halfway there, but I remembered the way, finding her waiting at the back, standing on the edge of the alley, looking for me. In a flash we were together again, in her little apartment, the weeks apart having disappeared like a puff of smoke blown away by a strong, sudden wind. Without saying a word, we had each other again, having reunited for the first but far from the last time, acting out a routine that'd become, in the short time we'd been together, ours and ours alone.

6. Present

When I was around a year old, my parents divorced under circumstances that remain unknown to me. My earliest memories are of my sister and I shuttling back and forth between our mother's and father's places, spending a week at one, then a week at the other, each located on the same street hardly a block and a half away. We moved in with our mother, full-time, when our father took a job in Edmonton and relinquished sole custody to her. (He would later tell us he'd always intended to be back in Vancouver within a year or so but wound up, due to circumstances beyond his control, living in Edmonton for many years, though I've never decided whether this was a lie). What followed was more than a decade of hatred and recrimination, with my sister and I caught in the crossfire like a pair of innocents in a war zone. We visited him, with holidays, summers, the odd long weekend seeing us fly, alone (the airlines labelled us as 'unaccompanied minors'), back and forth between Vancouver and Edmonton, while each of them plied us with gifts, with praise, while whispering, when no one was watching, that the other was to blame. I recall about this period only a profound sense of isolation, as even a small child can understand, on some level, how he is different from everyone else, being as I was made to serve as an example to classmates, friends, teachers, everyone. It was my fault, I felt, that I was *different*. It was my fault that I was *made* to feel *different*.

There came a time when our father moved, along with his second wife and her daughter, to the city of Carrollton, Texas, a suburb north of Dallas. We didn't see him for three years. Lisa said he refused to pay child support which meant the loss of his access to us. He said she had actively tried to cut him out of our lives and turn us against him. Both were probably true *and* false. At one point, our mother forbid us from answering the phone if he called at a time when she wasn't there. This all culminated in a night when he showed up, unannounced, at our front door, forced his way inside, and refused to leave, the police arriving shortly thereafter to drag him away in cuffs. He spent the night in a jail cell, or so he told me when he called the next day. Personally, I think he was drunk but couldn't admit it, and that 'jail cell' was just his euphemism for the drunk tank. Later, perhaps a year or so, the dispute was settled and we were allowed to see our father again, but not before my sister died suddenly in an experiment with inhalants gone awry. Her name was Sheila, and she was fifteen years old. Though it's been close to twenty years since she died, I'll never forget coming home after school to the sight of her lying, motionless, on the couch, her skin cold to the touch, her flesh having already begun to turn a deathly pale colour. Sometimes I still have nightmares where I walk in on her lying there, and just before I wake up her lifeless eyes open, their whites turned black.

As Karen and I had kept seeing each other, I never asked directly about her divorce, and she never told, instead our affair resuming as though it'd never stopped. She'd moved out of their place and rented an apartment on the same street a few blocks away; she wanted to live near work. I'd helped her move, hauling furniture and heavy boxes in my truck, shuttling back and forth between her old place and her new, but allowed only when her husband and son weren't home. Her new apartment was a one-bedroom unit, small, hardly larger than mine, and it soon became cluttered with so many boxes piled high, couches and beds and tables designed for much larger quarters shoehorned into the narrowest of spaces, looking very much like a hoarder's mess. One of the first things she'd unpacked was the little ceramic lovebirds I'd given her, setting it on the dresser in her bedroom. She'd kept it all those years, in her bedroom, only packing it up when she and Richard had moved in with each other, finally able to display it again without having to lie or give any awkward answers to uncomfortable questions. I was there when she'd put it out. In the midst of it all, she stood, her hair tied up into a bun, wearing an oversized sweatshirt and a pair of skin-tight jeans, then turned away and bent down to pick up a box, seeming to present to me her wide, shapely figure, daring, tempting me. Approaching her from behind, I gently rested my hands on her shoulders and lifted her back until we stood against one another. She pressed back into me and seemed to crane her neck as I planted little kisses on her bare skin, then licked the side of her face, working my way up, taking the lobe of her ear in my mouth and biting, softly, then harder, while she gasped slightly, soon us both shoving boxes off her couch, shedding our clothes, then setting ourselves against one another, laying over each other as I let my full weight fall onto her with every motion, our *lovemaking* suddenly raw, animalistic, frenetic, until I came, holding myself still as I strained to come inside her, pressing into her as if to become one with her. When the moment cleared, I became aware of my harsh, ragged breaths, the thin film of sweat covering my forehead and hers too. It was so sudden, over in an instant, even as we had all the time in the world to *make love* something compelling us to act as though we needed to *make love* as quickly as possible. We'd become like any other couple, seeing each other whenever the time spared itself, no longer needing the secrecy that had come with indulging in an affair. In that little apartment she'd come to call her own, all it took was one look in her eyes to tell that she'd lost exactly that, as I held her, naked, but from the way she seemed to recoil from me slightly once the after-sex glow had receded made me feel ashamed of myself, in a strange, roundabout sort of way, as though I'd hurt her. "Karen," I said, letting her slip from my grasp, "I still love you." For a moment, she said nothing, then managing to look me in the eye and say, "I know you do." By then she'd slid into a t-shirt and looked like she was tired. "It's fine," she said, "let's be...that was nice. You make me feel good about myself." But the reluctant tone in her voice seemed to betray her true feelings. Still, I let it be, and that night we fell asleep in each other's arms, my last thought a little mental note of the tension in her muscles, a mental note filed, then forgotten until it was too late.

Months after Karen had reappeared in my life the second time, it became painfully obvious that she wasn't altogether there. Karen's child, her son, around eight years old. His name was Lucas, and I knew him, then, only as a series of images glanced at every now and then. Her son's welfare hadn't been my concern, and I'd never given it much thought until first meeting him, whereupon memories came flooding back. I had become *the other*, he who would wreck a family by way of wedging myself between its two halves. A few days after Karen and I had moved the last of her things into her new apartment, there came a moment when she saw fit to introduce us, having me over for dinner on a night when he was there. She introduced me as "Keith," and from the sideways look he gave me it was immediately obvious that he wanted me gone. What followed was such an awkward night, with Karen and I exchanging nervous glances throughout, talking around each other, at each other, but never *with* each other. Later, as I began on the dishes, she appeared at my side, having sent Lucas into the living room so as to give us some time to talk. "He's my precious little boy," she said, her voice filled with a warmth, a love so unlike the kind I'd seen from her. "He'll always be my precious little boy," she said. "I understand," I said. "No, you don't," she said, "you can't understand until you've had kids of your own." Silence, broken only by the dull roar of a sitcom's laugh track emanating in from the living room. "I wish it hadn't come to this. I never should've cheated on Richard. It wasn't right. Now Lucas's never going to have a good and proper home and he's going to have only me to blame for it. I don't think I can ever forgive myself for that. My life may not have been perfect but at least I had a family." My hand found hers, and gave it a gentle squeeze, bringing the faintest of smiles to her face, allowing a hint to creep into the moment of things to come. But if we were such different people, it wasn't always immediately obvious, the age difference but the only thing that clued us apart; but still I wanted to make her feel good, so a few days later I made sure to take her for a night out, dinner, a show, then back to her little apartment where I laid her gently in bed and went to kiss her goodnight. Thinking, I told her, "tell me what's bothering you," meaning to help. But she looked over at me as we lay side by side in her bed and said, "it's nothing." So different was this Karen from the woman I'd fallen so hopelessly, so helplessly in love with as a teenager, yet underneath the woman she'd become was hints of the woman she'd been, sensuous, desirous, her deep, brown eyes hardly concealing the hope for a new tomorrow. Suddenly, then, I couldn't quite remember what'd made me fall *in love* with her to begin with, and as we lay next to each other in her bed, through the darkness of her bedroom I thought I could see her body beneath the sheets moving slightly, her chest rising and falling softly with each breath she took in and pushed out, took in, pushed out, in, out, until she seemed to blend into the darkness of a night's sleep. Though she'd been the one to decide it was time, that night, to introduce me to her son, I couldn't escape the notion that she already thought she'd made a mistake in doing so. It was a notion that would linger in the back of my mind over the coming months, finally coming to a head after it was too late.

Though Lisa and Randall had separated, they sort-of kept in touch. He wasn't to contest the divorce, or so she'd told me, but still the process required both their participation in filing and counter-filing, in applications and responses to applications, the whole thing seeming like a mess of paperwork to have recognized by some distant bureaucrat what'd already become a fact of life for them both. It'd been only days earlier that Lisa and Randall had been setting themselves apart; she'd begun seeing a counsellor by way of the local mental health authority, while he'd kept on drinking himself into an early grave. How he provided for himself was a mystery to me. His little delivery business had fallen apart completely, and she told me he spent most of his days dodging calls from debt collectors. As I drove along the highway to work one rainy afternoon, I thought to call Lisa, but the rain-slick road demanded my full attention, soon the warehouse passing around after I'd swapped my truck out for a dock-stocker, the day's work there to offer itself as a distraction from all that bothered me. The union was there, but Gerald Wang had stopped showing up for meetings even after having come back from his vacation, seeming to have taken a break, leaving the company to continue refining its proposal, but these concerns faded into the background as Karen's slowly falling-apart life demanded every last thought that strayed through my mind. Taking to the floor, I found a certain release in pulling pallets of product from inside trailers, by the dozens of them, until I'd filled an entire section of the dock with so much. It'd become something like an abstraction given form, to start with a nearly-empty stretch of floor and, over the hours, build stack upon stack of product until there was a huge wall of pallets I'd built. By the time I'd clocked out for the day, though, I'd recalled Lisa's troubles, and checked my phone; she'd called. But that night, I chose not to call her back for reasons I still can't explain, instead retreating into the safety, the security of my little apartment for the night, the next morning seeing me rise to face the consequences of my actions. It's an understanding thing, but in the cold, wet autumn's morning, with a light rain pattering against the thin, smooth glass of my apartment's windows, I sought to face myself with the most confident face I could manage, a stiff upper lip and a scowl muscled together, warning my co-workers that day to let me be.

With Karen, there was sustenance, a kind of satisfaction I fully believed couldn't have found in anyone else. Still it became hard to watch her in the midst of her marriage's breakup, and for a time I wondered what might've gone on in her life for those months we were separated from one another. She rarely talked about it openly, and I rarely asked; we had an unspoken agreement that anything to do with her young son was strictly off-limits but for the odd detail that she volunteered. Visiting the Lonsdale Quay in North Vancouver became a ritual we shared in, walking as far as the quay would allow at exactly the right moment to watch the sunset fill the skies with their lavender hues and their orange tint, slashed by the fading white trails left behind jets passing far overhead. But as we walked along the quay one night, the skies were overcast, leaving me to walk alongside her into the wind and look into that familiar spot on the horizon just beyond the towers of the city of Vancouver, imagining there was the sun's golden disc in its usual spot. At the quay's edge, we stopped, and leaned over slightly, the beginnings of rain falling. "Keith," she said, "do you remember what it was like when we were together at Eastmount?" "How could I forget?" I asked. "It was fun back then, wasn't it?" she asked. "It's still fun now," I said, and leaned in for a kiss, stopping halfway as she looked aside and shook her head. "I still love you," I said, my hand finding hers, giving a quick, firm squeeze. "I know you do," she said, "and I'm grateful. I just don't know about myself anymore. Maybe in a little while I'll feel better, but for now..." She let her voice trail off and looked out over the water. "Look," she said, "I'm going out of town for a couple of weeks with Lucas. We're visiting Richard's parents in Winnipeg." "Are you going with him?" I asked. "Yes," she said, "I know it seems odd for us all to be going together but, we're still trying to be friends, for Lucas's sake." A pause. "Karen, I love you," I said, "and I want to do everything I can to make you happy." "Thanks," she said, the beginnings of a smile crossing her face. That night in her apartment, we *made love*, this time she atop me, her hips moving in long, slow strokes, her breasts pressed against my chest, her hands on either side of my head as we kissed, our tongues mingling, the sensation of her thighs against mine seeming to complement feeling of her taste flooding my mouth. Her smooth motions took me in to the hilt, then back out, then back again, building me rapidly towards my climax as she had hers. After I'd come inside her, still she kissed me, on the lips, the cheek, the side of my neck, the moment lingering underneath a warmth that seemed so familiar even in its novelty. Later, after I was sure she'd fallen asleep, I whispered, "I love you." She stirred, saying, "I know," the words escaping her lips in a whisper barely heard against the night. It was such an amazing thing, to be so fully *in love* with a forty-six year old woman who lay, naked, next to me, so close I had only to reach out and touch her, but to be so far away.

But for the exchange of a few text messages here and there, Karen and I kept ourselves separate, the days filling themselves, each morning seeing me trundling off to work, each evening seeing me retreat home to that little box of air where time seemed to stop. There, the apartment's bare, white walls stood, stout, their whiteness faded, their paint chipped along the creases, the edges, with but the odd movie poster or two to add a dash of colour, a large American flag hanging, draped, its red, white, and blue dulled, faded. Each morning, each night, time flowed like a sludge, pooling at my feet, oozing from one patch of exposed floor to the next. Scarcely a few minutes had passed into the first day of the week when I found myself again speeding home at the week's end, another forty hours fading into a cloud of dust rising off the road, obscuring the rear-view mirror behind a haze. That night, I stayed over at Karen's new place, with her bent over before me, my hands on her hips as we *made love*, acting out a vague compulsion that came from some instinct hidden deep inside us, the lewd slap of skin against skin filling the air as we had our way with one another, our *lovemaking* long, slow, deliberate, the softness of her skin and the slickness of her sex fitting over my length, each forward motion into her, smooth, rhythmic, rehearsed, seeming to bring me that much closer to being together with her. "Karen," I said, later, after we'd come down from our orgasmic high, "I wish I could marry you." "You can," she said, lying against me, "soon." "When?" "Soon." She kissed the side of my cheek, then turned the light off, leaving us both to drift into sleep, the moment behind us dominated by the light pattering of rain against her bedroom's window. Then, it was months later, and suddenly I couldn't tell whether Karen, Miss Thoreson was in love with me or not. It was an unsettling feeling, but as the weeks turned into months, it became like a second set of eyes looking on us from a distance, watching, waiting for either of us to show weakness, to bare ourselves for everyone around us to see. Looking back, I can see, now, that she was in the midst of a long, slow breakdown, each day bringing her closer to the edge. But at the time, I was fully confident in the *love* we shared, in the sort of almost-belief that we were *meant to be*. Through the years after high school, I sometimes dreamt of her, only to wake and spend the days inspired to look forward to meeting her again. Then, suddenly, we were in the midst of her family's disintegration, with my almost-belief at the very centre.

But I hardly ever saw Lucas again after that one dinner, she keeping me well away even as I'd become, or so I thought, her partner, or boyfriend, if you'd prefer. Sometimes, now, I wonder what her son had told her husband about me, about having met me, and what her husband might've had to say about me; but then, whenever I begin to wonder, I can't help but feel a little guilty about thinking of what they thought of me, as if I should've been the centre of their slowly-unravelling lives. At some point in the time since we've last seen each other, Karen, I've come to realize something I should've known all along: it wasn't about me. It was never really about me. The real drama, I never saw, never heard, and it's only from taking my own experiences and the bits and pieces of yours that I've been able to thatch together an understanding of it all. But then there happened an event that seemed to come out of nowhere at first, but, on reflection I now understand to have been the only possible outcome, the natural extension of what'd happened in our lives so far. One night, a few months after Karen had moved into her new place, she and I were lying in her bed together after having *made love* for the first time in a couple of weeks when she said, "I'm pregnant." That night, neither of us slept, instead staring into the space above until the ceiling grew slowly brighter with the dawning of a new day.

7. Past

"Don't think this is over," Karen had said, that first weekend together, and it was on that first weekend together, that Saturday's morning, that we'd had a talk, brought on not by our having *made love* but by the simple act of looking out the window and spotting, in the distance, a plane slicing across the suddenly clear, blue sky. "Have you travelled much?" Karen asked, before quickly adding, "other than Texas, I mean." "Some," I said, "I lived in California, too." "When?" "I was too young to remember." "I see." "It was back when my parents were still together. My dad took a job in San Jose and we all moved down. My dad's moved around a lot. But I don't know why we moved back. No one's ever said. We never talked much about it. Dunno why." An awkward silence settled. Some time passed, not a long time, but just a half-second too long. "Keith," she said, finally, "I'd be lying if I told you I know what's supposed to come next. But I know that what we just did—it's wasn't supposed to happen." Nodding slightly, I put one arm around her shoulder and pulled her in, for a moment she just leaned against me, the differences between us suddenly seeming so small. Her apartment was too small for us to be apart from one another, even the thin walls between rooms allowing any noise to be heard from the unit's other end, but then, at the time, I wanted only to be *near her*, to touch her body, to approach her from behind and rest my hands on her hips while planting little kisses on the back of her neck, to listen to the sound of her voice and to feel her pulse racing at our touch. It was all a bad joke. I was scared and confused, only I didn't know it, just as she was scared and confused without knowing it. It was new ground for both of us. I hadn't the slightest idea what I was doing, but she was there to hold onto me. *It wasn't supposed to happen.*

After we'd *made love* for the first time, things changed between us, beginning the very next morning. (I think it wasn't the next morning, but I can't remember exactly). For her part, Karen had on a pair of loose-fitting jeans and a white sweatshirt with loose threads and frayed edges in places. Her hair was tied back haphazardly into a bun, with strands falling astray, framing her face. And I wore my faded, threadbare pants and a t-shirt stretched tight over my chest. Despite all that'd happened, I couldn't quite understand the way she might've felt, couldn't see things from her point of view. As she led me through her shoebox of an apartment, I let my thoughts wander, just far enough to wonder if we were meant to be. On a cabinet there were a row of framed photographs, the one furthest to the right her wearing a mortarboard and gown, posing with a wrinkles, grey-haired, bespectacled woman, both of them smiling. "My grandmother," she said, "both my parents died when I was very young, too young to remember. Car accident. My grandmother saved a newspaper clipping of it. Now I have it. I keep it in a shoebox in my closet along with other...mementos." "Why do you keep it?" I asked. "It's all I have of them," she said, "there's nothing else." Silence. "It's so strange, isn't it? I never knew them. Nobody ever talked about them to me, except for telling me things that don't really matter. What kind of car they drove. Where they went to school. You know, I was the first person in my family to go to university. A cousin went to BCIT but that's not a university. The rest of them wound up flipping burgers and stuff like that into their...well, into their thirties and forties. And here I am with a younger man in my bed. It's insane, isn't it?" At a loss for words, I sat silently at the dining room table while she turned and poured herself a glass of wine, then drank it all in one motion, setting the glass back on the counter. "Keith," she said, turning to face me. "I love you," I said. "I know," she said, "but this is illegal. If I'm caught I'll get in so much trouble. I've always been the good little girl, the one who worked hard and made herself into something. If I lost my job and went to jail because of this, then even the good girl of the family would be a disappointment. It's not that I don't want to be with you it's just that..." She stopped, turning to look at me. "Keith," she said, "I know this all must seem so sudden, but you have to understand there are things you just can't tell people. You make me feel so good about myself when you look at me the way you do. It's been so long since anyone's looked at me like that. It's scary. It's like I'm a teenaged girl again. I don't know why I'm telling you this now. I just don't want to be alone for even a second longer. I've been living like this for years and I—it's like I've been quietly working and keeping myself in check, day in, day out. And then you showed up. And all you had to do was look at me like you do and it was over for me. We're going to have to figure something out but in the meantime we'll just call this a good time for the both of us. We can't be more than that. Do you understand?" "I think so," I said. "I don't think you do," she said, "but that's okay. We'll work on that. Maybe. For now, all we need to do is keep this a secret. Rumours flying around would be a step in the wrong direction." The implicit assumption, I've since realized, was that she believed, on some level, that what she was doing with me was wrong. At the time, though, I couldn't see it, couldn't see past myself, couldn't see beyond the next day. Everyone knew me as a head-case already, for reasons I'll show you, but for now, it's enough to tell you, Karen, that I knew exactly what you were talking about. I know you teachers don't talk much with your students (most of them, anyways), but I'll tell you that if you had asked around about me, you might not've done the things that you did with me. But at least you had the courage to judge me by what you saw in me, not by what others saw.

Then, she'd relaxed, having gotten, I suppose, that much off her chest. It turned out that our *lovemaking* was not only taboo but outright criminal. Though the age of consent in Canada was sixteen, it was illegal for teachers to sleep with their students who were under the age of eighteen. As I was, then, a few months shy of my eighteenth birthday, the act of our having *made love* meant Miss Thoreson had committed a criminal offense, punishable by a prison sentence of up to several years. (This I realized later; she'd never told me and I'd never asked). Though it meant little to me at the time, given that I was at the age of seventeen and therefore possessed of an idea of our *love* as noble and pure and above the law, but, then, we all think like that when we're that age. It was ridiculous, self-indulgent, and melodramatic, but it felt so real, so honest and right. Though we spent the rest of the morning sitting on the couch, sipping coffee and watching the sky brighten, there was a sense of anticipation that built, with my arm wrapped loosely around her waist, while she held my hand in hers, the warmth of our bodies having become one. She stirred, standing, but I held onto her hands and pulled her back down onto me. With one hand I traced a path lightly along the edge of her forehead, letting the loose strands of her hair fall lazily back over her eyes while her lips pressed into an impish grin. We kissed. "Keith..." she said, sighing, before pulling away. At that moment, I thought to go after her, feeling that very same impulse that once compelled me to feel like I was falling in love with her soon after we'd first met. It was a deeply passionate sensation, a kind of surge of adrenaline that made me feel alive, and it was that very feeling that convinced me, then, that no matter what any law said, our *love* wasn't wrong. *Love* can't be *wrong*, can it? Even between teacher and student, so long as we *loved* each other it couldn't have been wrong, could it? These were my thoughts at the time, and it's only in the years since that I've come to entertain the notion that they weren't really *mine*, that they might've been a product of my youth, that I might've not yet gained the power to control my own thoughts and feelings, as if such a thing was possible at all. Karen became a different person after that first time we'd had together, the teacher giving way to the sensuous, sexual woman who'd, in time, come to be the love of my life. In her little bedroom, with hardly a metre of space between her bed's either side and the walls, it was hard to reconcile these two roles, these two completely different people with one another, not that I, at seventeen, knew how to do so, and at the time all I could think about was having her again. So late in the morning, the room was illuminated by the pale, white glow of the bright, late-winter's sky filtering in through the blinds, lending the scene a surreal atmosphere not entirely unlike the feeling of standing next to a falling-asleep child and wondering if the child's dreams were of you. "Karen," I said, "do you want me to leave?" "No," she said, "not yet, stay here. And in a few months it won't matter. I know you're in love with me Keith, and it makes me feel so good about myself, the way you look at me when we see each other in the halls. I don't know why this is coming out now and not before. You remind me so much of a guy I knew back in high school. Big, strong. Worked out every day. He never talked to me, never even knew I existed, probably. And now here I am, with a young man just like him in my apartment about to fuck me again. Good things come to those who wait, eh?" She drank another glass of wine, then approached me and grabbed me by the collar of my shirt, pulling me in for a kiss, the taste of cheap wine on her tongue. It was the first time I'd seen her, well, not drunk, but at least tipsy, and it seemed so at odds with the Karen I'd come to know, the Karen everyone else knew. We *made love* that night, this time in her bed, but on top of the covers with some of our clothes still on, afterwards she, for once, falling asleep before me; the wine, probably. Sometime later, I left, our first night together behind us, and already I felt as though we'd been apart for much, much longer. It was too strange to be like this with her, and I couldn't have known what'd prompted her sudden and jarring change in attitude, but I ignored it anyways, as though there was some subconscious part of my mind that carefully evaluated the change she'd presented and then discarded it, choosing to have me look on her exactly the same way.

We didn't speak again that Saturday, which saw me return to an empty home. Managing to keep away from the phone for the day, I busied myself, leafing through a book, passing my eyes over the pages, taking every word in but without actually reading. Randall spent much of the day in the living room, rising every now and then to head into the kitchen and make himself another drink, while Lisa was at work, having taken to Saturday shifts. (She never said why but with Randall seeming to have stopped working altogether her reason was clear). The look and feel of our little townhouse had begun to fall apart. Empty rum bottles littered the kitchen counters, some turned over on their sides. In the corner, there sat garbage bags full of empty pop cans, piled on top of one another. The sink was filled with dirty dishes in a pile that reached almost to the tap, with flies circling overhead. Sometime through that afternoon, I took to the kitchen, washing the dishes one after the other, scraping at the days' worth of caked-on grime, cleaning my way through nearly the whole sink before my hand slipped and I cut my finger on an exposed knife's blade. There was a moment of pain, but it passed, and I watched as the dirty dishwater around my hand turned a slight shade of crimson. It all made me feel more than a little bit lonely, and in my lonely state I couldn't help but look forward to the next time I was to see her. I didn't know what I was doing. Leaving the sink half-filled with dirty dishes and soapy water, I turned and leaned back against the edge of the counter, watching the clock on the far wall strike its way past noon.

At Eastmount, the first day back after that first weekend we'd *made love*, and still we hadn't spoken. At lunch, I was walking the hall outside her classroom when she and I crossed paths while the chatter of so many classmates carried on around us. Clutching a binder tight against her chest, she stopped for a moment, the two of us exchanging a furtive glance. It was as though we were alone. "Karen," I said. "Keith," she replied. "Are you—" "—No." "Okay." "What about—" "—No." "Fine." She stepped went to step past me, and as she came close, I said to her, "I love you," softly, as though it was the most natural thing in the world to say. She stopped again, a pained look crossing her face, and at once I realized my mistake. Later, sitting in my car, I waited for her, on seeing her shooting a look her way, receiving only a quick look back, the evening seeing me work through a shift at the thrift shop. Towards the end of my shift, I stood on the edge of the loading bay at the back of the thrift shop, letting a gaze linger into the night's sky, wondering what was yet to come. Never more confused than at that exact moment, I look back on it, now, and remember looking to the future and seeing myself somewhere, anywhere but there, seeing endless possibilities, a thousand-and-one adventures waiting just over the horizon, and after I'd gone in to help close the shift, I could only replay that little conversation with Karen that'd taken place in the hall that day, hardly twenty-four hours since she and I had last been in each other's arms. It was all building towards something, but, then, I hadn't the slightest idea what. Then, weeks later, I don't remember exactly how many weeks later but weeks later anyways, and already the halls had begun to talk, not that they'd ever stopped, and, I learned, they were talking about us. But I've always been the last to learn about these things, keeping to myself, unaware, then, of what everyone thought of me. Then, Karen.

After weeks apart, to be back in her arms was impossible. We'd *made love*, then laid in her bed, she resting on my chest. We remained like this for a while, motionless but for the gentle, rhythmic rise and fall of my chest with each breath, until at last she broke the silence. "Have you told anyone yet?" she asked, speaking as though she were talking to herself as much as me. "No," I replied. "Really?" "It's just like the last time you asked me. I haven't told anyone." She lifted her head to look at me, then away. "You're surprised?" I asked. "Not exactly," she said. "Have you told anyone?" I asked. A pause. "Yes," she said, "a girlfriend. We've known each other since I was your a—since I was in high school." "Why did you tell her?" She sighed. "Don't know. Needed to tell someone, I suppose." Silence, a lingering silence, broken only by the thrum of the city's streets fading in through an open window. "You know, I've never done anything like this before," she said, "slept with a student, I mean." "That's okay," I replied, without missing a beat, "I've never slept with a teacher, either." She laughed. "So this is new ground for both of us," she said. With one hand she reached over and traced a path lightly along my jaw, resting her thumb on my chin for a half-second before pushing gently in, her grin fading, slowly, replaced by a square-jawed strain. It was a look I'd become used to seeing on her, but still a look I didn't like. It just seemed so unlike her, even as it seemed exactly like her. "You are so beautiful," I said. "Is that all?" she asked. "No," I said, leaning over for a kiss. "What else?" she asked. "I don't understand," I said. "I don't doubt it," she said. But then she laughed, and let me have that kiss, with one hand reaching for the back of my neck and pulling me in, sharing the kiss for only a moment before breaking it, leaving me leaning forward, not knowing what to do next.

She pushed herself away, then sat on the edge of the bed, turning back slightly to look at me while she pulled on a pair of boxer shorts that looked much too big for her. "I'm serious, Keith. You have no idea how much trouble I'll be in if this gets out." "I know," I said. Some time passed, perhaps an hour or so. Finally, I had to say something. "What do we do now?" I asked. "I don't know," she said, "What do you want to do?" "I want to be with you." "How's that going to happen?" "I dunno." By then I'd sat up, with the sheets having fallen around my waist, leaving my chest bare, my arms free as I took one of her hands in mine and gently stroked her palm with my thumb. "This can't go on," she said. "I know," I said, though I couldn't help but remind myself it wasn't the first time I'd heard her say that. "When we go back to Eastmount tomorrow we can't act any different around each other," she said, "we have to go back to being just teacher and student, nothing more. Just like we've been doing the past few weeks.

It's got to stop. I need you to try and stay away from me whenever we're at Eastmount." "I know." "You promise?" "I've been doing that." "Oh, no you haven't." "I don't know what to say." "Oh fuck, listen to me," she said, as much to herself as me, "I can't believe what I'm doing." Rising, she made for the kitchen, turning a corner to disappear behind the thin wall separating it from the living room. Starting after her, I found her checking a cupboard, then another, then another. "What are you doing?" I asked. "Looking for a pack of cigarettes," she said, finding one, pulling a single cigarette out and placing it gently between her lips before lighting it. "You don't smoke." "I used to." She drew in a deep breath, holding it for a moment, then exhaling slowly, the thick, acrid smell of smoke filling her small kitchen. After she'd taken a couple more drags, I reached for the cigarette, took it from her, and mashed it out on the bottom of the sink. I thought she might've lit another, then another, then another, but she only looked at me with a kind of strain that was hard to gauge. I was only seventeen, almost eighteen, but with her in that little apartment I felt like I was becoming something more than another teenager, one of many, the act of having become Karen's *love* making me feel like a man. It's ridiculous, now, and even to write such a thing makes me half-cringe, maybe partly because it's true. She seemed so small. Holding her by the shoulders, I seemed to tower over her, my bulky, muscular body dwarfing her shapely, curvaceous form. It was as though we were made for each other, perfectly complimentary pieces, together greater than the sum of us. We kissed, but the taste of cigarettes in her mouth made me break the kiss. "Are we really going to do this?" she asked rhetorically. "Why not?" I replied. "I can't say no to you," she said, murmuring. "Do you want to?" I asked. "Not really," she said. We kissed, again, this time slowly, passionately, the strain in her body seeming to unwind through our touch.

Then came the first time she'd said to me she was leaving. "It doesn't matter," she said. "Why not?" I asked. "This is my last year at Eastmount anyways," she said, "next year I'm working at a school on the North Shore." "Why?" She shrugged. "I grew up there. I went to school there. I want to go back there." In her third year teaching at Eastmount, she was in the final year of her current contract and had already signed on with the North Vancouver school district. When the time came, she would move up there, not altogether far from where she'd lived when she was young. At the age of seventeen, I wanted to be anywhere but where I was, the whole world seeming to offer an endless array of possibilities, so many adventures waiting just out of sight. But the way she looked back made her voice soften and the tension in her evaporate a little. We had a few months to go, I thought, and then we could be together openly, like any other couple. A few months, that was all, but those were a few months which, then, seemed to stretch into years, as time does when you're so young. But I shouldn't, couldn't have been expected to know what was to happen in the meanwhile. Over the next few weeks, as Karen and I kept seeing each other, off and on, here and there, whenever a spare moment in her life presented itself, until, one afternoon, it became abundantly obvious, to me as it'd been to her all along, that she was just as lost as I was, but that, unlike me, she realized it, in the place where I'd felt fully confident I knew exactly what I was doing she felt adrift, looking for meaning, for something to believe. Through the little hints, here and there, I came to learn that she'd booked her escape to North Vancouver not because she wanted to go back home, I'd decided, but because after three years at Eastmount she'd needed to get away from me. That must've been it. I can't remember what prompted this line of thinking. Nor can I remember what it made me feel like when it came to me. All I can remember is that the sudden and inexplicable realization marked the beginning of the end of our affair, if only, then, at seventeen or eighteen I'd been able to realize it, and if only she, then, at thirty-five had the heart to break it to me. But by then we were too dependent on one another, too critically and emotionally dependent, made abundantly clear from the little glint in her eye whenever we crossed paths, whenever we exchanged looks over the last few months at Eastmount that year. It was all building towards something, but, then, I hadn't the slightest idea what.

At home, Lisa and Randall were there, but not there. He'd roped Lisa into helping him with early deliveries, while at work she'd transferred to a shift starting in the afternoon and ending late at night. This left her little time to spare idling at home, some days the only evidence she still lived there was the car parked out front and the disappearance of the stack of mail I'd bring in every afternoon during that small window of time between school and work. Though I couldn't have known it at the time, she was working herself exhausted, made to do so by a live-in boyfriend who didn't have a pot to piss in. She paid the rent, and he paid nothing. As soon as he'd moved in, it became a frequent occurrence that mail would arrive for him with "PAST DUE" or something like that stamped in big, bold, red letters on the front. He once answered the phone and, in a low voice, claimed he'd just been released from a length hospital stay and so hadn't had the time to pay a bill. The peak of all this came when Lisa asked me, her teenage son, for a couple of hundred dollars to help make rent that month, that very month when Karen and I had started our affair. She was embarrassed. She knew it wasn't right, just as she knew it was. It seemed impossible to conceive that things had become so bad in such a short time, but still she held firm. In the years since, I've come to appreciate just how scared Lisa was, scared as any of us were of our steady advance through crisis after crisis. Even as the unpaid bills piled up and the cracks in the walls widened with each passing day, I couldn't manage but the harshest of scorn. It's a strange thing, to be so full of— not anger, but disdain for someone so close to you, someone who'd given you so much, but it was just the way I felt. It was for this reason that I kept my *love* with Karen away from my rapidly deteriorating home life, and why I couldn't do anything to stop it. But then I was only seventeen, eighteen, somewhere in there, and it would've been *wrong* for her to expect me to do anything. That's what you want to hear. It's what everyone wants to hear. It's what everyone expects me to say. But I just can't bring myself to say it. It was all building towards something, but, then, I hadn't the slightest idea what.

The next few weeks passed without incident, February bleeding into March, March bleeding into April. Karen and I kept having each other whenever time permitted, whenever there was a moment in her schedule to spare. Naturally, these trysts became the highlight of my life, with the days made up mostly of staring off into space while filling my head with re-enactments of our times together, of her lying back on her dining room table with her legs hooked on my shoulders while her whole body jostled and jolted in time with my thrusts inside her, of her atop me of her naked, voluptuous body against mine. In a few short weeks we'd become the subject of so many rumours, so much gossip at Eastmount, drawn from someone catching us glimpsing at just the right time, from someone looking in through the door to her classroom at just the right angle to see me leaning over her desk suggestively. But all I could think of was Karen and the next time I'd have her. Being in love then was like an addiction, where I spent every waking moment either with her or thinking about the next time I'd be with her. At Eastmount, not the next day but sometime around then, Karen approached from behind, walking the hallway like she did, when I turned abruptly and found myself face to face with her. Maybe it was deliberate, but I reached out as she stepped past and let the back of my hand lightly touch her bum, the fabric of her jeans coarse, causing her to stop and toss a cross look back before continuing down the hall and out of sight. It was just like before we'd become a couple, only this time with so much more at stake. I was a teenager in love, *making love* with a *woman*, and for the first time in my life it felt like I had something worth having, something I shouldn't have been ashamed of, a feeling I haven't since had with anyone else. Months later, just a few months later as I walked across the stage and took my little diploma from the principal of Eastmount Secondary, I turned slightly and looked out across the crowd assembled in the school's gym, to see if Karen was there.

At home, Lisa and Randall were fighting, but they were always fighting, as though it was an act they put on, roles they'd learned from routine and were acting out. I was absent much of the time, days passing between the times Lisa and I crossed paths. When we ran into each other, I could hardly recognize her, the woman who'd been my mother replaced by someone totally unlike her. It wasn't anything specific, anything I could pick out and point at as proof of her change. The light in her hair had dimmed and dulled, and the little etches and grooves creasing her face had hardened and darkened. She seemed to have aged ten years in ten weeks. It was unsettling. And as I walked past her in our home's little dining room, she looked past her body and onto the wall behind, like a veteran's thousand-yard stare. But there was Randall. They'd fought the night before, of course they'd fought the night before, but when he came home that day they shared an embrace as though they'd forgotten all about their fight, he kissing her on the cheek, she wrapping her arms around him and letting off a sigh of relief as she held him tight. As I watched surreptitiously from the kitchen, it seemed as though they had become different people overnight, replaced with those who looked exactly like them but which couldn't quite pull off their fraud. Though I've since realized what she was going through, it was a transformation that I, at the age of seventeen, couldn't make sense of. One minute they were fighting, and the next they were in love.

Karen and I saw each other again that night, some night, one night or another, *making love* quickly, quietly between her sheets, she trembling as I touched her exactly as she'd shown me to, her eyes shutting and her jaw clenching tight as she let out a low, guttural groan. It was the first time I'd made her come. Afterwards, she gently patted the back of my neck as I lay atop her, the smell of sex and sweat overpowering my senses with each soft, shallow breath I drew in. Though our night was all but over, we still had left one bit of feeling to share. "I love you," I said. "I know," she said. Before falling asleep in her arms, I thought to the next day, for a moment wondering if it'd ever come at all. In the meanwhile, though, even after having heard the rumours, I knew they weren't true, knew they were easily denied, that so long as we were careful then there wasn't any risk, and if we were found out and she'd lost her job, well, then I still thought the trouble it'd caused would've been nothing when compared to the fact that we were in love. It was in this frame of mind that I, somehow, sometime, took to watching her from my seat in the back of the class, took to watching her work through a day's lesson, she stopping every now and then to look out across the classroom, for a split-second the sweep of her eyes meeting mine, for that half-second it seeming like we were alone even as we were surrounded by people, by her students, by my classmates, each of them having long since realized there was something going on between her and me.

7. Present

After Sheila's death, I flew to see our father for the first time in three years, alone. At twelve years old, I boarded an American Airlines flight that was to take me directly to Dallas/Fort Worth. Every previous flight to visit our father I'd taken with Sheila there, and although I can't recall all that much, I can recall a profound sense of isolation, of loneliness, one which has never let up. On that flight, I spent much of the time looking out the window at the array of landscapes passing underneath, the mountains eventually giving way to flat fields that were criss-crossed with arterial roads, interrupted only by the odd town that looked very much like a cluster of huts scraped up and dropped on the prairie for no rhyme or reason. It was a long flight, seeming much longer than it was, and when I saw my father, Roger, waiting in the lounge just outside the gate, I ran over to him and jumped up into a hug. It seemed like the right thing to do, what was expected of me after having not seen him in three years, even as I could've just as easily spent the summer at home had I chosen to (or so said Lisa). We walked along the airport's concourse, and he asked me what I wanted to do with our four weeks together. We went to Six Flags, took in a Rangers game, and went shooting at the range four or five times. Even at twelve years old I couldn't help but wish Sheila was there; her absence was something I've never been able to forgive her for. She'd left me alone to face the experience of being a stranger in a strange land. It'd been three years, and three years to a kid at that age was a lifetime. We were strangers. I couldn't articulate it as such, then, as I was just twelve, but it was the way it was, I'm sure of it.

It was the first time I'd visited Dallas, Texas, the city filled with big trucks and huge people. The moment I stepped out of the airport's terminal building and onto the sidewalk, a wall of heat struck, a scorching dry heat. The old joke I've since heard was that the United States had forty-four states, five commonwealths, and one Texas. In mid-June it was so hot in Texas that you could cook an egg on your driveway, and you couldn't walk barefoot on exposed pavement for the searing pain that felt like walking on a stove's element. Roger lived in a single-storey, three-bedroom rancher in Carrollton, alone; in the three years since we'd seen each other, he and his second wife divorced, leaving his spacious house eerily empty. When he was in the backyard relaxing, he'd have me go inside and mix his rum-and-cokes; I thought it was funny, then, to deliberately mix them way too strong. Soon, the summer had ended and I'd flown back to Vancouver, the events having made a lasting impact on the course of my life.

For my part, work continued, but at work I'd all but stopped paying attention to the union's negotiations, my full attention devoted instead to each of Karen and Lisa. After Karen and I had been discovered by her husband, Richard, they'd stayed together for a while, agreeing to stick it out for the sake of Lucas, their young son. But the months that'd followed saw arguments, suspicion, lies, Richard demanding she purge all evidence of me from her life, then looking through her phone's call logs and emails, with Karen at first insisting it'd been only that time we'd been caught, then that it'd been only a few times we'd been together, Richard seeing right through her, the truth like something to be negotiated, fought over, won through attrition. They began to fight over every little thing, from the bills, the credit card bills and the mortgage and the payments on the Mercedes-Benz he drove to and from work in that office tower in Downtown Vancouver every day. Any little thing was all it took to set off another fight, any possible reason seized on as an excuse to act out on their mutual distrust and acrimony. Finally, one day she'd come home, took one look at him, and without saying a word to each other they both realized it was over. Some of this she told me later, some of it I've come up with on my own. It wasn't hard to figure out; it's just how these things happen, I've since realized. He was everything I wasn't. Though I hadn't yet met him, I thought of him already as a fool—no, a tragic figure for having taken Karen's love for granted. It was in this frame of mind that Karen found me one night, having let myself into her apartment with the set of keys she'd given me, and took me by the hand into her bedroom where we had adequate, perfunctory sex, the kind that satisfies a need but can't quite quench a thirst.

We were in the middle of a summer's short night, with a dry heat bleeding in through her bedroom's open window, the blinds rattling gently against the sill. Karen sat up, and turned to let her legs hang off the edge of the bed. Lying back in bed propped up on my elbows, I looked on Karen as she reached for the nightstand and opened its drawer, leaning forward to look inside. She seemed so unlike the thirty-something woman I'd first fallen in love with more than a decade earlier, time having added little crow's feet behind her eyes, creases where there'd been bare smoothness, the odd blemish spotting her skin. But her hair was still the same dirty blonde, almost a light brown, an almond colour too perfect to be real. There was the Miss Thoreson I'd known, somewhere, I was sure of it, but I couldn't figure out how to get through to her the way I'd done before. On her finger, I imagined what it might've looked like to see her wearing a ring. When she leaned forward, the light from her bedside lamp cast a white glow on her face, making her look very much like a porcelain doll. "Karen," I said, "you've gotta tell me what's going on. You've gotta tell me what's wrong." She turned slightly, glancing back, but saying nothing. "Are you just gonna shut me out of your life?" I asked. "If that's what I wanted, you wouldn't even be here," she said. "Then what is it?" I asked. She let out a long, slow sigh, and said, "It's..."

Her divorce was underway, but it was a long, slow process marked by the filing of forms and the payment of fees small and large, to the court and to their lawyers. It was to take a year of them living separately in order for a divorce to be granted, and it'd been only a couple of months since she'd moved into her own place. In the meantime, they were going back and forth, negotiating rights to this and that, filing motions and responses to motions and requests for judgments and counter-requests for denials of judgment pending that and this. Before that one dinner Karen had me over for where I'd met her son, I felt an anxiety about inevitably meeting him. If Karen and I were to have our *relationship*, I knew, then it would happen, sooner or later. The thought turned my insides over, in exactly the same way they used to turn whenever Karen, then Miss Thoreson and I were together ten years earlier, when I was her student and she was my teacher. Besides standing by and providing her a sympathetic ear, there was little I could've done, little I should've done, the entire affair making me feel very much powerless to help after having caused so much harm. *Stand by her side*, I reassured myself, *it'll all work out in the end*. Little did I know, then, as Karen sat on the edge of her bed, her bare backside facing me while the thin sheets seemed to cover her like a light dusting of snow, that it would be some small miracle if we all made it through to the end of the year alive. As the season quickly turned and the skies darkened earlier and earlier each day, I began to wonder back to the last of the little moments we'd shared, before her husband had found us, before we'd become something more than secret lovers, and imagined ourselves *making love* as we'd once, indulging in a secret pleasure wherever time presented itself. With one finger, I traced a path along the curvature of her body, only lightly touching her, imagining myself touching her as a secret lover and not a young man who'd broken up her family. For a moment, I nearly convinced myself it was still real, even as it *was* still real.

And then, Karen had become pregnant. We hadn't discussed it much since she'd told me, but it was implicitly understood that she wouldn't carry the baby to term. We spent enough time at her place for me to see the signs, the little half-mumbled sentences and the way she seemed to sort-of deflate slightly whenever asked about it. Then, not altogether long after she'd first told me, she announced her intention to have an abortion. We were in bed, her bed, at the time, spending the night together like any other. She'd gone to bed first, and a little while later I sauntered in, walking up to the bed, then on my hands and knees inching across the bedspread towards her, taking the book from her hands and setting it on the nightstand before kissing her, trying to kiss her with all the passion and the intensity I'd kissed her with when we were younger. "Keith, I wanted to talk to you," she said, inching back slightly, sitting up against the headboard, while I leaned away and sat, cross-legged on the bed. "I'm getting an abortion." "When?" I asked. "Soon," she said. "How soon?" "In a couple of weeks." A pause while I thought how to respond. "What do you want me to do?" I asked. "Just be there for me," she said. Then she explained they wanted her to arrange to have someone drop her off and pick her up at the hospital on the day of the procedure, and I readily agreed to do that for her. We didn't *make love* that night, instead turning out the lights before quietly turning in. She fell asleep, but I stayed awake through the night, at three or four in the morning rising from bed and making for the washroom, splashing cold water over my face, looking at myself in the mirror, imagining myself in place of the person staring back. Then, some time later, Karen entered the washroom in her nightgown, stood at my side, and took my hand in hers. "Keith," she said, "you're a good guy. You've always been a good guy. But this isn't about you." "Then what?" I asked. "Keith…" I knew what she'd meant, but I wanted to hear her say it. But she, in turn, knew I only wanted to hear her say it, and met my try at her with one of those looks that seemed a blend of the irritated and the forlorn. I knew not to press the issue, but now, looking back on it, I wish that I had. It would've, might've saved us all a whole lot of heartbreak. "Karen," I said, "I'm here for you." She reached with one hand and rested it on my shoulder, giving a firm squeeze, her touch making it clear that there was nothing I could say or do to alleviate her stress, her strain, and that she understood that I still *loved* her as I'd *loved* her when I was her student and she was my teacher, only now it was a kind of *love* that wasn't as it'd been.

My feelings changed over time, and they'll continue to change, but between that night and the day of Karen's abortion I had little time to think about it. I never wanted a child, I knew I would've made an awful parent. But there was a part of me that was upset—no, disappointed with her decision to abort the child I'd given her. It was as though instinct in me wanted to start a family with her, to raise a child with her, to have a home with her, to kiss her when I come home in the evening after a long day of work and to sit at a dinner table with her and our children as a family. It was impossible. At forty-six she was too old to start a new family with a much younger man. And as her divorce from Richard proceeded slowly, day-by-day through its year-long separation phase, she kept tending to her young son. I rarely saw him, and whenever I did it was little more than a passing look as he was on his way between Karen's and Richard's. They had a provisional custody arrangement which meant he spent alternating weeks with his father and with his mother; this I knew from hearing about it from Karen. Whenever she talked about her son I said very little, listening intently while nodding along. There wasn't anything I could've said to help anyways. I was there to provide emotional support as a sounding board. Listening without acting made me feel small and impotent, but

I put those feelings aside as best I could. Even as these thoughts came to dominate my feelings, I worked to consciously remind myself of what Karen had said: it wasn't about me. This thought I used to assuage any misgivings about her coming abortion and resolved to simply be what she needed me to be. With all that was going on around us, the point, in fact, was to become whatever might've been for me to become. Sometimes I thought to ask directly what was going to happen with her son and I, what kind of place I would have in their life, if any, but I could never put myself up to it.

She hadn't been skiing in months. It was weighing on her, in the same sort of way, I imagine, a lifelong sailor might want to be back out at sea after months ashore. Karen must've known how I felt just from the way I looked at her, from the way I touched her, for a few days before the abortion she took me aside in her kitchen and asked me a simple, direct question: "what do you want?" "I don't know what you mean," I replied, feigning ignorance. "Yes, you do," she said, "I know you too well for that to work." She had her hand on my shoulder, and gave a quick, firm squeeze. On any other day, I might've told her, might've been honest with her, but on that Sunday, hardly a couple of hours before Richard was due to arrive to hand Lucas over to her for the coming week, I muscled a smile onto my face and insisted, "it's nothing." The light behind her eyes dimmed a bit, and she withdrew her hand from my shoulder, turning away. "I should get going," I said, gulping down the last of a mug of lukewarm coffee before making at the door. Taking Karen in my arms, I held her tight and kissed her goodbye, her hands resting lightly on my forearms, her lips parting, allowing her taste to mingle with mine. "I love you," I said. "I know," she said. Then, I was gone, obediently disappearing with an understanding between us that, other than texting and talking on the phone, we weren't to have much contact until her son was back at Richard's. As an interim arrangement, it seemed to work, she and I leaving the question of *us* to be dealt with *later*.

Meanwhile, Richard continued to occupy the better part of her days. He wanted sole custody of their son, while Karen wanted sole custody but with Richard allowed extensive visitation rights, weekends, holidays, the summer, and more. He intended to argue that his much greater income made his home a more suitable place for a young child to grow up. All this I learned from listening to Karen, here and there, over dinner, in bed at night, on the phone as I spent spare moments here and there, breaks at work, mornings at my place, even stuck in traffic, whenever a little sliver of time presented itself, listening to her. It was in the middle of one such conversation (I think it was while I sat in my truck waiting at a red light on East Hastings) that I realized it was over for me, that the passion, the intensity of feeling I'd had was gone, replaced by something I, then, couldn't quite understand, couldn't quite articulate, except to see myself as having fallen out of love with the woman I'd thought of, for more than ten years, as the love of my life. We saw each other that night, arriving with a surprise bouquet of flowers and a little heart-shaped box of chocolates, the light behind her eyes brightening in an instant, she taking me in her arms, kissing me while I still held the flowers and the chocolates, then taking them from me, setting them on a table, then sitting me on her living room's couch.

And then there was the pregnancy, the little baby slowly growing inside her. Before she'd told me, I wouldn't have known; but now, whenever I looked at her, I couldn't help but see her stomach expanding, even as she hadn't yet been pregnant for even six weeks. I didn't want to have a child. Her choice to abort, nevertheless, made me feel a little uneasy, as though I'd become *used* to the idea of having a child. I don't know. It's hard to explain. I don't really understand it myself. Maybe we all just have an instinctive desire to have children, to give permanence to ourselves by way of another, and in her decision to abort I'd lost that. But it was a decision she'd made. It became a daily occurrence to leave work tired, sore, but then to be unable to sleep, to toss and turn for hours, in the morning rising, still tired, sore. Every time I thought to complain, I reminded myself of one simple truth: 'this is the life I chose.' As the state of affairs at CylinderWorld worsened, I found myself having to silently utter that line on a daily, hourly basis, as if to will myself through the fatigue, the aching sensation behind my eyes. As if I could've had a child; I could hardly make it through the shift and all I had, then, was a woman who was my lover, she not even depending on me for anything more than a sexual and emotional release. The nights I'd spent with Karen, the secret rendezvous' we'd had in her marital bed, the mid-morning liaisons had in my little shoebox of an apartment, the spare time we'd found, a half-hour here, a couple of hours there, these were the moments that'd kept me going through the long, hard hours, even as these were the very moments that'd led to her becoming pregnant with the child I wouldn't have.

But other concerns were to intervene. Sometime a few days after Karen had told me she was pregnant with my child, it emerged that Richard was trying to take Lucas away from her, forever. It came out, one night, when Karen had had two or three glasses of wine with dinner, she'd later say, and she suddenly started blowing up my phone with her texts. At work, in the middle of picking an order from the racks, the texts started coming, one, then ten or twenty minutes later another, then a few minutes later another, then seconds later two more at almost the same time. Thinking, I texted her back, asking, "what can I do to help you?" But I received no further texts from her that night, staying up late, late, late into the early morning, waiting. He wanted sole custody. Karen was an adulteress, he'd argued through his lawyer, and that meant loose morals, in turn making her unfit to raise their child. Later, Karen would tell me her lawyer had assured her they were just words printed on a document handed in for the court to read, a generic, boilerplate line that was thrown in for good measure. And I assured her this was true, though I had no way of knowing. But it bothered her all the same. It made her cry. After all that'd happened, after Karen's having become pregnant with my child and her decision to have an abortion, after Lisa's having left Randall, it seemed, then, that all the wrangling, all the hand-wringing and the raised voices were so distant, that it was all an elaborate theatre, each of us there to play our roles in a real-life fiction unfolding before us.

8. Past

The weekend after Karen and I had first *made love* arrived, with it a break from the act we'd put on, the disinterest in each other we'd feigned since. Thinking of that week makes me, in turn, think of the months before, recalling the tantalizing glimpses she'd given me before, the little moments when I'd spot her across a busy hall and we'd exchange the briefest of glances, sharing something only we understood, or so I thought. Then, Karen and I were together again, this time in my car, overlooking the city. Across the darkened landscape, the city's bright lights looked like a sea of glittering stars smoothly undulating into the night. "Wow," she said. "Do you like it?" I asked. "Yes," she said, "on a clear enough night you can see all the way to the states." Leaning over, I placed one hand on her thigh, gently stroking. "This is the most amazing relationship I've ever been in," I said, "and you're the most beautiful woman I've ever seen." We kissed, slowly, softly. It'd been hardly a week or two since we'd first *made love*, but already I felt as though we'd been together forever, that we'd come to know each other so intimately it was as though we were one person. "Keith," she said, "we have to talk." A pause. "About what?" I asked, dreading her response. "This," she said, pushing me back slightly before continuing, "I've had a lot of time to think about it over the past week," her voice trembled slightly, "and we can't keep doing this. It has to stop now." "Karen," I said, "I don't understand." She sighed. After having *made love* and broken that barrier, it might've seemed we were about to begin some kind of *relationship*, but with the months left before I was to graduate from Eastmount, it wasn't in the cards for reasons I couldn't understand.

"I just heard from someone there's a rumour going around about us," she said, "from one of my co-workers. He said he heard from someone else that we're having an affair." I said nothing, instead watching, waiting as she stumbled over herself to push the words across her lips while I thought of the rumours I'd been hearing about for nearly a year. (I suppose there was that wall between teachers and students). "I really don't want to lose my job or go to jail for this," she said. "I haven't told anyone," I said. "I know you haven't. It doesn't really matter. With the way we've been acting someone was bound to start talking." Even at seventeen, almost eighteen, I knew what she was saying, but to actually hear her tell me that she wanted, needed to keep our *love* a secret still wounded my pride a little, as though there was some small part of me that believed we should've been open with one another, to hell with the consequences. "Karen," I said, "I think I love you." A pause. "I know," she said, "But this has to stop before it gets any worse." "Okay," I said. The rumours swirling around for a while amounted to classmates talking about my pursuit of Eastmount's Spanish teacher, about the leery stares and the sideways glances, about the propositions I'd made that she'd politely rejected, about the way she'd seemed to tolerate my awkward advances as though they'd made her feel good about herself. But the rumours running wild were so salacious, so lurid they were scarcely believable. But as I sat on the hood of my car next to her, looking out across the city's lights, all that mattered was the way she made me feel, the way I made her feel when we were alone, beyond the law. Slowly, I took her hand in mine, and kissed her, holding my lips against the back of her hand for a little while, just long enough to feel the tension evaporate from her body. It began to rain, and we retreated into the Oldsmobile, she lying on the backseat while I lay atop her, moving against her in awkward, stilted, clumsy motions as we *made love*, she clutching me tight, coaxing the come from my body, the moment ceded to our *love*. It was almost the end of the year, and with all that'd happened between us I never bothered much to look ahead, leaving me to come up with some plan for the immediate future in a short time. I thought to go somewhere no-one could follow, across the world, to some little town up the coast of Greenland, where I could sit on the deck of some colourful, brightly-painted house and watch the midnight sun circle the sky. I thought to buy a one-way bus ticket to the mining town of Sudbury, Ontario and find work in a bar, slinging beer at workers after the ends of their shifts, each of them always a day away from potential unemployment. I thought to hitchhike down to some little city in Arizona, somewhere not far from the Mexican border, and spend the days working alongside immigrants picking vegetables in the fields or cutting meat on a slaughterhouse's floor, retiring at night to some little cube of a bedroom where I could look ahead to another day of life on the margins. It was stupid of me even to fantasize like that. It was all a sham. I hadn't the slightest idea what I was doing even as I was fully confident that I had it all figured out. I only wanted to leave, to be anywhere but there. In the weeks that'd pass before Karen and I had each other again, I obediently stayed away from her, feeding the rumours by my sudden avoidance of her, but only half-listening as the rest of the school carried on without me.

In her apartment weeks later, we sat, until she pushed herself from the couch, then turned and in a half-step entered the kitchen where she looked through a cupboard, on her tiptoes as she reached up with one hand, her back to me, my eyes tracing a path along her body, my gaze lingering lovingly on her wide hips, her shapely, curvaceous figure, her behind. Suddenly I stood and moved on her from behind, reaching past her for the mug I knew her to be looking for, setting it on the counter before she took it, then turned to face me. We stood with our bodies lightly pressing into each other's, her stance wide as she leaned back slightly against the counter, my one step between hers, my one hand on the counter and the other resting on her hips. We were so close I felt her heart beating. We kissed. Though it'd been months since we first kissed, I still felt a surge of fear in my gut whenever we touched. It was like a pain, sharp, jagged. But I craved it. I needed it. Like an addict, I ran towards the pain, seeking more. Her hands found my arms. She broke the kiss, and looked at me with a gaze that seemed to peer into me and bare for her every part of me. *Don't be afraid*, her eyes said, *you're all right*. Emboldened, I spoke first. "I love you," I said. "I know," she said. "Do you love me?" I asked. It took every bit of courage to ask her. She sighed, reaching to muss up my hair a bit before saying, "we'll see." It makes little sense now, but it made complete sense then, being as I was a young man who fully believed he had it all figured out. "I wish you would just say it," I said. "Keith..." she said, "let's not get into this now." "Why not?" I asked. "It's not going to end well if we do..." she said. "It doesn't have to end at all," I said. This brought a smile to her face, a wry little smile that curved the sides of her face up even as it seemed to slide halfway into a frown. "Don't you ever change," she said, "don't stop being the way you are." We *made love* that night, but it was hard, fast, she on me, her hips moving in quick, short motions, my whole body stiffening as I came inside her, like all the other times we'd been together much too soon. But after I'd come down from my high, she looked into my eyes with a half-scowl that was so entirely unlike her, but like the little almost-frown she'd shown before we'd taken to bed. It was only later in the evening, after we'd *made love*, that she told me, in the way that she did, that she had to stop seeing me, "for a little while at least," as though she was trying to negotiate her way out of what we had, whatever it *was*. And I let it be.

The next day we didn't see each other at all. Avoiding her classroom, I spent much of the day's spare time at the smoke pit, leaning with my back against the wall, chain-smoking until I ran out of cigarettes, then turning away to head back inside. Halfway there, I came across Adrian and his girlfriend Alyssa Wong, on their way from one class to another. As soon as they saw me, they stopped talking, Alyssa looking away while Adrian looked me in the eye. At that moment, I knew he'd told her about me and Karen—Miss Thoreson to them, I suppose. And if he'd told her, then she'd told someone else, and instantly all of Eastmount had begun talking about Miss Thoreson and me. Looking back, it was inevitable that we. If this seems like it's meandering aimlessly, wandering into nothing, then all I can tell you is that I'm trying, trying my very best to make sense of it all, to take the events of my life and twist and turn them until they fit into some kind of narrative, but when it comes to real people's lives you can only mangle them so much until they begin to unravel completely. Driving between Eastmount and the thrift shop that afternoon, I thought about what Karen had said; no one actually *knew*. Rumours were one thing, but you can't get in trouble because of rumours, or so I thought at the age of seventeen, nearly eighteen. Wheeling into the day, I vowed silently to come up with a plan of action, so to speak, on how I'd— how we'd keep our secret, and tell Karen about it the next time we saw each other. No harm would come of it, not to Karen's career or her life, that harm delayed until ten years later when she would come to believe herself as having paid the price.

Early in the eleventh grade, sometime after I'd blown up at Karen and stormed out of her classroom, I took to using the daily planner given to me at the start of the school year as an improvised journal, jotting my thoughts down whenever a spare moment presented itself. Soon, I'd filled every available space with writings, random half-sentences like, 'don't you want to be like your own person,' or lyrics from some song I'd stumbled across while sorting through the racks of CDs at the thrift shop on my break. One day, not altogether long after I'd begun to find myself inexplicably drawn to the Spanish teacher everyone thought I'd hated, I wrote in my planner, in red ink, 'I love you Miss K. Thoreson.' When I wrote that line, I wasn't in her Spanish class, but the next time I set foot in her Spanish class I suddenly couldn't look her in the eye, even as I couldn't help myself from looking her right in the eye. She might've known something had changed, as the rest of the period she kept looking over at me, as if checking for something, maybe worried I'd have at her again. Things continued this way for a while, a month or two, each and every day seeing me devote more and more of my time withdrawing into a fantasy world where she and I already were. As December turned into January and January turned into February, I began to feel that tell-tale longing whenever I was in Miss Thoreson's classroom, whenever I stood near her, then, finally, whenever I thought about her. If there was something wrong with me, then I couldn't see it for all the *feelings* that'd come to control me so completely. For her part, the woman I, then, knew only as Miss Thoreson led the eleventh-grade Spanish class in which I sat while keeping an eye out for me, every now and then her glimpse catching mine in a rare moment of honesty. But, then, she'd always look away quickly, as if afraid, of what I couldn't, then, say, nor can I now.

In the halls, sometimes I'd come across people in the middle of a conversation that suddenly fell silent when I was near; a couple of girls in Karen's Spanish twelve class, Sylvia and Nazifa, were holding binders against their stomachs and looking my way, but when I smiled and waved they snickered, leaned towards each other, Nazifa whispering something into Sylvia's ear, both girls laughing. They kept whispering when I walked into Biology. We sat through the days in Eastmount's classrooms, breathing air pregnant with the perspiration of so many bored and listless teenagers, watching as rays of light slanted in through the tall, clouded windows, a fine dust swirling like a thousand grains of sand caught in the ocean's currents. I wanted to see her. It was all I thought about. In English, I sat at the back of the class drawing loops and whirls in the margins of my notes, imagining her at the head of the class. In History, I looked to a large map on the wall and traced a little path with my eyes along the contours of the Mexican coast, wondering which of the little indentations into the sea she'd seen. In Biology, I excused myself halfway through the period, telling the teacher I needed to use the washroom, then walked the hall slowly towards Karen's room, approaching at just the right angle to catch a glimpse of her in the middle of a lesson, instead finding her place taken by a substitute, a man who looked, at a glance, hardly older than the students he was teaching.

At the day's last bell, I walked out to the smoke pit, lit cigarette between my fingers. All the way there, whispers seemed to swirl through the air, rumours of Karen and I, of the things we'd done, the things we hadn't done. Arriving, I found a few of my classmates milling about, a couple of Indo-Canadians and a few others, some of them leaving shortly after I'd arrived. But I said nothing to them, leaning back against the wall to light a cigarette, taking one long drag on it before refocusing my attention. In the distance, I noticed Karen emerging from the school's side entrance, the first I'd seen her that day. I watched as Karen walked along the edge of the parking lot towards her car, my eyes tracking her with all the sharpness of an eagle; she must've known I was watching her from a distance, as even though she hadn't turned to look my way there was something deliberate about the way she walked, each step seeming halted, forced, her whole body having a rhythm I wouldn't have been able to sense before I'd come to know her as more lover than teacher. It wasn't right. And then, after reaching her car, she opened its door and suddenly stopped, then turned to toss a look my way, a look strained, yet subdued, from the distance my imagination tightening her jaw and furrowing her brows slightly, then a thin-lipped smile appearing, as if to incite me. Raising a hand, I waved, across the lot she nodding slightly before getting into her car and driving away. I know it sounds repetitive to keep saying it, but I was in love with that woman, so hopelessly in love, like I wanted to be with her for the rest of my life. I was sure of it. The teenager in me fully believed I'd found *true love*, that the intensity, the fear I felt whenever she and I were in the same room as each other was *true love* in its *truest* sense, whatever that means. And, that day, as I looked after the spot she'd stood in only minutes earlier, it seemed as though she was still there, and for a moment or two fear blended seamlessly into love, making me want to throw up. It was all so confusing, and from the pained expression she'd sometimes taken to shooting my way I could tell she, too, found it so confusing, too confusing to stand. But, we'd been at it for long enough to have become, almost, kind-of, sort-of used to it, she seeming to adjust to the constant tension in ways I couldn't understand but could admire, showing up relentlessly each and every day, powering through her work, even when the light seemed to catch her just so she still looked just as you might expect a teacher to look. After late shifts had ended, I'd sometimes drive past Eastmount, looking out over the faculty parking lot, as if some part of me expected her to still be there so late even though the rest of me knew campus had long since closed for the night. It was an act, it was all an act, and although I believed, then, I was in full control of myself, I know, now, that I was really just in obedience to my *feelings*, following vague *compulsions* for no other reason than I couldn't resist them.

In that span of a few weeks when Karen and I had agreed to stop seeing each other, all I could think of was plotting the next time we'd, by pure coincidence, cross paths, falling back into old habits like an addict relapsing after having broken a long sobriety streak. That night, I drove along the city's streets, threading the gas as I jockeyed for the clearest route there. Arriving at Karen's place, I sat in the Oldsmobile, parked a half-block away, looking ahead while trying to work up the courage to go any further. At the front door to her apartment's building, I let my index finger hover over the keypad, ready to punch in her number. It was insane. It was insane. She wasn't there. Ringing her once, twice, five times, I received no response, eventually giving up, then turning and leaning on the building's front railing, lighting a cigarette and watching as traffic sped this way and that along the street. It was in this frame of mind that Karen found me, as she'd parked on the street a little ways up. I'd watched her approach, and she watched me, holding her hand the guy I'd come to know, years later, as Richard, her apprehension seeming to grow as she drew nearer and nearer. "Can I help you?" she asked, her voice tinged with anxiety. "Sorry," I said, "I'm—I'm waiting for someone else." "I hope they get here soon," she said, "it's cold out." Richard looked at me quizzically, until she took him by the arm and walked him past. They disappeared into the building, at the last moment she turning back to shoot me a pained look I couldn't figure out. When next we saw each other, at Eastmount, it was like we'd gone back to being teacher and student, like any other, as though we both had learned how to lie. But with events at home mounting, slowly but surely, I needed the distraction more than anything else.

8. Present

Something had changed after Sheila's death. Lisa turned to drink, more often than not coming home in the evening with a two-litre bottle of cider, the kind that's sold in plastic jugs usually used for soft drinks. It wasn't anything specific about the way she acted when she drank; at the age of twelve I couldn't pick it out at the time. She smiled, laughed, the only time I'd seen her smile and laugh since Sheila's death. But then, the next morning she'd inevitably sober up, slowly making her way downstairs around breakfast time, rubbing her temples gently as she poured a cup of coffee and told me to turn the TV off. She began to miss work. Her car insurance lapsed. She went out one Friday night, and (I've since learned) a cop pulled her over and arrested her for driving an uninsured vehicle and doing so while under the influence. She didn't come home that night, and I lay in bed wide awake all night, staring at the ceiling, thinking. She came home the next morning, of course, picked up from jail by a friend. I was eating breakfast when she walked in the door. Her hair was a ratty, matted mess, and her eyes were red. She said nothing to me, turning and heading upstairs, until I heard the sound of her door swinging shut followed by bedsprings groaning. That day at school, I couldn't focus, and wound up spending most of it looking off into space, in the seventh grade already well behind the curve. Towards the end of the day, I looked at the map of North America on the wall, eyeing a little dot marking Dallas, Texas, and made my decision.

A few days later, when I was sure Lisa was sober, I approached her and said I wanted to live with my father in Texas. She said no. I called him and told him, and he said it only mattered what I wanted, because I was twelve years old and could decide for myself who I wanted to live with. What followed was months of acrimony and distrust between us all, with he and Lisa fighting, she telling me not to call him on the phone (claiming long-distance rates too expensive), he telling me to call him when she wasn't there and to lie about it to her. The peak of all this came when he asked me to write a letter to his lawyer stating plainly I wanted to live with him, which I did. But I didn't think to sign it, so he told me his lawyer couldn't use it, and I had to do it again, the second time making sure to sign the letter. But Lisa found out, and hid all the stamps in the house. By this time months had passed and I was beginning to lose interest in the whole business, and I didn't send another letter. He kept asking me to, and I kept avoiding it. Finally, on the phone with him one night, with Lisa listening in, I told him I didn't want to live with him. I may or may not have been crying. I had just turned thirteen. He might've been crying too. He said he'd tell his lawyer to stop the whole thing. He said it had cost each of them around ten thousand dollars. The next day I went to school and found a little card in my desk from my seventh-grade teacher (a fifty-something named Miss Leung), written inside a little note expressing sympathy.

Arriving at Lisa's new place, I found it to be a little, one-bedroom apartment, smaller even than mine. There to pick her up, she and I said very little, soon heading in my truck towards the last place she and Randall had shared. It was the first time I'd been, they having moved more than once since we'd last spoken, leaving a trail of unpaid rents and withheld deposits behind them. I can't remember what I was expecting. He was there, sitting in the living room, drinking and watching TV, mostly ignoring Lisa and I as we carried boxes of her things from the dining room and the kitchen out through the front door and loaded then into the back of my truck. But then, as I walked back in to take the last of the day's boxes, he was there, standing between the kitchen and the dining room, looking at me, glass of rum in his and. I stopped for a moment, then picked up that last box and turned for the door, only to hear him mutter, "fuckhead," under his breath. This time, I was able to keep walking, without missing a step. Lisa was waiting in my truck, seatbelt buckled. In the middle of an unusually cold Vancouver's winter, the trees were coated in a light dusting of snow that looked like confectioner sugar, and the skies were coloured a bright, brilliant grey that only just concealed the sun's warmth. But then it wasn't winter, in a blur summer having arrived in full force, the road ahead disappearing into shimmering pools of silver behind rising waves of heat. In the months that'd passed since Lisa and I had reconnected, much had happened, but without any way of knowing whether Randall would contest their divorce Lisa just couldn't seem to relax, nearly every time we'd get together finding some way to work it into every conversation. If it sounds like I didn't want to hear it, then that's probably because I didn't. It was like an obligation to be there; Lisa had been the first between us to stick her neck out and call us back into each other's lives after the unpleasantness that'd happened, and it was exactly her courage that'd made me feel like a coward next to her. I don't know, that's probably overstating it, but I can't think of any better way to put it. "When did you graduate from university?" she asked. "A few years back," I said. "Did you take any pictures?" "A few." "Who took them for you? Friends?" "I don't really have any friends." A pause. "Do you remember Barb Simpson?" I asked. "Of course," she said, "but I haven't spoken to her in years." "She came to the graduation ceremony. She was the only one there. It wasn't much of a ceremony, actually. And afterwards we just went for dinner. It seems like it was a long time ago..." Silence. "It sounds like it was nice," she said, "I wish I'd been there." "It's not your fault," I said. My grip on the wheel had tightened and the truck's seat had become uncomfortable. Soon, we'd arrived. Lisa invited me in, but I declined.

So late in the summer, it was so hot that even with the truck's air conditioning on full-blast I couldn't manage comfort. The windows were rolled down, allowing the summer's heat to mix with the coolness of the air rushing through the truck's cabin. Listening, I gunned the engine here and there just to hear its throbbing, satisfied by the groaning of its moving parts protesting having to surge and subside on command. In the time it'd taken to move Lisa out of the home she'd shared with Randall, I had asked her so little, but learned so much, the strained looks and the tensed air every time the three of us were in the same room together seeming to reflect on all those years apart. Leaving Lisa's, I took to the city's streets and slowly made my way home, fiddling with the radio at exactly the moment Karen had called, for a moment the temptation flaring to ignore her call and listen to traffic reports for roads and highways nowhere near me. But I couldn't ignore her. No matter how I tried, no matter what'd happened, I just couldn't turn away from Karen Thoreson, the woman I'd loved, the woman who'd become like a *soul mate* to me. With Lisa having been dropped off, the rest of the day was free to be spent however I wanted, and right then I wanted to be alone.

Right after that phone call we'd shared while I was sitting in my truck at a red light, I'd taken to trying at reliving the way I'd used to feel for Karen, as if by repetition I could've tricked myself into thinking we were the way we'd been ten years earlier. Rhythmically, mechanically, I put my body through the motions of making it through the day, as if, by some stroke of happenstance, to shift the focus of my *feelings* back onto *her*. But it was over. No matter how I tried, no matter what I tried, I can see, now, that there was nothing I could've done to make myself fall in love with her again. It was as though, somewhere along the way, I'd turned my back on the more than ten years since we'd come into each other's lives, and it made me feel helpless to be so unable to just *force* myself to *feel* a certain way for her, for anyone. Where once she'd been the thirty-something Spanish teacher standing at the head of the class, she'd become, to me, something else entirely, no longer a pole on which I could fixate, but a weight burdening itself on my back as I tried to move forward. Months later, as I'd come to grips with the fact that Karen was no longer the woman I'd fallen *in love* with more than a decade earlier, it suddenly seemed impossible to reconcile with the Karen she was fast becoming, her skin drained of its colour, her hair sprouting split ends here and there. When we took each other to bed, then, it'd become a staid, tasteless act, as though we were acting out on our urges in a mechanical way, the lewd slap of skin on skin having been replaced by a subdued groaning of the bedsprings beneath us as Karen lay on her back, clutching at my body as I made long, slow strokes inside her, she seeming to cling to me like she'd needed it. But it was a fraud. Working methodically, rhythmically to my release, I came inside her, at just the right moment she tensing up, arching her back, tightening her legs around my hips, in the aftermath it becoming abundantly obvious she'd learned to fake her orgasm but for the sake of vanity, my vanity. On reflection, I've realized she, then, wanted me to think I'd not lost the ability to *please* her, to *satisfy* her, but not because she'd become concerned for *me*, even if that's what she might've thought, but instead because she wanted to continue to think of *herself* as having the ability to engender in me the kind of fiery *passion*, the heated *love* I'd once felt for her those many years before. It seems stupid, and it is. After all that'd happened, we couldn't even trick ourselves into believing we were the same as we'd been, off and on, for more than ten years. And then, the baby growing slowly inside her seemed to mark her as having *made* something of our time together. It made no sense, but it was.

A week or two after she'd told me she was pregnant and we still hadn't talked about whether she was to have an abortion or carry it to term. I thought about it every day and every night. At times, I'd be standing in front of a supervisor, Maya, at work, receiving instructions, only to blank out and suddenly find myself standing alone, forgetting what I'd been told, having, then, to go back and ask Maya to repeat the instructions given to me minutes earlier. (But Maya, far from being irritated, seemed to understand). When driving on the highway, I'd suddenly find myself having driven halfway to work with no memory of having done so, as if I'd buckled my seatbelt, turned the key, and then been teleported halfway down the highway. Finally, when Lisa and I had carried a little couch up a flight of stairs, we'd stopped at a little landing, Lisa looking at me like I was pale and sick, my only response to clear my throat and fumble for the bottom of the couch. *You're going to be a grandmother*, I thought to tell her, *except that you're not*. But she knew, Lisa. Of course she knew. When I told Lisa that I'd had an affair with a married woman, later in her little suite, she said, "I knew something was bothering you." Then, she asked, "do you wanna talk about it?" I said, "maybe." But we didn't, not then, and when we saw each other next at a Tim Hortons for coffee it came up, she asking if my affair with a married woman was to go anywhere, my reply to wave it off by saying, "it's complicated." After the way we'd become estranged after I'd graduated from high school and moved out, I suppose we couldn't just open up to each other. Even just to have called me and broken the silence had used all the courage between us. It didn't matter. It mattered more than anything in the world, to us, at least.

Months later, more than a year later, well after Karen had called and re-entered my life, this time our relationship having made me into the guy who'd broken her home and she into the woman who'd cheated on her husband. After much thought, she'd said, Karen decided to have an abortion, feeling uncertain about the prospect of having another child to care for, this one from a different father. Still, I had mixed feelings about her decision, on the one hand thankful she'd relieved me of the responsibility, the burden of helping to raise a child, on the other upset—no, disappointed that she'd taken from me the chance at starting a family of my own. With my twenty-ninth birthday a few months away, these things had begun to weigh on my mind. In the six months Karen and I had our secret affair, we'd gingerly avoided talking about her family, but for the brief warning she'd given me after our first night together, "I have a family now," or something like that. As she'd sat on the edge of the little twin-sized bed in my apartment's just-as-little bedroom, she ran a hand through her hair, let out a little sigh, and tossed a glance back at me, looking at that moment just like she'd looked a decade earlier when *the future* was something I saw as so distant it may as well not've been at all. But, that first night together, after she'd glanced back at me, I sat up in bed, reached for her shoulders, and kissed her on the back of the neck, feeling a shiver run the length of her spine like a little electric current, then fell back, gently pulling her down on top of me, for the moment convincing myself (and I think her, too) that things were the way they'd been.

It'd only been a few weeks since Karen had told me she was pregnant, and still it hadn't begun to show. Turns out, not every woman's stomach begins to swell in exactly the same way, and not right from the moment of conception. I wondered how many people she'd told. One night, we were together on her couch, she sitting in my lap with my hands resting, linked, on her stomach, and I swore to myself I could feel her abdomen expanding, even by the minute. Late on a weeknight, I'd asked her if Richard knew we'd been together before. "He knows," she said, "I told him." I asked if he knew I'd been her student. "I told him that too." My insides turned to ice. "He doesn't know we slept together when you were my student," she said, "I sort of made it sound like we started seeing each other after you graduated." A pause. "I didn't think he'd use it against me. I mean, what does it matter whether you were my student or not? It doesn't change the fact that I cheated on him. Now he's making me out to be some kind of…deviant," she said, "my lawyer says it's just talk but I can't help it." Then she was crying, and my inability to soothe her pain and anxiety made me feel more impotent than anything else. Months earlier, when we'd chanced a rare public meeting, after weeks apart she excusing herself from the family for one of those 'professional development' days teachers get, her son still at elementary school, her husband at work, leaving us free to be together. In that little spot between the trees where we'd gone a decade earlier, we met, in the summer's half-shade *making love* in the backseat of her little SUV, she leaning over while I took her from behind, awkwardly leaning over her, my chest on her back, my hands on the seat to either side of her head as I pushed my length inside her on every forward thrust, a little whimper escaping her lips, her body quivering as she came. It was just the way we'd once *made love* in that very spot more than ten years earlier, as though we were trying to recapture the magic of our *love*. But it was a fraud. We'd *made love* many times without using a condom, and the idea of using the pill was never broached. (Not that it mattered; messing with hormones and risking side effects just to avoid pregnancy seemed kind of sketchy to me, especially when condoms are easier and cheaper). I suppose conception was inevitable. That day, after having come down from our after-orgasm highs, I leaned over her, my bulk resting atop her sumptuous, curvaceous form, and began to nuzzle against the back of her neck with my forehead, prompting a half-moan from her, with the slight swaying of her ample hips beneath me betraying her arousal. For a moment, I think, we might've succeeded in our self-deception, and although that moment can't have been the moment when I'd made her pregnant, I'd like to imagine it was, at least then it happening in a moment of happiness.

At Karen's, a month or two earlier. Reaching for the pack of cigarettes on the table, she drew one out, set it gently between her lips, and lit it, drawing on it with a look of dulled, muted satisfaction, relief. "My parents died when I was less than a year old," she said. "Car accident. A drunk driver ran a red light and swerved right into them, smashed them head-on, killed them both. He lived though." A pause. "That's what the case said. So I was given to my mother's parents. But my grandfather died a couple of years after that. He was sixty-eight.

Lung cancer." Another pause. "A lifetime of two packs a day will do that to you." Drawing on her cigarette, she inhaled, then exhaled slowly, a thin tendril of smoke snaking from her lips, rising lazily, blending into the early-morning's sky. "I don't like it when you smoke," I said. "Me neither," she said, then drew one more drag off her cigarette before mashing it hard into an ashtray. "Then why do you do it?" "You haven't figured that out yet?" she asked. "I guess so," I said, "but I'd like to hear you say it." "Why?" "You can make anything sound like it's heaven." She laughed. "You don't really talk like that, do you?" she asked. "Sometimes," I said, sneaking a grin. A silence settled, a peaceful silence set against the gentle thrum of the city's streets fading in from just beyond the sky. "Keith..." she said, "please don't leave me." "Never," I said, without hesitation. Leaning over, I placed one hand on her thigh, stroking gently as we kissed, the foul taste of her cigarettes flooding my mouth. She never stopped smoking, not that I know of, and although it made her smell awful, I have to admit that when she leaned back into a chair on the balcony and let a wick of smoke loose into the air, she looked sly.

But after she'd finished her cigarette, she reached for another, finding the pack empty. At first, I was relieved, but when she took the empty pack, crumpled it into a ball, and threw it as hard as it seemed she could over the railing and into the alley, then let out a sigh. "I can't even tell my own son and my own husband the truth," she said, "I have to lie to everyone. If they find out you were my student ten years ago then they might accuse me of sleeping with you back then and they could use that to take my son away from me." "You can tell me the truth," I said, trying to sound supportive, "you can tell me anything." She laughed. "Yeah," she said, "like the criminal can tell the victim only 'cause the victim already knows." "I'm no victim," I said, then asked, "do you think I was a victim of something when we were together back at Eastmount? When you were my teacher?" She paused, then, in a half-mumble, said, "sometimes." "How?" "I don't know." "It's not like I dropped out or got hooked on drugs or got into gangs because of what we did back then." "I know." "I think I turned out okay." "I know." "I'm never going to be a doctor or a lawyer or an engineer but that doesn't mean I've—" "Keith," she put a palm on my chest, stopping me, "I get it. I shouldn't have said anything. I just needed to get it off my chest. It's fine." Caught up in myself, I couldn't, really couldn't see she was fighting herself, teetering on the edge. All it might've taken, then, was one last push to send her over the edge. In the months that were to come, she'd spend less and less time with me, devoting herself, I imagined, to her young son. We were on hold. I missed her, again reverting to that state of mind where I spent days at a time imagining being with her or re-enacting in my mind times we'd been.

Then, it happened. One weekend Karen was up on the slopes of Grouse Mountain when she took a spill and tumbled right into the path of an oncoming snowmobile, seriously injuring her knee, causing a torn ACL. At least, that's how she told me a day later when I arrived to visit her in the hospital, she in the medical ward. She was to be discharged in a couple of days, with strict orders to stay off her feet indefinitely, with surgery to take place a few weeks later. Her family surrounded her, those that were nearby. But I wasn't her family, I wasn't anything that counted. I was her lover, the guy who was at fault for her son's parents' impending divorce. I was the guy who'd torn apart her home and set her on the path to self-destruction, if only I'd known it, if only any of us had known it at the time. Still, whenever I visited, Karen was glad to see me, each and every time she leaning back in her bed, the hospital's gowns lumpy, bland, her hair unkempt, the bags under her eyes a shade darker than usual, but her white teeth bared in a smile that seemed very much hers. Whenever a spare moment presented itself, I went to be with her, but those spare moments suddenly became sparse, my employer demanding overtime which left little time for her, the hours spent circling between the warehouse and the hospital on the North Shore where Karen was kept. Sitting in her room, I dozed off one night, only to wake to Karen looking at me from across the room. "Go home," she said, "you're tired." Nodding, I rose and made for the door, at the last second coming face to face with him, the light blocked by his imposing figure that seemed so much larger than it was. In the middle of the evening, tired after a half-night at work, I didn't recognize him right away, but as I excused myself to step past him, I suddenly recognized not his face but the face of the boy standing next to him, that of Karen's young son, Lucas.

Richard. It was a tense moment, as we looked at one another, too long to be a glance, too short to be a stare. I'd seen him before from a distance, but never had we been in the same room as one another, not counting the time he'd walked in on Karen and I, of course. We said nothing as we passed each other, though out of the corner of my eye I could've sworn he'd squinted slightly and muttered something. But it was Karen who was the centre of attention, as she should've been. So I sat in one of the hard plastic chairs outside Karen's room, wondering what they were talking about, imagining myself inside, as if to be. Around an hour must've passed, when I was startled awake by the door to her room swinging open, Richard walking past. Standing, I wasn't sure if I should've said something, until he turned to face me. "So," he said, "you're Keith." "Yes," I replied. "What are you doing here anyways?" he asked. "I'm here for her," I said. He forced a chuckle and then he said, "...right." He turned and made down the hall towards the elevator, disappearing around a turn. He'd left Lucas with her, and I couldn't think whether to join them or let them be. Before long, Richard returned to pick up their son and visiting hours were over, and after kissing Karen goodbye I, too, left, both looking ahead to and dreading the next time I'd visit her in that stuffy, sterile room at Lions Gate Hospital in North Vancouver which was her home for the time being. It was a feeling so unlike the craving I'd once felt for her, all those years earlier when I'd been a confused and restless young man and she'd been a newly-minted teacher staking her claim to a career. The fear was still there, but dulled, muted, blunted. After having met Richard, whenever I visited Karen in the hospital I wondered whether I might run into him again, looking around each corner with a kind of anticipation that was altogether uncomfortable.

In the following days, I learned the accident had done no damage to the foetus that she'd already decided to terminate, that she'd skipped out on one appointment at the abortion clinic only to have another scheduled for the very near future. But at the time, all I could think about was whether she'd make a full recovery. Some others visited her, friends mostly, with a few co-workers stopping by for good measure. Still, even in the aftermath of her accident it was impossible for me to be anything but *the other*, the young-ish man who'd wrecked her home and ruined her family's life. When she slept, if I happened to be in her room then I'd watch, waiting for her to need me, only to doze off and wake, later, to the nurse's gentle but firm reminder that visiting hours were over, the thought occurring to wake Karen to bid her one last goodbye, instead it seeming better to let her rest. Every time, I'd lean in and give her the lightest of kisses on her cheek, then turn to leave, in the doorway stopping to cast a quick look back, just to steal a second or two more with her. She looked peaceful, so serene, in an odd way, her body all but covered in a billowy hospital gown. Even after her discharge from the hospital some days later, she couldn't return to work, as she was under doctors' orders to stay off her feet. This meant, in turn, she couldn't keep up with her responsibilities, relying more and more on others, Richard's dropping off and picking up of their son from her place soon happening more and more often, making it harder and harder for Karen to keep her life so compartmentalized as she liked. I should've seen it coming, but, looking back on it, I can see, now, why I didn't; in times like those you only see what you want to see.

It was around this time, I learned, that Richard had begun to drink. Though details were scarce, I imagine it started innocuously enough, perhaps with a glass of wine to relax at the end of the day, or maybe a bit of scotch while reading a book before turning out the lights and falling asleep. It's how these things always happen. Then, one night, as I was sitting in on the couch Karen's apartment with her in my arms, not long after her discharge from the hospital, he called. It wasn't her phone that rang, but mine, buzzing silently in my back pocket. I didn't think much of it at the time, in fact I didn't even answer it, but later, after I'd returned to my place for the night I listened to the drunken, rambling message he'd left on my voicemail, hardly recognizing the sound of his voice. Were it not for the fact that he'd identified himself as "the guy whose wife you fucked" I might've thought it was a wrong number. I didn't know he had my number. He must've gone looking for it. For a little while I thought to tell Karen, even to play the message over for her, but in the morning I deleted it and moved on with my day. It was something, I thought, she didn't need to know about. The next time she and I met, she looked into my eyes and asked, "are you okay?" For a moment, it crossed my mind to tell her. "It's nothing," I said, pulling her in close and kissing her, "I'm just happy to see you. It's been a long week." "I know what you mean," she said, before taking me into the night. In the months that'd followed Karen's accident, I began to think less and less about the past and more about the future, thinking when it all might've been coming to an end.

9. Past

Early in the eleventh grade, well after having been admitted back into Karen's Spanish class, there came a particular week right in the middle of the second term. Presentations on another term project began that day in Karen's Spanish, but this time she called on me to go first, watching along with the rest of the class as I stumbled in broken Spanish through a project on the Cuban national holiday commemorating the expulsion of the American-backed dictator Fulgencio Batista from the country (the project's topic was to be a national holiday of a Spanish-speaking country, you see). Then, again, as the class filed out at the end of the period, she called me over to her desk. But as I stood in front of her desk and waited for her to have at me, she, instead, sat silently, staring up at me, brows creased, exasperated look on her face. She`d caught me, again. "This is not the first time you've done this," she said. "I'm curious. Did you actually think you'd get away with it or do you just not care?" Shifting my eyes to the side, I muscled a straight look onto my face. "No, don't look away," she said. "Look at me." And then I looked back, our eyes meeting. Like a policeman interrogating a suspect, she seemed to let the silence settle until I just *had* to say *something*.

"I don't know what to say," I said, suddenly aware of myself. "Well, obviously you get a zero for this project," she said. "I understand." "That's it? You understand?" "What's done is done. I can't go back and un-cheat." "So you admit it?" "There's no point in denying it." "Well, I suppose that's worth something." She picked up a red pen and drew a one next to the zero she'd scrawled on the front of my paper before handing the paper back to me. Looking back up at me, she'd let the stern look fade from her face, replaced by something halfway between exasperation and amusement. "I'm sorry," I said. "You're sorry for cheating *again?*" "No, for yelling at you." "You've already apologized for that." "Maybe, but I still feel bad about it." "Don't." "Don't?" "Don't." It was a small moment, looking back on it, but one that marked a half-understanding between her and me. Feelings for her, *feelings*, had begun to make themselves felt in me, but had yet to grow into the full-fledged *love* that'd later come to mean so much. It might've seemed strange that she and I should've fallen *in love* with each other after having made everyone around us think we *hated* each other, but then, perhaps, it was exactly *because* we hated each other at first that we wound up falling *in love*. I don't know, it just seems *right*.

In the eleventh grade, in the hall on my way to the shower the next morning, there was Karen, at a distance walking with a folder clutched against her chest. We locked eyes for a moment, and then it was over, I having entered the changing room and begun shedding my sweat-soaked clothes. In the shower, I turned the tap until the water was piping hot, with a thick steam rising all around as I stood with my face tilted up, directly underneath the head, while my hands pressed flat on the stall's wall. The water flowed around my body, curving along the muscles in my arms and chest, falling in streams to the tiled floor, pooling around the drain, swirling slowly. At the age of sixteen and halfway through the eleventh grade, I suddenly couldn't stop thinking about my thirty-something Spanish teacher, images of her flooding my mind. In the picture I had of her, she wore a pair of jeans under a white blouse, and she stood with her hands on her hips, her head cocked slightly, and impish grin on her face. A sudden creakiness of the door to the locker room swinging open, followed by the sound of footsteps padding against the floor, snapping me out of my reverie. At once, I finished showering, dressed, and left, navigating the halls filled with classmates and teachers. Looking this way and that, I checked for Karen, and on seeing no trace of her began towards my first class of the day. But there she was, in the office, standing behind the main counter, still holding file folders and binders clutched against her chest as she spoke with another teacher. It seemed out of the corner of her eye she spotted me, quickly glancing my way, then back on the other teacher, making me realize I'd been staring. Moving on, I soon found myself in first period biology, staring listlessly into space, imaging the glance she'd given me, replaying it in my mind, going over every little detail in search of meaning. Our little game was nearing the beginning of its end. But I hadn't the slightest clue what we were doing, even as I was fully confident that I'd had it all figured out. That was then.

A year passed, then a week or two. It was the twelfth grade, early in March, when the skies had thinned and the sun had begun to show itself after months of hiding. "What a long day," she said, falling onto her couch next to me. We were in her apartment, the TV turned to the hockey game, though neither of us were watching all that closely. (The pros were locked out, so we were watching the local junior team, players around my age hoping to be drafted to the majors). After she'd said we needed to keep our distance from each other, Karen had spent the better part of a week avoiding me, but without actually avoiding me. We couldn't keep ourselves apart. We were in love. She sat back against me, her softness steadied against my bulk, wile my hands rested gently on her stomach, my palms feeling the sensation of her ample body even as she seemed so small. The following weekend, we'd found one another, again, she calling for me to join her in the act of expressing our love for each other, our bodies like objects to manipulate until we were as one. But when I arrived at her apartment, she took me inside, closed the door, and leapt on me, her hands clutching at the back of my neck while I carried her into the bedroom. Tossing her on the bed, I tore out of my clothes and set myself on her, the two of us like a pair of rutting animals; I came inside her much too soon. But it wasn't the point to make her come. We were there, I think, to just be ourselves, free from the expectations of the world. "It's been so long since I've been this tired," she said, "thank God for the weekend. And for my doctor." With my head, I nuzzled at her bare neck, kissing her.

Much had happened. In the week we'd spent apart, Karen had been seeing to her own affairs, using the time to continue sorting out her move across the water to the city of North Vancouver. At some point, and I can't remember when, she'd started seeing a doctor; she didn't say what kind but I figured out it was a psychiatrist. (Don't ask how I figured it out). I wanted to moot the idea of living together after I finished high school, but couldn't think of a way to bring it up. It was too awkward a question just to put out there. Wherever she went, I would follow, even if it meant giving everything I had just to be with her, just to smell her hair in the morning before she'd even made it out of bed, just to try at rubbing her feet at the end of too long a day, just to hike to the top of Grouse Mountain in the middle of the summer and stand with the whole city splayed out before us as we held each other in embrace, as though to declare our love to everyone in the world. It seems silly now, melodramatic even, but at the time it was simply and plainly how I felt. But not all things have that way of working out just however we want, just however we wish. In the aftermath of our *lovemaking* that afternoon, as she and I lay next to each other in her little bed it seemed she was no more at ease than the last time we saw each other, the tension having set itself into her muscles, only for a brief time relaxed by the pleasure of us having been together. But it was a tense moment, each second seeming linked by the drawn-out holding of an energy in place, like a little ridge of pressure about to collapse down the leeward side of a steep mountain's slope. All I could've done, it seems now, to relieve her of the indecision she felt was to give her some space. But, then, I was eighteen years old and *in love*. When you're eighteen years old and *in love* staying away is the one thing you *can't* do.

Her psychiatrist had prescribed her some medication, an antidepressant she kept in her washroom's medicine cabinet between shaving cream and a little bottle of mouthwash. It'd probably been there for some time before I'd noticed it; though I never asked, she'd later confess she'd been taking the medication since before she started working at Eastmount. It wasn't anything I'd done, nor was it anything anyone in particular had done that drove her to need the medication. It was just something that was sort of there. "Don't you think so?" she asked. I hadn't been listening to a thing she'd been saying, and thought, quickly, what to do. Nodding, I reached for her and let my hands fall gently on her sides, the softness of her body so unlike the hardness of mine. "Keith," she said, "aren't you going to do something with yourself after you graduate?" "I don't want to do anything," I said, pulling her close until I felt her stomach pressing lightly against me, "except be with you." She sighed. With all that'd happened between us in the short time we'd been together, the few weeks since we'd first *made love*, it was as though the stars had aligned perfectly, just to make it possible for us to be together. It might seem like a silly thing to say, now, but back then, seized as I was by the passion of the moment, I fully believed it to be true. And she knew it. Of course she knew it. She could tell how I felt just by looking into my eyes and drawing from the feeling out of me in a way no one had before and no one has since.

Leaning over, she tried at it again. "Keith," she said, "this can't last." "Why not?" I asked. "Keith..." "Can't we just be together? People will understand. We're in love. Isn't that all we need to be happy?" "No, no it isn't," she said, "we've had our fun, haven't we?" She sounded unsure of herself, her voice wavering slightly. Instinctively, I seized on her indecision, saying, "I don't want to have fun." "Yeah," she said, "I can see that." She stopped. "Keith, I've got a lot of things to take care of." The moment had crept away, limping under the cover of darkness, leaving each of us to ourselves. "It's not just the moving away..." "Then what?" "Keith, don't be like this." It was so hard to think of a way to convince her of the way I felt, of the things I wanted, that I fully believed in the notion that we were bound to be happy together. It was like an almost religious devotion, not to her, but to the *idea* of her and I together, which I mistook, then, for *love*. But it mattered little, as I laid my hands gently on her ample backside, kneading softly, slowly, as if to coax the tension out of her. Actually, I hadn't the slightest clue what I was doing, governed as I was by the vaguest of impulses, the feeling inside me that pushed me towards her. *Don't think*, it the feeling seemed to say, *just keep doing what you're doing*. With hardly two months left until I'd graduate, passing half my grade twelve courses by a hair's width, it was as though I'd charted a course roundabout, sure to arrive at my intended destination, whatever that might've been, after having made it all as difficult for myself as possible, and, looking back on it, I can see, now, that Karen, then, knew it just from looking at me.

"Keith," she said, "this has to stop sooner or later. If it doesn't, then I don't know..." Her voice trailed off, seeming to fade into the kiss I let hang on her lips for a half-moment too long, then leaned back slightly, she almost leaning forward as if to find the kiss again. Trapped up in Karen's little apartment, I suddenly felt suffocated, smothered by the walls surrounding us, and at that very moment I wanted to be anywhere but there. Rising from her couch, I thought to pace myself across the room, but Karen reached up, took my hand in hers, and gently pulled me back down. But when I looked at her, there was an almost-regret behind her eyes, dulling the light a half-shade or two. Seizing the moment, I turned back to face her, let my hands fall on her bare leg, and gently, gingerly worked my fingers in towards her robe, finding the sides of her thighs. But she wouldn't have it, taking my hands and pushing them away from her. Time to change tack, I thought, and did my best to seem as big as I could, flexing my biceps beneath the skin-tight white shirt I wore, trying to loom over her, but succeeding only in pushing myself away.

"I can't stand the thought of not being with you," I said. "I know you can't," she said, "but it's not going to be like this forever. It's just for now. You'll find someone who'll show you a good time and you'll have lots of new experiences with them..." "I've done that already," I said, "I don't want to be with *someone*. I want to be with you, forever." "That's sweet of you to say," she said, "but it's—" "I mean it," I said, "more than I've ever meant anything." A pause, as she seemed to take a moment to think. "Keith," she said, "what brought this on?" A direct question, one I couldn't quite answer even as I knew the truth; I just didn't want to lose her. Even as the better part of me *fully understood* in the way it did that ours was a *love* that couldn't last, there was that instinctive part of me that sought to defy myself and convince me not just that it *could* last but that it was *certain* to last forever. "Listen," she said, "I'm going away for the week." "Spring Break?" I asked. "Yes," she said, "I'm going to visit a friend for the week. I'll be leaving after school on Friday and coming back late on the Sunday before classes start again. I just need to get away for a little while." A pause. "Not from you," she added quickly, "I just need a break. Everything's been so crazy and I know a girlfriend who lives in Ottawa. It's been a long time since we've..." She didn't know and I hadn't told her that the very first day of that week was my birthday, which I'd looked forward to spending with her. We couldn't. Smiling, I told her, "I hope you have a good time," then wrapped my arm around her and pulled her in, kissing her lightly on the forehead. Having become used to keeping secrets long before, I said nothing more, already silently looking ahead to the week after when we'd have each other again. I wondered if Karen was leaving to be away from me, the insecurity uncomfortable, yet strangely satisfying, reassuring, as though it meant I was doing something right even as I was doing something wrong. It left me some time to think. If nothing else, I felt like I *needed* the time to think, as if I could've figured myself out just by taking to the streets and passing the road under the wheels of my car. But it was a fraud. In Karen's little apartment, in her little bedroom, atop her little bed, we *made love* again that night, slow, mellow, like we were savouring the taste of each other, awkwardly fumbling around one another, my hands shaking slightly as I held onto her, the night ending.

There was a sequence of events that'd led to me apologizing to Lisa, beginning sometime in the first week of the month of March, when I came home after a day at Eastmount and found them in the living room, she sitting on the far side of the couch while he sat in his rocking chair. Lisa took one look at me, smiling faintly, and said, "it's my day off." Randall ignored me. The TV was on, turned to a sitcom he liked, the sound of canned laughter rolling across the room. With the day of their wedding fast arriving, I couldn't help but feel like I was being left behind them. Karen and I didn't see each other at all that week. I skipped all of my Spanish classes, and she dutifully gave me zeroes for all the work due. No reason. We simply arrived at an unspoken understanding. If she let me make it up then it'd look like something was there. No, that wasn't it. There was more than I could've seen at stake, more she had going on in her life, and as the month of March wore on, it became increasingly obvious that I just didn't have the strength to keep away from her. Karen, if you're reading this, please know that I never meant to hurt you, I only wanted to be with you like a man wants to be with a woman. All that's happened, all the pain and sorrow you've been through, I never meant for any of it to happen. But you knew that already. You've always known. Things just have their way of working themselves into a certain *way*. It's impossible to imagine, sometimes, but it is.

At home, I'd become all but invisible, the signs of my life slowly evaporating. And then there was Randall. Boxes stuffed with paperwork were piled up in the living room, with hardly a table or seat to spare. It seemed that in the time I'd spent away from home he'd turned the place into his own little kingdom, installing himself as the head of the household without anyone's knowledge or consent. It'd only been some months since the three of us had come to live together, but it felt like much longer, as though the way of things had made itself permanent, reaching back into memory to trick me into thinking it'd always been and always would be. Whatever the case might've been, that night I slipped in late, quickly and quietly tiptoeing up the stairs, on the way to my room catching a glimpse into Lisa's bedroom through the door left slightly ajar. Life at home was rapidly becoming unmanageable for us both, and I believed it was all Randall's doing. Retreating, I left. Imagining, I pictured Karen and I lying on a beach in Viet Nam, cerulean waters lapping lazily at the bright, white sands. But I was seventeen, eighteen, I can't remember exactly when we were, only that we were, the secret nature of our affair, the taboo character of our *love* meaning I'd kept little evidence aside from the sensations committed to memory, sensations warped and worn by the passage of time.

At home, I'd begun to plot my escape. All I needed was a path to the freedom I was sure lay on the way out. Lisa told me she loved me. She told me all the time, just as she'd told me nearly every day when I was little. Crashing down the stairs one morning, I found Lisa, alone, in the living room, nursing a cup of coffee and quietly watching the news. After having read the letter Lisa wrote to Randall, I didn't know what to think, even as I knew exactly what to think. When Lisa came home from a late shift at work that night, I waited in the kitchen, pretending to poke around in the fridge until I was sure she'd shut the door, then turned and approached her. "You're still up?" she asked, then said, "of course you are." As she turned away and began up the stairs, I said, "I'm sorry." She stopped, and said, "for what?" "For everything." A pause. "It's not your fault," she said, then started back up the stairs, while I listened for the sound of the floorboards creaking beneath her feet, their bedroom door swinging slowly open, then shut, the night settling into silence.

At Eastmount, I managed a whole day, one solid day from bell to bell without seeing Karen, without walking past her classroom and chancing a look inside, without looking over my shoulder on the off chance she was there. It was just like it'd been through my eleventh grade, but this time with the secret knowledge we shared of our having been together. In the hall outside her classroom, I stood, one day, leaning with one shoulder against a locker not far from the door to her room, watching for her to pass, chancing at a moment's glance I knew would've been the highlight of my day, maybe hers, too. Then, we were in her bed, with the door locked and the curtains shut, the thirty-six year-old woman and the eighteen year-old man (boy?), *making love* out of the compulsive urge to *make love*, doing what we needed to make ourselves whole again. But it was a fraud. In the weeks that followed, Karen and I met each and every day, sometimes just to exchange quick glances, she looking me up and down in that surreptitious way she'd come to like, and for a time it was enough. Then, as we lay in her bed one afternoon she turned on her side, looked me in the eye, and said, "it's over." Though it wasn't to be the last time we'd *make love* before meeting, again, ten years later, from the way she rested one hand on the side of my face and gently, gently stroked my chin, it became like a faded, old photograph that's lost its colour, left out in the hot summer's sun so long it's become stale. In the end, Karen, that night, let us have at least one more time, before events in her life took a turn I never saw coming.

At Eastmount, we kept away from each other, quieting the rumours that'd been swirling around us for months. It was the middle of that weeks-long stretch after Karen had first ended our affair, and it'd become hard to force myself away from her. Days passed without either of us seeing each other at all, other than in class, even then sticking to the teacher-student routine. Whenever I ducked out of the gym each morning, tired, sore, I'd look up and down the hall, hoping to catch a glimpse of her, a disappointment setting in each and every time as I couldn't find her. In the shower, I'd stand directly under the head, shoulders slumped, hands pressed flat against the tiled wall, scalding hot water striking the back of my neck, streaming along the hard edges of my body, making an obscene gurgling noise as it flowed down the drain. And then I'd imagine her there. In my imagination she'd undress slowly, letting her clothes slide to her feet, then she'd step into the shower and rest her hands gently against my chest, my hands finding her hips, the two of us swaying from side to side. And then we'd *make love*, the power of imagination turning me into a much better lover, I can now see, than I was. In class, then, I'd look up from my desk and watch as she scrawled on the whiteboard, my eyes tracing a path along the curvature of her body, wishing I could've had her again, one more time, always another time. But it was a fraud. She'd changed. Wearing jeans and a loose-fitting blouse, she seemed to take the recent turn of events in stride, looking out over her class with a half-grin and a little glint in her eye, fielding questions from students with a playful tone of voice that was so unlike her. It was as though she'd been relieved of a burden. Weeks later, sometime in the month of March, I was crossing the parking lot in the pouring rain, arriving at my car only to find Karen standing nearby. When I opened my door and stopped to look right at her, she just looked right back. I nodded. She nodded. Then, we were off, she driving ahead while I followed the way to her apartment, parking, this time, in the alley, she there at the building's back entrance. Without speaking, we hurried up the stairs and into her unit, inside, pausing for an embrace. I was scared and so was she, but I don't think we were scared of the same things. It was the first time we'd been close for nearly two months and I was so scared it almost hurt. But from the look in her eyes as we fell into bed, there was a part of me that just *knew* she was scared, too.

We were caught up in ourselves. We couldn't see what was happening. I couldn't. If she could've, then she wouldn't tell me, other than alluding to it sometimes when we lay, together, in her bed in the aftermath of having *made love* again, each time maybe the last. "I thought you'd forgotten about me," I said, but right away I regretted having said it. "I couldn't forget about you," she said. By then we were sitting on her couch, half-talking, half-listening to the music she'd put on, some Michael Jackson, at a low volume. "I thought you'd started going out with someone else," I said, afraid even to ask. "A friend," she said, though she seemed uncertain. Some time passed. A few minutes, maybe an hour or two. "I love you," I said. "I know," she said. We kissed. Holding her lightly by her jaw with both hands, I savoured her taste, while she'd rested one hand on my leg, applying the gentlest of pressure while she stroked against my thigh, seeming to slowly work her way in. It was like we were sealed away in a little glass box, for the few hours we had together that afternoon time seeming to stop and everything else fading to a distant blur. We *made love*, there on her couch, for a little while after just lying in each other's arms, spooning naked, her warmth draped across my body, her head seeming to sit delicately, perfectly atop my chest. In class the next day, Sylvia and Nazifa went to the front of the class, together, to ask Karen what her plans were for the weekend. She looked over at me for a half-second, just long enough to exchange looks, before she said, "just some work at home," nervously, then added, "I usually have pretty quiet weekends." But later, the next time we were together, I thought about it, mentally noting the quietness that'd set in throughout her little apartment, the same quietness that'd always set in every time we were together, and suddenly I wanted to say something, anything at all, just to break the silence. But neither of us could. It was awkward and unfulfilling. I wonder, now, if Karen, then, was as afraid of me as I was of her. Even as her weight lay on mine and it seemed as though our hearts were beating in time, there was still that bolt of fear tearing through my insides, twisting slowly like a screw, and if I could've left my body to get away from it, I would have. The following Monday, when that Sylvia and Nazifa asked Karen if she'd "got much work done on the weekend," Karen, again, looked over, not at me this time, but at the back of the class, just for a half-second, long enough. Sylvia and Nazifa giggled, then went back to their seats, whispering at each other all the way. By the time I'd managed to muscle the wide-eyed, thin-lipped look off my face, catching Karen, for the rest of the period, stealing a glance at me now and then, until we all left at the end of the period, on my way out the door looking back, looking on her as she'd turned to the whiteboard, wiping off the day's verbs, seeming to make it a point not to look back.

An interlude emerged. When the school year began, Karen would tell me later on, she'd made it her goal just to get through the year, to cope with whatever came at her. Whenever I went to her classroom after the last period of the day, there was always a four or five centimetre stack of work sitting on her desk by the time the last bell rang. She stayed late and arrived early. Through the winter, it meant she hardly saw the sun. It must've weakened her resistance. It must've drained her. By the time we'd first *made love*, it was more of an act of surrender, she'd later say. After I'd graduated, then we could be whatever it was we were to be, but she couldn't make it that far, giving in, her breakdown seeing us *make love* for the first time on that rainy afternoon in January when I was still seventeen. But I didn't tell her when I was to turn eighteen, and she continued not to ask, maybe preferring to imagine I'd already turned eighteen and made it not a crime to be with me. She could've found out easily enough, anyways, by rifling through some file folder in some cabinet in some room next to the office at Eastmount. But through the early weeks of March, that year, she came to look like she was in the midst of her own crisis, having taken to trying at avoiding me once again, leaving me more confused than ever. The next time we were alone, not in her apartment but her classroom, I said to her, "Karen, you've gotta let me in." But she just kept on working, without looking up from her paperwork, seeming to make it a point to mark a red tick against one page, then another, then another. Taking the hint, I left, coming across her in the hall once more, my eyes avoiding hers, hers avoiding mine, the blanked-out look on her face only just perceptible around the edges of view. And on reaching the end of the hall, just before turning down the main stairwell, without looking back some part of me *sensing* her looking down the hall over a sea of people.

Weeks earlier, weeks later, I can't remember when any of this happened; I'm just reconstructing it all from a memory that seems fragmented. A moment of clarity emerged, a moment I'll remember for the rest of my life as one where I managed thoughts so much like those of someone beyond his years, thoughts assembled in an orderly, mechanical fashion, thoughts that seemed to fall into place as though they'd been released from a height and allowed to drift gently, lazily to the ground. Karen was trying to let me back in her life, but without saying so. In her classroom, one day, I made sure to be the very last student to leave at the end of the period, on my way to the door looping around the room and stopping right in front of her desk, leaning in slightly and saying to her, "I still love you," under my breath. She looked at me. Trying again, I said, "I still love you," then paused for one, two, three before saying, "you're so fucking hot," a little lower, a little steadier, with the kind of even-keeled tone that belied the fear tearing my insides to shreds. "Don't," she said, and glanced at the door.

Nodding, I didn't know what to do next, pausing until she told me to leave. Though I didn't want to, I left, arriving home, walking right in and thumping up the stairs without checking to see if Lisa or Randall were home, the twisted knife of fear inside me only sliding itself from my stomach hours after I'd calmed down. Strange, I think now, to be so afraid of her after all that'd happened, after all the times we'd *made love*, after having bared ourselves to each other in ways I've never bared myself to anyone. In her bed, I can't remember whether it was before or after that day, we had each other, so much melodrama having built up a frustration between us, as I came inside her, shuddering, shaking, she just held onto me, clutching at me as though she was afraid to let me go. It was the little moments like that, when the slightest of movements and the lightest of touches said more than words ever could.

But events soon overtook either of us. Karen had been spoken to about the rumours swirling around us, I'd learn, first by a concerned colleague, then, as the rumours refused to die, by an official from the school district, with a rep from the teacher's union there to sit in. I don't know what prompted it. I didn't even learn about until Karen would tell me in the months after I'd graduated. At the time, though, I only wondered about her sudden distance, calling her, but never leaving a message, the next time we'd cross paths she shooting me a look from across the parking lot at Eastmount, prompting me to nod slightly, then wait until she'd driven away, out of sight before following her to her apartment, then letting myself in through the left-open fire escape, climbing the stairs, raising my fist to knock on her door, at just the right moment she opening the door and pulling me in. But later, after we'd both had the chance to calm, she said something I don't think she could've ever taken back. "Keith," she said, "I can't keep this up much longer." In the days that followed, whenever we had the chance, she explained part of why she'd suddenly become so distant, that she was at war with herself, the person she was pitted against the person she thought she needed to be. She didn't explain it using those words, and it's only in the years that've passed that I've come to understand, in the crude, fragmented way that I have, what was happening to her. At the time, though, I was controlled by the overwhelming need just to be near her, to take every inch she gave and turn it into a mile, the young man I was unable, then, to see anything but the chance for something more. But then, right around the time that I turned eighteen, a series of events began to take shape that would change all our lives forever.

9. Present

After I'd almost-moved to the States to live with my father, I finished the seventh grade and entered Eastmount for the eighth. (Karen had not yet started working there). That year, the Canucks made the playoffs for the first time in five years, and drew a first-round matchup against the heavily favoured Colorado Avalanche. When my father visited, staying at my grandmother's place in the suburbs, we watched as the Avalanche swept the Canucks, each game but the last decided by one goal. So confused and angry at only fourteen, I wanted to lash out any way, the only way I could. After my father had gone back to Texas, I told Lisa, again, that I wanted to live with him. This time, she agreed, but she insisted that I had to call him and tell him myself. Though I was only fourteen, or perhaps *because* I was only fourteen, it was a hard thing to do, on the phone the words just sort of creeping up from my throat. "My mum has said," I began, sitting on the bottom of the bunkbed I'd so recently shared with my sister, Sheila, "that I can...come and...live with you." By the end of July, two-thousand-one, months before the world was to change forever, I'd flown down to Dallas, moving into the little, three-bedroom ranch house he'd used to share with his second wife and her daughter but which seemed so empty, so airless, so unlike a place where people *lived*. Just a couple of months before the world was to change forever, the stage had been set for some of the most tumultuous years of my life.

After Karen had been released from the hospital following her skiing accident, there'd been a whirlwind of activity around her, little of it involving me. A few weeks later, the day of Karen's abortion came. Actually, the whole affair was, at first, almost anticlimactic. In the morning I picked her up and drove her to the clinic, dropping her off, promising, again, to be there when she was ready to leave. We weren't to see each other in the time between, and the hours offered a freedom to think, a freedom I hadn't made much use of in the months leading up to that day. Much had happened in those months, but little of it immediately obvious. The supervisor who'd once lectured me, who'd taken me to task for forgetting to fill out some little piece of paperwork had since decided to have it in for me, looking out for every little thing to nail me with, every punch a half-minute too late, every misplaced initial on some form mentioned. With all that'd happened since the day he'd lectured me, Karen's divorce, the pregnancy, Lisa's trying at putting her life back together, it seemed like so much harder to stand up for myself. He was right, after all. They're always right. As though I'm watching a movie, I can look back on myself and recognize fully that I was to blame for all my own problems, that every misstep, every act of disobedience whether deliberate or the result of an unlikely oversight was my own fault and no one else's. Then there were the little hints, here and there, that seemed to reaffirm my beliefs; one evening, not long after I'd shown up wearing my pink vest, Maya had asked me where I'd bought it, and when I told her the store she said, "my daughter needs one and I thought she might like one like yours," later that night, after I'd gone home, the thought suddenly occurring that Maya had been mocking me for wearing a pink vest. I even worked out the perfect comeback: make fun of her moustache. (I even imagined doing it in front of a group of people and getting laughs all around). This, as I held fast to the idea I'd been the target of a—well, not a *campaign*, but that there was something *about* me that led others to identify me as a problem to be handled, an issue to be dealt with where, in the rest of the workers, there was no such issue. Circular reasoning; I was being targeted because I was wrong, and I was wrong because I was being targeted. It recalled a conversation I had that day with Donovan, when we'd talked about the union's troubles. Someone had half-seriously suggested a walkout. But Donovan just said, "would you risk your job for someone else's?" I couldn't answer. There was still that little bit of spirit left in me that wanted me to say yes, but it wasn't as strong as it used to be. Maybe that's just something that happens as you get older. Maybe it's just something that happened to me. I wish it hadn't. At work, with our union seeming to work slowly in the background, I was left, with the others, to come up with my own version of what was happening behind closed doors, but with Karen about to get her abortion all I could think about was her. It might seem strange to recall all this in the middle of recounting the day Karen went in for that abortion, but I just can't help it. Maybe it's because it was this sequence of events at work that led up to, first, Karen's abortion, then a pair of shocks that'd destroy both our lives.

Still, Lisa, months later, after Karen had gone to the abortion clinic that first time. After having helped her move, there was still much to be done. "You'd think after all that I've been through I'd be experienced in dealing with relationships, but I'm not," Lisa said, "I don't really know what I'm doing." This Lisa admitted in a moment of weakness that came at exactly the wrong time. With the waiting period of their separation underway before the divorce could become finalized, Randall had taken to calling her at odd hours, sometimes three in the morning, sometimes just past noon, each and every time, she said, drunk. But this didn't register to me, then, as anything out of the ordinary; it's just what people *did* when getting a divorce. A crack, a snap, a blinding flash of light as I woke, early one morning, to the sound of the phone ringing, ringing, ringing, as I stumbled out of bed and fumbled for the light. The next thing I can remember is speeding along the streets of Surrey, ducking and dodging traffic, weaving in and out of lanes, running red lights as I chased after the ambulance rushing Lisa to the hospital. When I ran inside, I couldn't see her, eventually a nurse walking into the waiting room to tell me she'd been rushed into the operating room, with no word yet on whether she was expected to make it. I spent the rest of the evening sipping on coffee from a styrofoam cup and checking the clock on the wall every few minutes, wondering if I'd ever see Lisa alive again. It's an agonizing feeling I won't ever wish on anyone. But as the clock's hands slowly worked their way around its face and the hospital's waiting room filled and emptied and filled again with people, filled and emptied, filled, emptied, I slept off and on, the hospital's hard plastic chair hurting my back until I had to stand.

Weeks earlier, I picked Karen up from the clinic only to learn there'd been, in fact, no abortion after all. In the clinic, she was waiting to be showed into the room where it was to be done, when, as she put it, she became nervous and left, hastily cancelling the abortion literally minutes before it would've begun. It was so unlike her, to lose her nerve at exactly the wrong time, but, looking back on it, I can see, now, it was exactly like her. A year earlier, before Karen and I had reunited but after we'd been found in the shower, it'd become harder for me to make it through the day without *something* happening to drag my attention from the path laid out ahead of me. If it wasn't the isolation, then it was the pangs of loneliness that made me regret having gone to Karen's house that night, made me regret having been unable to just wait until the next opportunity presented itself. I recall one night, one of the few nights we'd spent together soon after her discharge from the hospital, sitting on her balcony, watching as the rain fell on the roofs of cars parked in the alley, down the street, the sound of a chattering, hissing rain drowning out the gentle thrum of the city that'd usually faded in from the sky. But we wouldn't talk about the abortion. We couldn't. Don't think this meant nothing to me; the part of me that wanted to have a child was only just contained by the part of me that knew it couldn't happen this way. It's a strange place to be. But we were both thinking about it. One look in her eyes, her stormy, murky eyes said what talk never could've. It was an open question, which neither of us ever answered.

After Karen's skiing accident and subsequent release from the hospital, she didn't return to work right away. Her son, Lucas, spent time with her, she'd told me, and from her awkward tone of voice I knew instantly what'd happened, reaching into my own memory to fill in the gaps left by her unease. Trading their son, week after week, had taken its toll on her, though, and after having been hurt while skiing she'd been under doctor's orders to stay off her feet, leaving her mostly stuck at home. Richard would drop Lucas off at her place, then picking him up each weekend, Karen's inability to drive making her unable to take care of their son during the week when he had to be taken to school in the morning and picked back up again in the afternoon. For the most part, I stayed away, working through the weeks, other than texting whenever I could having little contact with her while her family was in the midst of its disintegration. It was hard to tell, exactly, when I should've been there for her and when I should've given her and her family the space and the time they needed, wanting to be near her but, sometimes, understanding the need not to be. Through it all, she had yet to say whether she'd changed her mind on whether to abort our unborn child, and in my uncertain state I couldn't tell when (or if) it was appropriate to bring it up. So I didn't. There came an evening, I think a Tuesday evening, when, on break, I ducked out to my truck, called Karen on my phone, and listened as her disembodied voice invited me to leave a message on her voicemail, then hung up just as the beep sounded out. All I wanted was to see if hearing her voice after having not seen her for a couple of weeks would make me feel *something*, anything at all. It didn't.

After Karen's release from the hospital, following her skiing accident but before the date she'd scheduled for her abortion, events had taken a turn for the worse. The next Monday after I'd been talked to by that supervisor, he came to me in private and apologized, not for what he'd said but how he'd said it. Weeks passed, and the date of Karen's abortion arrived, after I'd dropped her off I milled about in the park nearby, imagining myself feeding the ducks like an old man would. Later that day, I picked her up; we sat together in the cab of my truck for a little while, saying very little, holding hands. The drive back to her place was quick, she living within a few kilometres of the hospital in North Vancouver, and that evening we spent together, the both of us standing on the balcony long after the sun had set, looking down the street, watching the darkness of the evening fill itself with the pale orange glow of so many streetlights, the sky overhead a blanket of billowing clouds seeming to be lit a dulled, greyed colour by the city's lights underneath. Still we said very little to each other, yielding to the sounds of the city fading in, the gentle thrum of traffic and the lapping of the tides. "Karen," I finally said, "why?" In the days that followed, Karen and I spoke more, but said less, until it seemed like a wall had thrown itself up between us. She never did explain why she cancelled the abortion that day, but I think I've been able to piece it together in the time that's passed. She was scared, of what I can't say, maybe of nothing at all. It's the same surge of fear that we all experience when we're doing something we know we *need* to do but which makes us so frightened and uncomfortable, like a survival instinct taking control from some primitive part of our brain. She was scared, of something, of nothing, and in my confusion, then, in trying to figure out *why*, I overlooked the importance of understanding simply that she *was*. It's one thing out of all this that I'd like to go back and do over. It might've saved her and me and everyone else a lot of heartache.

Karen's soon-to-be ex-husband, Richard, took a turn for the worse. Little of this I knew at the time, but I've learned about it after the fact, partly on what Karen told me her son had told her, but also partly on my own intuition (or imagination, if you'd prefer). His drinking became worse, costing him a day here, a day there, then days at a time missed from work. That's how it always starts. He'd come home with a brown paper bag carrying a couple of bottles of wine and a mickey of vodka, each and every night, drinking until he passed out, sometimes missing working the next day, sometimes staggering out of bed to get himself to the office, sometimes with hardly a minute to spare, sometimes a little late. Then, one night, he was caught driving while drunk, with their young son, Lucas, in the passenger seat. He spent the night in the drunk tank, and Karen picked Lucas up from the police station, keeping him overnight, interrupting what would've been a night out for us. But it was an interruption that needed to be made. Having gone home, I could only imagine what it must've been like for Karen to show up at the police station, dressed in an oversized sweatshirt and jeans thrown on hastily, her hair unkempt, her eyes bloodshot from the exasperation of it all. Strangely, as I lay awake that night, staring at the ceiling of my little apartment's bedroom while waiting for sleep to overtake me, I couldn't help but empathize with Richard, imagining myself not in his place but that of his young son, as I'd been so many years earlier when my parents were fighting over me. *This isn't what I wanted*, I thought, *when I was seventeen*. But I listened, thinking, recalling the way I'd pictured myself back then, imagining I walked along a dusty road on a dyke between two rice paddies on a farm in northern Thailand instead of a drab, grey, rain-soaked city on the edge of a country with a name like Canada. Then, there it was. Arriving at Karen's one Sunday afternoon, I was there to see her hand Lucas off to Richard, watching from a distance as she and her soon-to-be-ex-husband forced a politeness, I could tell for the sake of their son. Actually, I wasn't there, but I can, drawing on experience, imagine exactly as it went, fully confident as I was in the accuracy of my imagining, the next time I saw Karen the tired look on her face telling me I'd imagined it right. Lucas was the most important person in her life, and still she couldn't help but feel guilty for having forced him between his mother and father. It was an unspoken understanding, unlike all the other unspoken understandings we'd shared, even as it came close to being like the others, so close that if I squinted just right then I might've been able to confuse them. Don't think, just be whatever you are, right now. It's time to embrace the horror and let it all go. Looking back on the confident person I'd once been all those years before, it's hard to reconcile that person with the unsure person I'd become, the person whose tenuous grasp on his own life had become defined by things like his student loans and his credit cards and his truck. It happens when you get older, I think, it's part of becoming what you are. They take a young person full of ideas and hopes and dreams and they make him into a productive, functioning member of society, but, at least in my case, one who felt like he was always one bad day away from reverting to the person he'd been.

In my apartment, sometimes, I could hear angry voices and muffled shouting coming from the next unit over, but only when I stood in the washroom and listened just so, the voices carrying through the air vents and coming out through a grille along the washroom's wall. I couldn't pick out much, words like 'fucking' and 'fuck' being most clearly audible. Then there was the slamming of doors and the familiar sound of the back of a hand striking a cheek. Karen's son left to be with Richard for a few weeks on the island, leaving her and I free to have some time together, a freedom we'd had only in fits and spurts over the past year. But as we sat opposite one another at her little dining room's table, she seemed hardly able to lift her spirits, wearing the same half-blank, sort-of impassive look that'd come to be hers. In her son, Karen had something I couldn't imagine, the kind of longevity, the kind of immortality that came along with making part of herself into another person's. After the skiing accident, Karen had been prescribed painkillers; I don't remember which one. Maybe it was the combination of her antidepressants and the painkillers which pushed her to come to rely on the drugs just to get through the day. But then, one night, I wandered into her little apartment's bathroom, spotting in the medicine cabinet the empty bottles that'd held those very painkillers, some with their lids screwed on, others missing their lids, still others lay on their sides, only one in the front still holding any pills. It made me regretful to have broken up her family, a regret I'll never be able to shake; I don't think I should. After what she'd done, because of what he'd done, because of what I'd done, none of our lives will ever be salvageable, lost as we all are to the passage of time. If it seems like I'm being pessimistic, fatalistic even, well, I can't help it. It's just the way I've come to see the world. But we'll get to that later. For now, Karen, I hope you'll see things from my point of view and come to believe, truly believe I never meant you any harm, even if that's what I've wound up doing.

10. Past

In the eleventh grade, more than a year before Karen, then known to me strictly as Miss Thoreson, and I first *made love*, she'd come across the daily planner I'd taken to using as an impromptu journal, something I'd learned of only when she kept me after school one day, asking me to come to her classroom after the last bell. After the last of her students had left, she reached down into her backpack and drew out the planner, handing it to me as I stood in front of her desk. I don't remember exactly what she said, only that it was something to the effect of, "Keith, it's okay." But, at the age of sixteen, I blanked, saying nothing as I took the planner from her, then turned and walked out of her room. On the way out, I tossed the planner into the first garbage can I saw, then kept walking, making it all the way home before realizing what'd happened. The next time I set foot in her classroom, I thought, I should've just carried on as though nothing had happened, as though Miss Thoreson hadn't read some of the most intimate thoughts and feelings I'd ever committed to paper. A couple of days later when I made sure to walk into Spanish after most of the rest of the class had already taken their seats, I glanced at her once or twice, each time catching her glancing back only to quickly shift her look elsewhere. The seed had been planted. In the months that followed, it began to grow. By the time the summer between eleventh and twelfth grades had arrived, I was sure she'd come to feel about me just the way I'd come to feel about her. It was enough, for a little while, to make me forget—no, not forget, but fail to see the mounting problems at home, problems that were, then, gestating, Lisa spending her time with the new man in her life, soon enough to have him take his place in our family, a place he'd wind up refusing to let go without a fight.

But crisis loomed. In the twelfth grade, in March, hardly two months after Karen and I had first *made love*, and I felt as though I was failing in my goal of just making it through to the end of the year. There came a night, one night, when I bounded down the stairs at home and turned to make for the kitchen only to come face to face with Randall. There was booze on his breath. "Where the fuck have you been?" he asked. "None of your business," I said. "You live under my roof then it's my business," he said. "It's not your fuckin' roof," I said, then tried to push past him, but he leaned in and stopped me. "The fuck is your problem?" I asked. "You think you can just come and go whenever you want? That's my fuckin' problem." Lisa wasn't home. It was just him and me. This time, I thought, then, I wouldn't waste the chance he gave me. With one fist cocked, I took a swing, but halfway across the space between us I stopped, and suddenly became aware of myself. Randall hadn't flinched. He was laughing, a toothy grin on his face. But on my way out the door, later, I turned and said to him, "I hope you die," before walking out. When I returned, late, after a shift at the thrift shop, Lisa had already come home, and she was waiting for me, but instead of confronting me like I might've expected she waited until I'd gone to my bedroom before she knocked gently, then let herself in, leaving the door open slightly behind her before sitting on the edge of my bed, keeping as far from me as she could.

So late at night, the streets outside were quiet, their silence broken only by the shrieking of a police car's siren as it faded in, then out. "How have you been?" she asked. Her tone was guarded, but not confrontational. When I didn't answer right away, she continued, saying, "we don't see much of each other these days." "I've been working a lot," I said, thinking of Karen and all the nights we'd spent together. "Have you?" she asked. "Yeah," I said. A pause. The window's blinds rattled against the sill. Through the stairwell came the sound of the fridge opening, a bottle's cap screwing open, the cracking of ice cubes from a tray. "I tried to call you the other day," she said, "but you didn't pick up. I tried the thrift store but they said you weren't there. You didn't come home that night. I was worried. I almost called the police. But then you came home, the next morning." Another pause, this time long and awkward. She seemed to be expecting me to say something, maybe even something that we both knew wasn't true, but instead I let the silence linger. "Sometimes it seems like you don't even live here anymore," she said. "I thought you said you wanted me to move out," I said. "Yeah, I guess I did say that," she said, looking away, a half-exasperated look crossing her face for a moment, but only for a moment before she seemed to let it disappear, replaced by a look I couldn't understand. But she wasn't angry. While I sat sideways on an old wooden chair pulled out from my bedroom's desk with one arm resting on the chair's backrest and my hands linked together by my intertwined fingers, Lisa had bunched up the edge of my bedspread in her fists, but must've realized herself as I looked, letting the bedspread go and bringing her hands to rest on her thighs. It was jarring to see her that way, so indecisive and afraid, so unlike the Lisa who'd been fighting against something for as long as I could remember, since, I suspect, even before I was born. But it was a rare lapse, and even as she was in the middle of trying at making peace she seemed to realize herself, forcing a stern look back onto her face. Any other time and I might've seized on this indecisiveness, might've exploited the fact that she was at war with herself the same as anyone else might've been in her place, but that night I was caught off-guard, and could only think to say nothing, letting the awkward silence fill the room until she just had to say something, anything at all.

"You're just not around much anymore," Lisa said, "it makes me worry. Who are you spending all your time with?" "Work," I said. "You don't work overnight," she said, "are you...seeing someone?" "Not exactly." Another pause, and another unsettling silence. Just then, my phone buzzed with the arrival of a text, calling both Lisa's and my attention, and right away I knew it was Karen. But the phone was on top of my bedroom's dresser, closer to Lisa than me, and for a moment I thought she might've tried to reach for it and read the text, that half-paranoid feeling taking over. She didn't, though, instead looking back at me, cocking her head slightly and raising her eyebrows, as if to invite me to seize on the distraction and check the text, but I couldn't, or at least wouldn't, sitting right in that chair without having moved a muscle, working to keep my stance as relaxed and casual as possible, afraid to say or do anything that might've reveal the secret of Karen and I. It seems ridiculous, I know, that I'd eventually admit without much of a prompt to Lisa that I was involved, in the way that I was, with my thirty-something Spanish teacher, when, then, I worked to conceal it from her, but that's the way our family worked. You trust someone, and then you don't, and then you trust them again, without anything much having happened throughout to change the way things were between you and them. So much was about to change, and it's only now that I realize that the change had already taken place, and it was just me who'd refused, until then, to see it.

"Well, you should know that Randall and I are getting married," she said, "we've got a date picked. A couple of weeks from now. I don't know if you knew that already but there it is. We're going over to the island for the weekend. We're not..." she seemed to struggle on deciding how to say it "...we're not expecting you to be there. You don't want anything to do with it. We'll be taking the ferry over on Friday and coming back on Sunday." There was more, but I can't remember much of it, soon Lisa excusing herself, shutting my bedroom's door gently behind her, leaving me to sit, alone, in my bedroom, wondering what'd just happened. It hadn't been all that long since it'd been just the three of us, Lisa, Sheila, and I against the world. The next few days passed without incident. I went to school and to work, but said very little to either my classmates or my co-workers, even not bothering to spare much time for Karen, the usual little sideways glances exchanged in the hallways replaced by a cold stare ahead, the mornings seeing me in the weight room, working the strain from my body, pushing myself, with every rhythmic contraction of my muscles a burning sensation building in my arms, my biceps and my core, but I kept pushing myself anyway, pushing past the pain, feeding off it, until I couldn't stand it any longer and staggered over to a bench and slumped back against the wall. It was happening. I couldn't stop it. Randall had become an integral part of our home, I suddenly realized that morning in the gym, and there wasn't any way to change that fact, not that I'd tried; I'd just never expected it to last. At some point, I was sure, she'd become the woman I'd grown up with and kick him to the curb. But it wasn't happening. It wasn't happening. It was like I'd woken up one morning to find my family, whatever it might've been before, all but taken over. Karen had already told me she was going away for the week of Spring Break, but as the date of her departure neared, I spent those mornings in the weight room preferring to imagine she wasn't going anywhere.

In the eleventh grade, in the last week of classes before summer, I'd taken to *looking* at Karen from the other side of her classroom's window, walking along the concrete path outside, stopping at just the right moment to catch a glance at her as she sat at her desk. Sometimes, during the spare period I had that year, I'd walk past her window while she was in the middle of leading a class through a lesson, watching as she stood at her whiteboard, felt pen in hand, halfway through scribbling something when she noticed me, seeming to momentarily forget herself. But, then, she'd always realize herself, turning back to the class, awkwardly, slightly fumbling with then pen. That was then. Less than a year later, as I left the school's weight room with my muscles sore and tired, I thought to try it again, just to see what might've happened, just to see if her reaction would've been any different just because of all the times we'd been together in the last months. It was the last week of classes before Spring Break. After waiting for the day's first period to start, I wandered outside, through that very window catching her scribbling on the whiteboard, the cross look on her face not changing when she must've realized I was watching. The next time I tried, the blinds were drawn shut, and I don't think I saw then open even once for the rest of the year. When we were with each other next, she'd taken me into her bed, like all the other times we'd been together it was clumsy and awkward, but unlike all the other times we'd been together, this time it was clouded by the sudden realization that this, that each time could've been our last. But she wasn't angry, even though she was, as though each and every time I'd pushed her, even a little, had made it that much harder for her to maintain the lie that she'd resisted my advances. She'd pushed me back down on her bed before sitting on my midsection, reaching, taking me in her hand and guiding me inside her, seeming to tense up as she rested on me until our bodies were flush with one another's. She controlled the pace, whenever she did it slower and more deliberate, so unlike the awkwardness whenever I was on top of her. With her hands on my chest and her whole body held upright, she made short, quick strokes with her hips, each motion back and forth against me seeming to unwind the tension in her. It was over quickly. I came but she didn't. Afterwards, still with her lying on top of me, I let my mind wander, a sigh escaping my lips. "Keith," she said, is something wrong?" Looking at the ceiling, I wondered whether to tell her, wondered if she would've wanted to know. It's a hard thing, keeping yourself closed off from everyone around, trying to be someone you're not. It takes all your energy. It leaves you tired and sore. The temptation flared to let it out, and this one time I didn't want to fight it.

"It's not..." I began. "What?" she asked. "Things at—" "At home?" "Yeah." A pause. "My mother's getting married," I said. Another pause. "I don't know what to say," she said. "I didn't think you would," I said. "I take it you don't like the guy," she said. Looking back, I said, "what makes you say that?" It was a strange moment, one where I had no idea what to say next. It's always a strange thing, to show weakness—I know that's not the best way to put it, but I can't think of any other—to someone you love, but even then, to be afraid of it, as if there was a chance she'd run from me at the first sign of trouble. But it'd been that way all my life, even as a young child people avoiding me just because I was *different*, just because of things entirely beyond my control. It'd become like an instinct, to clam up, that instinct coming close to overpowering even the way I felt about her, the way she'd come to feel about me. But she knew me in ways that no one else ever has, or ever will, not from the things she'd learned about me or from the things I'd said to her but from the way she seemed to just look in my eyes and silently, wordlessly pull the truth from me as only she could. "Where is your father?" she asked, "is he in Texas?" "I don't know," I said, "last I heard, Edmonton." An awkward silence, like all the others, but seeming longer. Then, I reached over her back, took her by the shoulder, and gently rolled her off me, then turned and sat off the other side of the bed, letting my feet touch the floor while I gripped at the bedspread with each hand. But she leaned over, and rested a hand lightly on my back, at exactly the right place between my shoulders to send a shiver running the length of my spine, giving me away.

"Keith, it's okay," she said, "it's not your fault." "I didn't say it was," I said. "If it means anything, I know what you're going through," she said. "You do?" "Well, sort of." "How?" "You remember how I told you my parents died when I was very little?" she asked. "Yeah, but—" "And how my grandmother raised me?" "Yeah, but—" "I know, it's not quite the same thing, but it's close enough.

You go to school and they make you think that everyone else has a normal family and you're the only one who's different." "All my life I've been different," I said. "I know you have," she said, "and so have I." Turning back to face her, I thought to kiss her, but waited, she then resting her hands on my bare chest, seeming to lean forward slightly, kissing me not on the lips but on the cheek, then reaching around to pull me into an embrace, for a moment the two of us just touching each other, holding each other, together swaying slightly. But it couldn't last. Not then, but sometime in the days to come when we were alone in her classroom after school one day, we talked, casually, about her Spring Break plans to spend the week in Ottawa with an old friend from university. Thinking, I offered only half-seriously to give her a ride to the airport, but of course she said nothing, only, instead, looking at me with a sort-of sly grin that was there only for a moment before she muscled it off, in its place appearing a stoic, blank look as she turned her back to me and began packing some things up, folders, files, books, the silent understanding between us arriving that it was time for me to leave. So I left. But this time, I didn't wait for her in the parking lot, instead walking right to my car, getting in, and driving away, without looking to see if I could've spotted her. It'd been only days since we'd sat on the edge of her bed and had our understanding, again, but already I'd begun to feel as though we were further apart. I can't explain it. I just remember, now, that the act of having confessed made me, somehow, like it was something still to be ashamed of. If I had to *confess* something like that even to her, the thinking went, then that was proof; if it wasn't something to have been ashamed of then it wouldn't have needed to be *confessed* in the first place. It was distorted thinking, I can see now. My thinking's still distorted, but at least, now, I can see through the distortions and look on it for what it was. But as she left for the week, leaving on the day of my eighteenth birthday, I *still* only wanted to be near her.

We lay in bed, one night a couple of weeks earlier, after having *made love*, she seeming to bask in a warm, after-sex glow. It'd been soft, slow, mellow, she having taken me and laid me in bed before setting herself down on me, taking me inside her, her hips moving in long, slow strokes, I coming too soon but staying hard inside her anyways, she reaching down with one hand to the place where our bodies had joined, moving her fingers in quick, frenetic circles until she, too, came. In the aftermath, I looked down on her as she rested, half-slept, my eyes drinking in her luscious curves, her shapely hips, the sight of such a voluptuous woman enough to harden my erection again. Leaning over, I kissed her, and she began to stir. "Karen," I said, "don't move a muscle." But she raised a hand flat against my chest, pushing gently until I broke the kiss and put a confused look on my face. "Keith," she said, "we've got to stop this sooner or later. And I think it needs to be sooner rather than later." "Why?" "I've told you why." "Yeah, but—" "But what?" She'd sat up, the covers having fallen around her waist, her small, wideset breasts bared in the dim of the bedroom. "But I—" "Don't say it again," she said, "I don't think I can hold out if you keep saying it to me." It might seem repetitive, but it was, like I was slowly eroding her resistance to the idea of us being *together*, just as I'd, before, eroded her resistance to the idea of us *making love* at all. At Eastmount, the rumours had settled, but were there, lingering in the background, the whispers quieting whenever I walked past, the silence commanding attention. Each day I walked the halls between classes, sometimes making sure to avoid Karen, sometimes going out of my way to deliberately cross paths with her, if we weren't to be together on any given evening then the sight of her enough to sustain me until we were. But absent the most important of desperations, the halls themselves seemed to be lined with the feeling of loneliness. Recalling the times we'd spent the last year looking one another in the eye, for a split-second, I found myself standing in front of my opened locker, imagining there was, taped to the locker's inside, a little photo of Karen and I we might've taken in a photo booth at the mall like any other couple. Through the noise of class-change, it was almost possible to, for a moment, deceive myself into thinking my imagination was real.

Throughout the week she'd spend away, I'd sometimes re-enact our little conversations, the half-discussions and part-exchanges we'd had, given as I was to parsing every word, every glance, every inflection in search of some meaning hidden in plain sight. After I'd confessed to her the truth about what was going on in my home life, but before we'd *made love* a second time that night, she and I had taken to—not arguing, but as close as we'd come, back then, to arguing, sitting on the edge of her bed while we almost-argued over whether any of this was headed anywhere at all. "Try to see things from my point of view," she said, before asking, "would you risk your job just to be with someone?" "Absolutely," I said, without hesitation. She looked me over quickly, then forced a laugh said, "I don't doubt it," but in a sideways tone of voice. Even at seventeen, almost eighteen, I could see what she was thinking. "What's the point of having stuff if you're not happy?" I asked. "It's not about having *stuff*," she said, "or being happy." "Then what *is* it about?" I asked. "I haven't got a clue," she said. Back then, I took her admission as a kind-of vindication, but now, after I've gotten older, I'm not sure what to make of it, except to take what she'd said at face value: she didn't have a clue. Neither of us had a clue what we were doing. But at least she'd come to know herself well enough to be able to admit it, while I, at seventeen, almost eighteen, was still seized by the belief that I knew exactly what I was doing even as it should've been painfully obvious to everyone, except maybe Karen, that I was just making it up as I went along. She and I had that in common, at least, even if I couldn't have known it. It was all too real, but, at the same time, it was all so fake. When Karen left for Ottawa to spend her Spring Break with a friend, I looked ahead to her return as if it was years away, in the meantime my obsession with her leaving me completely blind to the crisis playing itself out right in front of us all.

By some stroke of coincidence, Lisa and Randall left on that same day, heading to the island to have their wedding on, I've since learned, a little acreage owned by a friend of one of Lisa's older brothers outside the city of Nanaimo. I wound up spending nearly all of Spring Break alone, working almost every day at the thrift shop, then coming home to a cold, dark, empty house. It wasn't what I'd wanted, it wasn't the way I'd ever thought I'd spend my eighteenth birthday. I almost want to make something up, maybe come up with a story about spending the day with Adrian, the lifelong best friend who'd forgotten the exact day of my birthday, but I'm tired of lying, Karen, to you and to everyone else around me. Though I tried to pass the week just by putting my head down and turning into the wind, it soon became hard to do so, the sudden loneliness imposed on me by circumstance making it seem like I woke up every morning with the end of the week somehow further away than when I'd gone to bed the night before. Then, a day before Lisa and Randall were to come home newly married, I went poking around one of the closets upstairs, finding on the top shelf behind a small pile of towels a grey case, unlocked, inside it a nine-millimetre handgun and some bullets. I'd never find out how or when Randall bought the gun; it wasn't the sort of thing I could just *ask*. It didn't matter, anyways. After I'd put the gun back in its case and the case back on the top shelf in the closet, I went back downstairs, having forgotten what I was looking for in the first place, and in the kitchen I looked at a calendar tacked to the wall, counting the days until Karen would be back. Still, the gun.

Look, I'd lived in a house with a gun before. In Texas my father had a little .22 pistol he took with me to the range and let me shoot even when I was just twelve or thirteen. When he was out of town, once, I'd wandered into his bedroom's walk-in closet and found it, in a case just like Randall's, just like Randall's the case unlocked. Back then, at only fourteen, I took the gun out of its case and played with it, at first just sitting on the couch with the gun in my lap, then, later, pointed it at the wall, the framed pictures and pulled the trigger, the gun clicking empty. Even once I might've pointed the gun at myself, pressing its muzzle against the bottom of my jaw and pulling the trigger, that satisfying click sounding out. It wasn't serious. It was like play. This time, though, at eighteen years and a few days old, I felt a kind of deadened realization, almost like a crushing certainty that I'd lost. This gun was bigger, heavier, and when I held it with one hand I felt a surge of anticipation. It was intimidating and it was emasculating. When Lisa and Randall came home the next day, rings on their fingers, I waited in my room until I was sure they'd left me a clear path to the front door, then made my way downstairs slowly, with each step carefully placed to avoid the little cricks and creaks in every stair, only to, on the last turn, find Lisa standing there, as if she'd been waiting for me the whole time. At once, I wondered if I'd left the gun out in the open somewhere, if she or Randall had found it and immediately realized I'd had it out, running through a checklist of excuses and explanations in my mind, finding none, opening my mouth to speak when she spoke first. "I'm sorry," she said. "It's not your fault," I said, without thinking. But it was, it was true. I knew it then, and I still know it now. I'd like to tell you, Karen, that it was the moment that marked the severance of that last, tenuous link between Lisa and I, when we became something unlike what we'd been. But, you know, I'm not sure anymore, if I ever was. There was never any one point I could've looked back on as having turned against me; it's always been one continuous blur.

But while Lisa had seemingly become a different person, Karen was still, to me, the same as she'd been, the week she'd spent away having made me feel, by the time we saw each other again, like we'd been apart for ages. That first Monday following the break, and we first saw each other like we'd seen each other so many times before, from across a wide hallway as I was leaving the locker rooms and as she was heading into the main office; although we were so far apart, it felt like I was so close to her but I couldn't just reach out and touch her. "Don't stop doing what you're doing," she'd said to me, once, as we were nearly naked, kneeling a few inches apart on her bed. She'd meant it as a reassurance, but, on reflection, I've come to think it was meant to reassure her more than me. That afternoon, Karen and I crossed paths in the hall, exchanging a glance that betrayed her conflicted state in a way only I could've picked up on, and instantly, instinctively I seized on her indecision, pursing my lips slightly, for a half-second almost blowing her a kiss, restraining myself at the last moment, the way her eyes, for a moment, widened only a hair's width telling me it'd hit her almost as a real kiss. But for the bolt of fear tearing my insides, it might've been one of those little moments I'd come to remember as something other than what it was. That night, we weren't to have each other, having agreed to keep apart for the sake of letting the rumours die, but as we kissed the feeling she put into the kiss made me realize, years later, that she'd already, in some place deep inside her, gone past the point of no return. The act of *making love*, to come later, was just that, an act. It's unbelievable, I know, that a teenager believes this things, that a teenaged boy (man?) could be *in love* as I was, then. But it's true. That night, rain chattered against the street outside, while passing cars sluiced through puddles of standing water, and I found myself in Karen's little apartment again. She'd brought me there with only one thing in mind, I knew it, and I knew she knew it, but still I was only afraid, just like she was. It was building, the pressure mounting, feeling like a sudden immersal in deep water. For all the pretense of needing to stay away from me, she couldn't make it a day without having me, without me having her again. It'd become like an addiction, for both of us. The evening was at hand. Whatever had happened to her in that week we'd been apart, the only thing that mattered right then was the smooth sensation of her skin against mine, of her curvaceous figure seeming to fit so snugly into the broadness of my shoulders and into the thickness of my chest.

Earlier in the day, during the ten-minute gap between classes, we would steal glances at each other from across the hall, just like the looks we'd been exchanging for more than a year, but now with a little twist, nothing I could quite *see* but something that made itself perfectly clear, the little twist in her eyes, the way the little strands of colour in her irises that I could pick out from ten metres away but that I don't think I could've seen if she'd been right in front of me, looking me in the eye. Sitting on the edge of the bed, I was only a half-metre apart from her. She stood in front of me, holding my hands in hers. My heart was slamming against my chest. She understood. She said something, I don't remember what exactly, but it was something like, "I shouldn't be doing this, but I just can't keep away from you." I nodded, trying to act as though I knew what I was doing. It was stupid to still be nervous and self-conscious around her, Karen, even after she'd crossed that red line months earlier and put her career in my hands, but, still, I couldn't help but feel that way. Then, she took a half-step back and let my hands almost-slip from hers, and she said something like, "this just never gets any easier." Then, suddenly, her phone rang, startling us both. She must've been thinking the same things I was. With one hand, she reached for the phone, nimbly extricating herself from our closeness, and at once were out of the room. Still sitting on the edge of the bed, I was suddenly alone in the bedroom, watching through the open door with a view into the living room as she sat on the couch, talking with the person on the other end of the line, every now and then nervously looking back at me, our shared glance seeming to make clear the understanding between us that neither she nor I knew what was supposed to happen next. We'd already crossed that last red line many time before, already made her into a criminal—no, into someone who'd broken the law many times over. But it hadn't, I realize now, made her any less uneasy about crossing that line again. There might've been more than one thread needling through the moment, but at the time I could only think to stay until asked to leave. But after I'd had a chance to process what'd happened, after I'd re-enacted the whole scene in my mind for the thousand-and-first time, I've decided it was the moment, that exact moment as she was on the phone while I sat on the edge of her bed, when Karen became irrevocably committed to the idea of being *in love* with me, just as I'd, months earlier, come to fall so hopelessly *in love* with her. It all seemed so *wrong*. Whatever she'd been through in that week away, I've realized in the time that's passed, it'd changed her, someway, somehow, it'd made her ashamed of herself, it'd made her feel more than anything else that she had to move on and try, again, to be an upstanding member of society, to be something she wasn't and to detach herself from herself.

"I'll go," I said, more to myself than to Karen, and rose, making for the door. "Keith," she said, the sound of her voice stopping me. Something happened next, but I can't remember what. She'd said, "this isn't what I'm supposed to be doing," but she'd said it half to herself, and at the time I'd thought she was talking about the rules against teachers being with their students, as if she could've *still* been divided against herself over that taboo after having violated it so many times in the three months that'd passed since our first night together. On her knees while I sat cross-legged, both of us on her bed, she leaned in, her hands on either side of me, the look on her face unsure. So close, I could feel the warmth of her breath against my face. She looked down, half-closed her eyes, and bit her lip. She was waiting for me to kiss her. But suddenly I was too scared, and felt the urge to step outside myself and leave the room. Kissing me, she pushed me back on the bed as we kissed, until I was lying flat on my back with her atop me, her taste flooding my mouth, she seeming to grind her hips down against my midsection, my erection straining against my jeans. It doesn't matter exactly what happened next. I won't say right now. That'll come later. Later, we sat, for a while, on the couch, in the warm, pleasant after-glow of having *made love*, as if to let the moment sink in, to let the mood settle, all the while that knot of fear in my stomach tightening, tightening, tightening until I felt like I was about to throw up. It was strange; she was so sure of herself, but at the same time she was so unsure of herself. The way her hands had nimbly reached inside the front of my jeans and unzipped them before pulling them down made it seem like she knew exactly what she was doing, even as those words, 'don't stop doing what you're doing,' made it seem like she was relying on me to overcome her own self-doubt.

We'd been through this before, and yet, then, it seemed like the first time we'd been together. Reaching for her shoulders, I pulled her back until we were eye to eye, then sat us both up, my jeans and underwear bunched awkwardly around my thighs. We kissed again. But then I became suddenly aware of myself. I was scared, so scared. But I wanted it. Twisting, I muscled her underneath me, the reached between her thighs and pulled her underwear to the side, my hands trembling slightly, then my palms coming to rest on either side of her shoulders as I clumsily pushed at her, missing the mark, missing again, about to try a third time before she reached down, took my length in her hand, and guided me inside her. Our *lovemaking* that night was like our first time together, built up like a thousand-volt charge, then over as quickly as it'd started. I didn't stay over that night, leaving an hour or two later. As I passed through the back door and out into the alley, I heard a window slide open somewhere above and behind. Looking back, I caught a glimpse of Karen watching, sitting by the open window with a look on her face I couldn't figure out for the distance between us. Days passed. I don't remember what prompted it, but in her apartment the next time we were together, alone, the thought suddenly occurred to say something to her she probably never thought she'd hear from me: "I want to be with you forever," followed by, "I wish I could marry you." She seemed taken aback, her brow furrowing slightly and her jaw tightening, but only for a moment before her look reconfigured itself into a thin-lipped grin. "It's sweet of you to say that," she said, after having paused for some time. "It's true," I said.

"Keith, don't—" "It's true." We were sitting upright, she still in her underwear while I was naked, my body only partly concealed from her by the thin sheets. In her little twin-sized bed, there was hardly any room for us to be apart, but, suddenly, it'd become awkward and uncomfortable for us to be together, with her sitting at the head of the bed on top of a pillow while I sat further down. Even in the dim, her blemished but tanned skin was visible. Her stomach stuck out slightly, and her breasts were held back neatly in the cups of her bra. With every breath she drew in, her stomach expanded and her shoulders rose. It all made her seem so much more *real*, as if the little flaws came together to make her something more. We talked a little while longer, before the night wound down, but, later, when I said to her, again, "I love you," and, "I want to be with you forever," she sort-of looked me up and down and then, in an almost-mumbling voice, said, "I know."

Then, it all began to come together. The next time we crossed paths in the halls at Eastmount, I deliberately waited until she was just past me, then made a trilling sound with the back of my tongue pressed against the roof of my mouth. But this time, she just kept walking, and I looked down the hall, watching as she turned a corner and passed out of sight, all without looking back at me. It was a small thing, but it wounded my pride a little. We saw each other later that day, in her Spanish class, but it wasn't until we were alone, again, that either of us had the opportunity to bring it up. But we didn't. Less than two full weeks after we'd first *made love*, and already I just couldn't control myself around her, at seventeen, nearly eighteen in full possession by the love I felt for her. And she understood. In her bed, under the sheets together, all it took was one shared look, not a glimpse but a long stare into each other's eyes for me to realize she understood the confusing, conflicting feelings pulling me in a thousand directions at once. But, whether she understood or not made little difference, I suppose, as it wouldn't have saved her if someone should've found out about our love. As she lay on her side, face resting by the cheek on a loose fist, I couldn't help but be overcome by a sudden honesty, and let it out. "I told someone," I said. Her thin smile warped into a frown. I don't remember what I was expecting. Maybe I wasn't expecting anything. But she seemed to take it well, almost as though she was expecting to hear it, sooner or later. What followed was a roller coaster from one peak to the next, each day bringing new surprises.

10. Present

After moving to the States to live with my father, I enrolled at the closest high school, a then-recently opened Hebron High School set square in the middle of a patchwork of open farmland boxed in by expanding suburban neighbourhoods consuming everything in their paths. Having so recently moved from Canada, I became an object of curiosity for classmates and teachers, in that thick-thin sort of almost-Southern drawl being asked about life in Canada, the most commonly repeated question being, "is it different?" But it was a good-natured curiosity, from a redheaded gym coach who taught the biology class I was in, to a couple of juniors I sat next to during the lunch period we shared. Theirs was a politeness that seemed altogether *Southern*, even if Dallas, Texas was cosmopolitan, metropolitan, not all that *Southern*, and their passing interest in my not-foreign origin made me different, but in a way that didn't threaten their way of life. I liked America, and I liked Americans, and I still like America and Americans. They're good people. They're kind and they're generous and they're tolerant. They might make mistakes, but then, we all make mistakes sometimes. Most of us make mistakes more often than they do. We should all strive to be as decent as them.

A few months after Lisa had called me and asked for my help, I waited in the hall outside the operating room, hoping against hope the doctor would come out and tell me she'd live through the night. In the meanwhile, Randall had already died. The police would tell me he died at the scene. The lights overhead buzzed and crackled. Nurses in scrubs walked past. Others, the families of patients I suppose, sat in the row of chairs lined up against the wall. Returning to my seat after having used the restroom I found it occupied, but by a young woman holding a little baby, and I leaned against the wall, resting my weight on my heels, closing my eyes just for a moment only to open them and find, suddenly, it'd become morning, a nearby window bleeding in the faint, light-blue early-morning's sky. Out of the corner of my eye, I spotted a lone nurse walking down the hall, and as she drew nearer I began to silently pray that she wasn't to talk to me, that she wasn't bringing news, that Lisa's condition hadn't changed overnight because, as I'd come to appreciate over the nearly-thirty years of my life, change meant something bad had happened, change meant someone, somewhere had made a mistake, meant something, somewhere had gone wrong. As the nurse walked up to me and asked me to talk, I thought, immediately, of a conversation Lisa and I had a few months earlier, not long after she'd called me. I don't know why it'd been so late in the year that she'd made the choice to try and let Randall get himself together before finalizing their divorce, and I'll never know for sure. She kept, or tried to keep secret the things he'd done since we'd moved her out, but I learned about them anyways, the harassing phone calls, the threats. But she'd wanted me to trust her to work through it; it makes me wonder why she'd asked for my help at all. I think she was still trying to get out from under his control, when she'd made that call still working her way out of her state which gave him that last influence to use to destroy her once and for all. If he couldn't have her, I think, he was determined that no one ever would, ever could again.

Lisa and I had sat down, once, for lunch at a little diner in East Van, not far from the Pacific Coliseum, old home of the Vancouver Canucks, still hosting hockey in one way or another despite its age. "I don't know if I've ever told you why your father and I divorced," she'd said, "actually, it wasn't his decision. I left him and we divorced after that. We'd just moved back down from Prince George to Vancouver and I'd just gotten a job. That's why I looked for a job. It was in the eighties when you could afford a little apartment on your own with pretty much any full-time job. So as soon as I started working and really got on my feet, I left. It wasn't easy. I don't think I've ever been more scared of anything in my life. You know, I was your age but I didn't have a degree and I didn't have a savings and I was just trying to strike out on my own for the first time in my life." The waitress walked past and topped up our coffees, though both were mostly still-full. "Your father wasn't happy when I told him I was leaving him. He didn't take it well. We..." She paused, and fiddled with her mug of coffee, rubbing her thumb lightly against the handle, seeming to draw close to touching the rim, the searing heat making her withdraw reflexively whenever her thumb drew *too* close. Then, there was Randall. "He came home one day with a new van," Lisa said, "he just, he gave me something to sign and I signed it. It turns out it was a loan

I couldn't afford for a van he wanted for his delivery business. My credit rating wasn't good to start with but that van absolutely wrecked it. And they came one day to take it back. Randall was out with the van but since my name was on the loan and I couldn't tell them exactly where it was, they called the police and had me arrested. When they got the van from Randall the police let me go. Randall blamed me for it. And he wasn't happy..." She reached for the side of her arm and seemed to shiver slightly, my imagination seeing the faint remains of a bruise halfway to her shoulder. It was all so much to take in. And, I couldn't help but think it was my fault for leaving her in Randall's grasp, for leaving her just so I could spend my twenties trying to find myself. I know it seems self-centred and egotistic to imagine these events all revolving around me, when I've learned, in the years since, that they always amount to the whole bunch of us revolving around a common centre.

"He wouldn't let me leave," she'd said, referring to my father, "he didn't want me to leave. He didn't want me to leave." As I'd been barely a year old at the time, I had no memory of any of these events; trying to picture them, I couldn't help but picture each of my parents exactly as they were in their late fifties, unable as I was to picture them in their late twenties when these events had happened. Childhood's strange like that, I suppose, as it becomes more and more clouded by the things you've come to believe in your adulthood. But that was *then*, when I was a young child. This was the *now*. As I made my way through the hospital's cavernous interior, leaving through the emergency entrance, taking in a deep breath, exhaling slowly, watching as the hotness of my breath blended with the bleak, grey sky. The day was beginning and I hadn't slept all night, an aching strain twisting from the backs of my eyes and a painful warmth flushing across my face. From across the city, that characteristic thrumming sound rolled lazily in, punctuated by the wailing of an ambulance's sirens and the bursting honks of a car's horn. After Randall had shot Lisa, he'd shot and killed himself, and although only a day had passed, already I'd begun to blame myself for not being there to protect her when she'd needed it the most. Still, I wouldn't tell Karen for a little while; from her point of view, I imagine, it was as though I'd just disappeared, prompting her to, then, ask why I'd suddenly become so distant, when I admitted to her what'd happened just a few days later she coming to the hospital and taking me in her arms and holding me close, and at that moment with my head buried in her shoulder and my tears burning like ice I felt small, so small.

But as Randall had taken Lisa from my life by force, there was Karen appearing uncertain whether to bring another into my life. The abortion. Weeks earlier, maybe it was months, I can't be sure, after Karen had walked out on her abortion only minutes before it was to begin, I'd wondered if it meant we were to have a child together after all. The life that was growing inside her, I'd put it there; it seems like something crashingly obvious, and it was, but the truth of it couldn't land until after at least some time had passed. "Karen," I'd said, one night, as we lay in her bed, together, "you don't have to do it if you don't want to." It seemed like the right thing to say. All I wanted was to make her feel better about herself, even as I'd come to have fallen out of love with her, something I'd not yet admitted but which I'm sure, from the way she looked at me, she knew. I still wonder, now, what she must've felt on realizing I'd fallen out of love with her, how cold and lonely it might've made her feel to know that the man for whom she'd destroyed her marriage and her family no longer *loved* her in the way she wanted to be *loved*. It's a feeling I'd never wish on anyone, even my worst enemy. Then, a few weeks later and just as she was becoming visibly pregnant, Karen went in and had the abortion, but without having asked me to drop her off or pick her up. At the time, I couldn't figure out why it made all the difference to her whether I was there, but, looking back on it, I can see, now, that it was an important step in her effort to strike out on her own. And as Karen became addicted to those painkillers, I was oblivious, but then she might've wanted it that way, as she couldn't decide whether to abort or carry the baby to term some small part of her taking those drugs day after day to try and induce her body to make that decision for her. If the baby survived her use, I think she'd reasoned, then it was meant to be, and if not, then it wasn't. Distorted thinking, sure, but the kind that you think is rational when you're under the influence of a disease like depression.

Over the night Lisa had been in emergency surgery, I'd slept off and on, a few minutes here, a half hour there, waking each time with the sort of tired, aching sensation that went along with having spent the night in a hard plastic chair. Still in my clothes, the dirty, ratty clothes I'd worn to work the previous night, I felt unclean, sweaty, suddenly aware as I was of myself. "Christ," I said to myself, muttering under my breath, "what I wouldn't give to have you here with me now, Karen." It seemed like such an odd thing to say, but as Lisa's life hung in the balance, I couldn't think of anyone else to reach out to, anyone else to seek solace from. Calling her, I let it ring once, twice, three times, until, at the last moment she picked up. "Keith," she said. But I said nothing. It was too hard to say anything. "Keith," she said again. I hung up. I didn't know what I was doing. I still don't know what I was doing. It was all so confusing, so disorienting. When Karen called me back right away, I answered, and told her, at length what'd happened. So far away, she couldn't be there, but before hanging up she promised she'd come as soon as she could. "Okay..." I said. "I'm sorry," she said. And then we waited, each of us for the other to hang up first. I know I said I'd not yet told her what'd happened to Lisa, but the truth is that both are true and false, that I still can't bring myself to simply and frankly admit that I never could forgive myself for everything that's happened. Then, later, she arrived, walking through the doors of the hospital's main entrance, almost walking past before looking to the side and spotting me. I don't know what kind of moment it should've been, except to say that I knew it shouldn't have been and wasn't a happy moment, but from the way she and I shared an embrace it was clear we were both tired, so unlike the people we'd been when we'd first met.

After Karen had gone through with the abortion, but in the months before Randall had shot and killed Lisa, little changed immediately between Karen and I. But it was the small things, the things only noticeable from knowing someone so intimately, so closely. Whenever we'd *made love*, she seemed to let go, letting me have my release, but having none herself, her body almost limp as she just held herself in place, when it was over laying back, staring at the ceiling with the kind of vacant look that made it clear she was lost in thought. It bothered me, to have become so incapable of satisfying her, of pleasing her in the way I once had, all the experience I'd had in the decade since we'd first *made love* completely wasted, the awkward, fumbling, insincere teenager I'd been so much more capable of making her *feel* good about herself than the twenty-nine year-old I'd become. We never talked about the abortion, about the child we'd almost-had afterwards, and as I lay next to her in the aftermath of our having *made love*, it seemed as though she was holding something back, refusing to let me all the way into her self as she once had so readily. It was a frustrating feeling. One night, after we'd made perfunctory, unsatisfying *love*, I rose from her bed, excused myself, and after the lightest of kisses on her cheek, put my clothes back on and left, driving all the way home in the late-evening's darkness, arriving to a cold, dead, empty apartment, life having so suddenly and so thoroughly lost its colour. It recalled the way I'd left, ten years earlier, the little apartment she'd lived in then, after having graduated from Eastmount and thought to carry on our affair only to see it fade into nothing.

Sometime through this all, Maya had approached me while I'd been working and thanked me for all my hard work, noting that I was consistently the fastest and most accurate of all the pickers she supervised; later, I'd come to think of it as a 'peace offering' of sorts. Where once I'd been able to simply work myself through the motions like a machine, smoothly, rhythmically, automatically, then, after all that'd happened, I'd lost my focus, the day disappearing into a brightly-coloured blur. In the Roadsters, there was only the illusion of solidarity, of unity, an illusion that stood only so long as it wasn't challenged, then shattering into a hundred thousand little pieces that glittered in the pale moonlight. That day, after having finished my shift and clocked out, I knew, right then, that I wouldn't be able to return until things were made right. It's what I would've wanted. The next day, I showed up, clocked in, and worked through the day, each contraction and expansion of my body's muscles painful, as though my innards had been set alight. It was all an elaborate fraud. There was no bargain, no deal to be struck at the last minute, no intent on either side to compromise.

The doctors worked through the night to save Lisa. Every so often, a nurse would appear in the waiting room to give me an update on her condition. "Will she make it?" I asked, every time. "We're not sure," the nurse said, every time. Eventually, I stopped asking, leaving the waiting room to get a cup of coffee from one of the vending machines down the hall. As I walked in slow, measured paces along the hospital's smooth, linoleum floors, my thoughts were divided between two imaginings, one where Lisa miraculous made it through the night, the other where she died right there on the operating room table. As I slid some coins into the vending machine and watched as a thick, black sludge poured into a cup, I couldn't help but be torn between the two, caught between competing expectations, never sure in which one the truth lay. As I walked back to the waiting area, sipping on the scalding-hot coffee, I felt a tension develop in the back of my neck, like my muscles had wound themselves into a knot, tightening with every step I took. It was an odd feeling, but not a feeling that bothered me, as though the tension had become like an old friend there to comfort me during difficult times. Arriving, my seat was taken, the hall filled on one side with others waiting for loved ones, on the other spare equipment left outside. With little else to do and no idea when the end would come, I left, stepping outside through the hospital's main entrance, the cold, winter's air sending a shiver running the length of my spine. Home, I went home, and waited. Karen met me, arriving at my apartment, and for the small time she was with me that morning, I felt a little better. But it was all an elaborate fraud, just as it'd always been an elaborate fraud.

After her abortion, what we'd been seemed to subside. That night, after I'd left Karen and driven home, I couldn't sleep, instead spending the night lying awake in bed, some part of me certain she, too, couldn't sleep, that she, too, lay in bed, awake. In the weeks that followed, Karen and I spent less and less time together, our meetings marked by the drab, dispassionate sex that'd come to replace the warm, sensuous *lovemaking* we'd once had. Where once we might've seen each other daily, our meetings became two or three each week, then once a week, our *love* seeming to wither away under a sustained assault from the forces the *real world* had mustered against it. In her bed, one night, we lay on either side, the warmth of her body felt across the narrow gap between us. My hand found hers, my palm so large atop the back of her hand for a moment before she pulled away. Turning onto my side, I leaned over, and ran my fingers lightly, gingerly through her hair, provoking only the slightest of twitches in her. "Keith," she said, "don't." It was the first time we'd seen each other all week, as she'd been with her son, and I'd been working overtime. "Please..." I said, "just let me kiss you, that's all." She turned to face me, and at that exact moment., although there was only a few centimetres between us, we might as well have been a world apart. We *made love* that night, but it was dull, unsatisfying. Afterwards, as we lay awake, staring at the ceiling, it became immediately obvious that our little game was nearing its end. With all that'd happened between us, it seemed a harsh, crushing sensation to realize the inevitable was upon us, that the way I'd once felt for Karen was lost.

Then, in the night one night three weeks later, came the news I'd been dreading. Lisa didn't make it. They'd lost her in the ICU after the emergency surgery had failed. Like a bad dream I couldn't wake up from, the days to come were hell, and it's only because Karen was there to see me through that I made it each and every day, through the day, from one to the next. Little did I know this was to come at the expense of her own sanity, her own safety, and, nearly, her own life.

11. Past

When Lisa had come back from the island a married woman, she'd come seemingly bent on reconciliation, but I, then, wouldn't have any of it, spending as much time as I could away from home, on the rare occasion when we were home at the same time going out of my way to avoid her, faking sleep in the late afternoon, waiting until I was sure she'd gone to sleep herself in the evening before tiptoeing out of my bedroom to the kitchen, every motion slow, deliberate, with the rehearsed silence I'd come to learn. And then she'd be there, standing in the doorway to her (and Randall's) bedroom, watching as I quickly and quietly made back into my own bedroom. It was as though she'd immediately realized her mistake, whether it was excluding me from her wedding or marrying Randall at all, and I'd determined not to forgive her for it. During their week away, I couldn't have expected she'd try to make amends, and I don't think she could've expected I'd reject her attempts, even though, looking back on the thirty years we'd been part of each other's lives, it was exactly what we should've expected, it was the only way possible for either of us to respond. But there, too, was Karen, away for that very same week, and as the weekend before her return slowly turned from one day to the next, I felt a growing sensation, like that held by a lovesick young man, a feeling very deep in my chest. I couldn't understand it, couldn't find a place for it, and so instead drove to the local community centre and threw myself into the gym, working myself tired, sore, working myself until it was late at night and an attendant poked her head inside and said it was closing time. She looked like Karen. So many women looked like Karen. I saw her everywhere. It's like that old cliché, thinking the woman you loved was just around every corner, waiting behind every door, and all you had to do was turn that corner, open that door, and you'd be with her again. It was an agonizing feeling. And yet, as the days rolled slowly past, each seemed to take longer than the one before it, in that way every day of my life seeming to become the longest, the most drawn out, the slowest to pass. It all seems so silly, now, but as I was *eighteen* and *in love*, it was just the way I felt. Reluctantly, I wiped down the equipment and left without bothering to shower or change out of my dirty, sweaty clothes, driving home to an empty townhouse,

Randall and Lisa having disappeared, conveniently, for the night. At Eastmount, like the teacher she was, Karen had ditched the tight skirt and the snow white blouse for a pair of jeans and a t-shirt, and had taken to letting her shoulder-length hair flow freely down, framing her smile and her brown eyes. It seemed like such a small thing, but it made her look so unlike the strict, prim-and-proper teacher we'd all come to know. Keeping up with routine, I continued to work out in the morning before classes started, but after Karen had come back from her week away I couldn't take to the routine, and soon fell into an inconsistent pattern, one week working out a couple of mornings, the next four, the next just one, the next every morning, Monday through Friday.

At home, Lisa had seemingly reappeared; as what she called a 'peace offering' she took me to a hockey game one night, but I spent the evening in my seat at the arena thinking only about Karen. Then, at Eastmount, all eyes were on us. Events began to mount. I had to see her, I had to see her right away, and with all that'd happened between us it seemed the days left were to take forever to pass. We saw each other again that first Monday back, in her classroom an hour after the day's last bell. It was like any other day, but as I strolled through the door, then turned and made at her desk, she looked up from a book to meet my eyes with hers, a quick moment passing between us. "Keith," she said, "what are you doing here?" "This is not a good idea," she said, "you shouldn't be here." "Then where should I be?" "Keith..." The door swung open, and another teacher, a fat, balding, glasses-wearing math teacher, poked his head in, looking at me, saying something to her, I don't remember what, then leaving, although I remember thinking he was waiting just out of sight for her to make a mistake. "Karen," I said, hardly audible, "please..." She sighed, but it was a sigh of exasperation, left to linger for a half-moment until it'd passed. Nothing had happened in the time since she'd come back, and that nothing had begun to make me feel empty inside, like I was lacking in a kind of sustenance, whether it was air to breathe or food to eat, I felt parched, tired. And she could tell. I could tell she could tell just from the way she looked at me. After having spent the week apart from her, nine whole days from Saturday through the following Sunday, I was going crazy. Even though more than a few of my classmates, Adrian included, saw us leave her classroom, I just couldn't bring myself to care, stampeding through the hall, down the stairs, and out the door, making across the parking lot directly for my car, all the while that heated *feeling* flooding my face and making it impossible to think. It was the same *feeling* I felt whenever I was too angry to stop myself from acting out no matter who was watching.

We left separately, she driving ahead to get there first, while I waited a few minutes before speeding after her, threading the gas as I ducked and dodged traffic, weaving in and out of lanes, arriving to find her already there. "Are you out of your mind?" she asked. "No way," I said. "Keith, don't do this," she said. "I can't help it," I said. "I know you can't," she said, "but this can't happen anymore. We had our fun and we got away with it—I got away with it. But this can't last." "Why can't it?" "Keith..." So late in the afternoon, the sun's warmth had begun to wane, and I felt suddenly cold. "Keith, I wish I could stop myself from being with you," she said, before seemingly realizing what she'd said, "I'm trying. This can't last. We've had our fun, but now it's time to—" "I love you," I said. She sighed. "I know you do," she said, "and I..." But she couldn't bring herself to say it, even though it was clear how she felt. More was said, but little of it meant anything, the clock running out on our time together, some small part of me accepting it was nearing its end even as the better part of me refused to accept it. It was later that night that I'd told her I wished I could marry her and that I'd already told someone about us. But with all the rumours flying around at Eastmount, and after Karen had been spoken to not once, not twice, but three different times by three different teachers about the way I was acting around her, about the things my classmates were saying had happened between us, it was a miracle she'd—we'd not yet been caught, I now realize. When Adrian approached me in the halls between third and fourth periods the next day and told me everyone had seen me stampeding out the door, it hardly registered. "You don't have to worry about me," he said, looking away as he spoke, "but you better watch it, man. She's hot, she's a babe. Everybody sees you hanging around her." At that moment, I noticed Sylvia and Nazifa out of the corner of my eye, the two walking past, seeming to stifle their squeals and giggles as they saw me, briefly, looking at them. Shutting my locker, I said, "I don't care what people see," and turned to walk away. "She might," he said. Through the rest of the day, I couldn't help but notice all the people looking at me, some part of me imagining every little glance, every half-second of incidental eye contact as an interrogation.

But at home, it seemed I was determined to spurn Lisa's attempts to reconcile. A night came, just days later, when I fought with Lisa, in the stairs at home, just a few weeks before she and Randall were married. We said things that couldn't be taken back. "You're just washed up," I said, not really knowing what I meant but thinking it was something clever or cutting. "I'll pretend I didn't hear that," she said, "now fucking get down there and apologize to him for what you just said." She pointed down the stairs, and although Randall was out of sight she clearly spoke as if he stood right beside her. "Not a fucking chance," I said, and turned to make my way up the stairs and into my room. But Lisa reached out and grabbed me by the elbow. Instinctively, I snapped back and struck out with my arm, not hitting Lisa but shaking her off. She must've lost her balance because she tumbled back, slipping, falling forward at my feet, a thud marking her knees landing. Things had gotten out of hand. We were collapsing into ourselves. I don't remember exactly what happened after that, not immediately after, but what I do remember is the wailing of police sirens and the slamming of car doors. There were police officers standing around me, outside, in a little circle. I think I recognized one or two of them. They escorted me back inside and handed Lisa another card for some counselling, then left. I think Lisa understood I didn't mean to hurt her, and it was probably her understanding the led her to keep Randall from killing me that very night. But as much as we all felt we couldn't go on like that much longer, the truth was that we could, because we were used to it, like dogs barking at cars, not really knowing what we were doing even if we were fully convinced we'd had it all figured out. It had to end. That night, you might expect I couldn't have just walked back inside, but that's just what happened, our fight suddenly ending, our fight's climax left for another time. It was like a state where you can be scream and pulling your hair out at each other one moment, only to carry on like nothing had happened.

If it seems like Randall, Lisa, and I were stuck in a war zone, it's because we were. It was three months until graduation, three months that, then, seemed to stretch out over so many years, and all I could manage to do was imagine myself right there in the middle of an October's afternoon, then back, again, as a small child staring at the black screen of a turned-off TV and imagining what it might've looked like to someone watching me if the TV was turned on. At Eastmount, I was there, but not there, stuck in some ill-defined place between either, Karen having reverted to Miss Thoreson once again, herself caught in the middle of a long and difficult transition from one part of her life to another. We rarely saw each other, passing in the halls every now and then, avoiding each other's eyes nervously; you know that feeling you get when you can just *tell* someone's looking at you even though you're not looking at them? That's the feeling I had whenever Karen and I crossed paths, even as I was sure she wasn't looking. Through the twelfth grade I wondered what she thought, but I wasn't to wonder much longer. Adrian was there, but caught in the middle of his own mad drive towards university and a bright future beyond he sometimes had little time for me. When Lisa and Randall came home from the island, they brought back their own little way of settling the peace. He'd talked about having owned a gun earlier in his life, but it always struck me as talk, just talk. I never thought he'd buy one. We were, for all intents and purposes, like a family, and over the coming days, the weeks, it became possible for me to walk through my own home without worry, without that knot of fear tightening itself at the pit of my stomach. Even, a few times, Randall and I managed to exchange a few words; he'd say "hi" to me when I came home after a day at Eastmount, and I'd ask "what's going on?" From Lisa's point of view, I imagine, it might've looked like he and I were *trying* to get along, even if we couldn't quite pull it off. And then I'd found his gun, the act of having come across it during a rummage through the closet turning everything on its head. Sometimes I wonder, now, if Lisa knew Randall had a gun, if I'd found it so quickly and easily but she never had. That's stupid. No, it's not. She knew. It was one of those little facets of life that we all completely understood but had to act like we didn't. Trumped up on fear, I'd managed to make it look and sound exactly like I wasn't afraid of anything at all, even as it must've been obvious to Randall, Lisa, hell, even Karen and everyone at Eastmount that I was afraid of *something*, though none of them could've possibly known what.

After that night when Lisa and I had fought, she left a little card on my bed, which I found the next time I came home from work. It doesn't matter what the card said, except that it contained a handwritten apology, for what I wasn't sure, and I'm still not sure. Look, it wasn't the gun I was afraid of. It's hard to explain if you've never been there, but you never really get used to living in a constant state of fear. You never really *learn* to live with a level of anxiety that becomes entirely unlike your own, you only get worn down by it. Scared, I became acutely aware of myself, standing in the hall just outside my bedroom, listening as the thumping and the stamping of feet and fists sounded out through the night. We'd never been through anything like this. Randall stamped up the stairs and past me, into their bedroom where he opened the doors to the closet, at once the thought occurring that he was looking for the gun. I don't know why but right then I feared for my life. But Randall hadn't done anything, and he wouldn't yet do anything. Everything had changed, yet it all remained the same as it'd been. The next time I saw Randall, he was sitting in the living room on his favourite rocking chair, sipping on a drink, muttering something to himself as though he was unaware that I stood just above and behind him in the little space where the kitchen met the dining room. He'd bought Lisa flowers, a heart-shaped box of chocolates, a stuffed teddy bear, and taken her out for a night to see Harry Connick Jr. in concert. If it seems sometimes that they were only fighting, that they never showed each other any affection, it might occur to ask why they were together in the first place. But that's not the point. I suppose it's just my own thoughts, looking for something that wasn't there, turning the pages of memory, fixating on the negative, choosing to ignore—no, to *overlook* the positive. The truth, whatever that might've been, was that for all the fighting, for all the crying, I know there were times when he made my mother feel *good*, and those times must've been *good enough* for her to stick with him through the rough patches. In the seventh grade, we made a little wooden model of the ancient Greek city of Sparta, with dust and dirt glued on, complete with a little temple at the centre; it earned me a rare A-grade. As Randall mellowed out over the weeks, I learned to check my fear, soon instead gliding up and down the stairs without let or hindrance, comfortable in my own home once again. The day after I'd run into Lisa on the stairs, I approached her in the living room, sat next to her on the couch, and apologized for having made her fall. "I don't know what's happening to me," I said, "but I'm really, really sorry." "Forget about it," she said, "I already have." A look. "Dinner's at seven," she said, "if you're gonna be around, that is." It was like an unspoken agreement had been reached, but without a clear line I could know not to cross.

  With less than three months left until graduation, I kept myself from Karen by forcing myself back into routine, every morning in the gym working my body in hard, rhythmic motions, covered in sweat, muscles burning. It was on one of those mornings when, after showering and pulling my street clothes back on, I ducked out of the locker room and walked down the hall, turning a corner to come face-to-face with her. "Karen," I said. But she looked past me and after a moment's pause walked away. As she stepped past me, I turned and said, under my breath, "you're so fucking hot." But she didn't turn back to look. Not yet. Then, the next time we were alone in her apartment, I thought to tell her I loved her, again, but as I drew in a breath and was about to say it, she interrupted my train of thought and said, "don't." You'd think I'd have learned a valuable lesson that day, when to tell a relationship was well and truly *over*. But, Karen, I have never, and will never think of our *love* as having ended, even though, after all that happened after we found each other a second time, we'll never speak to each other again. In love with my teacher, I found myself imagining running away with—no, eloping with her, taking flight to some side-of-the-road chapel on the outskirts of Reno, Nevada, followed by a meandering trip through places like Albuquerque, El Paso, and into Mexico, hitching from here to there, riding on buses with farmers carrying chickens in cages and holes rusted through their wheel wells, reaching the sea somewhere down there, standing on the edge of some white, sandy beach, the tides lapping at our feet. We'd spent the year of my twelfth grade carrying out our covert affair like we lived in a serialized drama, of the kind you'd see on in the middle of a Friday night on Showtime, meeting every time we could, like lovers trying to spend every last second with our bodies pressed against one another, out of a vague but impossibly powerful need to be together. We'd hold onto one another in the warm, pleasant afterglow of our *lovemaking*, she nuzzling gently into the side of my neck while I drew loops on her back with one finger, tracing a path along. Her ample figure, the smell of sweat and sex lingering in the back of her car or mine. If I'm making our sex seem more romantic and passionate than it was, then it's probably because I'm remembering it that way; at seventeen, eighteen, I was so possessed by the *idea* of love that I couldn't see what would've been plainly obvious to anyone else in my place. And it was.

Though Adrian and most of the rest of my graduating class were in the middle of planning the first few years of the rest of their lives, picking out universities and filling out applications, for me the near-future still loomed in the distance, seeming to be a lifetime-and-a-half away. He took the time, though, here and there, to hang by me in the halls when I was looking through my locker, somehow the voice of reason. (Straight-A student, I guess?) I never told him Karen, known to him just as Miss Thoreson, and I were together in the way that we were, but, looking back on it, I can see, now, that he'd figured it out, like everyone else had. I don't know how, but all my classmates seemed to somehow just *know* we were having a secret affair, while the faculty seemed clueless as ever. Nobody actually knew anything. It was like an unspoken rumour that seemed to live in the halls. There was a dance coming up. Karen was going to supervise. I was just going. In the days that lead up to the dance, Karen and I avoided each other, deliberately, plotting courses that took one another around the places we'd usually have crossed paths. In the morning, I spent time in the weight room, but made sure to leave exactly ten minutes earlier, ducking quickly across the hall into the showers, then again out to my locker. Months later, it was the last time we saw each other at Eastmount, after the dance, after the last day of classes when I sat, along with a hundred other students, in the gymnasium, among desks arrayed in rows for us to take the last of our provincial exams, English I think. She was of the teachers mustered into service to watch us, and as the rest of that year's graduating class wrote, wrote, wrote, I couldn't focus, checking constantly up at the wall where Karen stood, leaning against the mats, hands behind her back, seeming at once to lock eyes with me, but only for a moment before looking aside. On my way out, we exchanged glances, but for a half-second she seeming to look on me with exactly the kind of forlorn look she'd once sent from across a crowded hall between periods. Then I left, without knowing when, or if we'd see each other again, yet, somehow, sure we would, and despite all that'd happened I was sure Karen and I would be together forever.

11. Present

Then, a month or two after Lisa's sudden death, it happened. At work, I received a series of calls from Karen, prompting me to leave early and rush to be with her. She wasn't at home, but in the waiting room outside the ER at Vancouver General. Through a stream of tears and ragged breaths, she explained that Richard had been in a serious car accident, and Lucas had been in his passenger seat. They were both in emergency surgery. Though she didn't say it, I immediately knew he'd been drinking, and so it turned out to have been the case. At the time, all I could do was sit close to her with one hand on her back as I searched in vain for something, anything to say. Ten hours later, a doctor approached and told her they'd both died on the operating room table. She cried long into the night, only to cry again the next day, until she could cry no more, her eyes bloodshot and her face flushed red, her voice hoarse, raw, her hair a matted mess, lit cigarette hanging from her lips as we sat on a street-level bench, watching the traffic flow past. At her side, all I could think to do was let her lean against me as we stared listlessly into the bright grey skies. Weeks passed, and in those weeks she spent much of her days in bed, though she rarely slept more than two hours a night, and when she rose there was an ashen look to her, as though the light behind her eyes had faded, making her look entirely unlike the Karen who'd once been so familiar. She stopped working, and then she stopped eating. The woman I'd known as Karen Thoreson seemed to become lost in the blackness, the pain, the despair. It was a hopeless tragedy, and, looking back on it, I don't think there was anything anyone could've done to stop her from doing what she did next.

You know, Karen, I lied to you earlier when I described reciting the Pledge of Allegiance in Texas. It's true the practice began shortly after the attacks on New York, and it's true I can recite the pledge from memory to this day, but it's not true that I participated in reciting it back then. Though I was only fourteen or fifteen, I thought, then, it would've been wrong to pledge allegiance to a country other than my own; I wasn't an American, I thought, just living in America. But it wasn't about me. It was about them. They'd just experienced a national trauma, and in so openly refusing to recite the pledge I had the temerity to make it all about me. I shouldn't have done it. I should've stood, put my hand over my heart, and read along with the rest of second period algebra as the words boomed out from the loudspeaker each and every morning. I wasn't an American, but that's not the point. They're just words, words that, by themselves, meant nothing. It's the show of solidarity that would've meant everything. In times like those, it's the responsibility of every one of us to do what we can to help each other through. I understand that now. Though I as, then, only fourteen or fifteen, I can't fall back on that as an excuse. Even if I couldn't have been expected to know any better, questionable in itself, it's just not an excuse. It's never an excuse. It was a good fifteen years later that Richard and Lucas had suddenly died, and in a way, it was like a violent trauma that'd shaken Karen in ways that I, unmarried and childless, could never truly understand.

Some time in the year before, in that months-long stretch after Karen and I were walked in on by her husband and Karen's calling for me to come back into her life, I'd taken to getting up in the morning and drinking my coffee before it'd cooled, the weeks uncertain but for the gradual dulling of my mouth to the scalding sensation of black sludge flooding in. It was during these uncertain weeks that, one day, I received a call from a number I'd not seen in years. It was Lisa. "I'm leaving Randall," she said, her voice full of dread, "and I need your help." What followed was a sequence of events that would change all our lives forever. If I'd known Randall would kill her, then, I don't know what I would've done. I might've taken that gun from him when he wasn't around and thrown it through a sewer grate where no one would've found it, where no one could've used it. As I drove to meet Lisa for the first time after years of having not spoken with her, the road seemed a little bumpier, a little rougher than it'd been, the wheels of my little Ford Ranger seeming to find every pothole, every groove, every loose patch of asphalt until I couldn't help but wonder if I should've turned around and made back for home, if I should've pretended Lisa had never called, if I should've taken the easy way out. Sometimes, I still wish I had. If I hadn't helped her, she might not've left him, and though she'd still be stuck in an abusive marriage, at least she'd still be *alive*. I know that sounds like a terrible thing to contemplate, but I can't help it.

In the weeks leading up to Lisa's having called me and asked for my help, I'd been without Karen ever since her husband had walked in on us. In bed, one night, one of the rare nights we'd spent together while she was separating from Richard, I'd sat with my back against the headboard, she laying draped atop me with her head resting against my chest as though she were listening to the slow beat of my heart. Running a hand through her hair, I felt the smoothness, but noticed the grey having begun to take over, the split ends, the firmness having softened, the years having taken their toll. Earlier in the evening, we'd *made love*, but it was dull, lacking in passion, as though we were rehearsing a series of motions, she underneath me with her legs hooked around my backside, heels digging into my thighs, hands at the back of my head while I thrust inside her, moving against her, rhythmically pushing myself into her to the hilt, then withdrawing, like a machine. It'd become so unlike the times we'd *made love* all those years earlier, when I'd been a teenager, when I'd come too quickly, when she'd taken me in secret even though I hadn't the slightest clue what I was doing. Now, our *lovemaking* had become sterile, formulaic, fulfilling a need but never satisfying. It couldn't distract either of us, the way it'd once, and after it'd ended we lay apart, the silence awkward and stiff.

There was one person, though, who'd seemed to be happy that Karen and I were still together, in the way that we were. The last conversation Lisa and I had before Randall killed her took place when I was in my truck, parked in the lot outside work, late enough that the sun had long set and bathed the inside of my truck's cabin in darkness. She'd figured out that I was seeing someone, and although it was a month or two before Karen tried to take her own life, it resonated anyways. We were on the phone. She'd gone home from work, while I was on break. We'd taken to texting, but, for reasons I still don't know, that night I decided to call her after having not spoken to her in over a week. I don't remember who brought it up or what prompted it. She asked me if I was seeing someone, though the concern edging into her voice suggested it wasn't so much a question. When I told her, "yes," it felt like an admission of guilt rather than the elation it'd once been to tell someone. "Is it the teacher you had in high school?" Lisa asked. "It is," I said. "Do you still love her?" Thinking for a half-moment, I said the first thing that came to mind: "yes." It makes me ashamed that I lied to her the last time we spoke, that I'll never be able to do right by telling her it was a lie. A little lie, it doesn't matter. It's still a lie, to my own mother. She might not've been perfect, she might've made more mistakes than most but she's the only mother I'll ever have. It took me too long to appreciate it. If I could go back and do over the years we'd spent apart, the years we'd spent not speaking to each other, then she might be alive today. At least, though, it brought a smile to her face, she, maybe, happy at the thought I'd made something beautiful last. If nothing else, I'll take some small solace in having made her smile one last time.

But after Randall had shot and killed Lisa, I remember that I regressed, looking forward, but in such a way that was unlike the way I *used* to look forward, like I'd picked up some childhood toys and begun trying to play with them again, but instead of using them to conjure up magical fantasies finding myself just holding pieces of coloured plastic and making stupid noises with the back of my throat. But it's not the same. It can't ever be the same. Nearly thirty, I just can't muster the same power of imagination I once had, even just ten years earlier, as though the power has been taken from me, and all this is some vain attempt to pinpoint the exact moment when that happened. Driving to the ferry terminal at Horseshoe Bay, on my way to pick up an uncle for Lisa's funeral, I wasn't ready to let go, but still I had no choice. It was my fault, I thought; I was supposed to be there for her in her time of need. If only there'd been some reason for me to have been with her on that day, then I might've been able to stop Randall from killing her. But I chose not to be there. I chose not to be there for her when it could've made a difference. It's impossible to put into words the guilt I felt in the immediate aftermath.

After the police had finished their investigation into Lisa's murder, there wasn't anything more to be done. Randall killing himself after killing Lisa meant there was no one to arrest, no one to put on trial, no one to send to prison for the rest of his life. A few of Lisa's co-workers and her two older brothers were the only people besides me at the little service we held, on a rocky outcropping somewhere on the southern shore of Vancouver's Burrard Inlet, not far from the Ironworkers' Memorial Bridge. It fell to me to pour her ashes into the water. It's something we'd all agreed she'd have wanted. After the others had left, I stayed behind, watching as the late-autumn's winds pushed the water's whitecaps high, in the distance a grain-carrier ship pushing its way under the bridge and slowly out to sea.

12. Past

"You're making this harder than it has to be," Karen said. "What?" I asked. "You're making this harder on me," she said, "I can't be in love with you." I won't lie, Karen, it hurt me a little to hear you say it. But I asked, "why not?" without missing a beat. We were together, in her apartment, me having invited myself over without calling first, she letting me in, then, after having awkwardly, clumsily *made love*, talking but finding it hard to say anything at all. It recalled the way things were between us back in the beginning of the school year, when our *affair* still, for all intents and purposes, fell within the bounds of the normal student-teacher relationship, even if I'd already begun pushing at those very boundaries, taking an inch here, an inch there, until, some time later, it must've seemed to her she'd just suddenly woken up one day with her seventeen or eighteen year old student in bed next to her, without a clue how it'd happened or what to do next. At least, that's how I imagine it must've seemed to her, prompting her to, then, in April or May try to set things straight, talking as though she half-wanted, half-didn't to stop. It came as a shock, then, to walk into her classroom one Wednesday's lunch hour and see a substitute teacher in her place, Karen missing, her absence punching a hole in my day. She'd seemed to be absent more and more often as we'd fallen deeper and deeper *in love*, and as I'd taken note of her absence the thought occurred to me that she might've been avoiding me. But then, some months later after we'd first *made love*, she said it was true, she'd been avoiding me, but for all the right reasons. Every time she'd wavered, every time she'd given in to her feelings, there was a part of me that took it as a vindication. She'd tell me, "you're just no good for me." Then she'd kiss me, her hands exploring my chest, her palms burning hot against my skin. It was like a dream. She was either there or not there depending on the exact moment I checked, and each day until I checked it was as though she was both there and not there at the same time. But so late in the school year, there were fewer and fewer opportunities to check, to exchange surreptitious glances with her from across a crowded hall, to trade knowing nods. After I'd told her I'd told someone, she became more distant than ever before even as she seemed to fall deeper with each passing day.

After Randall and Lisa had married, not the day they came back but at some time in the weeks that followed, I began to plot my escape, half-seriously looking through listings for an apartment, finding none I could pay for on my own but looking anyways. That gun of his just made me want to do things I'd never imagined myself doing. There were moments when I thought to just grab whatever I could fit into my backpack and hit the road, without looking back, but whenever I felt close to leaving, prompted by some exchange with Randall, there was Lisa, standing at the bottom of our home's stairs or in front of the kitchen sink, looking at me with a kind-of regretful look, making me feel immediately ashamed of myself for having even thought about leaving her, alone, with him, even as that'd eventually come to be exactly what I'd do. And so, for at least a little while longer, I'd stay. But when I saw Randall, in the morning, he was on his way out the door, and from my bedroom's window I watched him walk with a half-trundling gait down the street, wearing a shirt and pants with holes and a pair of flip-flops, only to see him return, hardly fifteen minutes later, with a brown paper bag that made a clinking and clanging sound whenever he handled it, that day I staying home out of curiosity just to see what he would do. That day, I heard him answer the phone only once, and listened as he, in a low, forced voice, told the person on the other end of the line that he'd just gotten out of the hospital, this time after a devastating car accident that'd left him crippled, wheelchair-bound even, and after he'd hung up there was the sound of his chair creaking, footsteps across the floor, the swinging of a cabinet and the screwing open of a bottle, then footsteps back across the floor and the creaking of his chair again. Lisa would later tell me that some days were slower than others for Randall's little home business, and I'd stayed home on one of those rare days when he'd taken no delivery orders at all. And I didn't argue with her even though I wanted to do nothing but argue with her. She just had a tired, half-collapsed look on her face that seemed to plead even as it demanded.

But Karen wanted to know more. "I can't be in love with you," she'd said, and when we were alone together, again, it seemed as though she'd come prepared. Earlier in the day, I'd gone to her classroom after classes had ended in the afternoon, only to find her on her way out, satchel clutched under one arm, the other across her chest holding a binder tight. "Karen," I said. "Keith," she said, stopping. "Please," I said. But she didn't respond, and as she walked past me I noticed, out of the corner of my eye, another teacher in the classroom on the other side of the hall, an older, balding math teacher named Mr. Zimmerman, seeming to look at me with his brow furrowed slightly and his glasses about to fall off the end of his nose. "You're no good for me," Karen had said, and as I walked down the hall away from her classroom, I felt him glaring after me, suddenly, then, the realization hitting me just what she'd meant, the understanding occurring to me in the way that it could occur to an eighteen year old who had no idea what he was doing even as he was absolutely positive he had it all figured out. The next time Karen and I had each other again, after I'd invited myself over, unannounced, to her apartment, I sat on the couch with her square in my lap, our hands on top of each other's resting on her stomach, the tension refusing to unwind from her body, building, until she just had to say something, anything at all. "Who have you told?" she asked. But it wasn't phrased like a demand, rather like she was asking herself more than me. "Someone," I said. "Why would you tell me you've told someone if you don't want to say who?" she asked. We talked, but later that night, after we'd finished talking, I left; or at least, I went to leave, pulling on my leather jacket, stepping into my shoes, leaning to tie them when she put a hand on my shoulder and stood me up, turning me to face her, telling me, "don't go," then, "I'm not upset," though the edge in her voice suggested it wasn't true. "What are you?" I asked. "I don't know," she admitted, "but I need to know who you've told. You know what can happen if we're found out." "I know," I said, "I didn't mean to tell anyone, it just came out." "Still," she said, and at that moment I thought back to the balding math teacher, imagining on his face a look probably sharper and meaner than there'd been, Karen surely sensing my anxiety as she let her hands fall to mine, reaching, gently pulling me just close enough to kiss me. But she still wanted to know more. We *made love* that night, but it was unlike any time we'd *made love* before. She was stiff and tense. Her hips, her thighs moved in long, slow strokes against me, with her hands resting against my chest as she began to move faster, faster, faster. The bedsprings creaked in time with her movements. With each of her strokes forward she took my length inside her to the hilt, then with each stroke back she drew me out nearly all the way. Later, after we'd turned out the lights, I turned aside, sat up, and let my legs hang off the side of her bed, the soles of my feet brushing gently at the floor as I swung them gently back and forth, back and forth, back and forth. Then, as I thought to quietly leave, I felt her hand on my back, softly, the only sound that of her bedroom's blinds rattling delicately in the cold winter's night. She left her window open, she'd never before left her window open. She'd left it open for me. The sounds of the city floated in, that faint, lingering, almost-sound always rising from the streets, like a not-silent humming from a machine's gears. In turn, Karen revealed, at last, why she'd done what she'd done, why she'd chosen me, why she'd risked her career and her hard-fought and hard-won good standing in the community for me. I should've been able to piece it together on my own by the time we'd been together for months already, but then, at eighteen, I couldn't see Karen for the woman lying in bed next to me.

Angry at Randall, angry all the time, I wanted to kill him, no I didn't, I would never kill anyone, but I'd like to say I wanted to kill him, it makes me feel like I could've done something that would've stopped what he'd do ten years later. After their wedding, three months before I'd graduate from Eastmount, and things between Lisa and Randall had settled. That look on Randall's face, that look of total victory that, looking back on it, I'd probably half-imagined, it was a look I couldn't stand, a look that had a toothy grin and behind his glasses eyes as bright as I could ever remember seeing. But events had begun to mount. It was late March, Easter Sunday, and it passed without the small turkey dinner Lisa and I had usually shared, the only gift coming in the form of a card from Lisa, a handwritten letter folded up and inserted inside which read half like a tearful apology and half like an angry rant. Whether she wanted me to stay or go, I couldn't tell, so I came to believe she wanted me out of there even as she confronted me with proof that she wanted me to stay. Weeks passed, Karen and I seeing each other off and on, Lisa and Randall fighting, always fighting, a night arriving, sometime in April, in May, I can't remember exactly, the little details aren't that important. That night, while Lisa and Randall were watching TV, a sitcom's canned laughter floating up the stairwell, I snuck out, making it to the Oldsmobile, parked in the street, before I looked back, like a criminal on the run checking behind him for any sign of pursuit, seeing only Lisa peeking out from behind the living room's curtains, a half-second later she stepping back quickly, letting the curtain fall back into place, the night disappearing as I drove away. Looking back, I wouldn't have needed to sneak out; I could've just walked down the stairs and out the door and neither Randall nor Lisa would've stopped me. I don't know what I was doing, and I don't know what she was doing; we were imitating roles, like children playing house. As I drove to be with Karen that night, I was suddenly overwhelmed by an awkward and clumsy but blunt and powerful feeling, almost an expectation that I would come home the next night to find something had changed.

"Don't ever leave me," Karen had said, once, in a moment of weakness, her tongue maybe loosened by a glass or two of wine. Still she wanted to know more, and still I couldn't, wouldn't quite tell her, and still she couldn't, wouldn't quite demand to know more, as though she was afraid of pushing my boundaries further than she already had. It was a game, I've come to believe, a challenge. The game, then, was to get as close as possible without crossing the line; to share so many surreptitious glances and half-formed gazes from across a crowded room, to exchange so many thinly-veiled flirtations whenever we found ourselves spared a moment or two alone, together, all without breaking the rules. She stood in the office, behind the counter, next to the secretary when I walked in, a thin-lipped smile crossing her face as we traded looks. When the secretary turned and left for a moment to gather something off the printer, I leaned in and asked, "so, do you come here often?" She laughed, I grinned, and it was as it was. I felt a growing boldness, and soon it was as though I was drunk off love, every day saw me taking greater risks, bothering less and less to conceal my intoxicated state from those around me. So compulsively drawn to her, I let my stares linger, and whistled at her when we crossed paths, imagining a cloistered place where she and I were alone. Then, one day, I spotted her from across the parking lot, either of us on our way home. Spotting me, she waved, and I raised a hand to my lips and blew her a kiss. It seemed to strike her as though it were a real, physical object that'd crossed the space between us, as she wavered for a moment, then turned, sat inside her CR-V, and waited, waited, waited while I stood and watched from a distance. Driven by an instinctual desire to be *near* her, in the year's final months I began spending my spare block in her classroom under the pretense of seeking her help. Most of the time we were alone, and we hardly keep herself hidden from me. She'd sit at her desk, thumbing through finished worksheets with a red pen in her hand, listening as I'd feed her lines picked up from late-night talk shows and prime-time sitcoms. "You know," I'd say, "if I had a nickel for every girl I know who's as hot as you, I'd have five cents." And she'd laugh, a wide grin emerging from behind her usual straight-faced look, for a moment her day seeming brightened. But it was a fraud, you see, as I still couldn't quite admit to her how I *felt*, couldn't yet articulate the way I *loved* her, as every time I thought to try every muscle in my body tensed up and it suddenly became difficult to breathe. And then, she'd turn up from her work, that wide grin fading, flattening into a look I couldn't quite decipher, a look that seemed to encourage even as it asked to be relieved. These were the moments where an understanding passed between us, a recognition of the other's difficulty. Either one of us had the power to relieve the other's; I could've stopped giving her attention, and she could've stopped receiving it. We didn't. We couldn't. At the age of eighteen, I was in love with a woman I still couldn't just reach out and touch, who couldn't just reach out and touch me. We'd had each other behind closed doors many, many times in those months, but all I wanted, then, was just to reach out and hold her hand in public, without having to hide. So close to the end of the school year and my impending graduation, I realize, now, it was like a noose slowly tightening around us, but with only her to risk paying the price. But it never happened. She was found out, I've learned in the years since, but not by anyone who thought to do anything about it, not by anyone who saw fit to turn her in for the crime of having fallen *in love* with her student, me. Back then, though, I saw only black and white, right and wrong, with no possible reason anyone could think to stop us but malice, hatred, and recrimination.

Then, we were speeding along East Hastings, ducking and dodging traffic, weaving in and out of lanes, finally arriving at her place, she taking me by the hand and leading the way into her apartment, shutting and locking the door before turning back to me. Towards her bedroom we tumbled, shedding clothes, until she fell back, pulling me down, our bodies pressed against one another as our tongues danced, her hot breath mingling with mine, her taste flooding my mouth. As we embraced, I felt a bolt of fear rip through my innards, as though I was suddenly aware of myself. Then, I was inside her, the jostling of the bedsprings, the harsh orange glow of the streetlamps filtering in through the blinds, the harsh, rapid-fire rattling of the night's heavy rain against the window as the storm intensified, surging, reaching its violent peak as I came, Karen clutching my body tight against hers, she suddenly motionless as I writhed in place, seeming to whisper something indistinctly into my ear all the while. As soon as it began, it was over, Miss Thoreson the thirty-something Spanish teacher holding me against her, as if basking in the warmth of the moment. I came much too soon, just as I'd always come much too soon, but that wasn't important. As it was that awkward time when the year and begun to move past winter but hadn't yet swung into summer, Karen had taken to leaving her window open, but had left the blinds drawn shut, allowing the sounds of traffic rolling along the distant streets and of jets soaring through the skies overhead to fade in, as we were there the warmth of her body striking a contrast against the coolness of the air floating in, a tension in her body, the very same tension I'd felt before, each and every time we'd *made love*, except for all the times we'd *made love* when I'd felt no tension at all. After all that'd happened between us, after she'd put her job in my hands, I still, then, couldn't see beyond the moment. But then neither could she.

As I lay atop her, she stroked the back of my neck with one hand, rubbing in soft, slow circles, the room silent but for the beating of our hearts in time with one another. Beneath me, her chest rose and fell slowly, rhythmically, her skin warm, her small, wideset breasts soft, yet firm, my head resting on her chest as I listened to the gentle throb and pulse of her heart's beat. My eyes were fixed on some unseen point on the bedroom's far wall as I peered through the darkness of the night, looking at nothing, as though my eyes were glazed over and the room lay shrouded behind a thick, black haze. And it was making love, soft, slow, sensuous, as though our sex was an afterthought, an epilogue to the night's events. Then she asked, "are you going to tell me who you told about us?" With both hands flat on either side of her, I pushed myself up off the bed until we were looking each other in the eye. Still I wouldn't tell her, except to say that "it's no one at Eastmount." Then, just as she parted her lips to say more, I leaned down and kiss her. She kissed back, her hot breath mingling with mine, our tongues dancing as her taste flooded my mouth. Breaking the kiss, I lowered my head to her neck and planted my lips on the nape of her neck, nuzzling gently. "Keith..." she said, her back arching as she lifted herself up against me. "Keith..." With my hips I ground against her awkwardly until she reached down, took me in her hand, and guided me inside her, soon the lewd slap of flesh against flesh filling the air as we made love, again, like a pair of rutting animals obeying instinct. We *made love*, a second time that night, this second time slower, more mellow, but without the *feeling* that'd been there the first time, I just doing it because I *had to*, she just letting me have my way. Afterwards, I thought to say something, but it took me a little while to figure out what. "Karen," I began, "do you love me?" She sighed, but it was a sigh of half-exasperation, half-resignation, I think. It was such a simple question, and then, at eighteen, I couldn't understand why it didn't have just as simple an answer. She didn't answer that night, spent as it was lying in bed together, and in the morning when I left for home she still hadn't answered, leaving me more confused than ever.

At some point, Lisa clued into what was happening. I don't know when she figured it out. I'd been so caught up in my affair with Karen that she could've figured it out from the very first time Karen and I had *made love* and I wouldn't have known. But the first she'd brought it up was late one night just after I'd come home from a closing shift at the thrift shop, in the kitchen she approaching me while I poked around in the fridge. "You're never here anymore," she said. I gave no response. "Are you seeing someone?" she asked. Thinking,

I knew to deny. "Yes," I said. "Is it that Spanish teacher?" Lisa asked. "Yeah," I said. "Is it...is it just sex?" "No." "So she says she's in love with you?" "Yeah." "Are you in love with her?" A long pause as I couldn't figure out what to say, defaulting to the truth. "Yeah," I said, "I am." "Well," she said, "I'm happy you've found someone." Turning, I faced her, and in the dim, almost-dark of the late-night, she seemed a little taller, her voice a little higher. But at the time, all I could think to say was, "thanks." We might've talked about it a couple more times, once a few days later, and again, I think, with a week or so before the last day of classes. She never told anyone, she's since said, and I believe her. After having spent so long at each other's throats, she seemed genuinely happy that I had something beautiful in my life. It might not seem credible, that a parent, a mother wouldn't have a problem with her son's teacher having an affair with him, and it isn't. But that's what happened. We'd arrived at an understanding. But even as Lisa and I had arrived at our mutual understanding, it seemed Karen and I had begun to drift apart, a coldness having infused itself into the way she'd look at me from across her twelfth-grade Spanish class, the whites of her eyes dulled a slightly darker shade, the beginnings of crow's feet reaching from their corners, though I can't remember if it was just my imagination playing tricks on me, if she really was drifting away from me or if I've come to imagine that she was. The person I've become, in the years that've passed, would say that this is how relationships sometimes end, not with a bang, but with a whimper, gradually fading into nothing, until, one day, you just wake up and realize it's been some time since you last were with each other. But we weren't there yet. I wasn't there yet. And the young man I was only wanted to hang on, to draw out the feeling of being near her for as long as I could in the hope she'd come around.

In Karen's classroom, there between periods right as the students from her last class had gone, leaving me the first of her next class to arrive. I approached her as she wiped down the whiteboard, but she wouldn't look my way, not right away, until I was hardly a metre away. After all that'd happened, it seemed such a waste to simply walk away from each other. We'd gotten away with it, so far, and we had the chance, at last, to be like any other couple, to walk the streets holding hands, to finish each other's sentences and spoon-feed ice cream to each other on a hot summer's day in the park, a few weeks, hardly a couple of months away as we were from my graduation. It was all I wanted, a simple fantasy, nothing more. "Keith," she said, looking over at me, "not now." "Then when?" I asked. We were interrupted by the swinging open of the classroom's door and the squeaking of wet sneakers across the tiled floor. Instantly I was in my seat, binder open, pen at the ready. That period, as Karen had the class bogged down in review, I braved the occasional glimpse over at her desk, chancing a look to see if she was, in turn, looking back at me. But she wasn't. She couldn't have been. Through the rest of the day and on into the night, I thought to stop by her class and press the issue, but every time I tried she had other students there, leading them through exercises or just plain talking. By the time I made it to her door at the end of the day, she was gone. We weren't to see each other again until that night, in the meantime, at home, I laid out my clothes for the dance on my bed, then sat on the edge of my bed, pulled out my phone, and scrolled through the texts Karen and I had exchanged, reading them over, as if to find in them some inspiration for the night to come. Another week or two passed. We weren't to see each other in the intervening time, not outside her grade twelve Spanish and the little glances we'd share from across a crowded hall, those little half-moments again becoming the highlights of my day. It was all so confusing and disorienting, for me and, I could tell, for her. As the night of the dance neared and the rumours refused to die, I began to spend time just watching for her, in the halls at lunch standing against the wall at the top of the main stairwell on the chance she'd walk right up and allow that momentary eye contact, only to see her walk across from one end of the hall to the other; I might've just gone to her apartment, and maybe she was expecting me to do so. It was a challenge, I can see, now. She was to withdraw, and I was to pursue. It was an act. It was all an elaborate act. But by the time I'd realized what was happening, we were so near to the end of the year that there was little time left, weeks at most, to indulge her in the game.

In Canada, or at least at Eastmount, there wasn't anything called a prom; we just had a class 'winter formal' in December which

I'd not attended, and then a 'dinner/dance' sometime in May, not long before the last day of classes. Finally, the evening of the dance had arrived, and I found myself driving into the parking lot at Eastmount, for the evening students allowed to park in the faculty lot. Spotting Karen still in her car, I pulled into the space next to hers, she backed in while I parked front-first so we were close to one another, each of us having to look back slightly as our eyes met. Just as I shut the engine off and went to say something, she opened her car's door and stepped outside, walking away as she threw the door shut, leaving me sitting alone. By the time I caught up with her, she was halfway into the gym, and hovering just a half-step behind her I leaned in and said, "you gonna dance tonight?" At first, she said nothing, but when I kept walking alongside her, refusing to take the hint, she said, "maybe." But then I noticed another teacher, the same fat, balding, glasses-wearing math teacher ahead, and I veered off, at once making the connection that he might've shown up just to watch out for Karen and I, just to see if I might've tried something, just to see how she might've responded. A little while later, after watching Adrian and Alyssa arrive, arm-in-arm, I wandered in, walking around the edge of the dance floor before sitting on the bleachers, watching as the night settled in, looking across the crowd, hoping to spot Karen. She stood on the far side of the dance floor, leaning casually with her back flat against the wall, watching the handful of students bravely taking to the pulsating beat of the pop music that filled the air. It was dark, and a thousand little points of light twisted lazily across the walls, reflected by a disco ball suspended from the ceiling. As that first song faded out, Miss Thoreson looked over at me, a moment passing between us, one which I couldn't quite decipher, but which seemed like a cross between desire and distress. At once, I thought it might've been a mistake to be there, and sought something, anything at all to distract myself from her. In the time it took me to come to, she'd disappeared, and I looked around, hoping to find her, again.

Wearing a white dress shirt with the collar unbuttoned and the waist hanging freely over a pair of jeans with a plain black tie left loose, I didn't look altogether out of place. Most of the rest of the students wore formal wear, dresses, tuxedos, but, there were a few of us, mostly sitting around the edge of the dance floor, wearing our ruffled, crumpled clothes, half-looking like we'd just shown up in whatever we'd thrown on that morning. Then, I found her. She stood, then, near the punch bowl, by a table at the back, next to a teacher she looked to be making small talk with, the pair of them surrounded by students, some jostling for the punch bowl, others just sort-of there. Stepping towards her, I looked right at her, the whites of her eyes visible against the gym's dim light. As I approached, she turned to the teacher standing next to her, pretending to talk, only looking back to me when I stopped right in front of her. That fear welled up from the bottom of my gut, making me almost nauseous. The teacher eyed me up, then left, excusing herself, leaving Karen and I alone, surrounded by people. "Wanna dance?" I asked. "No thanks," she said, her voice guarded, "I'm just here to chaperone." "Are they?" I asked, and pointed to a couple of teachers who were dancing with each other. "Yes," she said. But she still looked confident in herself. Looking back on it, I wonder, now, what she'd expected to happen when she'd volunteered to chaperone the dance, if she'd volunteered at all, that is. Maybe she wanted me to make a move on her. Maybe she thought I'd have known better than to try. Or maybe, just maybe, I've considered in the years since, she was just there to do her job. Anyways, I saw it as a last chance to have her, just as I'd see every time we'd meet in the months that followed as a last chance, living so completely in the moment as I was at eighteen.

The song faded out, a moment of silence settling before another faded in, this one slow, loud, but sedate. Leaning in, I tried again. "Come on," I said, "one dance?" I don't remember what she said, or what happened next, but soon we were on the dance floor, in the middle of a thick group of students, all eyes on us as I rested one hand on her hip and with the other took her hand, awkwardly leading her in a dance I'd never tried. It's hard to say exactly, but it was like being sealed in a little cone, unaware of the crowd surrounding us, as though it was all some little fantasy come to life. It doesn't matter. I was a teenager and in love, and all I wanted was to dance with the woman I loved. But what did she want? Did she, too, just want to dance with her secret boyfriend? Did she, too, just want, for one night, or even for part of one night to imagine she and I were like any other couple? "This is not a good idea," she said, almost whispering, barely heard over the music even though we were so close, "this is going to get me in trouble." But I was too caught up in the moment to respond. The song ended. As we began to separate, for a half-second I pulled her in close and leaned down to whisper in her ear. "Are you busy later?" I asked. "I'll be home by eleven," she said, before quickly adding, "I've got an early morning tomorrow." Nodding, I took a step back, allowing her the room to breathe. We exchanged one last nervous glance, before I turned and made back across the dance floor, disappearing into the crowd. The night was nearly over, and I had only half an hour to wait out, but while I sat back on the bleachers I couldn't help but feel like everyone in the gym was looking at me. We'd only been together, in the way that we were, for a few months, and already we were hardly able to hide it from everyone around us. I wonder what she'd told herself, that night, to reassure herself that our little public display hadn't gotten her in trouble; there's no rule against a friendly dance with a student, even if he's a student who rumours say she's already having an affair with. But by then, I imagine, she'd been looking for any excuse, however flimsy, however much of a reach, to she wasn't to lose her career that she'd worked so hard for so long to achieve. As the night ended and the lights came back on, the crowd of students thinned out, most headed for an after-dance party at whoever's parents were out of town. Adrian approached, Alyssa in tow, and he asked me, "you coming to the party?" Saying nothing, I looked right at him. "That's what I thought," he said, and walked away, leaving me to wait out those final moments before I could safely head to my car.

That night, late at night in her apartment we *made love*, she on her back, clutching at my body with her hands, her legs clasping my sides while I moved against her in awkward, halting motions, her whole body seeming to shudder in time with my movements. As we lay together on her bed in the aftermath of having *made love* she seemed to fold into my body as she sat in my lap and leaned back against me. We saw a full moon rise slowly from behind a row of apartment blocks, an unusually calm, clear night allowing a view so rarely seen. "I've found a new place to live on the North Shore," she said, "as soon as classes end, I'm going to move up there. By the end of July." There was a soft, slow mechanical hum, like that of a lamp burning itself out. I don't remember what I said next, or even if it was me, but one of us said *something* to prompt our conversation towards its inevitable end. "This can't last, Keith," she said. "Why not?" I asked. "It just can't. We're just two different people." "If two people love each other, isn't that enough?" I asked. "I wish it was," she said. "We'll always have our memories, won't we?" she asked. "Do you really talk like that?" I asked. She laughed. "I guess I do," she said. There was a long pause, marked by the sounding of a ship's horn and the clanging of a train's carriage trundling along a track. "This can't go anywhere," she said, "we've had our fun and we've gotten away with it. It has to end so we can both get on with our lives. You need to think about university and all the stuff you'll see and do there and I need to think about settling down and having a family. It's just got to end. I can't believe I've gotten away with it. After tonight it's just too close. People were already talking. I'm going to get an interrogation about it on Monday. It's got to end. It's just too close. We've had our fun, haven't we?" The way she repeated herself left open the possibility that she, too, wasn't convinced, a possibility I pounced on, not out of self-awareness but on impulse. After the dance, after having made us into a spectacle, there was a part of me that still refused to accept we couldn't be together forever.

"I just can't be in love with you," she said. As I went to say something, anything at all, she said, "but I can't keep myself away from you forever. It's so stupid of me to feel this way about you. A teenager. It can't happen." "Karen," I said, "I never want to be with anyone else. You're the most beautiful woman in the world. I want to be with you forever." Look, I know how it might sound, but it's what I said, what I felt. Young men aren't supposed to think like that, but it's the way I thought, even at eighteen. If I'm being honest with you, Karen, it's still the way I think, the way I feel, it'll never change. "We're too different," she said, "you've got your..." she seemed to search for the right thing to say, "you've got your whole life ahead of you. I've just got bills and debt, you don't even know what those are yet." A pause. "God, I want you so badly," she said, then kissed me, then kissed me again, breaking the kiss to look into my eyes, as she touched the back of my neck with one hand an aching sensation spreading between us, "but I just can't do this much longer." "Karen, I love you," I said, "I don't think I'll ever love anyone as much as I love you. I want to be with you. I want to be with you forever," I said. "No you don't," she said, sounding like she was trying to convince herself more than me, "you don't want this, Keith, you just don't." There was someone else talking, someone falling back on years of experience, as though she found the idea that someone wanted to be with her was impossible even after it'd been shown. It was years of rejection, of being made to feel like an outsider that'd made it so she couldn't stand the notion of someone being *in love* with her. It was a feeling I knew, a feeling I still know. It's what made us more like each other than anyone knew. She said, "I swear to God, you're going to be the end of me." We kissed. We kissed as lovers, she the thirty-something woman and I the eighteen-year-old in the act of becoming a man. When I'd first met her, just weeks after having moved from Texas, we were complete strangers, and I was but a boy so confused, so disoriented, only to emerge three years later as a young man on the verge of taking the next step into the rest of his life, tumbling about aimlessly like a feather caught in an updraft on a warm summer's day. With only a couple months left until graduation, I suddenly couldn't help but feel I was letting her go, and that was something I couldn't do. But, I've since realized, if only I'd let it play out as it would then it might've lasted a lot longer. As Randall had come to take over my home, I felt like I had nowhere to go, and some part of me, I can see now, had been half-expecting and half-hoping to find my way into Karen's life in ways I couldn't understand. None of it meant anything, even though it meant everything in the world to me. Love, that's really how I think, it was then and it is now, I don't want to be with anyone, no, I want to find love, I want to fall in love with someone, I want a connection, I need a connection with someone who wants the same thing as me, just thinking about it makes me sad. Even back then, at eighteen, I had that with Karen, the thirty-something Spanish teacher from the North Shore. Sometimes I think of what it must be like for everyone else to just meet people and take those meetings and turn them into relationships; but for me it's the other way around. I've never really been *in love* with anyone but you, Karen, and whenever I think there might be someone out there I could *love*, it's just, it feels wrong. It's all wrong, it's all malformed, grotesque, but out of it came something beautiful, something we had that I'd never trade the memory of for anything in the world, even after all that's happened, even after what I've become. I wish I could go back and fall *in love* with you again, but failing that I wish there was *someone* out there who could take what I had to give. It's hard to go through your life feeling like you're sitting at a desk, looking out a window, and watching as everyone else passes you by. It's why you wound up marrying Richard, wasn't it? It's not that he was a bad person; he wasn't. He gave you your son, even if he wound up taking that very son from you (I know you probably still blame yourself, as you blamed yourself the last time we spoke, but I swear to you that if I'm sure of one thing it's that you were not to blame for your son's death). It was all one big mess. It came about because I just happened to move back to Canada right when you just happened to take that job at Eastmount and we just happened to fall *in love*. But I can't do it again. In the time we were together, Karen, whether it was when I was a teenager and you were my teacher or when I was in my late twenties and you were in your forties, I gave everything I had to you. There's nothing left to give to anyone else. There never will be anything left to give to anyone else. It's all gone. After all that's happened, I know we'll never see each other again, but if we do then I don't think I'd be able to fall *in love* with you again, a third time. There's nothing left. There'll never be anything left. It's all yours.

But, that night, the line had been crossed, not a line drawn by the law but by something deeper, something more basic. I wasn't interested any longer in things like the age difference, the law, her career, my family; it was as though something else was there, something that came from inside her that was the same as something that came from inside me. It's awful, but it's true. It seemed impossible to think of her as the prim-and-proper Miss Thoreson as I once thought of her, she having bared herself fully, revealing to me not only her body but also her soul, and making me feel like a real man. We *made love* that night, again, but it was slow, mellow, a footnote to the night's events, as though we were both tired of pretending. Afterwards, we lay against one another in the dull black and blue light of her bedroom, our bodies relaxing, conserving ourselves before embarking on the first day of the rest of our lives. At the time, I thought we were meant to be, that there was some kind of connection between us more spiritual than physical, that our *love* was something not consisting of our *lovemaking* but expressed by it, an essence connecting us on a level deeper, more profound than anything either of us would ever have. It might silly, now, to look back on it and reflect, but the teenager in me still yearns for the excitement of our secret liaisons in her little apartment, for the feeling of anticipation that grew from the need to see her each and every day. It wasn't the last time Karen and I saw each other, nor was it the last time we'd *make love* before running into each other by pure coincidence in that grocery store's aisle late at night, but to this day it sticks out in my mind as the last *real* time we'd had together, the last of the little moments when we were ourselves. It might seem not at all like what you'd expect a young man to think, to feel, but even at the age of eighteen I'd always been given to fits and bursts of melodrama, to the idea that somewhere in the world there was a little piece of happiness just waiting for me to find it. In Karen, I was sure I'd found it, and then, in the time it took the twelfth grade to end, lost it, as though it'd slipped through my fingers like a fistful of sand. As I sat in my car and went to turn the key, I caught a glimpse of her looking through her living room's window right at me. Raising a hand, I thought to wave, but couldn't, and we gazed at each other for a while until it seemed she just couldn't bear to share our gaze any longer. The next couple of months passed, and in the time it took them to pass all the feelings I couldn't control seemed to flood back, hitting me again in full force. Karen and I kept seeing each other. Of course we kept seeing each other. We were never found out. I'll never know exactly what kind of suspicion she'd fallen under at Eastmount. It's too late to ask, now. In the weeks that were to come, I'd show up at Eastmount to write my provincial exams, passing just barely. I recall sitting in the gymnasium, somewhere in the middle of a field of students all taking exams, while our teachers patrolled the floor. Karen was there, but she stayed at the front of the gym, leaning back slightly against the wall's padded mat, hands behind her back as she looked right at me. Amid a sea of people, we shared a moment, a silent understanding passing through our shared gaze, before I turned back to my exam and she swept her eyes across the room. Though it wasn't the last we were to see of each other before our first affair had ended, I couldn't shake the feeling that I'd done something wrong. I made sure to be one of the last students to finish, on my way out deliberately avoiding her, using the exit furthest from her, on walking outside into the summer's head making straight for my car and driving away into the afternoon.

12. Present

In the hospital, Vancouver General Hospital, there was a little room not far from the main entrance, a room I imagine the staff referred to by a name like 'the cooler' or 'the icebox.' It was in this room that Richard and Lucas were both taken after their deaths, and it was in this room that they were to stay until arrangements were made by their closest living relative, Karen. But she couldn't face them. Not after what'd happened. In the months that were to follow, I learned his family blamed her for their son's and grandson's deaths, seeing her infidelity as the cause of Richard's descent into a drunken depression; in their eyes she had all but murdered them. She couldn't bear it all. Some months later, Karen called me at work, her voice slurring. She'd taken an overdose. It dawned on me. She'd tried to kill herself. Frantically, I kept her on the line while I found another phone and called nine-one-one, directing the paramedics to her place. Leaving work, I rushed down the highway, talking, to her, to myself, choking on tears, halfway there her voice falling silent but the line still clear. At last, she was lying in a bed in the ICU at Lions Gate Hospital in North Vancouver, hooked up to life support, the next few days passing as I waited for her to open her eyes. She'd gone, in ten short years, from a woman in love with a young man to losing almost everything, lying in the hospital, clinging to life.

III

13. Past

After having graduated from Eastmount, passing from one milestone to the next in the blink of an eye, Karen and I kept seeing each other, off and on, for a little while, but as the danger had passed it was as though, for her at least, the thrill of it all had, too, passed. There wasn't any one event that marked the end of our affair, no one point that clearly and carefully delineated the boundary between 'together' and 'not together' for us. We just sort-of drifted apart. No, that's not what happened; it's what the adult I've *become* would've done, then. As that summer bled into fall and fall bled into winter, I kept working at the thrift shop, until the time came when Lisa and Randall told me I had to start paying rent. Shortly thereafter, I moved out, into a little place I found, sharing a one-bedroom apartment with a young woman from Ukraine who spoke two or three words of English and kept the bedroom to herself, leaving me to sleep on a couch in the living room, the summer's warm, sticky nights seeing me look out over the hedge running along the parking lot's far side while I looked forward to nothing but the next time Karen and I would have each other again.

At the dinner/dance, with Karen among the smattering of teachers there to watch, it was after we`d danced, after I`d invited myself over to her place but before we`d left. She mingled around the edges of the crowd with an older biology teacher, and it was only when a little Asian girl named Isabella roped me into a dance that I saw, out of the corner of my eye, Karen looking across the hall at me. We locked eyes for a half-moment, and it was a half-moment when the whites of her eyes seemed to gleam against the darkness and the dim of the hall. But then Isabella led me away, turning to grind her rear against my groin, the dance taking us into the middle of a pack of our now ex-classmates, the evening drowning beneath a thumping bass and a kaleidoscope of brightly coloured lights. But then it was over. Kicking at the ground, I milled about the hall's steps, watching the last of my ex-classmates make an end to the night, surreptitiously eyeing them up one by one, hoping that each swing of the door open might've yielded

Karen, only when the lights went out and the door was locked giving up and sighing inwardly, resisting the urge to draw my cell phone out of my pocket, leaving in defeat. But it wasn't over, it couldn't have been over, not after all that we'd done, after all she'd risked, even then, at the age of eighteen, I somehow *knew* it wasn't over, as if some kind of divine influence had taken over and filled me the certainty we'd be together again. It seems silly, now, to have been so easily and so completely given to fantasy, but then I was stuck in that part of my life when I believed, as we all believe at one time or another in our youths, in the notion of *true love* as something pure, something pristine, the notion having not yet been stamped out by so much experience. As I made my way down the street, I imagined myself walking towards Karen, each step forward, each second that passed bringing me inexorably towards *her*; it was as if I thought all I had to do was allow the passage of time, like we were still in the same space as one another, still walking up and down those same halls day after day, even though I was alone on that sidewalk, with only the pale, orange glow of the streetlights and the rolling of cars down the road to keep me company. A light wind picked up, tugging at the jacket I was wearing, and for a moment it seemed as though it might've been about to start raining even though it was the middle of July.

Like a dream you can half-remember right after waking up but which fades from memory over the day, the time Karen and I shared when I was so young has all come together in the years since, blending to form a mess of memories I can't quite sort out. After the evening had wound down and I'd waited everyone out, I turned for home, walking towards the main drag to look for the nearest bus stop. But as I turned to start up the street, along came Karen, pulling up in her CR-V, stopping to let me jump in before peeling off down the road. Maybe it was that night, maybe it was weeks, even months earlier, I can't remember; but then, it doesn't really matter *exactly* when any of this happened. In her bedroom she took me by the shoulders and pushed me onto my back, her hair falling around my face as she leaned forward and kissed me, for a half-second or two our lips seeming to come within a hair's width of each other, hanging, never touching, a thousand-volt charge building up, keeping us apart, but so close it was as though we were already there. With one hand she reached between us, took hold of my length, and delicately but surely guided me inside her, the act of our having *made love* seeming to, at once, lift a weight off our shoulders. That night, our *lovemaking* was soft and slow, then hard and fast, that familiar lewd sound of skin slapping against skin filling the air, until, as quickly as it'd begun, I came inside her, my climax marking the night like an exclamation point at the end of a long, long sentence. Afterwards—there always was an afterwards, wasn't there?—we lay in her little bed, the signs of her having begun to pack up her life all around us, the boxes on top of boxes, the little holes in the walls where nails had hung pictures, the indentations in the carpet pressed-in by furniture. Turning onto my side, I lay face-to-face with her, and for a little while we stared into each other's eyes, the whites of hers visible starkly against the darkness of the room. Neither of us spoke, but the act of looking at each other said more than words could've.

But I was still a teenager, still stuck in that adolescent frame of mind where all that mattered was being together, where all the respectability and all the trappings of a good, honest life meant nothing so long as we were together. I cringe, now, as I recall having such a melodramatic, fatalistic outlook on life, but then I really was that young. "So are we going to do this?" I asked. "No," she said, "but that doesn't mean we can't try, right?" "I don't know what you're talking about," I said. "Of course you don't," she said, "it doesn't make any sense, does it?" "It doesn't have to." "I wish that was true." So late at night, I think it was after midnight, the street outside was quiet, so quiet I could hear the sound of my own heart thumping against my chest. But when I leaned over to run my hand around the curvature of her neck, I felt her heart thumping, too. "I have no idea what I'm doing," she said, seeming to talk to herself as much as to me. But it was all a fraud. Karen hadn't been there, hadn't picked me up, hadn't taken me back to her little eastside apartment to *make love*; it's all an elaborate fiction, created by and for that part of me that *still* refuses to accept that our affair had simply and quietly ended, with a whimper rather than a bang, that the memories I'll have could ever be augmented by the memories I've made up. When the dust settled and the smoke cleared, there was little left to hold on to, little to breathe life into the person I was rapidly becoming, the person I am now, the person I wish I wasn't. The last time Karen and I saw each other before that night in that grocery store ten years later was unremarkable save that we simply met and talked, we hadn't *made love* in a little while and we weren't to *make love* then. It was around a year after I'd graduated from Eastmount. We'd met at that same little place near the Ironworkers bridge, surrounded by a thick, leafy forest, with only a clear view over the water and across to the North Shore. It was over quickly. I don't remember exactly what she said—actually I do, but I choose not to put it here. It's too much. Anyways, you're the only person it really means anything to, Karen, and you know what you said. You said what you needed to say, you said what I needed to hear, I just didn't know it then. But then, that's always the way, isn't it? You only know what any of it means when you're a little older and you can look back on it all with the kind of *perspective* you wish you'd had. Karen, I still love you. Even after all that's happened, perhaps *because* of all that's happened, I will always love you.

It was all so sudden, and in my memory this whole sequence of events has blurred into a seamless continuum, so many events, so many people, so many thoughts and feelings compressing themselves into a single point. I can`t remember any of this; it makes no sense, and I`m sure half of it I`ve just made up but then come to believe in as the truth. Still I thought of myself as Karen's *lover*, but for the importance of appearances her *boyfriend*, her *not-partner*, her *other*, as if such ideas were even real to me back the, at the age of eighteen or nineteen. Later, after we'd eased off the high induced by our having *made love*, in the heat of the night it seemed like the moment might've frozen, might've held itself, fixed, in place, forever, only to yield to the flow of time around it like a rock being gradually eroded, swept away by a river's slow-moving waters. If there'd been a way to quickly and neatly extricate myself from the situation I'd found myself stuck in, I might've taken it, might've leapt out of her little apartment and run far away. The fear was still there, twisting my stomach into knots, having become like an old friend. Rising, Karen let the sheets fall around her waist, then turned and stepped across the floor, through the door, so unlike the woman I'd known anymore, stopping at that place that was exactly *hers* to toss a glance back my way, an impish glance that was only *hers*, with the whites of her eyes slimming and her lips twisting into a wicked, wry grin. Her skin was lightly-tanned, and her hair was a mild brown. Disappearing into the hall, she let the door half-close behind her, seeming to invite me to join her. In the washroom, she stood in front of the sink, watching in the mirror as I approached her from behind, rested my hands on her hips, and through the fear, the blinding white fear, kissed her on the side of her neck.

That summer, Hurricane Katrina destroyed the city of New Orleans, in full view of the cameras bodies floating lifelessly through the muddy, oil-slick waters, entire neighbourhoods laid waste. Under the watch of then-President Bush, more than a thousand people lost their lives, most of them poor black people who hadn't the means to get out before the storm hit, left to die slowly in the aftermath like human garbage. In stark contrast to the rapid and vigorous response to the devastation in New York not four years earlier, this time the world watched as people were simply left to die. As for me, I remember very clearly sitting in the waiting room at a call centre, watching CNN show pictures of refugees taking shelter in a football stadium, while I had shown up to be interviewed for a job, one of the many I'd work over the next few months, stuck as I was in that awkward, uncomfortable transition from adolescence into adulthood. For three or four weeks, I sold tickets in a barely-legal European lottery to pensioners in Australia and New Zealand—or rather, I *tried* to sell to them, succeeding in making a single sale over that period, before giving up and moving on to the next job, then the next, then the next, winding up working in another call centre answering calls from frustrated Americans looking for an explanation on why the toys they'd ordered online weren't going to be delivered in time for Christmas, ruining the holidays for their little children. Through it all, I secretly held fast to the fantasy that, one day, I'd be with Karen again, at eighteen investing an religious faith in the idea that we'd be together again. Even after all the pain and suffering I've caused her in the years since, I can't help but look back on myself, then, and wonder what I was thinking. When I write, here, what might seem like my thoughts weren't; they're just an educated guess at what my thoughts might've been, back then, aided by looking over old pictures, letters, little notes scribbled in the margins of notebooks found crammed in a box between a high school yearbook and an old Biology text I never gave back. Eventually, I wound up back at the thrift shop, whacking soup cans off the loading dock with an old golf club, under the flickering, orange glow of the building's lights another cold winter's night spent.

At the dinner/dance, Karen and I spoke, briefly, although it was no longer a risk to her career for us to be together she was, still, looking to appearances. We didn't touch. We didn't kiss or hold hands. We just exchanged small talk, concealed beneath it a talk only we could've understood. "Nice night, eh?" she asked. "Not bad," I said. "Could be better?" "I guess." "Well, enjoy it." "I just wish it was over." "Isn't it?" "Not really." I nearly said to her, 'I love you,' but caught myself just in time, the words lodging in my throat, making it sound like I was choking on them. Then she said, in a low voice hardly audible against the background noise, "I know." It was a small moment, looking back on it, but I think I can see, now, it was exactly the moment I should've left it at. It didn't happen. After we'd danced, we'd avoided each other until later that night in her apartment, and the exchange I just described is something I came up with on my own out of my imagination. But it's a nice thought. As Karen left early that night, I watched from the top of the hall's front steps, tracking her across the parking lot and into her car, then following her as she drove into the night. It took a little while, but, eventually, I found my way out, suddenly sad at having let a last chance to have her pass, all the times we'd been together disappearing in the time it took her to drive away. But it wasn't over. It couldn't have been over. Not after all that'd happened. At the thrift shop, after having returned from my months-long wandering from job to job, I felt a sudden surge of emotion whenever I thought of Miss Karen Thoreson, so sad as I was at the certainty I'd let her slip away so unceremoniously that we might as well never have been together at all.

13. Present

After Lisa's sudden death, I took a leave of absence from work, events having overtaken things like that. It was just as I was about to return when I found Karen lying, comatose, on her living room's couch, little bottle of pills half-spilled on the couch and onto the floor. A week or two later, I visited her on the psychiatric ward for the first time, in the little room she shared with another patient the two of us sitting on the edge of her twin-sized bed, making conversation about anything except what'd happened. "...But do you know when they're going to let you go home?" I asked. "No," she said, her voice flat, the look in her eyes dull. "How's the food?" I asked. "Fine," she said, flat, dull. "Do you want me to be here?" I asked. She tightened her jaw and looked over at me, pausing a moment before saying, "yes." So I stayed, right until visiting hours were over, Karen and I saying nothing to each other, but sitting together all the while. Then, as the nurse poked her head into the room and said it was time for me to leave, I delayed, reaching for her hand, placing my palm on hers, giving a quick, firm squeeze. It was enough to prompt on her face, for a half-second or two, the beginnings of a smile. That glimpse of the Karen I used to know was enough to sustain me for a little while, at least until we were to see each other next. But it was a fleeting thought. Having grown past the point where a feeling was enough to sustain me even as that very feeling was, in fact, enough to sustain me, I went home, on the way stopping at the liquor store, and drank until I blacked out. It wasn't the first time I'd drank myself numb, and it wouldn't be the last. The next morning, I woke, lying face-down in bed, still in my clothes, pounding headache magnifying every sound a thousand times, a hollow sensation lingering.

At the hospital the next day. After all that'd happened, she looked hardly recognizable from the woman I'd fallen *in love* with as a teenager. Her hair was frazzled, greyed, with split-ends, strands that clumped together, making her look like she'd not had a shower in days. Her eyes were red, but she'd never cried. Her hospital gown, loose-fitting, ungainly, seemed to just hang from her body like an oversized coat, making even her shapely figure seem small and lanky. But then she'd been hardly eating. Visitors were allowed to stay until eight o'clock, and it was until eight o'clock that I stayed. That first day I'd visited her on the psychiatric ward, it took until I was on my way out to notice the little details, the way the wall's paint had thinned in places, the lights in the ceiling flickering in exactly the same way as those had at Eastmount, the names of each patient scribbled on pieces of paper which were slid into a holder on the doors to each room. Before the doors to the elevator closed, the last thing I saw was a nurse taking Karen gently by the shoulder and walking her back into the ward, making me feel suddenly ashamed of myself, aware of myself, producing a surge of sadness I could only suppress by turning to my side and burying my face in my elbow, for a few seconds before the door slid open and I made quickly out of the building and onto the sidewalk. Outside, a cold, hard rain pounded the city, as if to beat it into submission, the walk to my truck drenching me to the bone. In the hospital's parkade, I waited a little while, taking out my phone and scrolling through the messages we'd exchanged, not over the past few months, but the messages from earlier, before Richard had walked in on us and set the final disintegration of her life into motion. The texts were so unlike her, lewd, salacious, interrupted by the odd picture, one of her, taken in a rare moment alone, standing in front of her mirror, naked, with her arm strategically placed across her breasts, her face bearing that impish grin. But her skin was creased in places, the little crow's feet out of the corner of her eyes and the stretch marks around the sides of her stomach and the veins on the backs of her hands standing out all making her seem so unlike the woman I'd fallen *in love* with more than ten years earlier. But it was the grin that made her who she was. It was the same grin she'd worn as a thirty-something teacher, a grin I'd, then, not really known the real meaning of, the teenager I was sure only it meant she *wanted* me, somehow, in some way. But it was a fraud. When Karen sat on the edge of the bed in that room on the psychiatric ward at the Lions Gate Hospital in North Vancouver, she must've felt more alone than she'd ever felt before, and as I drove home that evening I turned the stereo up until the hard rock music drowned out that incessant doubt and left me free from my own thoughts. But they came back. They always came back.

The little ceramic lovebirds I'd given her all those years earlier was still there; it'd been one of the first things she'd unpacked when she moved in. While Karen was on the psychiatric ward, I'd gone to her apartment, once, to pick up her dog and take him to my place. But I broke the lovebirds figurine. It was an accident. I'd stopped and picked up the lovebirds from their resting place on the bedroom's nightstand, just to hold it for a moment or two, only to fumble with it slightly and drop it, watching as it smashed against the hardwood floor. When she came home from the hospital, later, she must've seen it missing, she must've gone looking and found it in the kitchen, in a little box where I'd left it. Standing behind her when she looked inside the box, I said, "it was an accident," before adding, "I'm sorry." "It's fine," she said, her voice flat and dull as she pushed the box aside. "I'm really sorry," I said. "It's fine," she said. But I don't think we were still talking about the figurine. Still reeling in my own life from the shock of Lisa's sudden murder, it was as though I couldn't process the true implications of Karen's having tried to commit suicide, the image of her lying on the couch seared into my mind's eye like a little hole burned in place from looking at the sun a half-second too long. Time, it seemed, had become like a force, compressing memories into a single point that defied all attempts to drag meaning out from inside it. But in the months after Karen's discharge from the psychiatric ward, I found myself consumed by a lingering regret, the understanding settling that I'd lost sight of that one feeling that'd compelled me to do so much. Love, I've learned, can be like a religious cult; you're chasing a feeling, a chase that leads you to do things you'd never thought you'd do, even past the point where it's clear that feeling you're chasing is gone forever. But it's all a fraud, it's always been a fraud, it'll always be a fraud, even as it's the most honest and genuine experience I've ever had. I want it back. I'll never get it back. It's wrong. It was in this frame of mind that I met Tina, Karen's old friend from Ottawa.

"It's not your fault," Tina said. We'd run into each other at the little café in the hospital next to the main entrance, and over coffee and doughnuts we'd gotten to talking. "Who said it was?" I asked. "Lots of people," she said. "Who's left?" I asked. "Me," she said, "and her in-laws." "They're not her in-laws anymore," I said, then thought about it for a half-second, and asked, "are they?" "Listen," she said, "you shouldn't think this is all about you. Yeah, it's been twenty-five years since Karen and I were together, but don't think that means I don't know her. She's always been looking for, I don't know, herself I guess. That's why we were together in college. She didn't know anything about the world. We were eighteen. I knew I was a lesbian but she was just experimenting, just looking for herself. She'll be looking for the rest of her life, I think. So she thought with her husband and the kid they had she might've found herself. And then she ran into you again." "It's not my fault," I said. "Yeah, I said that," Tina said, drawing a drag off her cigarette before exhaling smoke in one long breath, "but listen, I'm going to be in town for a couple more weeks." "And then?" I asked. "Then I fly back to Ottawa," she said, "but let's see her together sometime. I don't know. Maybe it'll make her feel better if there's two of us there at the same time." "Might just make her feel overwhelmed," I said. "It might," she said, cocking her head slightly and raising her eyebrows for a half-second, "but I think it'll help." "All right," I said, "need a ride?" Tina was staying at Karen's place, and on the drive back over there we kept talking, at a red light Tina dropping the suggestion that maybe, just maybe I should've thought about preparing for a near-future where I'd "leave Karen's life for good." It took me a second to process. A car's horn blared, and I suddenly realized the light was green. "I won't leave her now," I said, pushing down on the gas, throttling off just as I spoke, "not when she needs me the most." "She needs someone," Tina said, "but that someone doesn't have to be you." When I was a teenager I'd have taken offense at that, but then, at almost thirty, it gave me pause for thought. Later, it'd emerge the psychiatrist had recommended electro-convulsive therapy to treat her chronic depression, but she'd decided against it, favouring medication and therapy. But that'd take a while. In the meantime, the nurse said, she had to be carefully watched, even after the immediate crisis had passed. When Karen called to tell me she'd be discharged the next day, I insisted on picking her up and driving her home, but she seemed reluctant, only agreeing when she saw I wouldn't take no for an answer. The drive home was long and quiet. It was over too quickly. It's always over too quickly. Looking back, now, on the thirteen or fourteen years we'd known each other, Karen, it's like we've never known each other. We've only known the ideas we've had about each other, the parodies of ourselves who've lived in each other's heads. No, that's not fair. It's just become impossible to summon the kind of energy and imagination that once came to me so easily and in such abundance. Where once I'd been so fully confident of myself, where once I could've so convinced myself that I knew exactly what I was doing even when I knew nothing at all I now can't help but feel as though every day I wake up to stare down an uncertainty that can't be overcome. The world, or at least my place in it, has gone from black and white to all grey.

After her discharge from the psychiatric ward, the psychiatrist sent Karen back home, alone, with a referral to the local mental health authority. For a while, I stayed with her, spending my nights on her little apartment's couch while she slept in the bedroom. Every once in a while, I'd give up trying to sleep and poked my head in through the door to check on her, sometimes watching her sleep for what seemed like hours before turning back to my spot on the couch, then staring at the ceiling, through the darkness of the night trying to muster the power of imagination against the hopeless situation Karen and I had found ourselves in, succeeding only in seeing through each day only to stare down another. Months later, after I hadn't heard from Karen for a few days despite my calls and texts, I left work early and drove right to her apartment, still in my dirty, ratty work clothes when I made it through the front door and into the living room, looking in that very place where once I'd found her lying limp and lifeless, finding only an empty seat, turning, about to pull out my phone and try her number again when I found her in the in the bedroom's doorway, a vague look between concern and irritation on her face. We talked for a while, but said very little, she explaining she'd just left her phone in her car overnight and forgotten about it, assuring me she was fine, that she wasn't thinking about trying to take her own life again, just before I was about to leave she adding that she'd made it past the mental block that'd kept her from seeing no other way out. It was hard to accept, but without any other reason to stay, I reluctantly left. That night was the last time we've seen each other, and although we'd speak on the phone and exchange text messages, off and on, for a few weeks, a couple of months or so, the detachment that'd come to slowly push us apart widening like a chasm with either of us standing on opposite sides, watching each other fade from view, growing smaller, smaller, smaller still, until we couldn't see each other at all.

The first thing Karen did when she arrived home was head to the balcony. I followed. When she reached for her pack, I took it from her, pulled a cigarette out, and lit it, drawing a long, slow drag off it before handing it to her. "You shouldn't smoke," she said, then took a drag and handed it back to me. "Neither should you," I said, taking one last drag, then gave it back to her. As if this all wasn't enough, something catastrophic happened next. Just weeks after her discharge, Karen sat me down on her apartment's little couch and said, in the calmest, most measured tone, that she was to "leave for a while," a sort of convalescence from everything that'd come to happen. As Karen had no family left in the immediate area, she'd received few visitors besides Tina and I during her stay on the psychiatric ward, a few co-workers now and then, but no one else. "Where are you going?" I asked. "Ottawa," she said. "You're going to be with..." "...With Tina, for a little while." "Why?" It seemed a crass thing to ask, but I couldn't help myself, the word leaping from the back of my throat before I realized what I'd said. But she gave me no direct answer, not right then, and over time I've come to realize why. In the months that followed, as Karen struggled to overcome her crushing depression, she and Tina would talk on the phone, nearly every day at first, then two or three times a week, then not very often, that lifeline itself like a medication she was to slowly taper off from on her doctor's advice. None of this she ever told me. None of this I ever saw. It's all just part of the puzzle I've pieced together in the years since. It`s not important how. No matter how much I wanted to be a part of Karen's life, it seemed I was slipping away from her like a piece of driftwood slowly floating out to sea. It's lonely. It's still lonely. After dropping Karen off at her apartment following her discharge, I fought the loneliness by spending the long drive home imagining—no, fantasizing about having the old Karen back, the strict, confident, prim-and-proper teacher who I fell in love with as a naïve, impressionable youth, about having her in the backseat of that old CR-V she'd driven, about locking eyes with her from across a crowded hall and exchanging a glance that only we understood.

But on the psychiatric ward, it was stuffy, airless, and every time I visited Karen I looked at the tiles covering the ceiling and wondered, half-seriously, if the people who'd built the hospital were the same as the people who'd built Eastmount. The whole place seemed sterile, used but not lived-in. It'd been more than a year since Karen and I had been walked in on by her husband, more than a year since her life had been turned on itself. Before Richard had wrecked his car on the side of the Trans-Canada Highway, it was always the little things that'd kept me going, the glint in Karen's eyes whenever I brought her a cheesecake I'd baked from scratch myself or sent her a bouquet of roses I'd bought from Safeway just because it was a Tuesday. No one could've taken those memories from me. There was one such occasion, not long after she'd suddenly called me to announce she and Richard were separating, when I'd arrived at her apartment after getting off work early one Friday, finding her in the bathtub with her body strategically concealed behind the bubble bath. Without saying a word, I'd lit a couple of candles she'd always kept in her bathroom, then slipped out of my dirty, ratty work clothes and slid into the tub behind her, when I'd settled in she laying back against me, her body seeming to fit perfectly onto mine, as though we'd been made for each other. We *made love* later that night, but the act of our having *made love* wasn't the memory from that night I'll cherish. It was the way she'd seemed to relax when we'd first touch after a long absence, the way she'd stay up until eleven thirty at night just to be there for me when I'd determined to spend the night with her after a long day of work. And she'd touch me, she'd rest her hands gingerly on my shoulders as we'd kiss. But for her young son's impending arrival to spend every other week with her, every night we were together, and for a while, for a little while it seemed as though it just might've worked. But it was a fraud. It was an illusion, a fantasy, something that, I can see now, existed only in my own head, a daydream that stood no chance against the overwhelming reality drawn against it. With her son, Karen was never going to have a lasting relationship with me. It just wouldn't have worked. It wouldn't have been workable. Still, it was those little moments that'd kept me going, if it was a fantasy then the fantasy enough to give me a reason to get out of bed in the morning, a reason to come home at night. And then, after Karen had tried to kill herself, even the fantasy was gone. Driving from the hospital, it suddenly occurred to me that even visiting her on the psychiatric ward had become like a routine, as I turned to pull onto the little street where I lived the thought seeming to lose itself in the cold, dark night.

At some point during the drive home I began to silently cry, tears sliding down my face even as I kept perfectly still. It'd all come to this, I thought, it'd all come to this. It wasn't fair, I thought. It wasn't supposed to be like this. We were supposed to be *happy* together. We were *soul mates*. We'd been *soul mates* since before we'd met for the first time all those years ago, since before I'd moved back to Canada from Texas, since before that day when New York's Twin Towers fell into a pile of rubble and changed the world forever. The unlikely chain of coincidences that'd led to us finding each other when I was only a teenager and she was just starting out at thirty-five. But, more than ten years later, I'd become just a sad almost-thirty-something sitting in a little pickup truck I'd bought used and paid the asking price for. On the drive home that day the rain let up but the skies refused to clear, through the smoothly undulating clouds the bright, white sunlight burning like a fluorescent light left on too long. But by then I'd stopped crying, the tears drying on my cheeks, and as I pulled into that spot on the street in front of my apartment there was only the salty taste left on my lips. It'd been some weeks since I'd found Karen lying on her couch, and already it seemed as though she'd been locked up on the psychiatric ward for half a lifetime.

And then, Karen was released, discharged from the psychiatric ward a little over a month after she'd been admitted. In the night, there was loneliness, a crushing certainty that nothing would ever be as it was, not in our lives, but in our thoughts, our feelings, the love having disappeared forever. A bang, a crash, the screeching of tires and the shattering of glass, Karen's sudden release from the hospital like a stick of dynamite going off. When the fog had lifted and the light faded in, I was lying on my back, staring at the ceiling, bound by my arms and legs to the bed I lay in, each of my breaths slow and steady, marked by the gentle rise and fall of my chest, rise and fall, rise, fall. It was years earlier, not long after my twenty-sixth birthday, more than two-and-a-half years before Karen and I would run into each other in that grocery store's aisle so late at night. It wasn't the lowest point of my life in the years between losing touch with Karen and running into her, by chance, again, but in a way it was, looking back on it, exactly the moment when I'd begun a rapid spiral down into a personal hell.

14. Past

At Karen's, a few days before I wrote that last exam in the gym, with the danger, I thought, all but passed, she led me into her bedroom before turning, sitting on the edge of the bed, then pulled me down on top of her as we fell back together into the sheets. It wasn't like all the other times we'd *made love* before in that very apartment, in that very bed, this time she seeming to want it in ways she hadn't before, her sudden confidence overpowering my awkwardness and my clumsiness, even after all I'd learned she still having to lead me through our *lovemaking*, that fear snaking its way through my stomach, leaving me all but paralyzed. Gently rolling me over onto my back, she draped one leg over my hips, then the other as she slid on top of me, her hair falling against my cheeks while she kissed me, my hands finding the sides of her hips, grasping, gently gripping while we kissed. She brought both her hands to rest lightly on my face, the tips of her fingers touching my forehead, the palms of her hands to the sides on my eyes. Then, as I entered her, her mouth left mine and her kisses found their way down my cheek until she buried her face in my shoulder, her breaths coming quick, hard. "Fuck me," she said between short, shallow breaths. Then, I was aware she'd reached with one hand between her and me, circling with her fingers, while I put my hands on her hips and held on, she seeming to half-struggle with the act of making herself feel good while keeping a steady rhythm against me, the motions of her body becoming disjointed, halting, erratic. "Fuck me, fuck me, fuck me." Her voice was nearly hoarse, her breaths strained, or maybe it's just that I choose to remember it that way. "Karen, I—" The words dissolved in my mouth as I let go. "Karen, Karen, I—" Still she said nothing, opening her lips to kiss me, her mouth ill-fitting around mine, she, then, taking my lower lip in her teeth and biting down just hard enough to make me feel an almost-pain. It was over quickly, probably just a minute (or less) after it'd begun, but later, the last thing I felt before falling asleep was the sharp almost-pain on my lip, and to this day sometimes whenever I'm *having sex* I recall that almost-pain, the recollection almost enough to convince myself I'm with her again. I don't know what to make of it, don't know how to tie it all together into a neat, little package, except to say that, even after all we'd done together, I was still afraid of her, still afraid of being so close to her that it hurt. It was the fear that made me want to run from her even as it made me want to hold her, to be held by her forever. When the pale light struck her just right I could see the look on her face that said she was just as afraid as I was. At eighteen, I was frightened even as I was confident, headstrong even, full of ideas about how the world worked, never stopping to think that maybe, just maybe someone else had already had them, that these were the ideas we all had, as if having them was a revolutionary act, like a string of profanities I'd just learned and didn't really understand. When you're that age you have a feeling, but it's a feeling so confusing and disorienting even as it's reassuring and inspiring. That's why I'm writing this, now, to make a record, someway, somehow, of the way I felt and the way I thought when I was young before I finally forget what it means to be young. It's exactly as stupid as it sounds, but it's true, it's all true. That night, I wouldn't sleep over at Karen's place, after I was sure she'd fallen asleep I quietly slipped out of bed, pulled on my clothes, and made for the bedroom's door, at the last second the sound of the sheets rustling slightly making me stop and turn to look back, when I saw her looking up at me. Awkwardly, I left, too embarrassed for myself to stay, wishing I could step out of my own skin. The teenager I was might've expected her to tell me to stay, but she said nothing as I walked out the door, the next time we saw each other in the gym when I wrote that last exam, after that a few more days passing, maybe a week or two until we were together again, each day making me feel as empty as the last. It's who I was. When we saw each other privately again, not in her apartment but at one of those little hole-in-the-wall Vietnamese restaurants that occupied the ground floor of every third or fourth shop-house along Vancouver's Victoria Drive, through the restaurant's barred windows a view of the street showing the traffic sliding past, this time she and I sitting on stools and feeding each other noodles, that first time we were together openly she still looking like she was instinctively checking the door every time it swung open to see if it was anyone we might've known.

But it was all an elaborate act, not just me, at the age of eighteen, seventeen, even nineteen not really knowing what I was doing, Karen, too, having not the slightest clue what she was doing either, even as she worked hard to present an image to the world of herself as a strict, prim-and-proper teacher who was on the right track in life. Months earlier, on that day in January, after we'd already *made love* for the first time, I lay on my back with Karen draped over me, her head resting on my chest as though she was trying to listen to my heartbeat. Her skin was soft and smooth, and her body was warm, with her small, wideset breasts having flattened beneath me. I don't remember how much time had passed after our first time that night; at some point I began to stir, she putting her arms around my broad shoulders and looking me right in the eye with a look that seemed to urge me on, then I pushing myself off her slightly, just enough to reach down and awkwardly, clumsily guide myself into her again. But this second time that night, it was different. She lay underneath me, whispering something indistinctly into my ear as I moved against her. As I'd already come once before, I was able to last longer this time, though it still must've been just a minute or two after I'd entered her that I felt myself losing control and reaching towards my release. "Karen, please I—" Nothing, still nothing. "Karen, I don't—I don't—" There was only a vague desperation where once thought had been, a crass feeling, a need to have something, anything. And there she was. "Shhh..." But with her hands on the backs of my shoulders and her legs clutching at my sides, she seemed to coax the feeling from me, tightening her grip, moment by moment, she clinging to me tighter and tighter still until my mind blanked and I came inside her, she holding me still as I strained into her for one, two, three, then let myself still, she still whispering indistinctly into my ear as I caught my breath, she slowly relaxing her hold on me, until the fog cleared and I could make out what she was saying. That night, after having *made love* again, we fell asleep, I collapsing into bed next to her, she turning on her side and leaning in towards me, when I woke up she already out of bed, fiddling around in the kitchen loudly, in the late-morning's winter I suddenly becoming self-conscious and afraid of something, anything at all, muscling a blank look onto my face as I slid out of bed and into my clothes as quietly as possible, approaching her in the kitchen, unable as I was to stop the churning feeling in my stomach, without the slightest idea what I was expected to do next. But then, I realize now, you, too, couldn't have possibly known what *you* were expected to do next, either of us just as confused as the other, only you able to make it look like you knew, I, at seventeen, able only to make it look like I was *trying* to *seem* like I knew. If it was all in my head, then none of it means anything, and after all that's wound up happening I don't know if I could deal with that. It's frightening, the idea that you never loved me, that I never loved you, that either of us were just in love with the idea of each other, I having the excuse of adolescence, you, I think, falling back on the need to feel alive.

At Eastmount, in the months after that first night we'd been together, we crossed paths like we had, but I was terrified of her even as I felt like I needed to be close to her. I remember skipping Spanish class, only to run into her in the parking lot, no, on the way through the main building's side entrance, on the way through the doors finding myself suddenly face-to-face with her, she looking flustered, while I felt my insides turn ice cold. It only lasted a moment, but without saying a word to each other we exchanged nods, either of us leaving separately, staying away from one another until the next time we were together, alone, in her apartment, far enough away from Eastmount for her to be safe, again in her bed, again naked or nearly so, at seventeen, almost eighteen I was so eager just to be with her that I couldn't see past my own feelings, my own thoughts, controlled as I was by the urge to be with the older woman I'd happened into an affair with. It was like the last time we'd been with each other, but without the urgency, without the impulse, this time the tension having unwound itself from her body, I realize, now, that she'd waited out the time and found herself still safe from being found out. This time, she was on top of me, but with her body lying against mine, she moving against me while I could only hold onto her, each of my hands on her sides, on her hips, then feeling back until my palms were against her bottom. She reached down to the place where our bodies had joined, and began a quick, slim circular motion with her hand, while I instinctively pushed up into her in motions that were halting, disjointed, her inner thighs beginning to quiver, her body shaking, her orgasm drawing out from her, snaking through her body like electric currents, the whites of her eyes beaming through the darkness as she let out a long, low groan. We came, her, then me, not at the same time but as close as we'd ever make it, our bodies suddenly still, rigid, holding each other tight. It was the first time she'd come while I was with her. It's only on reflection that I've realized she might've tried to time it to make sure we'd come at the same time, as if to trick herself into believing that I wasn't out of my element. Then, she lay with her head resting on my chest, the rise and fall of my body with each long, slow breath gently raising her, too, the only sound of the blinds rattling gently against the windowsill. This is how I'll remember those times we had together, not by the secret glances traded across a busy hall, not by the times we'd had in the car, but by those little moments in the after-sex warmth. No, that's wrong. It's just that I was overwhelmed by the feeling of being *in love* that I couldn't figure out what was *really* happening, leaving it to my thirty-something Spanish teacher to lead me through an awkward and confusing adolescence. I know it seems unbelievable that a teenaged boy—man?—should've fallen in love like I did, should've thought in terms like I did, and maybe it seems unbelievable because it is. But it's just the way I thought. There are others, you know. There are young men who think like I did, like I still do. How many, I'm not sure. Maybe not many. But they're out there. It might take a long time for you to find them. They might not even admit it. But they're out there. Even if there aren't any of them left anywhere in the world, they're out there, somewhere. I'm sure of it. They have to be. I can't have been the only one.

And then, after having risked her career and her good standing in the community for the sake of an affair with her student, Karen seemed not to have the heart to just tell me it couldn't be anything more than what it was, an affair, even as there was still that little sliver of *feeling* that made her want to try and be with me forever. I can see, now, that it was the good sense in her that overcome the urges she had and made her *decide* that it couldn't go on, even as she wanted it to. Look, I know it might seem anticlimactic to say that Karen and I just stopped seeing each other, but it's just the way it happened. When exactly Karen and I last saw each other doesn't really matter; I'll say it took place before my twentieth birthday and that we didn't have sex just as we hadn't had sex the past three or four times we'd spent time together, but that's it. After having spent the past three-ish years being consumed by my feelings for Karen, I found myself confronted with the unknown. But it wasn't a confusing time, not as I saw it, the confidence of my adolescence burning through, keeping me locked firmly in with the belief that I knew exactly what I was doing even as, looking back on it, I hadn't the slightest clue. At home, one night Lisa came home sometime between nine and ten, stumbling through the front door smelling of a thick, pungent booze. Glancing outside through the window, I saw a taxi pull away, illuminated faintly by the streetlamps. Standing uneasily in the foyer, she explained there'd been a fight with Randall, and he'd told her to leave. (At least, that's what I was able to get out of her drunken rambling). Stepping past, she fumbled about in the kitchen for a bottle of cider, knocking a loose roll of paper towels onto the floor before finding what she was after. Then, after having looked at me with the kind of dizzying, steadying eyes that seemed unable to focus, she made for the stairwell, and I listened as her slow, stilted steps sounded up to her bedroom on the second floor, followed by the swinging open of her door and the loud creaking and groaning of bedsprings as she collapsed into bed. Venturing up, I didn't bother to conceal my approach, knowing she was too drunk to be woken, and on my way past cast a glance in her room, finding her sound asleep, still in her clothes, on top of the bedspread. Her alarm hadn't been set, so I set it for eight in the morning, then retired to my bedroom where I finished the last of a novel I'd been reading and then listened to the radio with the volume low. Not long after that, I left home, moving into that apartment across the city which I shared with that young Ukrainian woman for about seven months before moving again into a basement suite in the city of Surrey, paying rent to a family of Indo-Canadians who used my payments to subsidized the mortgage on a house they could, still, afford only with their combined incomes. But still I kept seeing Karen for a little while even though she, too, had moved, she moving to the city of North Vancouver, in exactly the opposite direction as me, in my mind the easy access to the highway making it possible for us to keep on seeing each other despite the growing distance between us, only in the years since have I realized that distance, then, wasn't just physical. And then, there, was Lisa.

It hadn't been all that long since Lisa had made it a point of avoiding alcohol; I'd seen her flatly refuse free drinks at a family reunion just a few years earlier. That was before I'd spent a year living with my father, her ex-husband, in Texas. Still, when I'd returned, she had taken to drinking several two-litre bottles of cider a week, the empties frequently piling up on the kitchen counters, the dinner table, sometimes knocked over only to be left lying on the floor for days. Then she'd gather them all in plastic garbage bags and take them to the recycling depot, putting the money received towards the next night's drinking, using it all up in one fell swoop. This went on for a while, until she came home from running errands one Saturday in a brand new Mazda hatchback, thereafter a muttered comment from me prompting an argument about money which soon escalated into a full-blown shouting match. She yelled at me to "get a job if you think you know so much about money!" A little while later, I found work at a local thrift shop, using the money earned to buy that cheap Oldsmobile sedan, a battleship of a car that had so many kilometres on it to have taken it two-thirds of the way to the moon. That quieted things for a while. Then she asked me to lend her money to help with rent. Which I did. That night, as I passed the time watching old taped episodes of Star Trek: The Next Generation, there was a rustling sound from behind the wall, as Lisa climbed out of bed and felt her way down to the kitchen, then back up, ice cubes in her glass chattering with every step. The last time I saw Lisa before she called and asked for my help, she sat in the passenger seat of my car as I drove her to the ferry terminal at Tsawwassen, just a few hundred metres from the American border. It was a cold day, not long after Thanksgiving, the late-October's rains not deterring the ferries from running exactly on time. As I pulled up to drop her off, Lisa seemed uneasy, as if she instinctively *knew* what was about to happen. After dropping her off, I drove away, and for nearly ten years Lisa and I never saw each other once. It wasn't that I'd made the conscious decision to cut her out of my life, nor was it, I assume, hers to cut me out of her life. I should've asked her that before she was killed. No, for a decade neither of us bothered to pick up the phone and call the other. I'd like to believe that Randall manipulated her into not trying to find me, so I will. But there's nothing I can think of that explains my failure—no, my *choice* not to speak to her. And now she's dead. Back then, at nineteen, though, I drove back along the causeway connecting the ferry terminal to the mainland without knowing what I was doing even as I believed, as we all do when we're nineteen, that I knew exactly what I was doing. Arriving to the apartment I'd moved into, finding my roommate out for the evening, I stepped out onto the balcony, lit a cigarette, and watched the sky slowly darken and the stars flicker on one by one.

Almost immediately after I'd graduated from Eastmount, I'd lost contact with virtually everyone who'd graduated with me. Adrian and I kept touch for a few more years, then losing touch; last I heard, he'd graduated from the University of British Columbia's prestigious Sauder School of Business, then moved away, first to Toronto, then to San Francisco, while I remained, in one place or another, stuck in Vancouver, for all my daydreaming and fantasizing about adventure never managing to venture very far from home. Still, for a little while I had Karen, only once we'd not seen each other for a few weeks did I come to believe it'd ended. After gaining admission to Kwantlen University College just a couple of years before it became Kwantlen Polytechnic University, I had an easy in to a degree program despite mediocre grades in high school. University took me five years to complete a four-year degree. The university experience wasn't all it should've been, but it wasn't a waste either, those five years exposing me to viewpoints I'd never known existed. But I always fantasized about being with Karen again. In the time until we'd meet again, I had sex with exactly one woman, a tall, thin girl named Carolyn who wore all-black outfits with chains hanging from her pants and her jet-black hair flowing halfway down her back. But it wouldn't last with her longer than a few months. Then, the depression set in, and until that night in the grocery store when Karen and I ran into each other by chance I just couldn't manage the energy, the gumption to have at any other woman. There are so many women in the world worth the effort, so many outgoing, vivacious, so many empathetic, good-hearted, so many with figures shapely and curvaceous, but when it took every ounce of strength I had just to get out of bed in the morning there wasn't anything left. I remember lying on my couch in the living room of that little basement suite and looking up at the ceiling, with all the lights turned off, and in a despaired state of mind thinking to myself that I'd never find a way out of the pit I'd fallen into. It was not me but the depression that forced these thoughts into my mind, in this self-imposed isolation that began to let up not long before Karen and I would find each other again. In fact, just three or four years before we ran into each other again, I tried to take my own life; I'll explain in a bit. It happens, sometimes, to a lot of people, often to the last you'd expect. From the bottom, I had to work my way up slowly, each step forward seeming to move me two steps back, my twenties becoming a blur that I've only begun to parse out. Much of what I think I remember is probably false—I'm sure it's *all* false. But it's all true. It can't be anything but true. Because if it is, then none of this means anything, and I can't stand the thought. It's all too much, even as it's not enough, even as it's nothing at all.

You know the bare facts, Karen, and it's my hope that you now know what it all meant to me when we were together and that you'll come to forgive yourself for what's happened; I want to tell you that none of it was your fault, that it was all mine, but that would be equal parts insensitive and self-centred. It's not about me, even if my own point of view is the only one I can give. A few years after I'd spent time on the psychiatric ward myself but hardly a couple of months before we'd meet again, I took a vacation, driving, alone, for six or seven hours up into the Rockies where I camped for a week in a provincial park at the foot of Mount Robson. The air was clean and fresh, smelling entirely unlike the toxic fumes we've become used to in the cities. On the way home my truck broke down along the highway forty-six kilometres from some small town, and it took a two hundred dollar tow to get me into a junkyard on the edge of town, a junkyard with old cars and trucks right out of the fifties lying around with rust reaching up their sides. Spending the night in the cab of my truck, I found it hard to sleep sitting upright and sometime around two-thirty in the morning I stepped out to take a leak, but instead found myself looking up at the sky, taking in the sight of so many thousands of stars set against the thick, silky band of the Milky Way arching overhead. It was one of those moments when you stand back and realize just how small you really are.

14. Present

After Karen's discharge from the psychiatric ward, I watched her like a hawk, seized as I was by the fear she might've tried to kill herself again. I made sure her bedroom door was left open as she slept, and stayed up the whole night watching her, paying close attention to the slow rise and fall of her chest as she slept, mentally timing each breath she took, even the slightest difference from one to the next noted. But then, morning came, and I woke to the feeling of Karen touching my shoulder, she standing over me, with a look on her face that seemed somewhere between confusion and a kind of muted disdain, like she both could and couldn't understand why I was there. In the time it took Karen to work her way back to passable mental health, much happened. There were interviews with police, with courts, with counsellors and psychiatrists, the bureaucracy lurching into action only after tragedy had struck, each point of contact scrutinized, each and every detail of our lives examined in an effort, it seemed, to excuse themselves of any wrongdoing in her son's death, to make sure that none of them would be held accountable for their mistakes, all the while, by implication, blaming Karen for everything that'd happened. Once the dust had settled and the bureaucracy was satisfied it'd exonerated itself, the phone stopped ringing, the letters stopped arriving every day, and the appointments had ended, with only her psychiatrist left to see her every other week, tweaking her medication regimen, even those appointments ending when the psychiatrist was satisfied she was no longer a threat to harm herself. Then it was just us, Karen, me, Tina from the other side of the country, and her dog, Tango, the shaggy, shaggy dog who leapt into her lap whenever she sat on the couch and who waited patiently, faithfully at the door whenever she went out. It was heartbreaking to see Karen so abandoned when she needed help the most, and I resolved, then, to support her in any way I could, even as I'd come to reflect on our love having faded into nothing in the months that passed. But first, there was much work left, lingering over it an uncertainty like a cloud.

At some point in these months, I began to sort-of fade; I'm not sure how to put it. The days lost their colour. The days drowned, quietly, slowly. On the edge of thirty, I had little to show for it but broken relationships and death where there should've been life. I began taking medication. It doesn't matter what kind. I never told you about it because, well, I figured you'd had enough heartache, and I didn't want to run the risk of giving you something else to drag you down. So I took it on the chin, allowing it out only when I was alone in my apartment where no one could hear me. About this I recall only waking in the morning, struggling to find the energy to get out of bed, spending entire weekends hardly moving, sometimes falling asleep on the couch in my living room because it took too much energy to walk to my bedroom, staring at the ceiling, imagining little patterns in the whiteness of the drywall. You were there, Karen, but you weren't. Whenever we saw each other, meeting for a casual coffee or having a quiet evening at your apartment, I muscled the difficulty off my face, forcing a smile I'm sure you saw right through, as we lay back in that familiar spot on your couch the touch that'd once been a source of strength now becoming a shared depression. But we tried. We tried. As you sat in my lap, I rested my palms against your stomach, my fingers interlocking across your abdomen, your head resting against my collar, the warmth gone, the fire gone, replaced by a dulled almost-feeling I can't describe, even after having reflected on it for the past couple of years since we've last seen each other.

Months earlier, when Karen had aborted the pregnancy I'd given her, I thought of it, then, as the closest I'd ever come to having a child, a family of my own. This isn't to say that I was one of *those* people; I agreed, then, and I agree, now, with her decision. Bringing a child into the world, making him the centre of an endless circle of hatred and recrimination, giving him a family tree that would've looked more like a web wouldn't have been right. At least I've reached the point where I can make those judgement calls. No I can't. It's all visceral. And it was probably exactly that visceral compulsion that made me turn on Karen that made me fall out of love with her just as readily and inexplicably as I'd once fallen in love. She'd taken, as was her right, the child who would've been mine from me before even I had a chance to be with him. If this sounds like I'm resentful, know that I'm not; you did the right thing, Karen. It's just there's a part of me that can't accept it's happened, that I did nothing to try and stop it. It's a primal part, the part I'm trying to be better than, the part that sometimes I just can't help but wonder if it might be right even as I'm dead certain it's wrong. At some point, there came a day when the sun seemed to disappear altogether, where the mornings saw the skies dark, frigid, the evenings black, murky, with the light confined to a narrow space of time between, a time spent trundling about indoors under the watchful eye of the time clock. It became a routine to rouse myself in darkness and pass the day with only the harsh, pale glow of the warehouse's lights to illuminate the hours, as it had during the winters of so many years past. Still, every now and then, an open bay door would yield a clear view of the sky, revealing a deep, dark twilight that tempted an extended gaze, a lingered stare, as if to take the dulled light and commit it to the pages of memory, to impress an image of its brightness into the coming night. But it was a ruse, there for but a moment before disappearing in a flash, replaced by that darkness, that darkness that'd become like a friend returning home after so many months, so many years abroad. And then, Karen.

Halfway through her stay on the psychiatric ward, Karen had taken to playing solitaire in her room, and nearly every time I visited I found her sitting at the little desk next to her bed with a deck of cards laid out. When I asked, she said it was the only way to "pass the time." Sometimes, she'd keep on playing even after I'd arrived, and we'd sit in silence while she lose game after game. "Why don't you cheat?" I'd ask her. "Cheat at solitaire?" she'd ask, "can't even beat myself." And then she'd take the cards and gather them into a pile, some face up, some face down, and turn to me. We'd sit, saying very little, but then it was very little that we needed to say. If it seems I'm fixated on Karen's time on the psychiatric ward, it's probably because I am. I'm convinced she changed, somehow, in those weeks she spent locked up; I only wish I could know how. Maybe she'd hit rock bottom. Maybe she'd come to believe, in a roundabout sort of way, that after having failed at killing herself she had no other choice but to keep on living. It wasn't that she *wanted* to live; she'd just defaulted to living. I don't know. It's just a half-baked theory I've come up with on my own, based only on the nearly-indecipherable look on her face whenever I visited her on the ward, the way she seemed to look right through me, as if she was looking into the sky beyond and imagining whether she'd woken up after her overdose into a completely different world, one that only *seemed* like the one that she'd lived in all her life. Having met Tina earlier, I wondered if I might've had the chance to speak with her again, uncertain as I was of my continued place in Karen's life. We never made time outside the hospital, but in the little coffee and doughnut shop near the hospital's main entrance we sat more than once and talked about the very near future, about what was to happen after Karen's impending discharge. "She doesn't have anyone," Tina said. "She has me," I said. "For how long?" Tina asked. "Forever," I said, the word leaping from my lips before I had the chance even to think about it. "How long's that?" Tina asked. A pause. "I have no idea," I said. "Exactly," Tina said, between sips on her coffee letting the littlest sigh. Still I hadn't the slightest clue what I was doing, even after all that'd happened, after all I'd been through, after all I'd put others, put Karen through. It's a small thing, maybe, but as we were, then, stuck in that place between crises when it all seemed to have settled in a way that was eerily calm, like emerging from a shelter to walk around outside, not realizing it was just the eye of the storm. Months later, after Karen's discharge, I came to wake up each morning expecting a new crisis to strike that day, only to be half-disappointed as the day's end brought a quiet night at home. I don't know what Tina said to convince you to leave, Karen, but whatever she said, I think, now, it was the right thing to say because it was exactly what you needed to hear. Whatever my intentions might've been, I'd become an impediment to your well-being, a drain on the strength and the vivaciousness that'd drawn me, as a teenager, to you. But I hadn't realized this yet, in the months after your discharge from the psychiatric ward, hadn't realized it when you began packing for the move to Ottawa, hadn't realized it when last we saw each other some weeks before you drove away for the last time.

The winter's cold, hard rains lashed at the city, the thick, fast-moving currents running down the street like a river's rapids violently churning water with jagged, ragged rocks. Everything had burned, and with each passing day the remains of my life continued to smoulder, the foul, toxic smoke lingering in the air no matter how much time had passed. Days became weeks. A storm threatened, its ominous black clouds slowly rolling in from the west, pushed along by the warm oceanic winds streaming in from the far side of the pacific. Seated on the plastic lawn-chair in the corner of my apartment's tiny balcony, I watched the darkening skies, so vast as they were, so immense as they pressed themselves down on the city below, their oppression seeming to intensify, their edges thin, razor-like, their bulk bearing the curved edges and the broken ridges of a violent convection of air turning against itself. With my phone in hand, I scrolled through texts exchanged between Karen and me, then through pictures of her, one in which she lay next to me, naked, but a thin bed sheet concealing her bare body, an impish grin on her face, her hair a matted mess. So distracted as I was that it seemed scarcely possible to move, and with that autumn's first rains threatening, the city beneath spread across view, its stout, squat concrete buildings at once teetering, swaying slightly, as if resonating on some frequency barely above the range of human hearing. The apartment's balcony facing the south, I had a view of the street, on its far side a series of squat shophouses, of Korean, Thai, Malay restaurants, of thrift stores and pawn shops, of a makeshift church built out of an old video rental outlet, of a Jamaican-import business that never seemed to have any customers but always saw the same two old men sitting out front smoking marijuana and talking animatedly while playing chess. Through it all, Karen. With holes in my socks and dirt under my nails every day, I made my way through the next few years without a clue what I was doing, even as I was fully confident that I knew everything there was to know.

The last time Karen and I saw each other took place on a late-April's afternoon, and it was an unremarkable afternoon, a light rain pattering against the roof of my truck as I sat in the driver's seat looking out across a parking lot for Karen's car, checking my phone every few minutes for the time, mentally tracking how long past due she was over the agreed-upon time. And then, there she was. Though we both knew it was the last time we'd see each other in a very long time, I don't think either of us believed, then, it would've been the last time we'd see each other at all. In the parking lot we shared an embrace, but it was cold, stiff, withdrawn quickly, replaced by an uncertain glance. We met for coffee that one last time, and as had become our way we said very little to each other. Still, she had news. "Tina flies in from Ottawa in a couple of weeks," she said, her voice dull and flat, "she's going to help me drive there. It'll be easier with someone. Maybe we'll drive in shifts. Fifty hours is a long drive..." Taking a sip of coffee, she seemed to cringe at the taste of it. "Must be a bad pot," she said, forcing a laugh. "Karen..." I said. "Keith..." she said. But all I could manage was to put my hand over hers, give a quick, firm squeeze, and say, "I'm sorry. For everything." She looked right at me and said, "it's okay. It wasn't your fault." That was all. It was over. Though I still couldn't bring myself to believe it was the end, there was a part of me, small but growing, slowly asserting dominance, that'd come to accept it. That part of me, I now understand, was only trying to ease the transition, to bring the rest of me into alignment with what the rest of the world expected of me.

But no matter. It's *all* in the past now. Looking back on it, I can now see this, this stage, this part of my life was merely the prelude to another, the beginning to some unknown, unseen end. And there'd been Karen, Miss Thoreson, the woman who'd helped me become a man by way of *her*, her shapely figure, her wide hips, her luscious curves and her small, wide set breasts, she, then, seeming the perfect picture of a kind of raw, unvarnished femininity, at odds with the image of the strict, stern teacher she sought to project. But it hadn't just been that she was attractive. It couldn't have been just that. She came to me when I'd been at my worst, at my most vulnerable, and she gave me something beautiful, risking her career even as there was little I had to give her in return, little except all the love I'll ever have.

15. Past

Sometime after my nineteenth birthday, well past the point when she'd begun working at Carlisle Secondary on the North Shore, Karen and I were in her bed, *making love* like we'd done many times before; although I couldn't have known it'd be our last time before meeting, again, in that grocery store's aisle late at night, in retrospect she had likely already decided we weren't to be together after that evening even if she hadn't yet realized it herself. With the lights turned off, we lay against one another afterwards, but her mind seemed elsewhere. "Keith," she said, at last, "are you still..." "...What?" I asked, with one hand lazily, lightly rubbing against the small of her back. "...Are you still interested in travelling?" she asked. At first, I didn't understand the question—I understood the meaning of the words, I suppose, but I couldn't figure out what'd prompted it. More was said, but little of it meant anything as I chose not to answer her question. I'd never told her I wanted to travel. But then ours was the kind of connection where she had come to just divine my thoughts and feelings from looking at me, or so I'd believed. It recalled her own travels, when she was ten years younger, through Mexico, Guatemala, El Salvador, and back up, settling in the city of Zacatecas in the Mexican interior, and gave, or so she said, serious thought to just staying there for the rest of her life. She'd been as I was. She knew, I can now see, that it wasn't going to end so long as I refused to make that decision, leaving it up to her, whether she thought it was what I wanted or not. It must've been hard for her to make the decision, to cut herself off from the *feeling* of us being together. It's what that's like, to resist the urge to chase a *feeling* when you've spent your whole life resisting that very urge, with no relief in sight. As a teenager, I was completely at the mercy of feelings so new, so powerful they had seized me so thoroughly, as though they'd turned me into a vessel through which they could give themselves expression. It was insane, and yet it was. The night after that, and the night after that, we were apart; I worked past midnight hauling carts full of product across the back of the store, pausing every once in a while to read her texts and quickly reply, she working her way through grading assignments, planning lessons, her last text of the night announcing she was finally caught up.

And as I sat in my car reading over her texts, she sent another, this last one slyly half-suggesting we'd have each other the next night. No, she'd sent no text. It was the last time we'd *made love* before—I don't want to say *breaking up* since we didn't, but I can't think of anything else to call it but a *breakup*. But whatever you want to call it, whatever it was that we had, it was over. We were just *apart*. You know, it's just how these things start, sometimes; you catch someone at just the right time with just the right touch, no lighter, no stronger, the simple act of two completely different people meeting inadvertently setting of a chain of events that wouldn't have been possible if either had been slightly different, had done something slightly different at all, the result blending the worst pain with the most satisfying pleasure into something you would've never thought possible. There wasn't anything special about either of us, no reason for us to choose each other over anyone else, not when you were my teacher and I was your student and not ten years later when we were both just looking for something that might've made us feel good. It's not love. It's a feeling. Love isn't a feeling. I wish it hadn't taken me so many years to realize it. I suppose it just takes some of us longer than others. It's made me relate to Lisa; she paired up with Randall just because, at the right moment, he'd made just the right impression, giving her a feeling that she'd spend more than ten years chasing before she finally called me and asked for my help in trying to break free.

Nearly ten years later, not the first time Karen and I had each other after reuniting, not the second time either, but somewhere in there, before that night when we'd been walked in on by her husband and her young son. The night before, I'd left work and driven directly to the Trans-Canada Highway and followed it north until I'd arrived in the city of North Vancouver. There, I'd parked on the street a half-block up from an intersection, the location carefully chosen to be close enough for a quick walk the rest of the way but far enough so none of her neighbours would be able to see me coming. Arriving at her door at precisely the appointed time, I'd raised my fist to knock, only for the door to open at just the right moment, Karen standing there wearing her old University of British Columbia sweatshirt and a pair of jeans. She'd pulled me inside and shut the door quick, locking it tight, then turned to face me. With my hands on her hips, I'd gently slid my palms along the curvature of her figure as she leaned forward, pressing into me, her small, firm breasts pushing against my broad, hardened chest, lips joining with mine, my back against the door to her bedroom, until we fell back onto her marital bed, soon her ragged breath the lewd slap of skin against skin filling the darkened night. We had so little time together. It was a kind of deeply satisfying bliss. I don't remember when, exactly, this happened; it might've been before our secret affair had ended, or it might've been more than ten years later, after it'd begun again. It doesn't really matter, anyways, because it's all gone now, and it's never coming back.

There'd been a time when Karen, then Miss Thoreson, took note of me from the head of the class, and I wonder what, exactly, she saw in me, then. She'd taken an interest, that much I knew. In the eleventh grade, before I'd begun to fall *in love* with her. Having learned her age only some months earlier (I overheard her tell another student, though given her sideways, reluctant tone it seemed at the time she might've been subtracting a year or two from the truth), I'd realized she'd been my age in the mid-to-late-eighties, and over the a weekend I found myself obsessively seeking out and listening to all manner of eighties music. She seemed the sort who would've listened to new wave, and so it was new wave on which I focused, headphones soon filling my ears with the likes of Blondie, A Flock of Seagulls, and the Eurythmics, twenty years after they had faded from the scene. Listening on my portable CD player (it was that time just as dedicated mp3 players were becoming popular), I found my seat at the front of the class and waited for Miss Thoreson to tell me to put it away. It was a deliberate provocation, though, meant to incite attention, any attention, to induce a conversation which, in my intoxicated state would surely lead towards *something*, anything at all. She might've, I thought, asked what I was listening to, leading to her surprise at our shared tastes. As other students arrived, slowly streaming in, she stood, and moved to her podium at the head of the class, and between shuffling her notes she looked down at me, briefly, but without the hard, tight-jawed strain that'd worn her before. "Are you going to Texas this Christmas?" she asked. "I'm not sure," I replied. "Why not?" "Haven't heard from anyone." "Think you will?" "Probably not." Talking with her, then, made me tense up, a rigidity setting in through the muscles in my upper back. As if sensing my discomfort, she relented, taking a felt marker in hand before turning her attention to the whiteboard. Later that day, as I sat alone in my spot at the top of the stairs, I chastised myself for failing to take advantage of an opportunity offered, still watching as she walked slowly past on her way through to her class, the moment seeing our eyes meet, briefly, a shared glance at once making up for it. This, as the song 'I Ran' played itself out in my earphones, fading out, the sound of a hundred voices and a hundred feet fading in. It may have been little more than an overactive imagination mixing with raw, teenaged hormones, but I believed with every ounce of my person that she saw something, anything at all, in me. Pen in hand, I wrote thoughts, so many scattered, disordered thoughts on whatever loose scrap of paper was available, giving up on the notion of a single journal, ceding the part of my mind from which those thoughts spawned free reign.

The next day. In class, given time to work on an assignment, most of the students instead carried on with their own conversations, the room a hubbub of so many voices rising to form a carpet of noise. Her repeated attempts to incite us to work bore no fruit, with each of her protestations seeming to only to goad the class to further disorder, her voice barely heard even as she brought herself to the brink of shouting, her face bearing a slight flush as she looked this way and that, as if searching the room for something, anything for help. Then, she looked down at me, baring the slightest weakness, frustration, defeat, as if to invite me to add my voice to the cacophony of noise. But I didn't. As more students joined in, the noise built, feeding off itself, until she reached for her podium and slammed its textbook shut. "That's it, I'm just," she said, turning, grabbing her backpack from her desk and storming out of the room, leaving the door open and the class to its own devices. The room quieted for a moment, but only a moment, a dozen conversations blending into one, an indistinct rising, contained within those walls, those white, whitened walls, set against the crackling buzz of a hundred thousand and one pinpricks tumbling over one another, the morning's seconds drawing slowly, slowly,

slowly past. Soon, the period had ended, its passing marked by the dull, computerized clang broadcast over the loudspeakers, and as Miss K. Thoreson had not yet returned it was up to us, her students, to show ourselves out, a look back as I headed for the door revealing the room empty, a sight it seemed none had seen since she had assumed her duties as the school's Spanish teacher just a year and a half earlier. With one hand on the door's frame, I reached over with the other and flipped the lights off, then taking but one step forward before reaching back and flipping them on, leaving the room brightly lit.

Three o'clock came, the bell's final ring sounding out, releasing students from their last classes of the day. As the new year had since passed, the winter's cold, grey skies lay above, a smoothly undulating blanket spreading from one horizon to the other. Walking along a gravel path leading towards the road that marked the school's rear limits, it suddenly occurred to me that I hadn't seen the sun in days, weeks even, the only light being that which penetrated through the thick, murky veil laid overhead. At the edge of the back field, with the school's parking lot behind a chain-link fence, there sat a navy-blue, no, perhaps a dark-green sport-utility-vehicle, its driver's side door open, Miss Thoreson leaning out slightly. Our eyes met, a shared gaze lingering for a half-moment too long, a twitch of excitement flicking up through my chest. Instinctively, I raised a hand, offering the beginning of a wave. She nodded slightly, then seemed to allow a faint smile to cross her face. A shot of happiness, a rush of excitement struck through the moment, lasting but a heart's beat. Then she was gone, and I was gone, that happiness fading, ceding ground in the face of a rapidly advancing cloud of black and blue. Even after we found each other again, I was never satisfied with what I'd done with myself, and for that, I know, I have only myself to blame. It's one of the few things I'm absolutely sure of, one of the others being that I'll never meet another person like you. Take it for what you will.

There's not much time left. It's getting dark and the wind is starting to pick up. I should go home before the storm hits and driving on the highway turns dicey. I still have the Ford Ranger, but it's beginning to get on in years; I'd like an F-150, but the idea of trading up and having to maneuver such a large truck through parking lots and narrow streets and alleys is a little too intimidating for me to try it. All I want to say, now, is that as I turned twenty I still looked forward to seeing you again, seized as I was by the almost-religious certainty in the permanence of our *love*. In university, I don't know what happened to me, except to say that I fell under the influence of that all-encompassing disease we call *depression*, but in five years I'd emerge another person, and it was soon after that we'd meet again.

15. Present

Eventually, I returned to work, the company's patience with my extended bereavement having run out. On my first day back, I'd expected to face a barrage of questions from my coworkers about my lengthy absence, but hardly anyone showed interest. It was like I'd become someone who was just *there*, whose only asset lay in his ability to occupy space. In my absence, they'd had no trouble finding a replacement for me, and the company carried on like the well-oiled machine it was. In my absence, I'd missed the vote on a new agreement, and came back to find it passed by only a few votes, with only thirty or forty people having voted out of two hundred, most of them the senior workers. When I was a teenager, it might've made me angry, but then, at nearly thirty, it just made me tired. Trying, I put my mind aside and became like a machine, each movement rehearsed from memory, each contraction and expansion of my muscles smooth and deliberate, passing the days by simply switching off my mind and allowing my body to carry on. But it wasn't the same. Tired all the time, I pushed through it, forcing myself at each and every day, forcing myself through the pain even without an end in sight. It can't last. It can't. I can try to make it last, but *something* will happen, I'll do *something* that'll blow it all up. Every day I drove in my truck from within that narrow little corner of the world in which I lived, heading over a bridge and along a highway, then gliding gently atop a narrow country road, arriving at a plain, white building, a heap of wood and cement and metal scraped up and dumped down on the city's edge, within spitting distance of the Fraser River. That morning, that Monday saw the temperature dipping a degree or two below zero, each breath loosing a wick of steam into the bright, azure sky. The concrete walkways snaking around the parking lot bore a thin film of whiteness, the night's frost clinging steadfastly to its hard-won ground, crunching faintly beneath my feet with every measured pace that brought me closer, closer, closer to the unseen thing lurking in the distance, each second, each half-second that passed pushing Karen and the memories of her further into the past. And then, one day, I took a bottle of benzos I'd been prescribed for a sleep problem I'd had, off and on, for years, and swallowed all that were left, winding up, myself, in the psychiatric ward, in a ward just like the one, Karen, that you'd once been in. It wasn't that I wanted to die, I think. It's just that life had lost its colour. Everything had greyed. And then, three years later, I met you, again.

In the weeks between that last time we'd seen each other and the day when you left Vancouver for good, I spent the weeks working as much as possible, showing up early and staying late, volunteering to work every Saturday and even the odd Sunday shift that materialized as business picked up towards the end of the year as it does every year. But then I burned out. After taking two weeks off and spending those weeks almost entirely in bed, I returned to work to face a lengthy sit-down with management. The shop steward assured me they couldn't fire me, but I thought they'd start gunning for me anyways. I wish I could say that I quit, but in this day and age union jobs that pay as well as that don't come around very often. So I stayed. It hasn't been that long. Maybe one day I'll tell you what happened. For now, though, I'll just say that I've got a roof over my head and a half-tank of gas in my truck, and that'll have to do. Actually, I still work at CylinderWorld. I've even become a shop steward. With my degree in the social sciences, maybe one day I'll be able to parlay my newfound interest in the union into a career. It's a little late, but it's something. Like teachers, union organizers don't earn much money, but then, like with teachers, with union organizers it's not supposed to be about the money. Even still, I can't help but feel like I've become just another cog, like I'm part of something that's moving forward, always moving forward without ever being under anyone's direction or control, events having taken on a life of their own. It's all something that can't be changed, like it's expected that I'll take my place and do what is asked to keep the machine lurching forward, the whole thing having long since grown beyond any one person's control, assuming a life and a character all its own. But then, I know there's nothing that could compare to what we had, even if I can't figure out exactly what that was.

Karen, we've left each other's lives, this time for good. I'm still afraid of *something*, but I'm no longer afraid of *you*. I wish it hadn't taken all we've been through together for me to finally be able to say that. It's been a terrible end to the last years of my youth, a heartrending ordeal I wouldn't wish on my worst enemy. But it's happened. Neither of us can walk it back. I'm seeing a psychiatrist now, or, at least, I've been seeing one. She's got me on antidepressants, the same antidepressants you used to take. They smooth out the valleys. They keep me from falling into the lowest of the lows, those spells when I couldn't see a way out, a way forward. But I never thought about trying to kill myself. It never occurred to me. It was never that kind of depression; for me, it was more about struggling to get out of bed in the morning, and although I'll eventually stop taking the medications I don't think I'll ever be able to get out of bed as easily as I used to, as easily as when I had the possibility of a day with you to look forward to. All I can do, now, is try to make sure that I come home at night.

When I was seventeen and you were my thirty-something Spanish teacher, it was the only time I'd ever been *in love* with anyone in my life. If I'd been in your position, a young-ish teacher with feelings for a seventeen-year-old girl in one of my classes, I don't think I would've done what you did. It's not that I think you did something wrong; nothing that brings two people together in the way that we were could ever be wrong. It's just that I don't think I'd have the—not courage, but I can't think of a better word for it—courage to take the plunge and risk so much for so little. You're a courageous person, Karen, and you've always been, even if you've never realized it, even if you've never been able to fully articulate it like I have. Some people might take exception to my characterization of a teacher who'd slept with her student as courageous, but I don't care what those people think. Maybe that's the problem. It wasn't just you, that time I yelled and swore at you. There are still times, or at least, there *have been* times when I can't help myself. It's never cost me a job and it's never landed me in cuffs, but then, maybe I'm just lucky for that. I've never hurt anyone. I've never hit a woman and I never will. Men who do are scum. My father never had any impulse control at all, and I have only a very weak impulse control. If I ever have a son, then maybe he'll have it better than me, and his son better than him, and one day, somewhere down the line, there'll be a man who'll be a normal, well-adjusted person, in control of his emotions, something that's eluded us since before I was born. But it's all a wash, anyways, because we can't take back our mistakes, no matter how we'd like to. It's something you come to accept, I've learned, when you get to a certain age. It takes some people longer than others. Maybe there are people out there who never learn. Have you? It feels presumptuous even to ask. But I never took the opportunity to ask when I had it, and I don't have any way of finding you now, not easily anyways. Though, even if I did, I probably wouldn't.

After all that's happened, Karen, I want you to know that I will always love you. You're the love of my life. Even though we'll never see each other again, you'll always be the love of my life. Though it's only been a couple of years since we've last seen each other, I don't live in Vancouver; I've met a woman and together we've moved in with each other, sharing a place in the city of Surrey not far from where Lisa last lived. I'm a little younger than she is, but nowhere near as much younger as I was than you. She and I haven't planned much for the future, but it seems the sort-of unspoken agreement that we'll marry someday, if only because both of us are on the wrong side of thirty and feel the pressure to marry *someone, anyone at all.* We both have stable jobs, don't do any drugs, own our own vehicles, and no other prospects for the future; we've kind-of defaulted to one another. I met her not long after we last spoke. I haven't told her all that much about the life I came from, the life I left behind. If she, someday, reads this, maybe she'll ask, but I prefer to imagine that, by then, she'll know me well enough *not* to ask. But she could never know me as you have. No one could. It's a strange thing to bare your soul to someone, exposing yourself in all your weaknesses and all your insecurities that it hurts just to be with her, but wanting nothing more than to *be* with her any way you can. We had that, Karen, and we lost it, we lost it to all the little things that don't matter and to all the big things that matter more than anything else in the world. My greatest fear, though, is that it all means nothing, that it *can't* mean *anything.* I don't think I could handle it if all we've been through hasn't meant a thing.

Now that you've had the chance to see our relationship from my point of view, Karen, I hope it's a little clearer why I've done all the things I've done, why I never could move on from you, why I'll never be able to give to anyone what I've given to you. We'll never see each other again, but you'll always be the love of my life. Back when I was a teenager and you were my teacher, we made each other happy, in the way we did, for at least the little while we did. That counts for something. And now, things have found their place, in the way that they have. It's early in an unseasonably cold and stormy winter, late at night with a flurry laying a new coat on the street, and from the little apartment I live in with my girlfriend the road looks like a smoothly undulating bank of snow, the trucks moments away from pushing through with their ploughs and churning the whiteness into a grey mush on the side of the road. She's still asleep. She'll wake soon, actually. I don't have much time. In the last moments I have to myself, I look out into the sky at a plane flying far overhead, and I imagine you and me on board, together, flying away somewhere, anywhere at all, to start a new life together, to be with each other again.

The End

Printed in July 2019
by Rotomail Italia S.p.A., Vignate (MI) - Italy